Another Annunaki was out there

The mother ship had detected his presence immediately, identified him as one of her children.

"Ullikummis," Enlil muttered, the name lost in the sharp intake of his breath. "So you have returned, my son."

It should have been impossible, Enlil knew. He had expelled his child into space, sent him to float among the stars for the duration of his near-endless life. And yet here he stood on Earth once again, and with an army of apekin at his beck and call.

But Enlil did not question the facts presented to him. Ullikummis had beaten the odds and returned, and that was only right because he was his son—and what would any son of Enlil be if he could not defy the odds?

Tapping a quick sequence out on the palm link to *Tiamat*, Enlil called forth the Igigi who hid within the shells of the reborn Annunaki. "We still have much to do." He spoke to the empty room as if reminding himself. "More than I conceived. Let us begin."

Tiamat trembled as her mighty cargo doors opened for the very first time.

D0456428

Other titles in this series:

James Axler
Outlanders®

GOD WAR

A GOLD EAGLE BOOK FROM
WORLDWIDE®

TORONTO • NEW YORK • LONDON
AMSTERDAM • PARIS • SYDNEY • HAMBURG
STOCKHOLM • ATHENS • TOKYO • MILAN
MADRID • WARSAW • BUDAPEST • AUCKLAND

Recycling programs
for this product may
not exist in your area.

First edition August 2012

ISBN-13: 978-0-373-63875-8

GOD WAR

Copyright © 2012 by Worldwide Library

Special thanks to Rik Hoskin for his contribution to this work.

Printed in U.S.A.

There is undoubtedly something religious about it: everyone believes that they are special, that they are chosen, that they have a special relationship with fate. Here is the test: you turn over card after card to see in which way that is true. If you can defy the odds, you may be saved. And when you are cleaned out, the last penny gone, you are enlightened at last, free perhaps, exhilarated like an ascetic by the falling away of the material world.
—Andrei Codrescu
1946–

The Road to Outlands—
From Secret Government Files to the Future

Almost two hundred years after the global holocaust, Kane, a former Magistrate of Cobaltville, often thought the world had been lucky to survive at all after a nuclear device detonated in the Russian embassy in Washington, D.C. The aftermath—forever known as skydark—reshaped continents and turned civilization into ashes.

Nearly depopulated, America became the Deathlands—poisoned by radiation, home to chaos and mutated life forms. Feudal rule reappeared in the form of baronies, while remote outposts clung to a brutish existence.

What eventually helped shape this wasteland were the redoubts, the secret preholocaust military installations with stores of weapons, and the home of gateways, the locational matter-transfer facilities. Some of the redoubts hid clues that had once fed wild theories of government cover-ups and alien visitations.

Rearmed from redoubt stockpiles, the barons consolidated their power and reclaimed technology for the villes. Their power, supported by some invisible authority, extended beyond their fortified walls to what was now called the Outlands. It was here that the rootstock of humanity survived, living with hellzones and chemical storms, hounded by Magistrates.

In the villes, rigid laws were enforced—to atone for the sins of the past and prepare the way for a better future. That was the barons' public credo and their right-to-rule.

Kane, along with friend and fellow Magistrate Grant, had upheld that claim until a fateful Outlands expedition. A displaced piece of technology...a question to a keeper of the archives...a vague clue about alien masters—and their world shifted radically. Suddenly, Brigid Baptiste, the archivist, faced summary execution, and Grant a quick termination. For Kane there was forgiveness if he pledged his unquestioning allegiance to Baron Cobalt and his unknown masters and abandoned his friends.

But that allegiance would make him support a mysterious and alien power and deny loyalty and friends. Then what else was there?

Kane had been brought up solely to serve the ville. Brigid's only link with her family was her mother's red-gold hair, green eyes and supple form. Grant's clues to his lineage were his ebony skin and powerful physique. But Domi, she of the white hair, was an Outlander pressed into sexual servitude in Cobaltville. She at least knew her roots and was a reminder to the exiles that the outcasts belonged in the human family.

Parents, friends, community—the very rootedness of humanity was denied. With no continuity, there was no forward momentum to the future. And that was the crux—when Kane began to wonder if there was a future.

For Kane, it wouldn't do. So the only way was out—way, way out.

After their escape, they found shelter at the forgotten Cerberus redoubt headed by Lakesh, a scientist, Cobaltville's head archivist, and secret opponent of the barons.

With their past turned into a lie, their future threatened, only one thing was left to give meaning to the outcasts. The hunger for freedom, the will to resist the hostile influences. And perhaps, by opposing, end them.

Chapter 1

It was a little after dawn in Luilekkerville on the West Coast of what used to be known as the United States of America. The morning air still fresh and cool against his face, Minister Morrow rubbed his hand over his clean-shaved jaw and looked up at the golden ball of the sun as it rose over the cathedral. Placed in the exact center of the ville, the cathedral towered over the buildings around it, dominating the skyline.

The ville itself had the air of a construction site, half-built edifices poised along the straight streets, as if patiently waiting in line for their builders to return after a good night's sleep. So much had changed here since the days when this walled settlement had first grown up from the ashes of bombed-out Snakefishville. Back when it had been ruled by Baron Snakefish, the gates had been kept locked, the high walls patrolled by the Magistrates. Those were things of the past now. These days, under its new and hopeful name, Luilekkerville's gates were ever open, the new Magistrates welcoming all visitors that they might perhaps join the congregation. Minister Morrow took heart in that, feeling in part responsible thanks to his imparting of firm moral guidance to the newcomers to the ville, encouraging the work ethic that had seen so much rebuilding over the ruins of the old.

A balding middle-aged man with ruddy cheeks and

a square face, Morrow was dressed in his simple robes of office: a fustian cassock with a wide hood that could be pulled forward to hide his face in shadow. He was an Alpha, first priest in the New Order that had dedicated itself to a better world under the stone god who had returned from Heaven to spread his message of peace. The god's name was Ullikummis, but that hardly mattered. What he brought—what he was even now in the process of bringing—was utopia, Heaven on Earth.

Human society had suffered more than two hundred years of blight, first with the nuclear conflict that launched the twenty-first century and wiped out billions in what seemed a determined effort at mutual destruction. Then came the Deathlands era, a hundred years of radioactive hell that only the strongest could survive, clawing their way through the debris as they struggled to reassert some measure of order on the chaos. And then, approximately one hundred years ago, the Program of Unification had finally restored order to the ruined United States in the form of nine settlements called villes, each one named after its baron, who served as its absolute ruler. But even these villes were far from utopian. Unknown to most citizens, their rulers were engaged in a strictly regimented purge of the past, obliterating the details of humankind's advances prior to the nukecaust.

In their way, too, the villes were exclusive. Each housed a set number of individuals: five thousand aboveground, a further thousand in the Tartarus Pits at their lowest levels. Perimeter walls kept out the so-called outlanders, who were often viewed as dangerous in their nonconformity and many of whom were still affected by residual radiation from the nukecaust. If the baronies had been designed to provide some kind of respite, they had failed, ultimately sinking into chaos when the barons fled.

What Ullikummis and his adherents promised was a truly better tomorrow, a new society unlike anything seen before in the short history of humankind. What was more, the proof of this claim was already visible. The truly faithful, those blessed by the touch of Ullikummis himself, were able to channel his power, turning their flesh into something with the impenetrability of stone; Morrow had seen them in action. These people, the Stones, were the military arm of the new regime, the new Magistrates of the bright promised future.

As his ministerial robes billowed about him in the wind, Morrow stared at the towering structure of the cathedral. Its circular scarlet window dominated the spire like a cyclopean eye, and Morrow smiled. The future was here, so close he could taste it, smell it on the air.

His congregation was large, and even though the cathedral could seat more than eight hundred, it was frequently filled to brimming when he called the faithful to prayer. And not just with the people of the ville itself, but others, outlanders from the surrounding lands who came from near and far to pledge their commitment to the dream of a better world.

This day, however, Minister Morrow would have a special message to impart to his congregation. As he headed toward the always-open entrance to the towering cathedral, he saw the familiar figure waiting inside among the wooden pews. The man was in his late thirties and had the strong build of a farmer, his loose shirt buttoned low. His name was Christophe, and he was one of more than a hundred who had built the cathedral when Luilekkerville was just beginning to emerge from the debris of the old barony. These days,

Christophe helped Minister Morrow with the upkeep of the church, working as a handyman.

"Our love is a rock," Christophe said by way of greeting.

In response, Minister Morrow nodded. "What brings you here so early, Christophe?"

"Woke up early," Christophe told him. "Strange dreams, and then I couldn't get back to sleep. There's something coming," he explained vaguely.

"I felt it, too," the minister agreed.

"Then what should we do, Minister?" Christophe asked.

Morrow looked out across the interior of the vast, empty cathedral, its seats lined up in blocks, all of them facing the central dais, and he knew just what to do. "Ring the bell," he told Christophe. "Call the faithful. Call them home."

"GOOD MORNING, Haight."

Brigid Haight opened her eyes, the last whispers of the dream leaving her in that familiar whirl of colors, blue, gold and green. Across from the simple cot that she slept in—its bedding made up of an untidy blanket rolled in on itself beneath her head to provide some form of pillow—waited the great giant Ullikummis, her lord and master. He stood eight feet tall, his body formed of rock dark as mud with a weather-beaten look to it that made one think of the ocean batting against cliffs. Veins of magma hurried between the plates of his chest and along the joints of his arms and legs, their orange glow shimmering in the dark room like the ebbing rays of sunset. His tree-trunk-like legs ended in two flaring stumps, the feet long since hacked away in a vicious battle with his uncle, Enki. His body was unclothed, for he needed none. Indeed, he simply *was,* needing no adornments for his powerful form. Pointing struts reached up from his shoulder blades, forming twin ridges like the horns of a stag, mismatched and pointing inward toward his head in great scything curves. The head itself seemed ugly, misshapen, its ridges hard and uneven. Formed of rock like the rest of him, Ullikummis's was the face of nightmare, dark stone eroded by weather rather than carved with the delicacy of a statue. A slash of mouth waited grimly beneath a flattened nose, twin eyes burning with magma like pits beneath a thick brow. Humanoid in form, the creature known as Ullikummis was entirely hairless.

He stood in the doorway, the familiar charcoallike muster of his body wafting to Brigid's nostrils as he waited there, so tall he dominated the room before he had fully entered. A child stood before him, a girl no more than three years old, her long, wispy hair reaching midway down her back in feathery waves of a blond so pale it was almost white. She wore a simple dress, its creamy yellow somehow enhancing the paleness of her skin. The girl was called Quavell or Quav, named after her mother, and she was a hybrid of human and alien DNA. But Ullikummis called her only by her true name, the name of the programmed template hidden within her genetic code—Ninlil, the name of his mother. He stood now with his stone-clad hands resting gently on the girl's shoulders, protective, possessive.

Seeing Brigid's confusion, Ullikummis spoke again, his voice rumbling like the grinding stones of a mill. "You seem ill at ease, my hand in darkness."

Brigid shook her head momentarily, willing the feeling of sleep from her body. "I dreamed of shapes…"

she muttered, "colors." Her words seemed confused, as if she was trying to describe a thing just out of sight.

She was a beautiful woman in her late twenties, with porcelain skin and vibrant red hair that ran down her back in a cascade of tangled curls. Twin emerald orbs peered from beneath dark makeup that had been smeared like a black shadow across her eyes. Her full lips were darkened to the harsh purple of a bruise, and her cheeks seemed narrow and drawn. While those full lips invoked a tender, sultry side, her high forehead hinted at her formidable intelligence. Brigid pushed the blanket away from her naked body, revealing the trim, slender form of a trained athlete, strong but remaining enviably feminine.

They were inside a sea fortress off the East Coast of North America. The fortress had been named Bensalem by its originator Ullikummis, who had drawn it alone from the depths of the ocean stone by stone, shaping it with the power of his formidable will the way a sculptress might carve a pot. The placement of the fortress had been paramount, sitting atop a hidden parallax point—one of a network of nodes across the globe that served to function as access points for a teleportational system.

Brigid's room itself was small and cold with a narrow opening in its stone wall that served as a window. Through this, she could hear the waves crashing against the high stone sides of the island fortress, feel the billowing breeze from the ocean and smell its briny aroma as the sun rose. The walls of the room were hard rock, rough and unfinished as if a cliff face had been sheared away. Embedded within those walls, faint lines of orange-red glowed in jagged rents, each no wider than half an inch and splayed across the walls like the shards of a shattered windshield. Throbbing and pulsing, those orange rents seemed uncannily alive.

As Brigid shrugged aside her covers, feeling the cold dawn air on her skin, Ullikummis spoke again in that voice like grinding millstones. "The stars are aligned," he said. "The day is upon us."

Her body revealed, there were bruises there, too, circles in the deepest purples and blues as if her mouth had been made up in sympathy. The white-blond girl, Little Quav, trotted across the room to Brigid as she pulled herself from the bunk, an innocent smile in her eyes. The girl tottered a little, neither walking nor running but instead a kind of combination of the two as she hurried over to Brigid's arms. "Brigly," she said, excitement in her voice.

Brigid held her arms open, encircling the girl as she sat at the edge of the bunk. The hybrid girl felt warm as she pressed against Brigid's breasts.

"Good morning, munchkin," Brigid said. The epithet seemed strange to her, distant, like something made of mist.

The girl had been with them for six days now. Though fearless, she had cast Brigid as a mother figure in the echoing stone fortress. That was only natural; to an extent, Brigid had been a mother to her since her birth almost three years earlier. Little Quav's hybrid mother had died shortly after childbirth, leaving the child orphaned. A key player in the genetic arms race between humans and Annunaki, Quav had been in danger from the very moment of her birth. For her own safety, the hybrid child was entrusted into the foster care of Balam, the last of a race known as the First Folk. For the past few years, Balam had raised the child as his own in the abandoned city of Agartha, hidden deep beneath the

Altyn Tagh region of Tibet. However, as she had become older and hence more self-aware, the outwardly
human Quav had begun to question the obvious dif-
ferences between herself and her foster father. She had
delighted in the few contacts she had had with people,
understandably feeling a kind of instant kinship with
them after her time with Balam. Brigid had been one
of those people; she and Quav had met on brief occasions where the girl had formed her attachment. Haight
had been known by another name then, however—her
birth name of Brigid Baptiste, and she had worked for
the Cerberus organization tasked with the protection of
humanity from the alien machinations of the insidious
race called the Annunaki.

   The Annunaki were a race of aliens who had first
visited Earth many millennia ago, back when humankind was still hiding in trees from saber-toothed tigers.
With their strange, reptilian appearance and incredible
technology, the Annunaki had been mistaken for gods
by the primitive local populace, an error that they had
reveled in, encouraging their worship as false idols, and
they constructed their vast golden cities of Eridu, Nippur, Babylon and others on the virgin soils of Earth.
Though hailed in Sumerian mythology as gods, the Annunaki themselves were in fact a near-immortal race
from the planet Nibiru, whose group memories were
passed on—complete—to their descendants and the others of their race. By the time they arrived on Earth, the
Annunaki had become bored with their lives, gripped
by a self-destructive ennui engendered by the nature
of their vast shared memories. With no individual experience in living memory, it was hoped that the con-
quering of this new planet would stave off the crushing
boredom of their lives—and for a time it had. Here were

new territories to control, new creatures to toy with and experiment on. For a while, the gods had warred, battling for territory, for supremacy, for the adulation of the primitives that littered the planet all about them. But finally—perhaps, inevitably—they had become bored with their new playthings, and Overlord Enlil, the cruelest of their number and the master of the city of Nippur, had unleashed a great torrent to wipe the planet of the scourge of humankind like a spoiled child tossing aside his toys. This torrent had been enshrined in man's history under various names, most notably as the Great Flood of the Judeo-Christian tradition.

Enlil's plot failed thanks to the deceptions of his own brother, Enki, and the Great Flood did not wipe humankind from the face of the planet. Thus, while the Annunaki retreated into the shadows, humanity flourished. For the subsequent four thousand years, humanity reigned until, on January 20, 2001, a devastating nuclear holocaust had been unleashed by the antagonistic powers of East and West. This war, and the subsequent Deathlands era of privation that followed, had in fact been part of a long-term plan by the Annunaki to reassert their own dominance over the indigenous race, thinning the herd before reemerging two hundred years after the nuke-caust to finally take their place as rulers of the world. That audacious plan had involved the creation of artificially evolved bodies in the forms of the hybrid barons, of whom Little Quav was the ultimate progeny. Each of these hybrids had been prepped to accept a genetic download from the starship *Tiamat,* literally a mother ship for the Annunaki.

However, once the nine barons had been reborn in their original, lizardlike forms as the royal family of the Annunaki, old rivalries and prejudices had rapidly

emerged, and the nine overlords were soon at war with
one another for ultimate control of the territories once
more. Stuck between the factions, a plucky group of
human adventurers working together under the ban-
ner of Cerberus managed to turn the Annunaki's plans
back on themselves, destroying their mother ship and
leaving the various overlords for dead.

Or so it had appeared.

Over recent months, several Annunaki had reappeared, including Enlil and the mad goddess called vari-
ously Lilitu, Lilith or Ezili Coeur Noir. Nearly ruined
by the destruction of their womb ship, each of these old
gods had struggled to gain a new foothold on the power
they all craved. However, unknown to the Annunaki,
things had become more complicated than they realized when Ullikummis, errant son of Overlord Enlil,
had returned to Earth after a four-and-a-half-thousand-
year exile.

Far from being a typical Annunaki, Ullikummis was
a genetic freak whose DNA had been twisted beyond
recognition at his father's behest, turning him into a
monster even among his own people. Heartless in the
execution of his plan, Ullikummis's father, the Overlord
Enlil, had altered his son to become an assassin, a slayer
of gods. Enlil had called the child his hand in darkness
and sent him on a mission to destroy Teshub and gain
the operational codes for *Tiamat* with which he might
preside over the Annunaki. But the plan had backfired,
and Ullikummis—along with his tutor, the disease-
ridden Upelluri—had been ambushed by Enlil's brother,
Enki. That brutal exchange had resulted in Ullikummis
losing both feet at the keen edge of Enki's sword and
subsequently being disowned by his father, imprisoned
in an asteroid and exiled into space. A by-blow child of

rape, two contentions had driven Ullikummis to survive through the long period of his exile—that his father had orchestrated his downfall for his own insidious needs, and that his mother, Ninlil, was an innocent in need of rescue from this monster.

Now Ninlil's genetic code was contained within the child known as Little Quav, whom Brigid Haight had enticed from Balam's protection in the buried city of Agartha just six days earlier. The child seemed remarkably human, inquisitive and often finding pleasure in her own thoughts. Raised by Balam in the abandoned city, it was only natural that she should find joy in her own company, and Brigid had watched her at play in the cold, cavernous corridors of Fort Bensalem. The child would make a plaything of whatever came to hand, giving stones and material personalities and little voices when she thought no one was looking, frequently making up songs that she would sing to herself, endless loops of rhyming noises that—as often as not—were not words at all.

Although the child looked automatically to Brigid for compassion and comfort, she expressed no fear of Ullikummis, in spite of his monstrous appearance. Seeing the two of them together made for an incongruous sight: the girl not yet three feet in height with the tiny, birdlike build of the hybrids, while he was eight feet tall and as solid as living stone. Brigid had been surprised to see that, despite his appearance and eminent practicality, Ullikummis was capable of tenderness. He befriended the child by honoring her, the way a child will honor a parent, a man or a god.

In the curtailed week that Quav had spent at the rock-walled fortress, Ullikummis had lavished long hours speaking with her, patiently explaining her role in the

Annunaki royal family, her destiny and importance to his own plans. He had done this both as a teacher and a friend, never once berating the young child for her impatience or because her attention span did not equal his.

Ullikummis was exceptionally patient, Brigid had observed as he conversed with the child, something she had not really credited before now. She had first met Ullikummis in her other life, when she had been a Cerberus warrior opposed to all things Annunaki. Ullikummis had returned to Earth in his space prison, landing in the wilds of Canada, and he had immediately set about building his own army within the structure he called Tenth City. While he was monstrous and harsh in his manner, looking back Brigid realized he had never been impatient. Even as he suffered an attack and seemingly ignoble defeat, Ullikummis himself had simply stepped back, hiding himself in the shadows and letting the Cerberus warriors see what they wanted to see, believing him killed in an incinerator explosion. At heart he was an assassin, his father's one-time hand in darkness, and so his natural inclination was to step back, to merge with the shadows and let the world turn around him while things ran their course, secure in the knowledge he could strike when the time was right.

Brigid's second meeting with Ullikummis had come in the Ontic Library, an undersea storeroom that housed the blueprints to reality itself. Ullikummis had accessed the library to amass more knowledge about his father from its sentient datastream, but his brutal incursion had damaged the structures of the library itself. Brigid had joined her then-colleagues from Cerberus in expelling Ullikummis from the incredible library before the damage proved irrevocable, and it had been her consciousness that had been melded with the living data to shore up the library's defenses. Ullikummis had encountered her then, their astral forms meeting, but his perception had been so altered by the library that he had been unable to recognize her. It was only later, once the Annunaki prince was freed from the datastream, that he had realized who it was he had come in touch with—and he had decided at that moment that he needed to recruit this fearsome intellect for his own cause, lest she prove his downfall.

Ullikummis enacted a bold plan against Cerberus shortly thereafter, amassing his nascent army to attack and overwhelm their hidden base in the Bitterroot Mountains. Ullikummis had left the task of running the overthrown base in the hands of his first priest, a man called Dylan, whose primary job was to turn Brigid's partner, Kane, into a military leader for his stone army. Dylan had failed, and Kane had turned on him and overthrown the briefly victorious regime of his enemies. But Ullikummis himself had already exited the redoubt with Brigid, bringing her to Bensalem, where he had brainwashed and reconstructed her mind for his own means. Brigid, an eminently capable woman of fearsome intellect, had tried to resist, but ultimately her personality had been broken down and remade in the form of her new self, Brigid Haight. Now Haight was Ullikummis's new first priest, his so-called hand in darkness, as he had been for his father. And with her help, Ullikummis would bring about the next reign of the mighty Annunaki, an era over which he and Ninlil would preside.

Outside, through the open window of the rock-walled room, Brigid perceived the rays of the early-morning sun playing across the ever-changing ocean surface. It was barely dawn, the night chill still clinging heavily in the air. Gently pushing aside Little Quav, Brigid reached for the clothes that were draped over the stone chair at the end of her bed. Like everything else in Bensalem, the chair was constructed of rock and had a rough, weather-beaten look to it. As she took her single garment from the seat, two doglike creatures came wandering past the open door. They were huge, the size of lions with that same grace and majesty. Their bodies were rough, coated in a living stone that seemed to match the walls and the furniture of the room. One stared into the room for a moment, its nose in the air, and Brigid saw that it had eyes that looked sad and unmistakably human. She pushed the thought from her mind as she stepped into the leather leggings of the catsuit.

In a few moments, Brigid closed the front of the formfitting black leather suit she favored, stretching her arms out before her to affix its sleeves in place. The suit clung to her supple curves like a second skin, reflecting the faint red glow that emanated from the roiling veins in the walls. Now dressed, Brigid bent to retrieve the heavy fur cloak that she had tossed to the floor before retiring the previous evening, pulling it over her shoulders. Then, cinching the ties on the cloak, she stared across the room once more to Ullikummis, who waited in the doorway like some rudimentary statue from a primitive culture.

Meeting his hellish eyes, Brigid repeated Ullikummis's words back to him. "The stars are aligned," she said, knowing full well what it meant. "Thus it's time."

With a single nod, Ullikummis turned and left the room, his footsteps like pounding jackhammer blows on the hard stone floor. Little Quav remained in the middle of the room, abandoned and looking to Brigid for direction. The red-haired woman called Haight reached her hand down to take that of the hybrid girl's.

"Come on, little one," she said. "Time to meet with destiny."

Together, Brigid and Quav followed Ullikummis through the cool, echoing corridors of the rocky fortress in some perversion of the family unit, the stone hounds trotting along at their sides like the family dogs. It was the closest Little Quav had ever known in her short life to being a part of a real family.

THE THRONE ROOM was as simple as Brigid's living quarters, albeit larger. There were few decorations on the rough stone walls, just patterns on the rocks like veins on a leaf, along with two thick, moth-eaten curtains that had been used to partition lesser sections of the room. The windows were open, as no glass existed in the fortress island of Bensalem. Several of the windows were narrow slits, while one was wider, a circular hole in the wall behind the rock throne itself. The throne was massive, and sturdy enough to accommodate the hulking body of Ullikummis. He sat there now, his magma eyes pulsing. Two of his faithful hounds curled around the throne, their rough stone bodies melding together in the half-light of the room.

Brigid entered with Quav at her side, her pace slower than normal in deference to the girl's shorter legs. She looked across the room to where the raised platform waited. This was the parallax point, a key site in a network of linked locations that could be accessed via a teleportational device called an interphaser. The interphasers worked by accessing these naturally occurring hyperdimensional vortices, which could be found all over the world and beyond. Interphasers then opened a quantum window between the two points, allowing their users to step through the gateway to a place that may be a thousand miles or more away. While eminently adaptable, interphasers were limited in the points they could access, although Ullikummis had tapped them in a different manner to that seen before. By applying knowledge he had retrieved from the Ontic Library, that undersea storehouse of the rules governing reality, Ullikummis could fold space during the interphase jump, subtly shifting his destination point and transferring whole armies to specific places. It was through this technique that his attack on the Cerberus redoubt had been so successful two months earlier. Once the interphaser was activated, the journey itself was instantaneous and would be over in the blink of an eye.

The parallax point itself, like the rest of the room, was carved of simple rock, seemingly not shaped by hand but by the elements themselves. It stood two feet higher than the floor of the room, with twin circles marked out on its surface concentrically. The circles were carved channels no deeper than a knuckle joint, the widest of them reaching out to just a foot before the edge of the platform itself.

Ullikummis was concentrating now, reknitting the pathways so that he could utilize the interphase gateway in a subtly different way. Brigid watched as his bright eyes dimmed, his thoughts turning within himself.

"Come on, child," Brigid whispered to Quav, keeping her voice low. "We need to be ready for when the time comes."

Quav clung to Brigid's hand as the flame-haired woman led her to the dais, helping the hybrid girl up over the low step. Then, instructing the girl to remain in place, Brigid strode from the platform to an area that was masked behind one of the thick velvet curtains. She pushed the drape back, stone rings holding it in place on a stone strut that ran from wall to wall.

Behind the curtain lay a series of shelves like a bookcase, each one constructed from the same rough stone as the rest of the nightmarish sea palace. There were weapons arrayed on the upper shelves: a heavy mace constructed of stone, a leather bag filled with throwing stones, a TP-9 semiautomatic pistol with several clips of bullets.

Brigid plucked up the semiautomatic, her favored weapon when entering a combat situation, checking its breech before loading a new magazine and securing the extras in a pocket sewn into the lining of her cloak. The TP-9 was a compact but bulky pistol with a covered targeting scope across the top, all finished in molded matte black. The grip was set just off center beneath the barrel, and in the user's hand, the unit appeared to form a lopsided square, hand and wrist making the final side and corner. Satisfied, Brigid shoved the pistol into a hip holster, twisting it slightly to secure it.

Then Brigid crouched, reaching for one of two objects that waited on the lowest shelf of the wall unit, resting on the floor. The two items were identical in design, and it was impossible to tell them apart. Pyramidal in shape, the items stood twelve inches from apex to square base, and each side of the base measured twelve inches in length. The sides were plated in a shimmering mirrored metal, its surface curved randomly so as to reflect in a strange, almost disconcerting way. These were the interphasers, the teleportational units that could be used to access a parallax point and transfer a person or persons across the quantum ether.

Gingerly, Brigid picked up the unit to the right and carried it in both hands to the platform where Little

Quav was waiting. Kneeling for a moment, she flipped open a hidden door at the base of the pyramid-shaped machine, and her slender fingers traced a quick tattoo across the control buttons revealed within. The interphaser bleeped a moment, chirruping to itself as it accessed the cosmic pathways that would be used for this journey outside of traditional space.

Brigid stepped back as the interphaser began its automated ignition sequence, reaching for Quav's hand as the unit came to life.

In his throne, Ullikummis dropped out of the meditative state he had been in, his eyes resuming their fearsome glow like the lighting of a fire.

"The final sequence begins," he stated, the words rumbling through the throne room like distant thunder. "The endgame has arrived."

The three-year-old child known as Quav grasped Brigid's hand, squeezing it tighter as Ullikummis— genetically her son from four millennia before—drew himself out of the throne and strode across the room toward the raised platform containing the parallax point. Around them, the interphaser seemed to be splitting apart, a cone of many colors launching all around it, widening as it clambered upward through the room and, nonsensically, mirroring this action deep into the floor, the sight replacing the stone tiles there. Witchfire crackled within that dark swirl of colors, firing across its depths like lightning.

"I am the bringer of death," Ullikummis chanted, "the destroyer of souls, the alpha and the omega, the vanishing point. I am the Godkiller."

With those words, Ullikummis stepped onto the raised platform, the dogs trotting obediently along at his heels as he joined Brigid Haight and the girl who would be Ninlil amid the glowing quantum portal of the interphaser. The jump had begun.

THE CATHEDRAL BELL was chiming in Luilekkerville, a continuous droning clang pressing against the silence. Inside, the cathedral was packed. Almost one thousand individuals had crammed themselves within its confines, listening to the bell's droning as Minister Morrow strode proudly among them, a broad, toothy grin on his heavily jowled face. Many of the congregation had seats but some were forced to stand, piling in through several doorways where the shadow of a man—elongated and alien—stretched into the aisle beyond through some quirk of the architecture. Every last building in the ville had emptied, disgorging its occupants, young or old, to attend this special service.

"Alone we were weak, lost, we were victims," Morrow intoned as he strode up to the cathedral's central plinth. "Alone we were afraid. Those who grew up here, who witnessed the fall of Snakefish, will recall the feelings of real fear that gripped them as their world collapsed about their ears."

There were voices of assent from the congregation, calls of support and a hubbub of agreement from farther back among the swilling crowds.

"But together," Minister Morrow called, thrusting his clenched right fist in the air above his head where everyone could see, "together we are strong. Together we cannot be defeated. Together we are the heralds of the glorious future, together we are the heralds of god.

"Each one of you here today is my brother, my sister," Morrow continued. "Each one of you is a part of the future body, each one of you a building block for eternity.

"We are strong because we are stone!" Morrow

shouted, opening the fist he held straight above his head. Revealed within, a rock rested on his palm, just three inches across and dark as a shadow. As the congregation cheered and whooped their support, the rock began to glow, at first faintly in a soft peachy orange, before rapidly becoming brighter until it was burning a lustrous red as rich as lava.

"We are stone," Morrow chanted, and the people of the congregation took up the chant, shouting their allegiance to the glorious future of Ullikummis.

In Morrow's hand, the stone glowed brighter still, illuminating the altar where the minister stood, painting his simple robes in rich scarlet and vermilion.

"We are stone," Morrow called, and a thousand voices echoed the same words back to him. "We are stone."

As the voices became louder, calling in time with the chiming bell, the air began to change above the minister's head, poised as he was at the very center of the towering structure. The air seemed to take on a tangibility as a swirl of color began to form, small and faint at first but unmistakably present all the same.

The congregation continued to chant as the swirl above the minister grew bigger and more pronounced. The colors pulsed and swirled, dancing with one another like the aurora borealis, changing as they swam in the air. And somewhere deep in the midst of that multihued pattern, pencil-thin fingers of lightning began to crackle and flash.

Morrow continued to chant, his open hand raised in the air, brandishing the glowing stone like Prometheus bringing fire from the gods. The stone felt hotter now, not burning but like the feel of another person's skin, lover to lover.

"I am stone."

The crowd continued to repeat the phrase over and over as the wormhole opened behind their leader, widening like a circular window into the quantum ether.

Unknown to the congregation, all across the country, dozens more of the wormholes were opening as the faithful were called by Ullikummis, a widely scattered flock of believers called into service by their savior.

In Luilekkerville, the hole in space was as tall as a house now, taking up two stories of the cathedral's innards, poised like a disk in the center of the massive enclosed space, like an eye looking into the infinite. The colors swirled and clashed and witchfire flashed across its depths, the call of Ullikummis echoing from the infinity rent to tug at the souls of the chanting congregation.

Suddenly, Morrow turned to face the expanding circular disk, seeing it properly for the first time where it swirled behind him. His lips continued to mouth the chant—"We are stone"—but the sound died before it left his throat, snatched away by the swirling elemental forces that he was staring into. Minister Morrow looked into the abyss, his human eyes trying to make sense of the fractal patterns of the quantum ether, as he led his congregation into its shining depths. The disk looked like a bruise, blacks and purples and indigo blues all mixing together as it grew larger and larger, a hundred other shades swirling within its tesseract depths.

And if the end of the world had a color, then this was it.

Chapter 2

The spaceship *Tiamat* was crumbling about them, chunks of its wall plating fracturing away, dropping into the ankle-deep water that seemed to fill every passageway. A man and woman were racing through the curving artery that ran in a loop at the exterior wall of the ship's hull, and the man carried another figure in his muscular arms. He was much larger than the woman in his arms, and he made the task of carrying her seem effortless as he and his companion sought the makeshift entryway they had blasted in the ship's hull just a few hours earlier.

Grant was an ex-Magistrate from Cobaltville who now served the Cerberus operation. He was a huge man in his late thirties, wide-shouldered with skin like polished mahogany. His head was shaved clean, and he wore a trim goatee beard that surrounded his broad mouth in a black circle. His clothes were in disarray, as were those of his companions, and his heavy boots splashed in the water as he leaped over the riblike protrusions that lined the circular-walled corridor. Grant wore a long coat over his shadow suit, both of them made of black fabric, the former fabricated from a Kevlar weave. The shadow suit boasted remarkable properties. Snugly fitting its wearer like a second skin, the one-piece garment had armorlike features sufficient to deflect a blade, redistribute kinetic shock and offer protection from environmental hazards.

Grant continued to run, ducking as another chunk of the walls tumbled away in a crash of shell-like material. "Keep moving," he instructed his companion, though the command was unnecessary. Perhaps he was really talking to himself, driving himself on as they both hurried toward the rent in the hull through which they might escape this nightmare.

Running just a few paces behind Grant was his companion, a beautiful woman with olive skin and long dark hair that swung behind her in a ponytail. In her early twenties, Rosalia was a mercenary who had recently hooked up with the Cerberus organization during the ongoing Ullikummis infiltration. She had tucked the cuffs of her combat pants into the supple leather boots she wore, kicking out with long legs to keep pace with her taller companion. Her open denim jacket showed the shadow suit she wore beneath, and she had a Ruger P-85 pistol stashed in a low-slung holster on her right hip and a *katana* sword tucked through her belt loop across the opposing hip. The sword was two feet in length, and the blade had been blackened by flames to the color of charcoal. Rosalia's chest rose and fell as she took deep breaths to keep up with Grant's long strides, and her deep brown eyes seemed to burn with rage.

Grant carried another woman in his arms, her petite frame much smaller than Rosalia's. Her name was Domi and she was an albino, her skin a deathly white, her short hair the creamy color of bone where it framed her sharp-planed face in a pixie cut. Right now her pale flesh was marred with streaks of black where ash had smeared across her skin, and her eyes were closed in slumber. Open, those eyes were a vibrant, satanic red, like two pure rubies. Domi wore simple combat clothes in dark colors, but the clothes had been torn in places following a recent struggle.

As the group reached sight of the hole in the hull of the crumbling spaceship, Grant heard someone calling to him. Up ahead, he saw the familiar form of their other companion—a modern-day samurai warrior called Kudo, who was dressed in supple armor and had a long sword sheath depending from his belt. Kudo was one of the Tigers of Heaven, a group of fearsome warriors who had joined forces with the Cerberus exiles as they defended themselves from the hostile campaign by Ullikummis.

As Grant and Rosalia got closer, they saw that Kudo's face was streaked red across the left-hand side where something had marred and puckered the skin, and the white of his left eye had turned a chilling bloodred. His dark hair was plastered to his head in short, wet curls.

"What happened to you?" Grant asked as they made their way together to the hole in the ruined hull.

"I mistimed the charge," Kudo explained wryly before asking about his missing partner, Kishiro.

"He didn't make it," Grant admitted solemnly as he ducked through the door-sized hole that an explosive charge had left in the ship's outer hull.

The ship was grounded. In fact, it had never flown, at least not in its current form. An Annunaki starship of legendary repute, *Tiamat* had been mistakenly identified in ancient Sumerian mythology as the mother to the Annunaki race of space gods. More accurately, she was a mother ship, an organic machine that housed the genetic templates of the Annunaki. She had returned to Earth's orbit several years ago at the start of the twenty-third century, downloading the genetic codes that brought about the Annunaki royal family's rebirth from their co-coonlike shells as the nine hybrid barons, but had later self-destructed in an explosion that rocked the skies. Grant had been there when the destruct order had been given, and he had watched from the porthole of a flee-ing lifeboat as *Tiamat* went up in flames.

However, the spacecraft had reappeared just a few weeks before on the banks of the River Euphrates, Iraq, her familiar dragon shape towering over an empty city formed of her skeletal wings. Grant had no possible way of knowing, but the ship had been grown from a seed planted by Enlil, the cruelest of the Annunaki over-lords. Enlil had tapped the ship's incredible reservoir of knowledge to fast-track an army of Annunaki, warping the DNA of any human who came close to the skeletal city. However, something had been wrong deep within the codes of *Tiamat* herself, and the ship was now de-teriorating at an incredible rate, falling apart as its huge water tanks bled out.

Outside, the sun sat high in the sky, its midmorning burn pounding warmly against Grant's skin.

"We should destroy it," Kudo insisted, staring an-grily back at the shovel-shaped head of the spaceship that rested on the riverbank.

"We don't have anything that can do that," Grant told him as Rosalia emerged from the raw-edged hole in the hull, "but we can come back. Bomb the wicked thing out of existence once and for all."

DEEP INSIDE the dragon-form ship, deep in the belly of the beast, Enlil was fighting for his life.

Enlil, a high-ranking member of Annunaki royalty, and self-styled overlord of the human race, was a beau-tiful creature. He stood over six feet tall, with a crest of spines atop his head that added almost a foot to his already impressive height. His scaled skin was the color of gold dipped in blood, of sunset in the tropics, and it covered his muscular body like a suit of malleable armor. His chest and arms were bare, as were his clawed feet, while his legs were covered in loose, billowing breeks. Other than that, Enlil wore a bloodred cloak cinched around his shoulders that trailed down to brush at the tops of his ankles. The cloak was torn, for it had suffered during the current struggle with his enemies.

His enemies were even now swarming at him from all sides, like a cloud of insects attacking an intruder. Naked, it was clear that each of them came from the same race as Enlil, their muscular lizard bodies moving with the same eerie grace that characterized the overlord's gestures. They were adult Annunaki, full-grown yet they had only just come to life. The experiment engineered by Overlord Enlil had backfired terribly in the final moments thanks to the intervention of the Cerberus crew. The Annunaki had been grown in the vats of *Tiamat,* twisted around the DNA templates of trapped human bodies to create a new pantheon of Annunaki space gods. Even now, their egglike birthing pods stood silently around the scene of carnage, lining the sides of the vast room where streams of water burbled and catwalks grown from bone ran overhead.

Ill lit, the room was approximately the size of two football fields, with railless stairwells dotted around, each reaching up to the second level where the catwalks ran. To one side, a burning column belched smoke into the vast room, spewing out lightninglike shards of electricity toward the arched ceiling high above, illuminating the room in violent staccato bursts. Swathes of the roof were falling away in great chunks, crashing to the floor in explosions of dust and water.

And amid all of this, Enlil was struggling with the reborn forms of the Annunaki. There were 213 of them in all. Each one was unique, some male, some female, their scales a rainbow of achingly beautiful colors shimmering in the half-light that ebbed through the birthing chamber. Some had spines across their brows like Enlil's, while others featured a crown of bony protrusions around their skulls.

Believing himself to be the last survivor of his race, Enlil had grown these bodies to re-create the glory of the Age of the Annunaki, who had ruled the Earth more than five thousand years before. Prior to Enlil's experimentation, the rebirth of the Annunaki had involved a slow procedure of growing hybrid bodies that could accommodate the genetic changes needed to transform, chrysalis-like, into their Annunaki final form. Enlil had altered that, utilizing a much quicker—though far more traumatic—process to skip a step and change the basic human template into one suitable for the Annunaki. His plans had been interrupted by Grant, Domi, Rosalia and Kudo, and the waiting bodies had been awoken too soon, their memory downloads incomplete. In place of the memories of his brethren, Enlil found that an unexpected third party had been at play, prepped to snatch the bodies for their own. This group were the Igigi, the one-time slave caste of the Annunaki who were recorded in legend as "those who watch and see." Without doubt, the Igigi had "watched and seen" the moment to finally strike against their one-time master.

According to Sumerian myth, there had been one thousand Igigi who served the Annunaki, and each one was considered to be a god by the human populace.

However, their role had been to facilitate the day-to-day running of the Annunaki empire on Earth, and they had never achieved names. When Enlil had unleashed the Great Flood to cleanse the Earth of the human race, he had dismissed the Igigi, leaving them to drown as nothing more than collateral damage. But a group of rebellious Igigi had been wise to his plan and had hidden their memories in a shadow box until such time as they had bodies that could house them once more. When Enlil had generated this new army of Annunaki gods, the Igigi had seized their chance and now their souls occupied the Annunaki shells in place of the planned downloads. Now 213 fiercely powerful bodies had turned on the Annunaki overlord who had tried to extinguish them many millennia ago—213 angry souls.

Enlil had been knocked down to the floor by their vicious attacks, and more of the Igigi-possessed Annunaki swarmed on him, kicking and punching him from all sides as he lay on his back. A mound of bodies pressed against him, crushing Enlil to the floor by the sheer weight of numbers. At the bottom of that mound, Enlil was struggling for breath as five or six strong Annunaki bodies crushed against his chest, clawed hands grasping for his throat, reaching for his eyes.

Then, with an almighty effort, Enlil flinched his body, sharp and sudden, and three of the monstrous forms were thrust away from him, careering into the canal streams that filtered across the room.

Enlil shoved upward with both hands, pushing two more of the figures away even as more attackers neared.

"Get away," Enlil snarled, batting at a clawed foot as it swung at his face.

The kicker lost his balance, toppling back as Enlil twisted his grip. As he did so, another Annunaki drove a heel into Enlil's flank, driving the breath from his lungs as he rolled across the hard floor.

Enlil sprawled on his face, his scarlet cloak in disarray about him. There was water here—a shallow channel that ran the length of the room. Four feet wide, it was used to transport items across the vast distance of the chamber. Enlil felt the water's coolness lash against his face, reviving him instantaneously as the Annunaki figures stalked toward him, the sharp claws of their feet clacking against the bonelike tiling in a rising drumbeat of hate.

Enlil pushed himself up, assuming a crouching position. Lightning ripped across the ceiling of the chamber, echoing with such fury that he could feel its pressure drum across his chest. Behind him, a blast of that wild electricity slammed against a stack of the cylindrical birthing pods and they burst into flame. Enlil felt the heat against his back as he watched the milling crowd of reborn Annunaki. Every eye was on him, and every pair of eyes showed the unrestrained fury that welled within. He had betrayed these Igigi, these slaves, betrayed them without a thought, casting them aside as if they meant nothing. But he was a god. Was this not his right?

"Get back, damn you," Enlil spit as the Igigi moved in on him. "I am your lord...your master..."

Enlil's words trailed off as another of the furious Igigi leaped at him, swiping at his face with a salmon-scaled hand that ended in a phalanx of razor-sharp claws. Each of the Annunaki bodies was subtly different, each with its own attributes, its own natural weapons. Enlil rolled aside as the clawed hand reached for his face, only to find he had stepped out of the path of one attack and straight into another. This Annunaki was a broad-shouldered male with skin a canary yellow freckled with brown spots like rust. The yellow-skinned figure cuffed Enlil's ear with a savage punch, the blow so hard it made the overlord's head ring. Then the creatures were following up on their attack, the yellow one driving his knee viciously at Enlil's gut while the red-scaled one got his arms around Enlil's throat from behind and snapped him backward.

Enlil howled in agony as the knee struck his stomach. He was bent so far back by the one holding him that he couldn't move with the blow, and so it seemed to rip through him in a paroxysm of straining muscles.

The yellow-hued creature came at Enlil again, drawing his arm back in readiness for a brutal punch to the face. Enlil watched that blow rushing at him, timing the attack in his mind before rolling his shoulders. Enlil's move served to shift his weight just slightly, but it was enough that he dropped beneath the nasty blow, leaving it to strike at the attacker who still held him from behind by the throat. His captor, the red-scaled Annunaki male, fell down in a flurry of limbs, releasing Enlil as he did so.

Enlil fell, too, unable to keep his balance as he was drawn down by the creature that had held him. His left palm slapped against the tiled floor in a loud clap, and his bent knee brushed the surface of one of the water channels. Then he was up again, spinning back to his feet with the speed of thought.

"I am your master," he repeated as more of the reanimated Annunaki crowded toward him. "You will bow down before me."

Still close, the yellow-hued Annunaki pressed his attack on the traitorous overlord, lashing out with a high kick to Enlil's jaw. The kick brushed against the bottom of Enlil's face, and he was driven up and back at the same time, plummeting down to the bonelike tiles once again in a swathe of billowing red cape.

The yellow Annunaki took a step toward him to renew his attack, but at that moment another lightning strike rocked the high rafters of the room and something large hurtled down from overhead, a boxy shadow in the darkness. It was a seven-foot-long section of one of the catwalks, its surface curved and bevelled, with no railings to prevent a user from stepping off. Now it tumbled through the air, crashing toward the floor beneath.

Enlil watched as the section of catwalk crashed down into the yellow figure's back, slamming him hard across both shoulders and back of the head before he could even react. A shock wave reverberated through the room as the catwalk landed, chunks breaking away with the impact. The yellow figure dropped to the floor, moaning in agony as the catwalk pinned him in place. Blood leaked from the sides of his mouth as he tried to lift himself, but the section of catwalk was too heavy for one Annunaki to move.

Yet there was no time for Enlil to turn this momentary respite to his advantage. Already more of the Igigi creatures were swarming toward him in their stolen bodies, encircling him and cutting off any possible chance of escape. Not one of them spoke; they just stared at him through the slit eyes of the Annunaki, their hate burning in those putrid yellow depths.

Enlil pushed against the hard floor, struggling to stand. But he was too slow. Already another combatant, this one in a beautiful female Annunaki body covered in scales of cobalt blue, was lunging at him with deadly purpose. The Igigi drove both knees down into Enlil's gut in a savage drop-blow before he could clamber off the floor. Enlil slammed back to the tiles, his spine jarring with the bone-crunching impact. Without hesitation, Enlil's arms snapped out and he grabbed his attacker by the throat, tightening his grip against the armorlike scale plate there.

"Look at me," Enlil insisted, biting the words through clenched teeth. "I am your master."

In response, the blue-scaled Annunaki hissed defiantly, spitting a glob of saliva into Enlil's face. With a swift twist of his hands, Enlil snapped the creature's neck, tossing her aside like so much worthless trash. They were not true Annunaki, Enlil sneered; killing them was easy. More than two hundred of the possessed bodies surrounded him, Enlil saw, and he struggled to his feet where a stream of water sparkled past him.

"I gave life unto you," Enlil insisted, his tattered cloak swirling about him as he turned to face each of the slave class, piercing them with his indomitable gaze. "*Tiamat* is your mother, but *I* fathered you."

He searched the crowd, eyes meeting and passing the glaring eyes of more than two hundred creatures who had spent millennia waiting for payback. Overhead, another great chunk of the ceiling peeled away like skin and crashed down, electricity playing across it like witchfire as it slammed to the plate floor behind the Annunaki forms.

"I am your master," Enlil reminded them. "Without me, you are nothing, simply purposeless creatures."

As one, the Igigi stepped toward Enlil, their minds working in unison, bringing their final, brutal judgment on this monster who had once ruled them. They were in uni-thought, the shared horror of spending over three thousand years without bodies creating a kind of melded mind, frayed and blurred, no longer able to differentiate between individuals.

Enlil's shoulders shook as he struggled for breath, the exertions of this battle so soon after he had fought with Grant and his Cerberus colleagues draining his inner resources. Once again, lightning flashed overhead, lancing across the ceiling like a white-hot claw.

"I am Enlil," the overlord stated. "Enlil the destroyer. The one known as Dagon, as Kumbari, as the Imperator. A hundred names for a million peoples, and every one of those peoples obeyed me."

As one, the Igigi in their Annunaki shells took another menacing step toward Enlil, blocking him off on all sides, caging him in place.

Enlil glared at them, the power of his will lancing through his eyes like the hypnotic stare of the cobra. "You will obey me," he told them, his voice firm despite his panting breath.

As one, the Igigi took another tentative step forward. And then, as one, they stopped.

Enlil turned to survey them, his gaze falling upon each in turn as more than two hundred lesser beings stood all around him, awaiting his orders once more. They had turned on him for a moment, three thousand years of torment twisting their minds, making them believe perhaps that they were his betters. But he was the overlord.

"Now," Enlil breathed ominously, "we have work yet to do."

Above, a triple flash of lightning hurtled across the ceiling of *Tiamat*'s birthing chamber, lancing down and destroying another clump of the birth pods that had been used to grow new bodies for the Annunaki. It didn't matter. The Igigi would do.

Enlil had his army, eternally obedient. He was overlord for a reason.

GRANT'S TEAM rushed through the bone city of the dragon, the empty streets echoing with their footsteps. As they ran, Grant engaged his Commtact, a hidden radio transceiver that was used to communicate with his colleagues in the field and back at Cerberus headquarters. Most of the members of the Cerberus field teams had a surgically embedded Commtact. The subdermal device was a top-of-the-line communications unit, the designs for which had been discovered among the artifacts in Redoubt Yankee several years before by the Cerberus exiles. Commtacts operated via sensor circuitry, incorporating an analog-to-digital voice encoder that was subcutaneously embedded in each subject's mastoid bone. Once the pintels made contact, transmissions were picked up by the wearer's auditory canals, and dermal sensors transmitted the electronic signals directly through the skull casing, vibrating the ear canal. In theory, even a completely deaf user would still be able to hear, after a fashion, courtesy of the Commtact device. Commtacts also functioned as real-time translation devices, providing they had enough raw vocabulary from a language programmed into their processor, and because they were directly connected to the body of the user, could amplify speech no matter how quiet.

"Encrypt alpha-niner," Grant murmured as he brought the Commtact to life, engaging the encryption protocols that had been added to the system over the past six weeks. "Cerberus, this is Grant."

There was a pause while Grant waited for one of his faraway colleagues to respond. The voice that came back was that of Donald Bry, a man who was loosely considered the second in command of the Cerberus operation and whose voice, like his manner, seemed ever fraught with worry. "Go ahead, Grant."

"Have just exited *Tiamat*," Grant explained. "Making our way out of the ville now. Kishiro didn't make it and we have wounded."

"How many?" Bry asked over the Commtact, his voice emotionless and professional now.

"Kudo took a face full of explosive," Grant explained, "and Domi's out of it right now. I want her checked over as soon as she wakes up. She's been through a shitload of trauma."

Still running, Grant turned to Rosalia with a raised eyebrow. "Rosie? Anything you want to add?"

"I can look after myself," the dark-haired mercenary said dismissively. "You worry about your people, Magistrate."

Unlike Grant, Rosalia had only served with Cerberus briefly. She valued her independence, and there had been no time for her to have the minor surgery necessary to implant a Commtact receiver, even had she agreed to it. Grant eyeballed her a moment longer before relating her response back to Bry. Dark streaks of ash and soot marred her otherwise beautiful features, and her clothes were ripped in places, but otherwise she seemed fine.

"We lost our transport," Grant continued, speaking into his Commtact, "so we're going to need an exit strategy. You have anything showing, Donald?"

The Cerberus organization favored several specific methods for transporting their personnel over vast distances. Although its staff frequently utilized air and ground vehicles, the operation itself had taken its name from a twentieth-century military project devoted to a teleportation system that relied on mat-trans units. More recently, Cerberus had applied that knowledge to the alien design of the interphaser, accessing parallax points to transport staff across the globe and beyond.

"Scanning for mat-trans locations now," Bry assured Grant.

"Stay on it," Grant acknowledged. "We're maybe fifteen minutes from city limits yet."

With that the communication broke off at Grant's command.

SOMEWHERE ON THE West Coast of what had historically been known as the United States of America, Cerberus operator Donald Bry was flipping through computer screen data trying to find a suitable exit point for Grant and his team. Until recently, the Cerberus headquarters had been located in the Bitterroot Mountains of Montana. However, following the devastating attack by Ullikummis, the redoubt had been evacuated, and the core personnel had taken up temporary residence on the West Coast. For the moment, Cerberus was much diminished while it struggled to recover, many of its surviving staff forced into hiding.

Bry was a slender man with an unruly mop of copper curls and an expression that ranged from worried to fearful. He was a man given to stressing over a given situation, be it the health of his operatives or simply what the best filling would be for his lunchtime sandwich. He was, however, a remarkable computer expert whose dedication to his job made him an irreplaceable asset to the Cerberus organization.

Bry sat amid a bank of laptops, each wired through a mainframe to boost their power and link their attributes. Across the room, Brewster Philboyd worked at his own terminal, scanning information from several satellite feeds and location marker points. Tall with swept-back blond hair, Philboyd was an astrophysicist. He wore the standard white jumpsuit of Cerberus staff along with his usual black-framed spectacles.

As the two worked at their separate tasks, another call came over the Commtact system. This one was from a field operative called Kane, and it caused some excitement in the temporary Cerberus hideout. Kane had located the base of their enemy, Ullikummis, and Philboyd and Bry combined their resources to bring the location up on screen. As they did so, the founder of the Cerberus operation, Mohandas Lakesh Singh, joined them to review the situation and speak directly with Kane.

Thus, by the time Bry got back to the question that Grant had posed, a full twenty-two minutes had passed.

"It seems that the easiest way to evac your team is to use the interphaser," Bry explained to Grant.

"We don't have one with us," was Grant's patient response.

"I'll send someone out to meet you, and you can all come home together," Bry said, eminently logical.

"Makes sense," Grant agreed. "Where do you need us?"

Bry tapped out a sequence of commands on his computer keyboard, bringing up a map of parallax points, which he combined with the location transponder that Grant had with him at all times. Hidden beneath his flesh, the transponder relayed his location as well as crucial data regarding his state of health. "I'm getting a parallax reading about twelve miles to your west," Bry explained as he watched the map light up.

"That's gonna be a trek," Grant complained. "Nothing closer?"

"Wait," Bry replied, speaking as much to himself as to the man on the other end of the communication link. Before Bry's eyes, the on-screen map glowed with the crucial locations of the parallax points. They looked like a grid of stars, sprayed across Iran, Iraq and the rest of the Arab world. As Bry watched, a new point lit up on the map just outside the dragon-shaped settlement, less than a half mile from where Grant's transponder was showing. It was as if a new parallax point had just come into existence. But, that wasn't possible, was it?

"Grant, I'm picking up a point close to you...." Bry began warily. "It seems to have just appeared."

ON THE OUTSKIRTS of the dragon-shaped structure on the banks of the Euphrates, Grant, Rosalia and Kudo were staring in amazement as a huge rift opened in the air before them. Twin cones of light ebbed up and downward, growing larger as they watched. The multicolored blur within those cones was tinged with darkness as if painted on a black canvas, streaks of lightninglike witchfire playing within its depths. The Cerberus field team watched, incredulous, as the rift expanded, those twin cones spreading up from a central point at ground level, like some incredible hourglass poised in the air. For a moment it simply stood there, uncanny colors swirling in its depths. And then, even as Grant's team struggled to take in what they were looking at, the rift in space began to disgorge hundreds upon hundreds of people, each one walking in step from its impossible depths like some incredible army. Striding at the head

of that army was the unique stone figure of Ullikummis, the magmalike veins trailing across his body with
a fierce, red-gold glow. Grant recognized someone else,
too, walking purposefully just beside the ancient stone
god—it was the unmistakable figure of missing Cerberus operative Brigid Baptiste, her red-gold hair in
sympathy with those glowing strands of lava that criss-
crossed Ullikummis's frame.

Distantly, Grant was aware of Bry's words trailing
off over the Commtact receiver and he engaged the microphone pickup. "Thanks for the heads-up, Donald,"
he said. "We see it. And it ain't pretty."

Chapter 3

Some fifteen minutes earlier, the temporary Cerberus ops room had come to excited life as a communication was received from Kane. Accompanied by an old ally of the Cerberus team, Kane revealed that he had finally discovered the location of Bensalem, the fortress island that Ullikummis had designated his headquarters.

The Cerberus operation was connected to the external world via a web of communication and surveillance devices, the core of which was made up of two satellites in geosynchronous Earth orbit. Cerberus employed concealed uplinks that chattered continuously with these orbiting satellites to provide much of the empirical data its operatives relied upon. Gaining access to the satellites had taken many hours of intense trial-and-error work by the top scientists at the original Cerberus redoubt. Now the Cerberus crew could draw on live feeds from an orbiting Vela-class reconnaissance satellite and the Keyhole Comsat.

Speaking in real time to Kane, Brewster Philboyd accessed the reconnaissance satellite to track his position. Aged somewhere in his midforties, Brewster Philboyd was a long-serving Cerberus desk jockey. His lanky six-foot frame seemed hunched as he sat at the laptop and fed information to the satellite following Kane's instruction. Philboyd had joined the Cerberus team along with a number of other Moon exiles about two years

earlier, and had proved to be a valuable addition to the
staff. His dogged determination to find the cause of a
problem or uncover the basic workings of a system had
helped reveal the operating secrets of the interphaser.
While he wasn't a fighter, Philboyd was as determined
as a dog with a bone when he was faced with a scientific or engineering problem.

As Brewster worked, Donald Bry took over the communication feed, discussing the situation with Kane.
As he spoke, Lakesh walked into the sunny back room
that had been transformed into the operations center.

Lakesh was not a tall man, but he stood with a regal
bearing. He had dusky skin, thick black hair with slight
hints of white at the temples and above the ears, and
a refined mouth beneath an aquiline nose. He looked
to be a man of perhaps fifty years of age, but in fact
Lakesh was far older. Having spent more than a century
in cryogenic suspension, Lakesh was truthfully a man of
250 years of age, and until quite recently he had looked
to be exactly that. A contrivance of circumstances had
served to allow Lakesh to renegotiate his age, bringing
him back to a healthy fifty-something after a period of
accelerated decrepitude. A physicist and cybernetics authority, Lakesh had been present when the U.S. military
had first begun testing the mat-trans system. Not given
to panic, Lakesh provided leadership that formed a calm
center around which the Cerberus operation rotated.

"What has happened?" Lakesh asked, having heard
the raised voices as he approached from the corridor
outside.

"It's Kane," Bry explained.

"Put him on speaker," Lakesh instructed. Though
he seemed outwardly calm, a range of conflicting emotions vied for attention in Lakesh's mind. Kane was a

long-trusted member of the Cerberus team, one of the
most gifted field operatives Lakesh had ever known.
However, he was suffering some kind of infection that
created a paralysis of his face and was affecting his
vision, causing him agonizing moments of blindness.
Right now Kane should be restricted to bed rest, but
with personnel so thinly spread the brave ex-Magistrate
had volunteered to check out an alert beacon detected
coming from their old headquarters roughly six hours
earlier. It was there that Kane had found their old ally
Balam, with whom he now traveled.

"Kane?" Lakesh said, clipping a portable microphone
pickup over one ear. The pickup angled before his mouth
like a hard plastic straw, capturing his every utterance
and relaying it to Kane. "This is Lakesh. Donald is just
bringing me up to speed now."

Hidden speakers on Donald Bry's computer terminal
resounded with Kane's calm voice as the field agent replied, "Just tell me when you can see it," he said.

There was a momentary discussion while Donald
Bry explained to his mentor what was going on, and
then the satellite feed on Brewster's terminal screen
centered on an overhead view of a vast island of slate-
gray rock. The island was like an insect dropped into
the ocean, hard, jutting planes reaching out at nightmarish angles, hooks and narrow channels dotting its
brutal lines. Lakesh guessed that those channels would
be almost impossible to navigate by boat.

"What is it?" Lakesh breathed, his words just about
audible. "What have they found?"

"Do you see it?" Kane asked over the speakers, ignoring or not hearing Lakesh's query.

"Yes," Lakesh replied instantly, "but what is it?"

"Ullikummis's home," Kane stated matter-of-factly,

his words somehow lacking the impossible gravity with which Lakesh expected they would be expressed.

Lakesh stared at the image from the satellite feed for a long moment, unaware that he was holding his breath. "Are you there now?" he asked finally.

SEVERAL HUNDRED MILES away, just off the coast of what had once been New England, two figures skulked through the throne room of Ullikummis. Crouching together in the shadows of the stone castle, the two figures could not have been more different.

The first was Kane, a powerfully built man in his early thirties, battle hardened with a tension in his body that came from years of combat readiness. A dark beard shaded his chin and jowls, while his dark hair had grown long, reaching past his collar in trailing curlicues like snakes' tails. Kane was an ex-Magistrate turned warrior for the rebellious operation known as Cerberus. His clothes looked worn and dirty, and his denim jacket was frayed at the edges where the cuffs and hem had begun to unravel. There was something else about him, too, a bony protrusion that stabbed out from his left eye like a half-buried seashell on the beach, arcing down his cheek and marring his otherwise handsome features.

"Yeah, we're here," Kane said quietly, his voice picked up by the hidden Commtact implant he wore. He checked the open window as he spoke, peering out into the dark, uninviting waves that crashed through the narrow channels that cut their labyrinthine way through the island from the sea. Those would be hell to navigate, he realized.

Crouching beside Kane was the shorter figure of Balam, humanoid but not human, with a bulbous head and black eyes like limpid pools of water. Hairless,

Balam's skin was a pallid gray-white, the color a human might associate with seasickness. In contrast to Kane's tattered combat clothes, Balam wore a long, shapeless robe that reached almost to his ankles. The robe was woven of a soft material and dyed the indigo color of a summer night's sky. It had no pattern beyond the weave itself, but close to the collar, a darker patch showed around a frayed section where the robe had been torn during a scuffle. The dark stain was blood; Balam had been shot in the chest six days before when his charge, the foster girl known as Little Quav, had been taken from his protection by Brigid Haight.

Now Balam had joined Kane in his quest to find Quav and Brigid. The two of them had discovered this place utilizing an alien artifact in Balam's possession, a chair that could navigate through space.

Balam watched Kane as the taller man walked warily through the empty throne room, discussing with his colleagues over the Commtact.

"We're going to do a recon," Kane explained to Lakesh. "I'll have to get back to you."

With that, he cut off the communication link, and Balam was suddenly aware that Kane was staring at him, blue-gray eyes piercing into his.

"How is your sight, friend Kane?" Balam asked, his voice reedy and eerily alien in pitch and delivery.

The thing that lay in Kane's flesh seemed to have disrupted his vision, throwing him into bouts of temporary blindness, often accompanied by vivid hallucinations of another life—the life of his foe, Ullikummis. These problems were exacerbated by teleportation travel, be it through interphaser or the more traditional mat-trans, and Balam had speculated it was linked to the breakdown and re-forming of Kane's molecules at a quantum level, that shock event somehow triggering the stone fleck that had become embedded in Kane's face. The problem was so serious that, when they had met up earlier that day, Balam had proposed a mind-link that would grant Kane a clarity of vision, albeit one that was alien to his normal perception. The mind-link operated by proximity, which meant it would fail if Kane and Balam became too far separated. Even now, Kane was utilizing Balam's link to see more clearly, to overcome the effects that the shard of rock was generating in his own vision. However, how well that was working was anyone's guess—Kane tended to play these things close to his chest.

"I'm okay for now," Kane replied noncommittally. "Let's just keep moving."

Without waiting for Balam to answer, Kane led the way through the chilly throne room, commanding the Sin Eater automatic pistol he had hidden in a wrist holster into his hand. The Sin Eater had once been the official side arm of the Magistrate Division, an automatic handblaster that folded in on itself so that it could be stored in a bulky holster strapped just above the user's wrist. Unfolding to its full extension, the automatic pistol was a little under fourteen inches in length and equipped with 9 mm rounds. Kane's holster reacted to a specific flinch movement of his wrist tendons, powering the pistol automatically into his hand. The trigger had no guard; the necessity had never been foreseen that any kind of safety features would ever be required since the Magistrates were considered infallible. Thus, if the user's index finger was crooked at the time it reached his hand, the pistol would begin firing automatically. Though no longer a Magistrate himself, Kane had retained his weapon from his days in Cobaltville, and he still felt at his most comfortable with the weapon in his hand. It was an extension to his body that seemed second nature now, like the comforting weight of a wristwatch. By contrast, Balam was unarmed, his brief use of a blaster indirectly causing him to get shot.

The cold throne room was empty, and despite the sounds of the crashing waves and the caws of gulls from its open window, it seemed somehow abandoned to Kane. He had taken the lead because of his experience in the field—Kane was a soldier while Balam was, if push came to shove, nothing more than a glorified negotiator. Furthermore, going back to his days as a hard-contact Magistrate, Kane had been infamous for his so-called point-man sense, a near-psychic ability to detect danger before it happened. While that perhaps seemed superhuman to many casual observers, it was in fact a combination of Kane's finely tuned five senses, creating an awareness of his surroundings that was almost Zenlike in its comprehension.

Right now, Kane didn't detect anything much in the room, and he swiftly made his way out through the open doorway and into the corridor that lay beyond. Like the throne room, the corridor was empty, the stone walls cold and echoing the nearby waves as they crashed against the rough sides of the fortress island.

It was a strange feeling, walking through that corridor. On the one hand it was recognizably a corridor to Kane's eyes. And yet, on the other hand, it also had the properties of something eroded through the ages, weathered rock ripped through by shearing winds or surging water, cutting pathways through it over the aeons. It felt cold, lifeless, charmless. Whatever had crafted this, it lacked any sense of artistry, any desire for anything beyond function. The floor was hard and rough and unstable, the coolness of the stone so cold that it penetrated the soles of Kane's scuffed leather boots. Window slits were hacked into the walls here and there, haphazard and open to the elements, green moss growing along their sills where the seawater had pooled.

Kane continued down the corridor on silent tread, efficiently peering left and right into open doorways that led off the tunnellike passageway. Balam kept ten paces behind him, trotting along as lightly as possible to keep his own steps quiet. Kane peered over his shoulder, checking that the diminutive alien was keeping pace.

"Don't get too far behind," Kane instructed in a whisper. "If I have to shoot something, I'm going to want you close by. Or something bad will happen."

Balam looked at Kane apologetically. "I'm sorry, Kane," he whispered. "I'm unused to the application of stealth in this manner."

Kane nodded. "Just don't get shot if it kicks off," he warned, and then he continued on his way, hurrying down the corridor at a jog.

Following the ex-Magistrate, Balam was searching the vast fortress in his own way. A telepath, Balam had nurtured an especially close bond with his foster child, the missing Quav. He had sensed her essence here the very moment that they arrived, feeling it like some vibrant tapestry hanging on the stone walls. Little Quav was the culmination of the Annunaki experiments with rebirth, and she had been placed in Balam's care shortly after her birth to protect her from forces that might use her for ill. In that way, Balam had acted as a neutral party, siding neither with the Annunaki nor humanity but rather shielding the child from the dark destiny contained within her genetic code. Losing the child had hurt Balam, and he knew he had been played for a fool by the wily Ullikummis, tricked by the familiar face of Brigid Baptiste when she had appeared in Agartha. Balam had swiftly realized that Brigid was an agent for an antagonistic party, but with supreme irony, his very seclusion to protect Quav had also meant he was out of touch with developments in the wider world.

Whether foreknowledge of the rise of Ullikummis would have changed things, Balam could not say. As things stood, Balam felt Quav's loss like a scar, a wound on his own body that had cut far deeper than the bullet he had taken to the chest from Brigid Haight's gun during the kidnapping. In this, Balam and Kane had shared a tragedy, for Kane had also been shot by Brigid in her new guise as Ullikummis's hand in darkness. For Kane, that blow had cut even deeper. Physically, the bullet had left merely a bruise on Kane's chest, failing to pierce his armor and hence his flesh. But he and the woman now calling herself Haight were linked, a spiritual bond that entwined both of them through time immemorial. They shared the bond of *anam charas,* or "soul friends," and it seemed to carry over to different incarnations of the two of them, despite where they found themselves. To many, it sounded like mumbo jumbo, but Kane's bond to Brigid was deep and semimystical, despite his own eminently practical nature.

Kane moved through the arching doorway of a room, stepping quietly over the threshold. He could tell immediately that this room had a presence, something indefinable in the air that seemed to act as a warning. It stank of meat and burning, an almost physical wall of stench that made a person's nose wrinkle and eyes sting. Kane had encountered numerous incredible situations in his life, from ghostly hauntings to alien possession, and he had developed something of an instinct for the unusual. Wary now, he scanned the room, the Sin Eater poised before him, tracking the movements of his eyes. This room was large—more than fifty feet in length—and square, with a high ceiling that added to the sense of space. Like the rest of the fortress isle, the walls, ceiling and floor were carved from the same slatelike rock, roughly finished with bumps and chips all around, everything left unadorned by decoration.

There was a pit in the center of the floor, Kane saw, and it dominated the room with its unspoken sense of purpose. Kane stepped toward it without hesitation, still scanning the room for signs of anyone else. Balam hurried along behind him, stepping just inside the doorway and feeling the chill of the room immediately.

Turning to Balam, Kane raised his empty hand, signaling that he should wait where he was. Then the Cerberus warrior continued on, remaining on high alert as he approached the pit. Twenty feet across, the pit was shallow and it was darker around its edges than the surrounding rock where something had charred it.

Kane peered into the pit, already suspecting what he would see there. A deep pile of ashes was spread across the circular indentation, and amid them Kane could see a few bones, several of which were broken, viciously snapped in two. He had seen this before, months earlier when Ullikummis had first arrived on Earth and set up Tenth City, his first attempt at indoctrinating the peoples of the world. There Ullikummis had forced his recruits into brutal bouts of combat to determine both their physical prowess and their loyalty to him. A vast chimney dominated the skyline of that primitive settlement, and those who failed him had been cremated within its eerie confines. Here, once again, Ullikummis had burned those who had failed him, Kane realized, pilgrims who had risked the arduous journey through the narrow, chasmlike channels weaving through the sea fortress to meet their god.

As he looked at the hard, pebblelike flecks among the ashes, something caught Kane's eye. It was a bone, covered in ashes that rested along its length in a little mound. Leaning down, Kane poked at the bone with the nose of his pistol, pushing the worst of the dirt aside. The ashes fell away in silence. It was a bone, all right, no question of that. But when Kane looked at it more closely, he was surprised by the length of it. It looked like a leg bone, maybe a femur, but it was incredibly long. Furthermore, it bulged and featured a subtle twist. Kane had seen many skeletons in his days with Cerberus, but this was unlike anything he had seen before.

"Balam?" Kane called quietly. "What do you make of this?"

Balam shuffled over to join Kane, peering down into the pit where Kane nudged his pistol against his grisly find. "Leg bone?" Balam asked.

"Yeah, but from what?"

Unblinking, Balam looked at it and considered, recalling what he knew of human anatomy. "It looks human in the first instance, but there is something... untoward to its nature. As if it has been..."

Kane glanced up at him. "Changed?" he prompted when Balam left the sentence hanging.

"'Changed' is as adequate a word as any," Balam agreed.

"But how, and by what?" Kane asked, voicing his thoughts.

"The Annunaki are masters of genetic manipulation," Balam reminded him. "Ullikummis himself is a horror by their standards, but only because of the genetic changes wrought upon him at his father's insistence."

"Yeah, I remember," Kane said, nodding. That was not simply old information to Kane; his senses had been assaulted with flashes of Ullikummis's memories each time he had made a teleportation jump over the past weeks—and so, in some sense, he had experienced much of the nightmarish surgery that had featured in the Annunaki prince's earliest years. If nothing else, it had given Kane an insight into why the son hated his father with such fury.

"Something's changed these people," Balam proposed. "Something altered them—"

"Or tried to. Look at this junk," he said, riffling through the ash with the muzzle of his blaster. "Someone's been cooking up a storm, and I'll bet you it was someone who wanted to destroy the evidence of his failures."

"The Annunaki do not have failures," Balam stated wistfully. "They suffer disappointments, nothing more."

"Well," Kane said, drawing his Sin Eater out of the sifting sands of ash, "someone's had a shitload of disappointments in here.

"And we should keep moving," he added.

With that, Kane stood and led the way through the huge room with Balam trotting along at his heels. Balam looked back a moment, staring at the black smudge of the pit that dominated the room. Death seemed to follow Kane, lying in wait wherever he went.

IN THE WEST COAST operations room, Lakesh studied the satellite view of the island of Bensalem and consulted several reference documents.

"This island did not exist a year ago," he stated, shaking his head.

Brewster Philboyd looked at the map that Lakesh had brought up on his own computer screen. "This Ullikummis has pulled things out of thin air before now," he said miserably.

"No, not thin air, Mr. Philboyd," Lakesh corrected. "Rock. He has an affinity to rock, it seems, and is able to employ a form of telekinesis to call on such to do his bidding. That was, by our best guess, how he created his Tenth City. The rock itself was pulled up from beneath the soil—bedrock."

"So, this island—he's pulled it from the sea?" Philboyd theorized.

"It seems probable."

Philboyd shrugged. "I guess even monsters need somewhere to live," he said, nervously pushing the spectacles back up the bridge of his nose.

"No," Lakesh said, "there's more to it than that. Look at the design. Almost circular, with the highest towers based in its center. This is the same design that the nine villes followed."

Brewster moved his face a little closer to the screen, watching the live feed from the satellite as the dark blurs of gulls passed through the overhead image. "That's been cropping up a lot lately, huh?"

"It is the open secret we never noticed," Lakesh said cryptically. Seeing Brewster's quizzical look, Lakesh smiled apologetically and cleared his throat. "This design, the circular pattern of lower buildings rising to a peak in the center—this is the form that every city in the history of humankind has taken. After Brigid's experience of attempted mind control in Tenth City, she theorized that there was something in the architectural design itself that focused a person's thoughts in specific ways, perhaps making them more susceptible to instruction. As such, it is a way of controlling people, a sigil that traverses time. This is the same design of the cities that you and I inhabited in the twentieth century. We may presume that the subtle control of humanity by the Annunaki is long-lived, Mr. Philboyd."

While it seemed fanciful, the use of sigils—or magical symbols—that Lakesh referred to was prevalent throughout human history. Most infamous among these was the Nazi swastika, a reversed symbol for peace that, in its mirrored form, was believed to have wrought conflict.

Lakesh and Brewster stared at the image on the latter's terminal screen in silence while, across the room, Donald Bry became more animated in his conversation with Grant about the mysteriously appearing parallax point. At the same time, one of the Tigers of Heaven, the modern-day samurai warriors whose property the Cerberus base had temporarily commandeered, took two paces into the room before subtly attracting Lakesh's attention.

"Dr. Singh," the squat, broad-shouldered warrior urged, "your presence is required outside by Mistress Shizuka."

Lakesh nodded. "Keep an eye on the situation here," he told Brewster Philboyd, glancing across to Donald Bry as he did so. "If anything changes, I want to know."

"Sir," Brewster acknowledged with a curt nod.

THOUGH FULL OF OMINOUS shadows, the fortress of Ullikummis appeared to be empty, and after a while Kane stated that conclusion out loud. "If we haven't bumped into anyone by now, my guess is we ain't gonna."

The fortress had several levels, connected by rough, uneven staircases or spiraling ramps. While its passageways were wide, the rooms felt haphazard and cramped, like things that had budded from the main walkways rather than been intentionally connected. That was disquieting to Kane, who felt there was something almost living about the structure itself despite its lack of movement. It felt grown, formed organically. In some way, walking through the fortress felt a little like walking through a body.

They found rooms that contained possessions, obviously human. One room had a bunch of letters on the hard stone cot that stretched against one wall, tied with a ribbon and inexpertly hidden in the folds of a fur blanket. Another room, this one featuring two stone bunks, had a simple game board carved of wood, a jointed hinge along its center so that the pieces could be cleverly stored within. None of the rooms had doors, and Kane recalled how the cells had worked in Life Camp Zero, the prison that Ullikummis had used to hold the Cerberus exiles. Those cells had seemed to be hollows in the rock like honeycombs, and their doors only appeared when necessary, a shifting of a rock wall that seemed almost to have the properties of a liquid and a solid in one item.

Balam stopped as they walked past another open doorway, turning and walking to the room as if in a trance. Kane continued on, peering in each open doorway in turn, glancing across the shadow-dappled interiors before moving to the next. Three rooms along, he saw something odd resting on the floor. Clearly broken, it looked like a bucket seat or a gigantic vase, the top torn free to leave a jagged line. As Kane stepped closer, something fluttered across his vision and he found his sight turning dark. Kane looked around, realizing for the first time that Balam was no longer with him. He hadn't noticed his silent companion had stopped some doors away from him, and it only dawned on him now when his vision started to fade, the colors ebbing away to be replaced by grayness, the subtle edges of the stone walls and the shattered bowllike object diminished to a blur.

"Balam?" Kane called, turning.

The two were linked, and it was in this way that Kane could see, using their telepathic tie to overcome his own blindness. Proximity affected the bond, lessening its effectiveness as Kane well knew from a similar event while they had been searching the old Cerberus redoubt. So many new limitations to remember and to juggle, Kane cursed as he stepped out of the room. So many hazards to navigate at each turn.

"Balam? Where did you go?"

The weight of the Sin Eater still in his hand, Kane marched back down the corridor where he had just been. One advantage of their link was that he couldn't lose Balam for long, he thought cheerlessly; he just had to walk around until his vision became clear again.

When Kane found Balam, the smaller humanoid was standing in the middle of a small room. The room contained a simple bed, a stone base with a little padding from several furs, a blanket made of the same. There was a narrow window on one wall that was little bigger than a letter slot, but the room was otherwise unremarkable. Balam was poised silently in the center of the room, his hands clasped together before him, his eyes closed.

"Balam? Everything okay?" Kane urged.

"She was here," the gray-skinned creature said. He

spoke quietly, and his eyes remained closed in meditation.

"Who?" Kane asked and stopped himself, realizing that the question was redundant. Balam meant Little Quav, of course.

"She's not afraid," Balam continued. "Merely...curious. She was told things here, taught things."

"Some learning curve," Kane muttered. "Imprisoning a three-year-old girl in a big stone fortress."

Balam's eyes flickered open, their dark orbs peering wistfully into Kane's. "I do not believe she was imprisoned, Kane. This was a family reunion, mother and son."

"Well, she ain't here now," Kane said, indicating the empty room.

"No," Balam agreed. "So where is she? Where is Ullikummis?"

Kane racked his brain for a moment, trying to think in the manner of the Annunaki. They were multidimensional beings whose malice was just one aspect of their eternal boredom with their lives. So where would Ullikummis go next?

"Enlil," Kane said slowly. "That's the piece that's missing from this family reunion."

Balam's bulbous head rocked back and forth on his spindly neck as he nodded his agreement. "The child is not ready," he said after some consideration. "Her Ninlil aspect has yet to be teased out of her. She remains the little girl that you and I know as Quav. It will be years before that changes."

"There's something you should see," Kane said, gesturing to the corridor. "Maybe you can make sense of it." He was talking about the bowllike thing he had found, but he chose not to add that he had been unable to analyze it because his vision had failed. It wouldn't help to remind Balam of this; the First Folk diplomat was jumpy enough as it was.

Thus, Kane led the way from the room with Balam at his side. There were no doors in the gloomy palace, so everything here was open to view now.

Three doorways along, Kane stepped into the room, encouraging Balam to follow. There, in the center of the room, lay the broken bowllike structure. Kane could see it better now with his eyes recovered, and he studied it properly for the first time. Bigger than an armchair, the bowl seemed to be made of some kind of stone and rested on a very low plinth that raised it a quarter inch above the stone floor. The top edge was jagged as if the rest of it had been snapped away and, looking at it now, Kane was reminded of an egg. There were shards of the broken remains all around, quartz within it like plates of stained glass twinkling in the light from the arrow-slit windows that lined the room on three sides.

"Any ideas?" Kane prompted.

"A chrysalis," Balam said. There was no hint of doubt in his voice.

"You seen this before?" Kane challenged.

Balam inclined his head in a nod. "They are one of the ways that the Annunaki employed to stave off their immense boredom," he explained as he leaned down to pick through the wreckage strewed about the cuplike object. "You will have heard of how the gods of the Annunaki wore different faces and thus appeared to different cultures in different ways. Overlord Enlil was also Kumbari. Zu was Anzu…"

"Lilitu, Lilith," Kane added, nodding.

"On occasion this would involve a period of cosmetic change," Balam elaborated, "a minor amusement to the

Annunaki. The chrysalis was one manner by which this was achieved."

"So, Ullikummis has been—what—changing his face?" Kane questioned. "Ugly bastard like that's going to take a lot of work."

"No, not Ullikummis," Balam said, studying one of the broken fragments of the rock shell. "This pod is too small for an adult form. It was used on a child."

Kane fixed Balam with his stare. "I think we both know what that means, right?"

Balam nodded. "Quav."

Chapter 4

"There's got to be a thousand of them," Grant muttered as he watched the massing army step from the crazed pattern of colors and light that swam in the air over the banks of the Euphrates.

"More than that, Magistrate," Rosalia corrected, indicating the center of the rift.

Grant turned to where the dark-haired woman had indicated and saw the rift in space growing larger, its hourglass shape swelling in the center to disgorge more people with increased vigor. The rift crackled with lightning against a deep nothingness, swirling colors spinning and fraying in its depths, splitting apart to form even more colors as Grant watched. He estimated that the rift was a quarter mile across now, and as it increased in size it became harder to look it, burning against the rods and cones of his retina like some grisly optical illusion. It was an interphase window, Grant knew, but one so large as to reach a scale he had never seen before. The interphaser was designed for personal transport, carrying just a few people and limited matériel at a time. This, however, was on a scale he had never imagined, like some great monument tunneling through the very air over the sun-dappled surface of the Euphrates. Grant had never seen anything like it.

"Where the fuck are they all coming from?" he muttered, shaking his head.

"I attended a few of the rallies for Ullikummis," Rosalia spoke, her voice low. "Held in the old bombed-out sports stadiums and parking lots, they would regularly attract a thousand, fifteen hundred people at a time. It was quite something seeing that many people chanting in unison."

Grant turned to look at Rosalia, his brow furrowed, as the army massed behind him. "'Quite something,'" he repeated. "Huh."

"What?" Rosalia asked, challenge in her voice.

"It's never 'scary' with you, is it?" Grant observed. "Always just something that happened."

"The world's as scary as we choose for it to be, Grant," Rosalia told him cryptically. "You look at things the way you choose to. No one else makes you frightened but you yourself."

The rift continued to expel more and more people of all ages and body types. Many of them wore the familiar robes of Ullikummis's enforcers, some with the red badge shining over their left breast like those of the old Magistrates. There were dogs there, too, Grant saw— strange dogs with long bodies and heavy, loping movements, their shapes carved from living stone.

Ullikummis himself waited at the head of the army, backing slowly away from the rift to allow his followers space to spread out, Brigid and the little girl at his side.

"We're going to need to get closer," Grant decided. He was still hefting Domi's unconscious form in his arms, and despite the burden he showed no signs of tiredness.

Rosalia indicated the albino woman. "Planning on taking her?"

"No," Grant replied. Then he turned to Kudo, the man who'd lost half his face to the acid spillage inside the bowels of *Tiamat*. "Kudo, you good to get home if I leave you in charge of Domi?"

Kudo nodded, bringing forth a portable communications device from its secure place in a belt pouch. "I can tap Cerberus comms and ask them to guide me," he said without arguing. Like all Tigers of Heaven, Kudo was a fearless warrior who would never shy away from a fight. However, he also recognized the need for authority, and bowed to Grant's decisions as squad leader.

"Great," Grant said as he passed his pale burden to Kudo. The modern-day samurai took the petite woman, hefting her over one shoulder in a fireman's carry. "Tell Donald to trace Domi's transponder. He can use that to guide you to the nearest safe haven from which you can make the jump home."

Kudo nodded once. "As you command." Then he walked away from the scene, speaking into the comm unit.

Within moments, Grant and Rosalia were alone at the edge of the citylike dragon ship, watching as the tear in the air continued spilling more of the mismatched troops to the ground.

Rosalia reached down to the handle of her sword, her hand brushing against it to ensure it was still there. "How do you propose we do this?" she asked.

Grant held his right arm out, palm open, and his Sin Eater slapped into his hand from its hiding place beneath his sleeve. "Let's play it by ear."

SELA STONE HEARD the call like a racing drumbeat in her skull, its urgency increasing until it became impossible to ignore. A black-skinned woman, slender and hungry-looking, she had a body that was all toned muscle, no flab. She had not always been called Sela Stone; three months earlier she had been Sela Sinclair, one of the security experts for Cerberus before their redoubt had been infiltrated and all personnel had been taken prisoner. It was a distant memory now, that first vision of Ullikummis as he strode through the familiar corridors of the redoubt with his army of followers, overcoming all attempts to stop them. He had touched her, a fleck of himself embedding in her head like a living thing. The stone put Sela in touch with Ullikummis, helped her to comprehend his will, to accept him as her god.

Since that day, Sela had heard the quiet drums beating over and over in her head. The noise had become reassuring, a heartbeat from another world, the heartbeat of her god and savior. The drumming increased whenever Ullikummis was near, and also when those most important to him—such as the warrior woman known as Haight—came close. And this day, as Sela sat before a small congregation in the old province of Samariumville, preaching the word of Stone, she felt the drums beat louder and faster. As a believer in the future under Ullikummis, Sela had taken her first steps in spreading the word, gathering just a dozen of the outlander farmers in a dilapidated barn to tell them of the glorious utopia that was coming. A few days before, she had still been undercover, hiding in the shadows with her Cerberus teammate, Farrell, giving no indication that she had been turned. Now she was an Alpha, promoting the word of the new god.

"His love is stone, unbreakable, unconquerable," Sela assured them. "His embrace is the embrace of the all. His future is the pinnacle of achievement, the glory of utopia."

As she spoke, she could hear the drums inside her head getting faster and faster. She saw the farmers' eyes widen as something changed behind her, and she turned, her own words turning to silence on her lips. Where the barn wall had been just a moment before now stood a swirling hole of blackness, dark colors twisting within its newly impossible depths, lightning strikes ravaging within. The hole seemed to pulse, subtly changing shape like a living creature breathing in and out. Sela recognized it from her time with Cerberus; it was a rift window created by an interphaser.

She stepped back automatically, giving room for the interphaser's user to step out—but no one did. Behind her, the congregation of farmers and the hardy-looking women they had taken for their wives watched in awe. "Is this the utopia?" one of them asked. "Has it arrived?"

Sela peered deep into the impossible depths of the quantum window, watching those swirling colors coalesce and part over and over, no two patterns alike. There, deep in the swimming burst of light, fingers seemed to be moving, an upturned hand pulling back as if giving Sela the go-ahead signal. The hand was rough and crudely formed, as if it had been hewed from solid rock. When she saw this, Sela Stone knew just what to do. Without a second's hesitation, she stepped into the pulsing swirl of darkness, letting the quantum window wash over her like the tide on a beach, bathing her in its power.

An instant later, Sela Stone found herself stepping out of the rift onto an expanse of sand close to a riverbank. Hundreds of people were massing there—perhaps thousands—each one loyal to her master, Ullikummis, a vast sea of people clamoring for space.

Up ahead, Sela could see the silhouette of a dragon, its craning neck lunging into the skies as if to smell the low clouds that danced before the morning sun. The

dragon was five or six miles away, at least, yet it was
so immense that its head towered over the vista of the
Euphrates River, and its wings spread out, reaching to
perhaps a mile away from where she stood. The wings
were ragged and skeletal, their bones pale-colored struts
like some weird panorama of buildings.

Behind Sela, the dozen farmers had followed, stepping from the rift in space to add their bodies to the
burgeoning army of Ullikummis. They followed not because of the obedience stone—unlike Sela, they hadn't
received an implant—but because they wanted to believe that there could be this golden future, the one that
Ullikummis, their stone-clad fallen angel, had promised.

Sela, like a number of others among the thousands-
strong crowd, felt the call because of the stone that had
been implanted in her head. Known as an obedience
stone, it was a tiny chip from Ullikummis's own body.
He could grow these at will, tearing them from his body
like buds from a plant. All of them had a droplet of rudimentary sentience, enough that they could speak to
their hosts, bonding with them and influencing their
thoughts. Accepting the obedience stone was traumatic,
for the stone had to push through the skin to bond itself
to the user, but this pain had come to be seen as a rite
of passage among the faithful, a sacrifice they made
in their devotion to the new god. After all, the faithful
preached, the stone created a new way of understanding the world, a new life, and as such, it was a birth
and any birth was characterized as much by pain as by
joy, was it not?

The stone pulsed within Sela, hugging the lobes of
her brain, its tendrils enveloping her mind. The stone
brought an enlightenment, a freedom for the bearer. It

was an entheogen, bringing to all people who used it a sense of being a part of their god. The stones acted as markers, too, the same way that the transponders were used by the Cerberus people, and it was through these locators that Ullikummis had reached out for his most faithful, opening the multiwindow of the quantum interphase jump in a way that had never been seen before. A hundred quantum gateways had all opened upon the same location—on *this* location. This, too, was something that Ullikummis had learned in the Ontic Library, accessing its sentient banks of knowledge to discover new ways to utilize the Annunaki technology. These were old secrets, things that had been forgotten millennia ago. Ullikummis could generate parallax points where there were none, and he could fold quantum space in such a way that he could jump between parallax points, ambushing even the most wary of opponents. The old ways were the new ways.

"DAMMIT!" ROSALIA CURSED as she and Grant prowled warily along the edge of the city, as close as they dared get to the massing army on the banks of the Euphrates.

Grant glared at her. "You want to keep it down?" he warned.

When he looked he saw that Rosalia was holding her left wrist and her teeth were clenched in pain.

"What is it?" Grant asked more gently, regretting his knee-jerk reaction.

"Stone's playing up," the dark-haired woman answered, breathing hard through her nostrils.

"Run that by me again?" Grant requested, clearly confused.

"I have the stone inside me," Rosalia said, "you know that. Damn thing's pounding against my nerve like a fucking metronome." She winced, holding down hard on her wrist until the pain passed.

Like Sela Sinclair, Rosalia had one of the obedience stones implanted beneath her skin. But through her own subtle manipulations of her flesh, her stone had remained locked at her wrist, unable to attach itself properly and so bond with her. The stone was of a different variety to Sinclair's, as it had come not from Ullikummis but from one of his faithful troops. Besides affecting a person's thought processes, the stone was also used to operate hidden stone locks designed by Ullikummis within his bases, a little like a remote control opened a garage door.

In the earliest days of the Ullikummis religious movement, those with stones would identify those without by just being in their presence. That facet had become less important over time, as more people had joined the Ullikummis movement willingly, truly believing that a new and better world was coming.

Left unchecked, the stones would affect the thinking of anyone who had one, but Rosalia had assured the Cerberus people that she had hers under control. "It only works on the weak-minded," she had dismissed contemptuously. However, few people knew how much effort Rosalia put in to maintaining the rock's position beneath her skin, using a needle to cut into her own flesh daily to prevent it from locking there and so forming a more permanent—and dangerous—bond.

Now the rock inside her was drumming against her nerves like something alive.

"You're all right?" Grant asked.

Rosalia nodded. "Just go."

Ahead of them, the rift continued to swell, a great wound in the sky. Lightning crackled in its depths as it blurted out more people into the already swollen ranks of Ullikummis's troops. Among them were the hooded security teams who had assumed the place of the Magistrates, their malleable flesh as hard as stone. There were so many people now that it seemed chaotic.

The buildings around them were not buildings at all. In fact, they were the jutting bones of *Tiamat*'s wings, reminders that the great organic spaceship had regrown her body from a seed. The structures had indentations and steps and hooded porches, but they had no doors or windows. These things had been grown over with bone, leaving just the ghost of a building that never was.

Grant indicated one of the lower buildings, where a run of steps jutted along its back wall. The steps ended midway up the wall, leaving a whole other story above them. The wall itself bent forward as if it might topple, and another nearby structure did the same, creating a narrow channel between the two at their closest points.

Grant was up the steps in an instant, with Rosalia following. She waited poised at the foot of the steps, keeping a sharp lookout for anybody who might spot them among the long shadows of the early-morning sun before she clambered up the steps after the ex-Mag.

Bolting to the top of the bone steps, Grant reached up with his free hand and grasped high on the wall where it met with the lip of the roof. Without slowing, he pulled himself up, his feet kicking out as he continued to move. In less than two seconds, Grant had flipped himself onto the roof, three stories above ground level. He crouched there, crab-walking to the far edge of the roof where he would have a better view of the massing army.

Rosalia followed a moment later. Her swift strides brought her up the pale steps at a run before springing toward the wall of the adjacent building and using it to kick herself higher and land on the rooftop with Grant, making just the bare minimum of noise. Keeping her head low, Rosalia hurried to join Grant at its edge.

Beyond the roof, they could see the quantum gateway hovering next to the Euphrates, its impossible depths churning with a swirl of beautiful colors. Grant and Rosalia watched in awe as Ullikummis turned to the people from the head of that vast column of loyal followers, raising his long, stone-clad arms. In a moment, the crowd fell to silence, two thousand or more people hushed without so much as a word. It was quite something to behold.

The stone giant stood on a hillock by the river, a raised mound of dirt beside the rippling surface. Brigid stood beside him, her red-gold hair shimmering with the sunlight, clutching the hand of the little girl in the indigo dress.

"Behold the tools of the future," Ullikummis said, his voice carrying across the burgeoning group of arrivals. He indicated the dragon shape that stood behind him, its arrow-shaped head looming high above, his voice echoing through the abandoned streets. "Here is *Tiamat,* the engine that will change the world. Here is your future, waiting to be freed from terrible bondage.

"Will you stand with me as I free *Tiamat?*"

The crowd cheered in response, hanging on Ullikummis's every word.

"Will you embrace the future for the betterment of all?"

Again the crowd cheered.

"Onward, bearers of the future," Ullikummis yelled, "onward to utopia."

With that, the stone god turned and began to stride toward the outskirts of the dragon city, his tree-trunk-like feet stomping against the sandy soil in brutal, punishing blows. Brigid Haight strode with him, hurrying little Quav along at her side, the army of two thousand or more following briskly in their wake.

The people could not imagine how the wars of the Annunaki were to be fought. All they knew was what they saw: here was a leader who led, not a general who hid behind his troops as they went into battle.

Ullikummis spread out his hands, and the ground began to shake, a tremor running through it deep below the surface.

Holding his Sin Eater ready as he crouched atop of the chalk-white roof, Grant felt that tremor rock through his boots and against his knees, pounding deep through his body like a low bass note.

"The hell is that?" Grant muttered.

Before Rosalia could answer, something began to change beyond the edges of *Tiamat*'s broad wings. Those wings stretched out for eight miles, a huge structure that dominated the landscape. Now, around the outskirts, the ground rumbled and split as sharp prongs of stone were pulled from the soil, ripped from the bedrock itself to form a spiky cage around the perimeter of the spaceship. The prongs pointed into the air, their sharp tips climbing twelve feet into the sky like eerie monuments. More spikes tore through the ground as Ullikummis passed, and Grant watched as they spread out from where he was walking, new prongs jutting from the soil at an increasingly greater distance from where the stone god stepped.

"What is he doing?" Grant whispered.

"The same thing he did at Cerberus," Rosalia replied. "Creating a lockdown."

As she said it, the jutting columns began to dwindle,

and those farthest from Ullikummis appeared much shorter, some just two or three feet in height. From their high vantage point, Grant and Rosalia could see that the pointed columns did not wrap around the whole of the grounded spaceship but instead ran in a crescent shape around this, the southwest quarter. Even so, the bowed line of spikes took in almost a mile in its length, a vast line of bars caging in the spaceship where she waited poised on the soil.

Behind the Cerberus warriors, the citylike form of *Tiamat* waited in silence, never acknowledging the barricade that had been erected before her. Though she looked like a city, the streets and buildings had been left vacant, a ghost town on the banks of the river. Every person who had stepped into the city had disappeared, abducted by its lone ruler, the Annunaki Overlord Enlil. But now Enlil was gone—*wasn't he?*—and Ullikummis had arrived to take control of the genetic factory womb that *Tiamat* contained, his first bold step in reordering the world.

"We have to stop him," Grant blurted, scrambling back toward the area of the rooftop that dropped to the staircase.

Rosalia grabbed his arm, pulling the ex-Mag up short. "Are you insane, Grant? There are probably two thousand people down there, maybe more. We can't take them all on."

Grant stared at her. "I don't know a lot about all this stuff," he said, "but I do know that when *Tiamat*'s involved, bad things happen."

"I thought the ship was dead," Rosalia stated angrily.

"If I've learned one thing about the Annunaki it's this," Grant told her grimly. "Things die only to be reborn. And when they come back, they come back worse than ever.

"We have to stop him."

"Okay," Rosalia agreed reluctantly. "Then we figure out a way. I'm not going out there with you, all guns blazing against a whole fucking army, hoping that's somehow going to do the job."

Grant nodded in agreement. "Always a way," he said. "Just have to figure out what it is."

Below them, the vast, ragtag army of Ullikummis stormed through the streets to the southwest of *Tiamat*'s skeletal structure, their chants echoing from the hard walls around them.

"We are stone," they called. "Stone is strength."

They reminded Rosalia of locusts, the way they swarmed across the wings of the fallen spaceship.

Chapter 5

The armies were massing elsewhere, too.

Halfway around the world, on the Pacific Coast of the old United States, Lakesh stood on the balcony of the temporary Cerberus base and sighed. Beside him, a beautiful samurai woman of petite stature waited for the Cerberus leader to take everything in.

The pair stood on the wooden balcony that ran right around the single-story structure, its steeple roofs and the railings of the balconies painted a bright, festive red. The woman was called Shizuka and she was the leader of the Tigers of Heaven, a position that placed many great responsibilities upon her shoulders. Dressed in the supple leather armor that she preferred, Shizuka was a warrior born, and she could outmatch any of the warriors in her team. She wore a *katana* sword in an ornate sheath at her belt, along with a shorter *wakizashi* blade nestled close to her back. Her black hair was cut in a long bob, the tips of which trailed down to brush her shoulders, and she had peach-tinted cheeks and rose-petal lips beneath the pleasing almond curves of her dark, attractive eyes.

The building where Cerberus had set up shop belonged to Shizuka, and it had been in her family for many generations. Surrounded by several acres of carefully manicured gardens, the building served as a lodge or winter palace, which her predecessors had visited for rest and relaxation. A tiny square garden stood at the rear of the property, dotted with winding paths and a simple water feature whose constant shushing sound added to the sense of tranquillity engendered by the flowering herbs that colored its carefully tended borders. Beyond that lay the vast lawns that stretched off toward the sea on one side and out to an untended private road at the other. A high wall ran along this side with a long, steel gate. Made up of a line of vertical bars painted the same red as the balcony, the gate stood more than eight feet in height and ran to a width of twelve, wide enough to let a vehicle like a Sandcat through. A simple sentry box stood to one side of the gate, located within the grounds themselves, where the operator could open the gate for visitors. The gate operated via an electromagnetic lock, which sealed it shut when not in use.

Out there, beyond the gate, Lakesh could see four men waiting. Pacing back and forth like caged tigers, the men wore heavy fustian robes like monks' habits, the hoods pulled low to obscure their faces. Lakesh knew just who—or what—they were. Firewalkers, the agents of Ullikummis.

"Our jackals are getting closer," Shizuka said, her tone betraying no emotion.

"Yes," Lakesh agreed, staring at the gate through a set of binoculars. Behind him, Ryochi, the Tiger of Heaven warrior who had brought him to meet Shizuka, waited patiently, his pose as still as an ancient tree. "First there was one. Now four."

"Six," Shizuka corrected dispassionately. "Two are hiding in the foliage across the path. More will likely follow. Even now, we may assume that they are on their way."

"How do they speak to one another?" Lakesh wondered aloud. "How are they communicating? I can't see any radio equipment."

"They each have the stone," Shizuka reminded him. "Rosalia said it can identify sympathizers, other bearers of the stone seed. Maybe it acts as a communication device, too."

Lakesh nodded wearily as he pulled the field glasses from his eyes. There was more to it than that, he felt sure. He had been present when pro-Ullikummis troops had sacked the previous Cerberus base, and he had observed the way they acted in tandem. The Annunaki's faithful warriors seemed to be linked at a cerebral level, often acting as one organism rather than many. The nearest equivalent he could think of was the way birds reacted in flight, turning together, responding as one majestic creature rather than as several. It was inhuman.

Lakesh wondered how long they would have to wait until the strangers were ready to mount their attack. Because he knew that they had to be here to attack. When it was just one of them he could believe that he might be here just to observe. But now—well, now an army was forming right outside his door.

Once again, Cerberus was about to be attacked. And even though he knew about it this time, Lakesh couldn't help but wonder how well they would fare with none of his warriors left on site to repel intruders.

ON THE FORTRESS ISLE of Bensalem, Kane and Balam stared at the wreckage of the chrysalis strewed across the stone floor. A breeze blew through the open window at the far end of the room, playing through Kane's unkempt hair as he worked out this latest puzzle.

"So, what?" Kane asked, his eyes fixed on the debris.

"He changed Quav's appearance? Ullikummis changed her appearance?"

Balam bent at the waist, sifting through the debris with his toe. "It's hard to say," he admitted. "The equipment—what's left of it—fractured. It shouldn't have done this, friend Kane. I've never known of this to happen before."

"How many times you seen this setup, Balam?" Kane asked.

Balam shook his head heavily. "Not often," he said. "The structures are Tuatha de Danaan, but it's ancient technology reinterpreted. I barely recognize it."

Kane took a pace forward, leaning down to look at the wreckage of the chrysalis. Then, still bent, he turned, looking directly up into Balam's face. "Balam, we need to find her. To find them. So you have got to get that great big brain of yours in gear and figure out exactly what it is we have here, get me?"

"Kane, I know that you are worried about Brigid—" Balam began but Kane halted him with a single gesture of irritation.

"Just figure it out," he instructed. "Get your hands dirty, for once, and get as much information as you can." Then, to Balam's surprise, Kane grasped a handful of his tunic and shoved him forward, pushing the bulbous-headed humanoid closer to the ruined chrysalis.

Balam staggered forward, his feet tromping over the broken fragments that were arrayed across the stone flagging. "Respectfully, friend Kane," he said, "I am ill prepared to make a full analysis."

Kane tamped down the rage that was welling inside him, reminding himself that Balam had little experience in the field like this. The two of them had been thrown together by circumstance, with Balam essentially a peaceful arbiter and Kane currently at his lowest physical and mental ebb. Yet here they stood, on the trail of a woman Kane considered close enough to be his sister and a child whom Balam had taken for his own. Kane was being too hard on him, he knew. Balam was hurt, emotionally drained. He put up a front, as he always did, reticent to share his emotions. But he had lost his foster daughter, a girl with whom he'd been in the solitary company of for almost three years, and his feelings had to be in turmoil right now.

Balam looked up from the ruined shell. "It broke on usage," he stated simply. "Which means it was imperfect. A prototype, perhaps."

"It's possible, I guess," Kane mused uncertainly.

"If you build something that fails," Balam reasoned, "you either improve upon it or you resign yourself to defeat. I do not believe that Ullikummis would resign himself to defeat."

"No," Kane agreed. "That's not his way. Let's look around some more."

Without much enthusiasm, Kane and Balam left the room and began checking the other doorways along the tunnellike corridor, each one of them open. There were wide areas of solid wall between each doorway, and Kane wondered whether more rooms might be hidden in this structure, built as it had been by Ullikummis.

The next room was empty, as was the one after, nothing but dust blowing about in the sea breeze from the open windows. No provision had been made to insulate this rock palace. Presumably it had been designed by Ullikummis for his own usage and as such there was no need, for his genetically altered body could survive in the cold vacuum of space.

The fourth doorway on the right-hand wall opened

into a small chamber that stank of something rotting. Kane peered inside, but he stepped back instantly as something leaped at him, hissing like a snake as it threw itself through the air. There were bars there, narrow jabs of rock stretched horizontally across a recess behind the doorway like a venetian blind. The thing in the room slammed against these bars, reaching through them with its tiny hands as it tried to grasp Kane's shirt.

Standing away from the doorway, Kane stared at it, reeling in horror at the thing. It stood two feet tall, human in shape but deformed, with a blur of face as if its head had been melted. There was anger in its wide-spaced blue eyes—anger and perhaps sorrow. The thing was naked, female, with skin a pink so pale that it was almost white. Around her, watery feces stained the stone floor, creating the stench. The girl hissed again, rattling the bars of her cell. She was bony, wasting away, her ribs running like the keys of a piano against the pale skin of her chest. She couldn't get through the bars, Kane realized—the first "door" he had seen here—and he moved closer once more, studying the strange figure.

"It's okay," Kane soothed. "I'm not here to hurt you."

The creature behind the bars watched him with feral eyes, hissing again as he stood there before her. At first glance the girl appeared hairless, but now Kane could see a few tufts of white along her scalp as he took a closer look. Her skin was puckered here and there, running like fish scales along the sides of her legs and around her throat. It reminded Kane of the Annunaki, and he realized in a moment what he was looking at.

"Have you found something?" Balam asked from behind him, disturbing Kane's thoughts.

The Cerberus warrior turned to Balam, a hard look on his face. "You don't want to see this, Balam," he said.

Less than a year earlier, Kane might have teased Balam about the thing in the cell, taking a childish pleasure in shocking friends like his colleagues in the Cerberus group. Something had changed inside him over these past few months, something that had dulled his happy-go-lucky streak, making him more ponderous, more introspective. The thing in the cell was Little Quav, he realized, or some approximation of her.

AT THE TEMPORARY Cerberus headquarters on the Pacific Coast, three operatives sat in heated discussion about another problem related to Ullikummis. The room itself was a small study with a desk along one wall where a portable computer screen glowed, and several comfy chairs that had been placed in such a way as to be behind the desk user's back when people sat in them. The man at the desk had turned his swivel chair to face the two women, both of whom were dressed in the white jumpsuits with blue vertical zippers that served as the uniform of the Cerberus personnel.

"Could focused ultrasound actually break down rock?" Reba DeFore asked with irritation in her tone. She was a stocky bronze-skinned woman with brown eyes and ash-blond hair tied up in an elaborate braid. She appeared tired and haunted, dark shadows massing around her eyes. It had been a trying couple of months for DeFore, once the on-site physician for the Cerberus redoubt.

From the desk, Dr. Kazuka shook his head uncertainly and he peered back to the screen of his electronic notebook. "There's a lot of theory dating back to before the nukecaust," he stated, "but I can find little in the way of evidence of its practical application." In his early forties, Kazuko had cropped black hair and the walnut complexion of his fellow Tigers of Heaven, for whom he was a field medic. He had been seconded by Shizuka to serve the Cerberus team in this, their hour of need. He wore a light cotton shirt, open at the collar, with cotton slacks and soft shoes, and he moved with a simple grace that was unusual in a man. Despite his light ensemble, Kazuka was sweating; the room was small and the three bodies within were making it warm.

The third person, another operative for Cerberus called Mariah Falk, rubbed at her leg irritably. She was a slender woman in her forties, with dark hair pebbled with streaks of gray. Though not conventionally attractive, Mariah had a winning smile and an amiable manner that put people at ease. Falk was a geologist and, unusually, her expertise had been called upon in this medical problem because it involved one of the obedience stones that had been planted by Ullikummis. She had a personal beef with Ullikummis—not only had he killed her would-be boyfriend, but he had also caused her to be shot in the leg just a few months before. Whenever the discussion turned to Ullikummis, Mariah remembered Clem Bryant's face as he lay dying on the floor of the Cerberus cafeteria, and she felt the determination well up within her.

"The physics behind it seems sound enough," Mariah said, wincing at her own accidental pun. "Seismic waves have been used for oceanographic studies, but really you'd want to ask Clem about th—" She stopped herself, realizing her error.

Reba reached over, placing her thin hand on Mariah's for a few seconds, patting her gently. "It's okay, Mariah."

Mariah thanked her, silently mouthing the word before she continued. "Point is, it's possible," she concluded. "But I'm talking in terms of rocks, not people. Employing focused ultrasound for surgery is a long way out of my league."

Reba and Kazuka nodded, grateful for the geologist's input.

"The real question, it seems to me," Kazuka said in his compassionate tone, "is what other options do we have left open to us. Your operative Edwards has this sentient stone growing inside his skull like a tumor, and it is affecting his judgment and ability to function."

It had done more than that, in fact. Edwards had been turned against his teammates by the obedience stone, and he was acting on external instructions to achieve the goals of his new master, Ullikummis. And he wasn't the only one—other members of the Cerberus team who had once been trusted had now gone rogue, working for the New Order in Ullikummis's name. Sela Sinclair and Brigid Baptiste were two such operatives, and there had been at least four others identified whose thoughts had been infiltrated. It was a dark day for Cerberus when they realized friends had been turned into enemies.

"Utilizing ultrasound is a noninvasive form of surgery," Kazuka continued thoughtfully. "We can use it to break down the stone without making an incision and thus avoid causing damage to the brain. This would seem to be desirable."

"Although we remain uncertain how much this thing has infiltrated Edwards's brain itself," DeFore reminded them both.

"We cannot really ever know that unless we cut Edwards open," Kazuka said. "Something we are loath to do for obvious reasons."

When DeFore saw the confusion in Mariah's face she added quietly, "He'd die."

"At the end of the twentieth century," Kazuka summarized from the computer screen, "this type of surgery was being explored as an alternative to radiation treatments for cancer. The precision of the technique—if applied correctly—is its strength."

The room fell silent for a moment as the three highly educated people considered the moral dilemma they faced.

"You just need to make a decision, don't you?" Mariah said.

"I don't like it," DeFore said. "We run the risk of permanently scrambling Edwards's brain, turning him into a vegetable or worse, killing him." She turned to Kazuka.

"Better to act than to do nothing," Kazuka said. "I vote yes, we perform the surgery."

The two doctors turned to Mariah.

"You have the deciding vote, Mariah," DeFore said gently.

"No," Mariah said. "I'm not a doctor. You guys should—" She stopped when she saw the haunted look in DeFore's eyes. She remembered Clem lying there, his skull crushed, remembered what had happened to her in Tenth City, when she had been shot in the leg to save her from killing herself by walking into the flames of a crematorium on the instructions of Ullikummis, whose brutal words had seemed to pierce her very skull. She took a deep breath, forcing the welling emotions aside.

"When Ullikummis first landed," Mariah began, "I had his thoughts forced on me, overlaying my own. I imagine it was a lot like the way the obedience stone is affecting Edwards, a prototype, if you will.

"I remember how that felt," Mariah continued solemnly, "the way it felt to have my own thoughts obliterated by the thoughts of someone else. Some*thing* alien. So, I vote yes to the surgery, because if it does kill Edwards—who is my respected colleague and my friend—then death wouldn't be so bad. Death would be a release."

The two doctors nodded, accepting Mariah's impassioned speech. They would operate. Mariah—a geologist and not a medical doctor—only hoped she had made the right decision, because it was one she would have to live with for the rest of her life.

"WHAT IS IT?" BALAM ASKED.

"Tell me, Balam," Kane said, avoiding the question, "can the Annunaki clone living things? Humans, say, or hybrids?"

"Their bodies are clone bodies," Balam said with that superior logic he often employed. "When you met with Enlil and his brethren, you were not looking on the same flesh that walked this planet thousands of years ago. You merely looked at things reborn, perfect copies. Clones by another name."

Kane stepped aside, letting Balam see into the cell for the first time. "I think he cloned her, or tried to," he warned.

Balam looked at the thing in the cell, and his face became a stony mask. "Scales," was all he said.

Kane looked back at the girl in the cell, aware now that his heart was drumming a tarantella against his chest. He willed it to slow, recalling the breathing exercises he had been taught when he had trained as a Magistrate in Cobaltville. The thing in the cell stared at him plaintively before baring her teeth and hissing once again. The teeth were thin and sharp like needles, and they faced inward, cutting into her mouth.

Quav.

Balam was nodding, as if reading Kane's thoughts.
The thing in the cell was his foster daughter, or at least
an approximation of her based on a flawed genetic template. She had been changed, twisted, turned into the
Annunaki form she might one day blossom into.

Balam reached through the stony bars of the cell, the
six long fingers of his hand shaking just slightly as he
went to touch the girl.

The girl-thing in the cell hissed, flinging her hands
at Balam's, the talons of her fingers sweeping across
the cell bars to rip into his pale flesh. Balam pulled his
hand away in surprise, whispering Quav's name sorrowfully as he did so. There was no recognition in the
girl's uneven eyes, just hate. She was an animal.

Balam stood in the tunnellike corridor, staring at the
cell door with his wide, expressive eyes. He was shaking, Kane saw, just a slight quiver to his shoulders. "A
clone," he confirmed, reading the thing's mind.

"Balam," Kane said slowly, "I want you to step away.
Go back down the corridor and wait for me."

"Kane, I see no sense in that," Balam replied. "I am
well able to cope with—"

"Just go down the corridor," Kane cut him off.

Wary of further argument, Balam stepped back,
making his way to the far end of the corridor. Beside
the cell, Kane brought his right hand up, pointing it
toward the thing grasping at him through the narrow
stone bars. With a practiced flinch of his wrist tendons,
the Sin Eater appeared in Kane's hand for just a second, launching from its hidden wrist holster and striking his palm comfortably, its guardless trigger meeting
with Kane's crooked index finger. A short burst of fire
erupted from the muzzle of the gun, filling the corridor

for just a moment with the cacophony of gunfire. Then the weapon had returned to its hiding place, and Kane came walking back down the corridor toward Balam.

At the far end of the corridor, Balam eyed Kane with a faint appreciation. "You killed her. There was no need to do that," he said.

"Yes, there was," Kane told him, his mouth a grim line across his tired face. "There may be more of these things, stillborn clones created to emulate Little Quav. No good can possibly come of cloning her."

"I do not believe he was cloning her," Balam said. "I suspect he was testing the limits of her endurance. That thing had Annunaki traits, as well as hybrid ones. He is looking to catalyze the change."

"Test subjects, then." Kane nodded. "We should stop that."

"Kane, the chrysalis wasn't to grow Quav," Balam said. "It was to test her cells. Ullikummis must be planning to bring forth his mother, Ninlil, from her genetic template. But to do that would require a genetic factory—it would require *Tiamat*."

"*Tiamat*'s gone," Kane dismissed. "I saw it with my own eyes. She blew up in the outer atmosphere."

"Things Annunaki seldom die entirely," Balam warned.

Kane was thinking faster now, beginning to see the angles involved. "But if *Tiamat* is alive, then how do we find her? She's a spaceship and space is pretty big."

"We can use the chair," Balam stated simply.

Chapter 6

"Where are we, Brigly?" Little Quav asked. She was looking up to Brigid Haight's ocean-colored eyes as they marched past the pillars of rock that Ullikummis had placed to cordon off the city. All around them, the army of Ullikummis grew from the impossible reaches of the swirling quantum portal, swarming into the deserted city of the dragon.

Brigid flicked her gaze down to take in the girl properly, seeing her sweet face looking up at her with that strange blend of curiosity and hope in her pale eyes. Brigid had been thinking about the colors hidden in the interphase jump, the sky blue with its golden swirls like lightning, the flecks of green and red hidden in its depths. For a moment, she could see that pattern as if it had been burned into her memory, could feel the serenity those colors seemed to bring. In that moment, she didn't know hate. In that moment, she was not Haight at all.

"What is it, child?" Brigid asked, recovering herself to the here, to the now.

"Where are we, Brigly?" Quav asked once more, looking around her as Ullikummis's troops hurried past on their way to the dragon's torso at the core of the dead city.

Brigid reached down with her free hand, running it

gently through Little Quav's downy hair. "You're almost home, darling," she said. "Almost home."

FROM ATOP the pale-colored rooftop in the city, Grant and Rosalia watched Ullikummis's loyal troops swarm into the streets of bone. Grant looked to where the great dragon head loomed above the buildings, waiting emotionlessly in the center of the strange structure. They were perhaps five miles from that central hull, but the pathways to it were labyrinthine, following the addling design of the corpuscles that should flood through the great dragon's wings. The wings themselves stretched as mighty crescents along the banks of the Euphrates, two great quarter moons poised and ready to take flight.

"So, Magistrate, what are we going to do?" Rosalia asked, as just below them hundreds of troops surged in from the city limits.

"Ullikummis will section off the city," Grant said, extrapolating from what he had just seen. "Close in on the center where Enlil is housed.

"Of course, he doesn't know Enlil's down for the count," the ex-Mag added sourly. "Ironically, that might have been the one thing that would stop him. I wouldn't have placed a wager on who would win in a fight between Enlil and Ullikummis."

"But now?" Rosalia prompted. Down below them, strange stone-skinned dogs howled as they trotted ahead through the streets, leading the way and searching for the best route to the center. The bodies of the hounds were long, and they weaved through the turn-around-again streets like liquid, their stone bodies darting ahead of the surging mob in dark blurs.

Grant pondered Rosalia's question for a moment. "Now, Ullikummis can take control of whatever's left of

Tiamat unchallenged," he reasoned. "And even though she's dying, that's still a whole lot wide of ideal for us. *Tiamat*'s full of Annunaki secrets, evolutionary sequencing codes that encourage perverted genetic tampering. Hell, you saw what the ship did to those people who got caught up in its grasp. They were turned into Annunaki, or at least Annunaki-lite. The ship's reeling just now, but…"

"Enlil regrew her," Rosalia realized. "So there's always the chance that Ullikummis—or someone else—could do the same."

"Exactly," Grant confirmed with a brisk nod. "It'll take too long to get that bombing raid set up. We have to find a way to stop him before he gets there."

As he spoke, one of the stone dogs trotted up the steps that clung to the side of the building. The dog's long snout twitched as it sniffed at the air, ears flicking as it listened. It had sensed them, strangers on the rooftop above it. The beast was powerfully built, its torso and limbs corded muscle that writhed like snakes beneath the stone-hard covering of its skin. Reaching the top of the steps, the dog sniffed at the air again, eyes narrowing as it sought a way to get higher. Then, with a grunt, the dog pounced up, hind legs slapping against the opposing wall, using its momentum to reach the roof.

"What th—?" Grant began, but already the dog had spied them and was barreling across the roof.

There was next to no time to react. Grant merely stood his ground, raising his right hand and commanding the Sin Eater into its palm once again, firing a swift burst as the dog leaped at them. A flurry of 9 mm molybdenum-shelled bullets struck the hound's stone body, impacting like hailstones against tarmac, bouncing away in the blink of an eye with sparks of angry light.

Then the dog was on Grant, knocking him a half-dozen steps backward and forcing him onto the hard surface of the roof.

Rosalia leaped aside, pulling the Ruger P-85 pistol from its holster at her hip as she whirled in the air. In a moment a triburst of Parabellum bullets drilled through the air, hurtling toward the muscular beast as it jostled for position over Grant, furiously snapping its jaws.

It was a powerful beast, and its body had the length and thickness of a circus strongman. Its legs were long and rangy, its jaw a pronounced snout lined with thick, blunted teeth, each of which was two inches wide. As Rosalia's bullets ricocheted from the creature's thick torso, Grant rammed the nose of his Sin Eater into its throat, driving it up and away from him with a powerful thrust.

"Get down, Fido," Grant snarled, squeezing the trigger of his Sin Eater.

A burst of fire cut the air, the loud shots echoing back to Grant from the high-walled buildings around. The dog grumbled something then fell back, a line of indentations along its neck where the bullets had struck at point-blank range.

With a powerful shove, Grant pushed the beast away from him, sending it rolling across the bone roof.

The hound struggled to recover for a moment as Rosalia fired another shot at it from her Ruger. The bullet struck straight between the beast's almost human eyes. Then the creature powered itself back to its feet and lunged for Grant once again where he was just pulling himself up off the rooftop. Without stopping to think, Grant threw his arms up and snagged the beast's monstrous forepaws, using its own momentum against it as he tossed it over his shoulder and over the side of the roof. He and Rosalia watched as the dog hurtled down to the street, falling amid a crowd of a dozen or so troopers. The loyal troops stopped in place, glaring up at the rooftop with angry eyes.

"Nice one, Magistrate," Rosalia hissed.

KUDO HURRIED away from the sounds of the massing army, the childlike form of Domi asleep in his arms. He had served as a Tiger of Heaven for many years, and had never once shown fear despite the dreadful tasks he had been occasioned to perform. Now, however, his voice shook as he spoke to Brewster Philboyd via the portable comm unit.

"I require the interphase portal to be opened at the earliest juncture," he urged as he ran past the clumped vegetation that lined the area close to the Euphrates. "There are sinister forces massing here. It would not do to wait too long."

"I have you at about two miles out now," Philboyd replied. "I'll track you until you're a half mile in sight, then we'll send someone out."

Kudo slowed his pace just slightly as he spotted figures moving about in the vegetation directly ahead of him. Farmers, or acolytes to Ullikummis, he couldn't be sure. "Do you have any idea whom that might be, Philboyd?" he asked quietly, speaking into the comm.

Kudo heard Brewster snort. "The way personnel is looking here, it could very likely be me," he said.

Crouching, Kudo placed the unconscious Domi on the ground before he rose again. "No field operatives with combat experience?" Kudo queried.

"Kane's out in the field already," Brewster told him,

"while Edwards is out of action. We don't have anyone. Why do you ask?"

"No matter," Kudo said, curtailing the conversation. A moment later, he drew the short *wakizashi* blade from its position by his hip, taking a deep, steadying breath as the tempered steel caught the rays of the morning sun. The blade was thirteen inches in length, more like a bread knife than a combat sword, but it was all that Kudo had left. His *katana* had been lost while he was aboard *Tiamat*. The *wakizashi* would have to do—its razor-sharp line was decorated with two Japanese characters forming a simple motto.

Kudo halted, watching as the three figures trekked toward him. He recognized the hooded robe of the lead figure before he heard the woman speak, challenging Kudo with a bark. "Faithless nonbeliever," she shouted. "Pledge allegiance on the battlefield of Ullikummis." Behind her, two people dressed in more normal clothes followed, but their expressions were intense as if suffering a fever.

Kudo held his free hand up before him, the short sword clutched behind his body at a downward angle. "Halt," he instructed. "Come no closer. I mean you no ill will."

"Faithless one," the lead woman snarled, "you will pledge your allegiance or you will be converted."

"I have no time for this," Kudo warned. "My friend is sick and I will pass. Step aside." They were still fifteen feet apart in the field of forgotten crops, but there was no cover that he might use. The tallest of the leafy plants in the field came only to his knees.

The robed woman reached to the crude leather pouch hanging at her waist, plucking a handful of stones from its contents. Kudo did not allow her to load her slingshot. His feet slapped against the hard-packed soil as he ran at her, his lips peeling back to reveal a grimace.

As the enforcer produced her catapult-like device—just a loop of leather that could be loaded with the stones—Kudo ducked and sprang, driving the tip of his tooled blade at her face. The woman launched the first of her stones at him, but he was already too close, weaving in past her attack. Then his blade whizzed past her face, missing her by just a quarter inch.

"I am stone," the woman hissed, entering the trance-like state that allowed those loyal to Ullikummis to tap his formidable strength.

Kudo had heard of this from the Cerberus crew, but he had not experienced it close-up before. He slashed at her again with his blade, slicing through the fustian robe and plunging its tip into her breast. She just stood there, not even wincing as the knife struck, and Kudo felt the tip of his blade hit something hard. He pulled his hand back and watched as the cut robe parted. Beneath, the woman wore a simple cotton undershirt, and this was ripped, too, in a line where the *wakizashi* had sliced it. And beneath that, her skin was unblemished, with no sign of blood on her exposed flesh.

With the heightened awareness of his surroundings that combat brought, Kudo was conscious that the other two figures were getting nearer, stragglers from Ullikummis's mighty land army. He spun on his heel, taking them in with a glance before turning back to the woman in the robe. She posed the biggest threat, he realized, since she was what had been dubbed a "fire-walker," those who could enter the trancelike state that made their bodies as hard as stone. Not so long ago, she would have been a normal woman, a wife or mother, someone's sister, perhaps. Yet now, here she was, enraptured in the thrall of Ullikummis—a monster from the stars.

The robed woman was loading her slingshot for a second assault, and Kudo sidestepped as the tiny shinglelike stones zipped through the air at him, cutting through the space between the two combatants like bullets. Kudo gasped as one of the stones caught him, slicing through the supple armor at his arm and leaving a bloody line across his deltoid.

With a fierce battle cry, Kudo lunged for the woman again, bringing the *wakizashi* in a short arc like a punch, driving it at her face. There was the crack of bone, a squelch and the woman was staggering backward, the leather slingshot dropping from her hand.

Kudo stood over her as she tripped and slumped to her knees with her hands coming up to her face. His blade had cut straight through her left eyeball, severing the optic nerve and cleaving the eye in two. It wasn't something he was proud to have done; it was simply the only weak spot he could think of in the woman's stonelike form.

Kudo turned to the approaching figures of the faithful, the congealing remains of the woman's eye dripping from his blade. "Step aside and let me pass," he told them in an ominous tone.

The figures looked at him blankly, uncertain what to do. After a moment they turned their attention to their fallen colleague, tending to her as she sobbed in agony. Her concentration was broken and her ability to tap the stone had departed.

Kudo ignored them, hurrying back to where he had left Domi and plucking her up in his strong arms. A moment later he was on his way, leaving the warriors for Ullikummis to whatever fate they sought. He had no time to deal with these people; he merely needed to get home.

ULLIKUMMIS WATCHED with pride as the surging crowds of his faithful hurried into the mazelike streets of the settlement that had been dubbed Dragon City. He recalled the armies of a bygone era, over four thousand years before, when thousands of these apekin had been recruited to do the bidding of their betters, the Annunaki, fighting to the death over narrow strips of territory. It had been a vainglorious exercise in those days, a way for the Annunaki to extract tribute from the primitives of this planet of mud and water. And it had served the purpose, too, of reminding the apekin who their betters were and just what they were capable of, when finally the two Annunaki overlords met in a showdown, striking each other savage blows amid the billowing winds and fertile ground of the Euphrates basin.

The tales of those clashes had become legend, recorded on stone tablets, many of which had survived even to this day. It had been artifice, of course, mere show disguising the true nature of the Annunaki squabbles. All that thunder and lightning, the drama of the god wars, had served to tell a story, a narrative that the apekin could follow and believe, never truly comprehending the real nature of those blood battles. Multidimensional beings, the Annunaki were gods and they hated as only gods could hate and they battled as only gods could battle. No apekin—no man—could ever witness the true arenas in which those battles were won or lost.

And now he brought true war to his father, Overlord Enlil. Now he came with one hundred thousand troops whom he had recruited or had recruited for him over the period since he had returned to Earth after his hasty exile on his father's command.

His father had genetically altered his child, Ullikummis, into this weapon, a living creature of stone who could strike down other Annunaki gods who threatened his reign. But when the attempted assassination of Teshub, who then held the key codes to *Tiamat*'s operational protocols, had failed, Enlil had banished Ullikummis forever, expelling him into space inside a prison of the strongest stone. Ullikummis had accepted his father's punishment, knowing all along that he was the scapegoat in his father's scheme, described as a rogue and used to disguise Enlil's hand in the audacious power struggle.

Ullikummis's mother—who had borne him after Enlil had raped her, taking her as his own as much through necessity as lust—had remained quiet throughout, but she had promised to help her son. It was through her machinations that the orbit of the meteor prison that held him had been altered just enough that he would eventually return to Earth, the planet where he had been born and raised. Ullikummis had spent four millennia trapped in a tiny, rock-walled cell in orbit through the solar system, and he had repeated just one single word throughout his long journey: "Enlil." It was the name of his father, the single object of his hate.

But when Ullikummis had arrived back on Earth he had found a planet much changed from the one he remembered. The Annunaki no longer ruled; in fact, their most recent bid for world domination had ended in the destruction of the *Tiamat* and the seeming end to their mighty, eternal feud. Even Enlil, Ullikummis's father, had gone to ground, hiding from the very apekin he should by all rights rule. The display had sickened Ullikummis.

Through touching the Ontic Library, the sentient database of all knowledge, Ullikummis had discovered his father's whereabouts and learned how the Cerberus people had repelled him in his quest to rule the apekin once more, slapping him down as if they did not accept their place in the natural order. Apekin, as foolish and passionate as ever. Ullikummis would deal with them, too, in time.

While he was in the Ontic Library, Ullikummis had learned of something else, too: that *Tiamat* yet lived, reborn from her own ouroboros seed.

Now he trekked toward the product of that seed with his army in tow, ready to wage battle with his father, to engage in the god war.

To believe that the conflicts of the Annunaki were waged purely on the physical realm, with an exchange of punches or the blast of a lightning weapon, was to misunderstand the nature of the Annunaki. Ullikummis had explained it once to Brigid, when he had set about converting her prodigious mind to his cause. "They started their current cycle as hybrids, half human, half advanced DNA," he had told her. "The human part clings, holding them back. If you saw the true battles between the gods, if you had witnessed the ways they fought across the planes millennia ago, you would never even recognize the creatures you fought as the Annunaki—you would think them a joke."

Now Ullikummis and Brigid strode into the colossal structure of *Tiamat*'s wings, surrounded by a throng of his loyal troopers, the hybrid girl Quav at Brigid's side. Ullikummis had once described the Annunaki creatures she had seen before as nothing more than actors on a stage, dressed in masks and rubber suits, humans in everything but appearance. Now, for the first time in her life, Brigid would witness a true battle between Annunaki space gods. Ullikummis had explained the Annunaki to her as "beautiful beings, multifaceted, crossing dimensions you cannot begin to comprehend." Their wars, he explained, were fought on many planes at once, the rules of their games intersecting only tangentially with Earth and its holding pen of stars. What she had seen was only a sliver of what the battle was, and to his mind, the Annunaki had shamed themselves in portraying it thus.

Ahead of them, the swanlike neck of the grounded *Tiamat* waited, her red eyes glistening in the sunlight like rubies. She was sleeping—Ullikummis could tell that even from this distance. Dozing as she waited for the battle to commence.

ROSALIA PEERED over the rooftop as the dozen faithful troops spied her and Grant. They were dressed in different manners, three of them in the infamous robes that looked like a monk's habit with the red shield over their breast in imitation of the old Magistrate uniform.

"Unfaithful!" one of the robed figures shrieked.

"Nonbeliever!" another cried as his hooded eyes spotted Grant on the rooftop.

As one, the robed soldiers reached for the leather pouches they wore tied to their simple belts, pulling out a handful of tiny, sharp stones, each no bigger than a bullet. From their other hands, a slingshot had appeared from its hiding place in their simple raiment, and they brought the ammunition to the weapon in a swift, well-oiled gesture that seemed to be second nature.

Rosalia ducked back, her arm up to warn Grant away as the robed warriors launched their first volley. The tiny stones struck with such force that they chipped the bone that made up the structure, sending hard flecks of it up into the air with loud pops.

"Come on, Magistrate," Rosalia urged, running to the far side of the building, "it's time we blew this party."

Grant didn't need telling twice. He was already half-way across the rooftop, looking for an escape route that didn't lead to the street where the warriors were waiting. "Head up," Grant instructed. "Keep to the high ground."

Assenting to Grant's suggestion, Rosalia sprinted across the roof while behind her she heard the rattle of more stones peppering the building's walls. As she reached the edge of the rooftop, Rosalia flung herself forward, kicking off with her back foot and springing higher into the air, throwing her hands forward. With a grunt of expelled breath, she struck the next roof over with her body, clambering up and over its chalk-colored lip in a couple of seconds and scurrying onward even as Grant leaped to join her.

"They sense we're different," Rosalia stated as she led the way across the next roof, this one several feet higher than the first.

"Then we're kind of screwed," Grant said as he returned his Sin Eater to its hidden holster. They were hurrying across the rooftops in parkour style, and he needed both hands if he was to keep up with the ferocious pace set by his beautiful companion. "It's too late to convert, I guess."

"No," Rosalia said as she bounded from one rooftop to the next, making her way gradually back into the heart of the city. "Just get some ground between us for now. I have an idea."

"Care to share it with the class?" Grant asked, irritated by the woman's cryptic nature.

Rosalia's dark eyes flashed as she glanced back at Grant. "Just keep up," she said, and Grant watched as her trim figure launched across the gap between buildings, twirling through the air like a sycamore seed and allowing her to change direction as she landed.

The forming mob was long behind them, all but forgotten already. Even so, Grant couldn't shake the feeling that they were trying to outrun the crest of a tidal wave.

ABOARD THE DRAGON SHIP, *Tiamat,* Enlil stood in the control room, studying the glasslike diagnostics displays as they filtered across the air, streaming into and through one another like so much smoke. *Tiamat* had been wounded in the conflict with the Cerberus people, and there had been significant damage to her water tanks which, in turn, had caused peripheral damage elsewhere. The ship was not full grown and, Enlil thought regretfully, he had perhaps been hasty in executing his plan to capture humans and work their primitive DNA into something suitable for use by the Annunaki.

Enlil held a palm computer in his clawed hand, mentally linked to his brain so that he could send commands to *Tiamat* at the speed of thought. Now he squeezed the device, which looked something like a seashell with a split center. *Tiamat* responded to that squeeze, adding a secondary layer of information across his yellow eyes with the vertical, black-slit pupils. She was hurt and her body was deteriorating. She had within her the power to regenerate, but she could not tap it. Something was obstructing her functionality, something relating to the damage she had sustained the night before.

Enlil cursed as another lightning strike rattled the mighty ship from the abandoned birthing chamber. The machinery there was going haywire thanks to the combined efforts of several Cerberus operatives. Damn them—did they have to insist on interfering in his plans time and again?

As Enlil studied the internal diagnostics, an alert flashed across one of the mistlike displays that hung in the air like smoke rings. He studied it for a moment, trying to make sense of the information being relayed to him. There were people outside, an army of apekin, hurrying through the dead corpuscles of *Tiamat*'s dry wings. Could this be Cerberus once more, sending a thousand or more of their people to attack him? Did they *have* a thousand people?

But there was something else in the display that caught Enlil's eye, and he enlarged the image so as better to study it. Another Annunaki was out there, heading toward the heart of *Tiamat* among the apekin throng. The mother ship had detected his presence immediately, identified him as one of her children.

Enlil studied the scan for a long moment, taking in the information it provided about that genetically altered Annunaki. Not Marduk, then, or Overlord Zu. Another, one who had altered his perfect Annunaki body for reasons that Enlil could not begin to guess. And then the realization struck him as the monitors droned on, pulling up a graphic representation of that Annunaki stranger who hurried toward Enlil's lair.

"Ullikummis," Enlil muttered, the words lost in the sharp intake of his breath. "So, you have returned, my son."

It should have been impossible, Enlil knew. He had expelled the child into space, sent him to float among the stars for the duration of his near-endless life. And yet, here he stood on Earth once again and with an army of apekin at his beck and call.

But Enlil did not question the facts presented to him. Ullikummis had beaten the odds and returned, and that was only right because he was his son—and what would any son of Enlil be if he could not defy the odds?

Tapping a quick sequence out on the palm link to *Tiamat,* Enlil called forth the Igigi who hid within the shells of the reborn Annunaki. "We still have much to do," he spoke to the empty room as if reminding himself. "More than I conceived. Let us begin."

Tiamat trembled as her mighty cargo doors opened for the very first time.

THE SOUNDS OF THE MOB were behind them now, their distant echoes like a half-remembered dream. Grant and Rosalia made their way through the citylike structure of the grounded spaceship via rooftops, leaping from one level to the next, turning back only occasionally when they ran out of routes. Rosalia had a natural talent for this, Grant noticed, and—not for the first time—he wondered momentarily about the mysterious young woman's background. Her movements and abilities spoke of long hours of training via repetition, and she seemed competent in a great many disciplines. Perhaps, he thought, her training mirrored a Magistrate's. Perhaps she was an ex-Magistrate herself.

Grant and Rosalia had traveled through this so-called city once before, just a half day earlier. It had taken time to navigate the labyrinthine roads then, constantly meeting dead ends as the streets snaked back on themselves like rats' tails. The rooftops proved a far quicker way across the settlement, something Grant had not considered before, having assumed—incorrectly as it transpired—that the structures were inhabited.

They stopped at one point on the roof of a three-story structure, now far distant from the burgeoning hordes of Ullikummis's army. Rosalia stood bent over, palms on her knees as she sucked in great breaths through her open mouth.

"You okay?" Grant asked.

From her bent position, Rosalia glanced up and gave a fixed smile. "Little run...never hurt anyone," she said between breaths. Grant watched as her slender shoulders heaved.

His own cardiovascular system was burning with effort, but Grant steadied his breathing and watched the far distance, searching for the city limits. Prongs of dark stone had appeared there, like thick lines of ink amid the whiteness of the spaceship's bone structures. Ullikummis was bringing them, just as he had guessed, tearing up the streets as he set his markers, each one blocking off yet another route of the mazelike city.

With casual indifference, Grant recalled the Sin Eater to his hand once again, then checked it over with studied professionalism. He emptied the dead magazine in its stock, reloading with a fresh magazine from his belt before sending it back to its hiding place in his sleeve. He was running low on ammo now—best be careful how he used it.

When he turned back he saw Rosalia looking at him. No, not at him—past him. Grant turned to peer behind him, saw what it was that had caught her eye. Another needle of dark stone was wending its way into the sky like a single nail, emerging between the chalk-white buildings perhaps a quarter-mile away, scraping against their walls.

"He's moving in," Rosalia said.

"Yeah," Grant agreed. "Adding a few personal touches, I guess, to make the place seem more homey."

They continued on, heading toward their goal of the dragon's torso at the center of the weird settlement. Grant led the way, picking up speed as he hurried across the rooftops, and he was gratified to see Rosalia keeping pace with him. Her endurance was exceptional, and he had never once heard her complain.

They leaped from the edge of the roof and onto the next, this one just eighteen inches from their launch point where the structures of the city bent inward against one another, vying for space like teeth in a crooked jaw.

While the massing army crowded the twisty-turny streets far behind them, Grant and Rosalia made good progress. Despite a couple of missteps, the two Cerberus rebels found themselves close to the city center in a little over ten minutes. They stood atop a two-story structure, its walls bone-white like everything else around them. The sun had risen, and the brightness of the bone-cobbled streets and buildings was dazzling. There, just two blocks ahead, loomed the great saurian body of the dragon, its head thrust toward the heavens with the inscrutable lizard smile formed along the line of its pressed lips.

"Once we pass her, we can exit town to the north," Rosalia said, but Grant was thinking about other strategies.

Grant looked at *Tiamat* up close once more, his head reeling to take in the immensity of her body. This was a space vehicle that served as a city, and its head alone would have covered a city block.

They had come toward *Tiamat* via a somewhat circuitous route, and they now stood closer to its left rump than they had previously. Standing beside Grant on the bone rooftop catching her breath, Rosalia eyed the body of the dragon with awe. The scales of its flesh were dark as if smoke-damaged, the color lost to the shadows cast by the morning sun. There were lights within the structure, glistening in the shadows like pinprick stars, their true size lost amid the grandeur of the dragon form itself.

"She's kind of beautiful, I guess," Rosalia admitted.

"Yeah," Grant agreed. "*Tiamat*. Mother of the gods."

Tiamat's skin was mottled, and as their eyes adjusted to the darkness of the shadows Grant and Rosalia began to notice where that skin was damaged, great rents in the flesh where it had spoiled like an overripe fruit. *Tiamat* had not been fully formed when they had mounted their attack the previous night, and the damage they had caused—despite being relatively minor— had spread through the structure, ripping away great hunks of her flesh.

The last time, they had gained entry via a series of explosive charges strapped to the spaceship's hull, carving a small hole just big enough to allow a person entry, but that hole was a quarter turnaround from where they were now, Grant guessed, and on a structure the size of *Tiamat* it would take some time to find it again.

As Grant pondered this, Rosalia pointed to something at the very rear of the structure, beneath the base of its huge tail.

"Magistrate, look."

Grant saw a straight line of light forming there, and as he watched the line became a rectangle, moving downward as it increased in size. A door was opening there, he realized, colossal in size and wide enough to allow thirty Sandcats to drive into it abreast. An easy way in or out.

"This ain't good," Grant muttered.

Then he stopped, the words turning to ashes in his mouth. Within that huge line of light, Grant and Rosalia could see humanoid figures, backlit shadows that waited in line at the edge of the hangar door. Despite the harsh light streaming from behind them, Grant recognized their silhouettes.

"We have a new problem," Grant stated.

They were Annunaki—hundreds of them.

Chapter 7

Brewster Philboyd hadn't been kidding when he had told Kudo that he might be the one who came to collect him from the field. Right now the gangly limbed astrophysicist was hurrying across the carefully manicured lawn that surrounded the south stretch of Shizuka's coastal property that he and his team had taken over as their temporary headquarters, making his way to the spot that served as a parallax point. The lanky scientist carried a metallic attaché case in one hand, swinging it to and fro as he rushed across the green lawn. The case contained an interphaser unit, one of two currently in use by the Cerberus personnel. Grant's team had gone into the field via a different method, leaving Cerberus with both units until Kane took one to respond to Balam's call.

Several hundred yards from the back windows of the temporary ops room, Brewster halted, checking the area he now stood in.

"Are you in place yet, Brewster?" Donald Bry asked via their linked Commtacts.

Brewster gazed around at the largely unremarkable stretch of lawn. Over to one side he could see the simple wooden fence that ran along the cliff's edge like a farmyard gate, beyond which was a sheer drop into the Pacific Ocean. "I believe so," he stated into his throat mike.

"Domi's showing at about a quarter mile from the

pickup point and moving fast," Donald informed him, relaying the information he saw on screen just a few hundred yards away.

Brewster nodded. "Check." He was busy now, working at the locks of the bulky attaché case and pulling the triangular interphaser unit free from its protective housing. In a few seconds Brewster had the unit set up on the ground, the case closed and locked beside it. His fingers briskly tapped out a sequence of information on the flip-down control panel at the interphaser's base, waiting while the interphaser went through its self-diagnosis.

There was nothing to distinguish this part of the lawn from any other, other than perhaps the fact that the grass looked a little patchy where people had walked across it, like the baseline of a grass tennis court. The interphaser required a parallax point to operate, but these came in many different forms. Frequently, parallax points were centers of worship or held great religious significance, but so much information had been lost that it was quite possible that any sign of a point's existence had become buried under centuries of changing terrain. Whatever this point had originally looked like, it was now just another strip of the neatly manicured lawn of Shizuka's property. The nukecaust had affected the old California coast, which meant that this coastal property had probably been much farther inland a few hundred years before, just another grand estate in the Hollywood hills.

As he thought on that, the interphaser came to life and Brewster stepped back as the eerily beautiful flower of energy opened up before his eyes, twin cones of churning color lunging above and—impossibly—below where the interphaser waited. In another second, the quantum gateway was open, joining this space to one thousands of miles away in the midst of old Iraq. Brewster girded himself before stepping through, feeling that discomforting sense of nonmovement wash over him in a surging rush.

"IMPOSSIBLE," ROSALIA spit as she watched the lizard-like Annunaki forms step from the lit rear doors of the dragon ship *Tiamat.*

Crouched beside her on the rooftop, Grant didn't bother to answer.

"The ship was falling apart…" Rosalia continued, doing nothing to disguise the irritation in her voice.

"It still is," Grant told her in a monotone.

Rosalia looked to where he indicated, saw the blotches of discolored—what was it, flesh, skin?—that showed all along the hull where there had not been any before.

"Those creatures are being controlled by something," Rosalia said, turning her attention back to the hundred or so Annunaki who were now swarming from the lowered deck plate that formed the back of the door. "I don't know what it is, Grant, but it came out of my dog. I—" she shook her head, trying to vocalize something at the very farthest reaches of plausibility "— felt it."

"I don't think they're friendly," Grant said.

"They saved us before. Saved you," Rosalia reminded him.

"No, they didn't." Grant shook his head. "They wanted Enlil—they made that pretty darn clear. We just happened to be along for the ride. Once they had what they wanted, they dismissed us from their thoughts. My guess is that now they've dealt with the big bad, they'll come after anything and anyone who gets in their way."

"You're speculating," Rosalia cautioned him.

"We need to get inside the ship," Grant announced, ignoring her complaints. "Now more than ever, we need to shut this baby down once and for all. Before Ullikummis gets there or these reborn things strip the ship of whatever it is they want."

LOCKED INSIDE THE ANNUNAKI bodies, the Igigi felt joyous as they hurried into the bone streets of the dragon. For more than three thousand years, they had been locked in a prison of their own devising, their memories trapped in the corrupted shadow box. Now they had bodies once again, the powerful bodies of the Annunaki, and they reveled in their use.

That they served Enlil, the mightiest and cruelest of Annunaki royalty, seemed only fitting; they had served him in their first life, when they had been "those who watch and see," organizing the world to his requirements and enforcing his will. To serve the Annunaki was an honor, and it was all that the Igigi had ever wanted, all that they had lived for. Their quest of rebellion, three-and-a-half millennia ago, was but a momentary lapse in a race of creatures bred only for servitude.

Now more than one hundred of them flooded out of the hull doors of the starship *Tiamat,* rushing into the maze of streets beyond. Their Annunaki bodies were powerful, perfect specimens of the grace and superiority of their masters in all things. To wear those flesh suits was an honor like no other, and each Igigi gloried in what he or she had become.

Around them, the bone-white buildings glimmered beneath the morning sun, a swathe of alabaster that seemed to stand as a monument to the might and wonderment of the Annunaki, like the old cities of Eridu and Nippur and Babylon that had sat on this very soil just a few thousand years before. The Annunaki forms hurried through the streets, their pace never slacking, things of beauty carved of flesh and scale and life. Ullikummis's army had entered from the east, and they, too, dashed through the streets, their numbers more than three thousand now and swelling with each pulse of the interphase window on the banks of the Euphrates. That these two forces would meet—one of one hundred or so, the other outnumbering them by thirty to one—was inevitable. The first clashes occurred less than a mile and a half from the center, where *Tiamat*'s body basked in the sunshine.

The human army turned another corner in the twisted streets and came face-to-face with three Annunaki. There were almost two dozen in the human party, and though they were armed with simple weapons, they felt confident that they could overpower these few humanoid creatures whose scales shimmered in the light.

"Kill them!" shouted the lead human, a man in his late twenties with a swish of black hair that was going prematurely gray at the temples.

His name was Davies and he had once lived a refined life in the towering city of Beausoleil out in the western territory of the old United States of America. His life had been devoted to engineering—he had helped perfect one of the processes used to externally coat the walls of Beausoleil. Davies had been overseeing a project to find a more durable roofing design for some of the towers on Alpha Level when the air raid had struck, mercilessly destroying whole chunks of the ville that had stood for almost a century against all intrusion, a monument to man's reborn desire for civilization under the auspices of the Program of Unification.

Davies had lost his home and his wife when the

bombs struck, watched through the windows of his office as dark smoke poured from the residential building he had lived in. He had been lucky to survive; in the highly organized microcosm of society that was Beausoleil, Davies had done something almost unthinkable that morning—he had gone into work early, better to address the roofing issue that had concerned the buildings along the east walls of the ville. It had been that dedication to his duty that had allowed Davies to survive, while the very buildings he had planned to reroof had been destroyed in the blink of an eye as the bombing raid leveled whole chunks of the settlement.

In that day, Davies had lost his family, his home and his ville. Escaping the crumbling ville as smoke billowed from its ruins, Davies had found himself adrift. He had never ventured outside the ville's protective walls, had never had cause to consider life as an outlander. For a while he wandered the vast territory that had belonged to Baroness Beausoleil, searching for food and shelter and a way to live. He had fallen in with a group of nomadic farmers who bred goats. They had taken him in, teaching him to be strong, to rear the disagreeable and pugnacious animals. He was damaged inside, his spirits at their lowest ebb, but Davies understood work and so he threw himself into this new task, rearing goats as the tribe moved from one location to the next. He often stopped to cock his head as he went about his business, imagining he heard his wife's voice calling him to share some idle observation, only to discover it was just his imagination, a ghost on the wind.

Like so many of the ville dwellers who had lost their homes, Davies had been a man cast spiritually adrift. The new church had arrived at an ideal time, with its promise of utopia, of Heaven on Earth. Beausoleil was just one of several villes that had been left in ruins across the great continent of North America, and the outflow of survivors and refugees was colossal. Ulli-kummis could not have chosen a better time to begin his religion with its promise of a better tomorrow; a whole segment of the population had become desperate to hear that very message. Davies was one of them, and he had joined the congregation in its raggedy meeting room in a spit of a town on the outskirts of Beausoleil's territory. He had recognized other people there from his years in the ville, though they looked thinner now, and many of the men had grown beards. Each day the congregation grew, and all that the minister demanded in return was the pledge to a better world. "Our love is stone," he had said, "and a stone can never be destroyed." The mes-sage had appealed to Davies more than most, for he had worked with stone in his ville life, knew its properties and limitations, appreciated the strength it represented.

Now Davies found himself at the forefront of a swiftly formed platoon of crusaders come to fight in the name of their god. He had not heard the call when it had come, but the minister had; the stone was embed-ded inside *him* and he could always hear the drums if he listened, while Davies, like many others in his congre-gation, remained a simple advocate, trusting the stone-blessed minister to instruct them in god's will. Thus, when the call had come, Davies had stepped through the quantum gateway with willing fervor, joining the others in his congregation as they stepped forth to fight in the war of gods.

Armed with a simple strut of wood pulled from the wreckage of a woodworm-ridden door destined for scrap, Davies lunged for the first of the Annunaki—an eight-foot-tall figure who dwarfed his own five-foot-seven frame. The length of wood cut through the air, arcing toward the powerfully muscled torso of the Annunaki warrior. With dazzling speed, the Annunaki's left arm jabbed out, swatting the hunk of wood aside before it could strike his naked purple-blue body. Davies had no time to react; already the Annunaki's other arm was up, striking him across the jaw in an open-palmed slap. Davies tumbled backward, stars bursting across his vision with the force of the blow.

Behind him, Davies's colleagues were rushing at the Annunaki trio, and one of them stepped on the dark-haired man's fingers as he fell to the ground. The lead Annunaki, the one with a shimmer of purple-blue scales and a spiny crest running the length of his scalp, swatted at the next human, knocking the man so hard he went careening into a bone wall.

There was barely any room to maneuver in this alley-like pathway. Far from being helpless, the three Annunaki were like a battering ram, a solid wall that hurtled into the human soldiers without any hesitation, let alone mercy. They fought for their master, the god Enlil; to back away would be heresy.

Human bodies fell backward, tossed against walls and ground, one thrown so high he slapped into the edge of a second-story roof, snapping his spine as his fragile body folded with the impact. The Annunaki drove onward, smashing aside two or three humans at a time, each one as powerful as a whole squadron of men. Twenty-four men fell in as many seconds to just those three Annunaki, and their lizard brothers were exacting a similar toll as they charged to meet the intruders to Enlil's majestic starcraft.

One of the humans, a brutal man called Thomersen who had a history of violence, ran at the Annunaki devils with a meat cleaver in his hand. Unlike the soft ville-raised people who had joined his congregation, Thomersen had been raised in the Outlands, and he knew how to take care of himself. When the call had come, he had picked up the first weapon he could find before entering the swirling portal that cut through space. He had used the meat cleaver the night before to carve up one of the goats his tribe raised for slaughter.

Thomersen's cleaver swished through the air as he ran at an orange-scaled Annunaki. Unarmed, the Annunaki held one arm up protectively and shrieked as the razor-edged blade sliced a line across his forearm from wrist to elbow, a great gob of flesh falling away in bloody slop. Thomersen smiled sadistically, eyeing the foul alien, little comprehending that it was of the very same species as the stone god he stood for.

In a blur of sunset-orange scales, the Annunaki spun on a heel, bringing one powerful leg out in a sweep and knocking the grinning apekin away in a flail of limbs.

Thomersen crashed to the ground with a woof of expelled breath, cursing as the meat cleaver slipped from his sweaty hand. He reached for it automatically, only to feel something crash down on his back, knocking him jaw-first back to the ground. It was the Annunaki, running across his back as he reached for the vicious implement. The next thing Thomersen saw was that wicked blade flashing through the air toward him as the lizard-man plucked it from the ground, striking so swiftly that he almost didn't feel it at all. Thomersen's face began to burn a moment later as the nerves sang with pain, and the vision in his left eye turned red with blood. What happened after that was mercifully swift as the Annunaki finished the kill.

As Thomersen slumped to the ground, his hacked-up

body twitching as his lifeblood spilled across the cobbled bones, the orange-scaled Annunaki turned, swiping at the next closest human with the cleaver he now wielded, lopping a great hunk of flesh from the woman's hip. The woman cried out as the material of her pants was shredded, the bloody gouge cutting through to the bone. The Annunaki grabbed her by her outstretched arm as she tried to run, hefting her from her feet and driving the bloody wedge of the meat cleaver into her torso. The woman shrieked, while others of her number came hurrying over to help or struggled with the other Annunaki warriors. The meat cleaver swept down in the Annunaki's clawed hand, driving into the woman's skull thrice before he turned his attention to his next foe.

This same bloody scene was played out again and again in various ways across the vastness of the city like the repeating chorus of some terrible death song, as the one hundred met three thousand. The skirmishes were tiny and brutal, taking place in alleyways and beneath grand hoardings that grew from the buildings like fingernails. On the outskirts of the dragon ship, the quantum gateway held in place, disgorging more and more warriors for Ullikummis, each man, woman and child armed with faith. The towering pillars of rock that Ullikummis had drawn from the earth helped guide them, directing them like a funnel into the battlefield. Ullikummis himself was somewhere amid the bone structures, striding purposefully into enemy territory with Brigid and the yet-born Ninlil at his side.

In some instances, the Annunaki found themselves facing those most loyal to Ullikummis, the so-called firewalkers who had submitted to the intrusive addition of the sentient stone into their bodies. These warriors were stronger, able to meditate and call upon the endurance of their master to better deflect blows, their flesh becoming like unto a thing of stone. They too fell, though they took many of the reborn Annunaki with them.

One group of firewalkers pinned an Annunaki with emerald-scaled skin within the tiny courtyard between low buildings, taking the higher ground and firing sharp stone flecks from the slingshots that they carried until the creature finally tumbled to his knees. Then they swarmed down upon their fallen foe, ripping into him with stony kicks and punches with all the force of an avalanche, pounding his body into pulp. The Annunaki lost consciousness at some point during the attack, but the crowd continued on, hating the others and all they represented.

Sela Stone was among the early waves of humans who rushed into the city to face the Annunaki, and the scene of carnage all around her reminded her of the horror she had witnessed at the Cerberus redoubt. There it had been Ullikummis's troops who had attacked her people, yet now she fought for them, her old identity of Sela Sinclair like a dream she had awoken from. Highly trained in the ways of combat from her days in the U.S. Navy, Sela used a pistol to blast not the Annunaki, whose skins were superhard, but to detonate explosive charges she tossed at them. It was a lot like skeet shooting, tossing those charges and blasting them while they were still in the air. She watched as the charges detonated, pouring fire over the relentless Annunaki warriors as they hurried down another of the alleylike streets. Though imperfect, her plan managed to down four Annunaki, two of them with one hit. She continued using it to push the line forward, getting herself and the human troops farther into the starship city.

Davies, meanwhile, had to have blacked out, and he awoke lying on the ground, shaking his head to try to clear it as the screams and sounds of violence echoed from the unadorned walls all around him. The bulk of the battle had moved farther into the city, little pockets of skirmishes occurring at almost every turn. There was blood on his lip, and he could taste it—acrid like iron—swilling between his front teeth. He pulled himself up, peering around as the world swam dizzily back into view. There were humans lying all about him, their limbs crushed or hacked off, their bodies stretched out at awkward angles.

Davies pulled himself warily to his feet, searching for possible threats. He guessed that he had survived because he looked dead, in some ironic twist of fate that he could not really put into words. Screams and shouts echoed from somewhere nearby, and the sudden cry of "Hold the line!" went out over the low buildings from behind him, though he could not pinpoint it. Then, up ahead, Davies saw five of the Annunaki troopers stomping along the narrow passageway in his direction, their lizard faces set in mean scowls.

Davies searched for a weapon that might have been discarded by one of his colleagues. His own length of door frame had disappeared amid the carnage, but there was a knife lying by a line of steps, and he hurried to snap it up. Streaked with blood, the knife was long and wide, shaped like a machete. Davies looked back up the claustrophobic street as the Annunaki marched toward him. He was outnumbered, and the knife in his hand looked decidedly small when compared to the muscular, naked bodies of the Annunaki.

Davies turned as he heard a noise from behind him—more footsteps, these heavy, the sound of them dominating the audio landscape for a moment. It was Ullikummis, rounding the corner. Davies felt himself tremble. Oh, to be in the presence of his god, a figure he had never actually seen before. Ullikummis was huge, taller than Davies had imagined, and his dark, rocky body was cut through with lines of lava that glowed intensely. He was magnificent. Behind him came his peculiar entourage—the beautiful redhead and the little girl with the feathery white-blond hair.

Ullikummis strode forth, taking in the quintet of Annunaki in a single dismissive glance. His hand flicked forward with disarming casualness and the ground beneath them rumbled. As the Annunaki ran at this, their most hated enemy, the cobbled pathway was rent apart, broad spikes of rock tearing through the surface and snagging the two lead Annunaki before they could step aside. The sharp lines of rock pierced their bodies and, immolated, they squirmed on them as Ullikummis strode past, never once slowing his pace. He had killed Annunaki in his youth, piercing their bodies with the stone knife Godkiller, a blade rent from the very fabric of his flesh. He thought nothing of killing them now, despite the tenacity of their superior bodies against common assault.

Ullikummis was upon the others in the group in an instant, batting the first of them aside with a sweep of his mighty arm. The creature's jaw cracked as he tumbled away, skull broken with the force of that blow.

Ullikummis lunged, his huge hand snatching for a face. The Annunaki ducked, driving a jabbing punch at the mighty rock lord's body. The blow slammed against Ullikummis with a sound like a toppling redwood, but he held his ground, pushed just two inches back on the flat, circular bases of his feet.

Davies watched in awe, blessed to see his idol in battle. He could not possibly guess the many hidden layers of this battle between Annunaki, even the pale imitations that the Igigi puppets were.

Then Ullikummis swept out again with one of his mighty arms, and the Annunaki trooper was flung backward, crashing into a wall with a shattering of bone. The one with the broken jaw was struggling back to his feet. Davies was about to cry out in warning, but Ullikummis was ahead of him, flicking his arm out to slam the outstretched fingers of his hand into the creature's windpipe, felling him instantly.

The last of the enemy charged at Ullikummis, and he flicked his arm out once again, the fiery glow in his eyes pulsing brighter for a single second. With a rumble of quaking earth, another line of stone prongs sprang from the ground, bursting through the lumpy bone cobbles that lined the street until they stood like the needles on a porcupine's back, each one seven feet in height. Davies shrieked as one of those sharp pointers drilled through his leg and up into his intestines, ripping out again at his breastbone in a gout of blood, his rib cage cracking open at the pressure. The Annunaki would-be attacker who had challenged Ullikummis hung in the air, another stone spike rammed through his body and up into his skull. He swung at a wicked angle, his own gore and brains sprayed across the stone, as Ullikummis marched onward, leading the way farther into the city of the dragon. Brigid Haight followed, with Little Quav in tow.

Davies died, staring into the dead eyes of the Annunaki as he swung like a washed sheet in the breeze.

THE SOUNDS OF WAR were long since behind him. Kudo could feel the exhaustion pulling at his muscles, weighing him down. He had taken most of the twelve miles to the parallax point at a jog, carrying Domi's slack body over first one shoulder then the other, alternating to try to stave off muscle fatigue. Prior to that, he had spent a day and night on mission, first flying to the drop zone as part of Grant's field team and battling with several waves of guardians before he could finally enter the dragon. While inside the spaceship *Tiamat,* he had sustained dreadful injuries to his face when an acid-laced charge had struck him. And yet, despite all of that, Kudo continued on—he was a Tiger of Heaven, honoring his duty would always be of paramount import.

The parallax point lay within the ruins of an ancient temple that had stood close to the Euphrates for at least four thousand years. The temple was a sprawling, low single-story building with a basement beneath, constructed of sandy-colored rock that camouflaged it from casual view. From the air it seemed to form an almost perfect pentagonal shape covering fifty yards at its widest axis.

Up close the temple was pockmarked with bullet wounds, and the wall surfaces had been eroded by wind over the millennia since it had been built. Even so, it still looked impressive, one of the earliest signs of civilization on planet Earth.

Over the portable comm device he wore against his right ear, Kudo heard Donald Bry confirming that he was in the right place. "An agent will meet you momentarily," Bry promised.

Kudo acknowledged Bry's report before striding the final few paces to the nearest wall of the ancient building. It was perhaps a little unusual that Donald Bry chose not to say anything else, but Kudo was grateful for the man's silence as he turned his concentration to the abandoned structure, searching for possible threats. He remained wary. Their enemies were all around, were they not? Parallax points were frequently hidden within special sites of religious interest, their uncanny power perhaps subconsciously influencing the humans around them. This temple was a typical location for one.

Hefting Domi over his left shoulder, Kudo paced between narrow walls, and his footsteps were appreciably silent despite the weight of the girl he carried. His eyes moved left and right as he searched for signs of habitation, listening to the desert winds scouring the walls. A figure moved up ahead, emerging from behind one of the sand-colored walls. Kudo felt relief when he recognized Brewster Philboyd.

"Mr. Kudo," Brewster said, smiling broadly beneath his bespectacled brow, "I believe you ordered a ride home."

Kudo nodded. "Philboyd, I am most gratified to see you. It has been one very long day."

"Twenty-four hours," Philboyd said agreeably as he led Kudo through the maze of open corridors to where he had set up the interphaser.

As they walked, Brewster inquired as to Domi's health, and Kudo assured him she hadn't stirred and that, as far as he could tell, nothing was broken.

The interphase unit waited on a wide stone tablet brushed with sand, its triangular sides glistening in the sunlight.

"How long were you waiting?" Kudo asked.

"Got here about twenty minutes ago," Brewster said. "Took a little look around while I was waiting. Place is utterly dead, thank goodness. Don't know what I'd have done if it hadn't been."

One of the fundamental problems with teleportation was that one could never quite be sure into which circumstances one would emerge. Since teleportation worked instantaneously, it required a sharp mind to react to whatever scenario one might face. As a rule, Brewster preferred to monitor things from the safety of his own desk.

"Still," Brewster said as he tapped in the code to send them home, "at least we know where we'll be jumping this time. Straight home and don't spare the horses, am I right?"

Brewster pulled his hand back as the control panel at the base of the interphaser came to life, and the two men watched as the eerie cones of light opened above and below the metal pyramid like a lotus blossom, witch-fire flashing within their churning depths. A moment later, Brewster and Kudo—with Domi's unconscious form slung over the latter's shoulder—stepped into that spectrum of patterned light and disappeared.

AT THE SAME MOMENT, identical twin cones of light seemed to emerge from nowhere, forming with the abruptness of a monsoon on a spot on the carefully manicured lawn of a villa overlooking the Pacific Ocean. Brewster breathed a sigh of relief as he and Kudo stepped out of the chaotic swirl of light, back on home ground once more. But as they turned to return to the single-story lodge that served as the temporary base for the Cerberus operation, they saw dark smoke billowing from its walls and heard sounds of gunfire. Cerberus was under attack.

Chapter 8

When Kane stepped into the quantum gateway of the interphaser with Balam, it had been like stepping into water. It seemed to splash all around him with that familiar shush-shushing of the ocean as breakers raced up the beach, the smell of brine piercing his thoughts.

Opening his eyes, Kane looked down and saw the spume of the sea lash against his feet once again. Gulls cawed overhead, their voices sounding as if they were berating one another. Kane watched as his foot left another great indentation in the soft sand, watched as the ocean's edge hurried up the beach to cover it, filling in the damage with its clear waters.

He was no longer Kane, he realized. He was Ullikummis, the stone feet leaving long indentations in the shining wet sand. He peered up, that sense of disorientation passing in a moment as he realized he had somehow switched bodies, delving into the memories of the stone implant that he wore like a scar across his face. Overlord Enlil was waiting up ahead on a bluff, and beside him stood Ningishzidda, the genetic engineer who had created Ullikummis's body. Shorter than Enlil, Ningishzidda's scales were jade-green and he wore lenses over his eyes, each one operating on a mechanical arm that could be lowered in place to increase the magnification of whatever he studied. Both Annunaki squinted against the rich afternoon sunlight, their cloaks catching in the wind.

"Come now, Ullikummis," Ningishzidda called, his voice duotonal. "The experiment begins."

AUTOMATICALLY, Kane-Ullikummis hurried across the beach and up the bluff where his father and the gengineer waited, clambering up the slope in great, loping strides. His body still felt new, and the legs ached with each movement. As part of the ongoing experiment to make him the perfect assassin, Ullikummis had had his legs stretched, and the pins holding them in place burned and throbbed as he moved his muscles.

Dispassionately, Enlil looked at his son as he reached the top of the cliff. His father gave little of himself, and his mother had once described him to the young child as "one who only knows how to take, never to give." At thirteen years old, Ullikummis failed to really understand what she meant. He saw his handsome father presiding over the golden city of Nippur and he idolized him while others worshipped this so-called god from space.

"Your hands," Ningishzidda prompted.

Ullikummis held them straight before him, pressing the wrists together as shown while Ningishzidda produced the binding wire. The wire was made of spun silver, and it twinkled in the sun's rays like a sliver of stolen moonlight. In a moment, Ullikummis's hands were bound before him, and he watched emotionlessly as Ningishzidda kneeled to bind his ankles.

"There is a possibility that the prince will not survive this," Ningishzidda said, addressing Lord Enlil.

"Then he will have been a disappointment," Enlil replied, gazing out over the caroming waves of the ocean.

They did this often, talked about Ullikummis in his presence as if he was not there, as if he were just an object, a thing. He was seven feet tall now, as tall as either lord, yet he felt dwarfed in their company, these great figures who ran the world.

"How did the water feel?" Ningishzidda asked Ullikummis.

"Warm, sir," Ullikummis replied, "I think."

It was hard to be sure. Ullikummis was a genetic freak now, his skin grown over by the stone cladding for which he would become known. Under the instruction of Enlil, the gengineer had altered Ullikummis at a basic level, retooling him since before birth. The building blocks had been injected into Ullikummis when he was but an egg grown from Ninlil's womb. Over the following thirteen years, Ningishzidda had activated each of the changes he had planted within Ullikummis's DNA, encouraging the child to grow in a certain manner in the way that a master horticulturalist will tend to a rosebush to shape it in a certain way. In essence, the genetic engineer had created this freak, this monster that stood apart from the rest of the Annunaki pantheon, feared and loathed in equal measure.

The strips tight, Ullikummis waddled to the cliff's edge, peering down at the rolling waves crashing against its side twenty feet below.

"The drop is not very far, Ullikummis," Ningishzidda reminded him. "Take a breath before you hit the water."

"Yes, sir…" Ullikummis began to reply, but before the second word had left his lips, Enlil struck him between the shoulder blades, driving the breath from his lungs and pushing him over the edge of the cliff. The great stone creature toppled like a pillar, falling over himself as he hurtled toward the waiting ocean. His chest hurt from the forceful blow he had been struck, and he gasped only the shallowest of breaths before he hit the surface, dropping beneath like a thrown spear.

He had no breath. He was beneath the water, and he had no breath. Ullikummis watched as the last few bubbles escaped from his mouth, racing upward and away even as he plummeted toward the ocean's bed.

It didn't matter. Ningishzidda had built things into his biological makeup that would allow him to survive for a while without breath—perhaps indefinitely. His teacher, Upelluri, had shown him breathing exercises, ways to slow his breathing and his need for oxygen. He slipped into the trancelike state immediately, stilling his mind and letting the water surge past him.

Warm where the sun touched it, the water was cooler as soon as he dropped away from its surface. Ullikummis dropped quickly, his body straight, arms and legs tied, falling like the proverbial stone. His body was covered by stone armor, he weighed more than six normal Annunaki of his size and he was still growing.

He opened his eyes, two yellow orbs, each one split with a vertical black line. They were lizard's eyes, the eyes of the Annunaki. In time, Ningishzidda would replace them, too, but for now they would suffice. They felt hard against the water, as if they wanted to pop out of his skull or to burst. Ullikummis saw the darkness increase around him as he fell farther away from the surface and peered above to see the dwindling light that swirled there in a series of broken white stripes.

Ullikummis was struck by how different things were down here. Broadly speaking, Earth was two environments—the land and the water. Things of the land relied on air to live, and they hurried to and fro on legs or wings or the bottom of their bellies as they tried to keep up with those molecules of oxygen buzzing all about them. Down here, in the water, things ran at a slower pace. The creatures moved with grace, and the plants waited for time to pass, doing little to attract others to them in that desperate struggle to reproduce and spread their seeds. The revelation struck Ullikummis with such obviousness that he almost kicked himself—in holding his breath he could work slower down here, too, no longer dancing to the urgent drumbeat of the surface world. A smile played across the stony crags of his face as the teenager settled down to the task at hand, no longer hurried by the pace set by those around him.

An air breather could drown in an inch of water as easily as he could drown in an ocean. Thus, the depth mattered little to Ullikummis, and the pressure of the ocean was just a minor irritation on his powerful body as he worked slowly at his bonds.

It took three days before he emerged from the ocean, the bonds removed, a way located back to the surface. Kane had been with him the whole time, reliving the memory like an old video film, experiencing every second of those days, Ullikummis's thoughts now his own.

Ningishzidda had been gratified to see Ullikummis step into the banqueting hall in Nippur, welcoming the lad as one might welcome a dog one thought had run away from home. Enlil was less fervent, acknowledging the boy's return with just two words:

"Well done."

"KANE?" BALAM ASKED. "Kane, are you okay?"

Kane's eyes snapped open, and he found himself staring into the upturned bulblike face of the pale-skinned Balam. His head ached, swimming still with the intrusive memories of his enemy. He had spent three days beneath the ocean in the company of that monster, it seemed, sharing his thoughts. To be brought back from that was jarring, and Kane tamped down the wave of nausea that threatened to overwhelm him.

He was on the floor of a dark room, its proportions so vast that he could not see the walls. There were shelves and containment units scattered all around, spreading out from him in all directions along great aisles that filled the vast room. Despite its size, the room was windowless, an underground store in the city of Agartha, and it was lit only in patches, small cones of light emanating from the ceiling and leaving much of the vast space in darkness.

"I'm okay," Kane slurred, pulling himself up to a sitting position and regretting it as soon as he did it. He slumped back, feeling the hard floor knock against the back of his skull and not caring. The ocean swam in his ears, the whisper of memory plucking at his thoughts.

"How long since we got here?" Kane asked, taking slow, meticulous breaths.

"Fifteen minutes," Balam told him. "I wasn't comfortable leaving you any longer than that. I'm sorry."

The chunk of stone embedded beside Kane's eye was having a terrible effect on him. Each time he traveled via interphaser it would reconstitute with his own flesh, overwhelming his senses with ancient memories of Ullikummis's life, fully formed reconstructions that Kane had to live through with no ability to change or control. It was like being trapped as a prisoner in one's own body. This had been the worst one yet, and coming out of it took Kane a few moments, trying desperately to cling to his own thoughts, his own ego.

Balam stood at his side, patiently watching as the ex-Magistrate recovered.

"Let's get moving," Kane said, pulling himself off the floor more slowly this time. "No time to waste, right?"

Balam watched the human in admiration as Kane got to his feet. His sense of dedication was exceptional; his bravery knew no limits.

"We shall use the chair," Balam said, leading the way from the parallax point that had been their destination. The point was marked by a series of concentric circles that would glow when it was in use. Those circles were dim now.

Kane glanced across the room, taking in what he could with a sweep of his eyes. Balam had previously described this as a museum, and it was filled with alien artifacts, shelved or stored in various ways. To Kane's eyes it seemed more like a storeroom, all the old junk from civilizations past and future tossed into one vast holding pen where they could rot without fear of causing damage, Inca crap next to Egyptian crap, on and on. Kane's gaze was drawn to a pile of metal machinery, vast turbines held in cylindrical cups like the engines of a jumbo jet. He wondered what they might be.

Balam was walking with a slight limp now, and he winced as he moved. He had suffered some internal damage from a gunshot when Brigid Haight had attacked him, and he had yet to seek proper medical attention. The last time Kane had raised this, just a few hours earlier, Balam had dismissed him in a rare display of pride.

After a brief walk through the wide aisles of the storeroom, Balam and Kane came upon a huge, curve-sided cube that rested beneath a bank of lights. The cube was twenty feet square, and its walls were opaque but shimmering. Scooping his hands together, Balam arrowed his fingertips at the shimmering surface and they cut through it, parting the wall like a waterfall cascade. Kane followed as Balam led the way into the strange, stand-alone room, the wall resealing behind them.

Within, the cube had the rich smell of plant life, the air heady with the scent of living things, a smell like mulch. Kane felt the air like a wall, its richness overwhelming his nostrils for a moment.

The strange room was empty apart from one item held in its very center: a chair. The chair had a curved back and ran down on a single, thick leg like a tree trunk that ended in a splayed structure arrayed across the floor. The back of the chair curved like a spine, and two arms struck out from its sides. The chair was Annunaki in design and Kane had seen its ilk before; in fact, he had used this one just a few hours earlier. It was an Annunaki navigator's chair designed for use in space travel. Within, the chair held a databank of information that could either be projected or fed directly to the user's mind, and it could be employed to scan for specific locations and items within the immediate area. In this case, the "immediate area" was of a scale that dwarfed comprehension, given the vast distances involved in space travel, where one navigated in terms of light-years rather than miles.

Balam and Kane had utilized this chair just a few hours before, when Kane had accessed its semiliving circuitry to track down Brigid via the *anam-chara* bond they shared. It was this investigation that had led them to the island fortress of Bensalem, but it transpired that the two of them had arrived too late.

"We shall try again," Balam said as Kane walked across the room to the lonely chair.

Kane sat down, tentatively placing his arms down on the armrests. After a moment, the chair engaged, and Kane felt a thrumming against his back as the chair itself seemed to come to life. Kane winced as the chair's arms fired spines into his flesh, piercing the heels of his hands and running along the underside of his forearms like a rush of insect feet. Kane braced himself as the back of the chair shook and thorny, plantlike tendrils emerged from the headrest and started to wrap around his face.

"You'll need to concentrate on Brigid," Balam reminded Kane, "focus on the bond you share with her."

Kane was not sure whether he had closed his eyes at first, as the chair's visions channeled through him; it was suddenly hard to remember. He was plunged into a new sensory world, a new way of looking, and it felt as if his brain was being pounded with snow. He was linked to Balam by the optical bond, and that link allowed Balam to see what he was seeing, too. Beside him, Balam closed his eyes in a slow blink, letting Kane's visions rush over him, oozing into them with more comfort than Kane felt.

"Persevere," Balam told Kane. "You shall survive this."

To Kane, Balam's voice seemed to come from a distance now, faraway and ethereal. He had to concentrate on the words as the visions of the chair hurtled through him, colors and patterns and shapes to his left and his right, up and down.

Before Kane's eyes, the world seemed to be spinning, breaking apart, the gaps between things widening. Taking a determined, deep breath, Kane thought about Brigid Baptiste, instructing the astrogation chair to guide him to her.

Symbiotically linked with Kane now, the chair cata-
lyzed his endorphins, bringing him a breath of happiness
as it reached out to find the person he was searching for.
The vision quest had begun.

Chapter 9

On a neatly manicured lawn on the Pacific Coast, Kudo and Brewster Philboyd turned to face each other, their mouths agape.

"What the hell...?" Brewster began.

Several hundred yards ahead of them, they could clearly see dark smoke billowing from the single-story structure where Cerberus had set up its temporary home. The smoke was thick and black, and orange tongues of flame danced within the plume that reached into the sky. There were gunshots, too, and shouting, all of it echoing out across the lawn, mingling with the repetitive shush-shushing sound of the ocean washing against the cliff to their left.

"We must do something," Kudo announced in a firm, no-nonsense tone.

Brewster eyed the man for a moment. His face was red, the skin damaged along his left jowl as if attacked with eczema. His body hung heavy, his movements weary as he carried the pale-skinned figure of Domi in his arms. He was exhausted, Brewster could tell.

"You're in no condition to fight," Brewster warned.

Kudo looked at him, his face a mask of contempt. "Survival does not wait for one to be in the right condition or frame of mind," the Tigers of Heaven warrior stated. "We are needed now."

Before Brewster could respond, another voice chipped

in. "Gotta listen to the man, Brewster." It was Domi, finally waking up in Kudo's strong arms.

"Domi, are you—?" Kudo began.

Domi answered with a long, slow blink, her demonic red eyes burning fiercely in the rays of the morning sun. "I'll be fine," she said. "Looks like you took a nasty hit yourself."

Self-consciously, Kudo reached his free hand to his marred face, stopped short of touching the stinging wound. "Things did not go quite to plan in the dragon ship," he understated. When Domi looked at him in confusion, he added, "The city we were in when you were kidnapped. It was a spaceship, its body in the center of the settlement."

Domi nodded in comprehension, then urged Kudo to put her down. "I can walk," she assured them both as he and Brewster watched her with worried expressions. "Now, let's get moving. Cerberus is in trouble."

Agreeing, Kudo started jogging toward the burning building while Brewster and Domi followed, the latter still a little unsteady on her feet as she tried to shake off the effects of recent trauma to her body. The night before, Enlil had tried to turn her into one of his new Annunaki. As she ran, Domi pulled the Detonics Combat Master .45 pistol from its hiding place at the small of her back, placed there by Grant during their exit from *Tiamat*.

WITHIN THE SINGLE-STORY lodge, Lakesh found himself fighting for his life. The loyal troops for Ullikummis had amassed outside the gates in just a few hours, and when they had finally attacked, it had been sudden and brutal. There were almost two dozen of them by that time, each one hooded in one of the simple, roughly hewn robes, the cowls masking their faces in shadow. With more than twenty in total, they outnumbered the personnel that Lakesh could call upon at the base—between Cerberus staffers and Shizuka's Tigers of Heaven, there were still just nineteen people, including Lakesh himself.

Lakesh had been watching from the balcony when the first wave charged at the gates in a group of three, clambering over the spearlike struts like insects, never so much as making a sound. As they climbed, Shizuka gave the order to electrify the gates, and a ten-thousand-volt charge was sent through their metal railings, jolting the attackers from its struts with sparking bursts of electricity. The figures were tossed back, thrown to the ground outside the property with smoke pouring from their robes. It didn't stop them.

The next wave had marched over the bodies of the first, climbing up the gates despite the electric current coursing through them.

"Firewalkers," Lakesh had said as he watched them do the near-impossible with no hint of reluctance.

These were troops for Ullikummis, stone men who could channel the gift of his hidden, symbiotic rocks to harden themselves, making their skin like armor.

In that moment, as the first group scaled over the gate, Shizuka told Lakesh to retreat into the shelter of the lodge. Lakesh had done so without discussion, reentering the building and hurrying through the corridors to the temporary ops room. Waiting there, Donald Bry peered up from his usual position at one of the laptops.

"What's going on?" he asked, pushing his mess of copper curls from his eyes.

"We're under attack," Lakesh said, his voice drained of all emotion. This had happened to them not so long ago. To suffer it again, now, when they were at their lowest ebb, was almost unthinkable.

Bry didn't hesitate. He had already patched through to the comm system, and he advised all personnel to stand ready. The call went through the lodge instantly, and the cries of surprise and outrage came back from nearby rooms.

Once Bry had finished his broadcast, he locked eyes with Lakesh sorrowfully, like an obedient hound awaiting his master's orders.

"Can we do this again, Donald?" Lakesh asked wistfully.

"We did it once," Bry replied. "Surviving is in our nature, Lakesh."

Lakesh had nodded. "It had better be," he said ominously.

Outside, Shizuka had called upon the ten Tigers of Heaven who patrolled the lodge, and together they formed a human barricade through which the infiltrators would have to pass before they could reach the personnel within. Shizuka drew her sword, a twenty-four-inch *katana* blade with intricate gold inset along its center line and drizzled across its ceremonial handle.

Without a word, her loyal troops did the same, a line of *katanas* glinting in the morning sunlight like stripped-down trees in a metal forest. The first group of firewalkers charged up the long pathway that led to the lodge, utterly silent as they swiftly made their way to their objective. Quite why Ullikummis had singled out Cerberus for this punishment no one knew, but the Cerberus personnel had evidently been identified as enemies to the New Order. The reality was that Ullikummis had relived parts of recent history while imbibing data in the Ontic Library, and he had witnessed the crucial role that Cerberus had played in the defeat of the Annunaki following their recent rebirth. Such a force needed to be cut down swiftly, he reasoned, and given no opportunity to regroup and secure its power base. With that in mind, his attack on the Cerberus redoubt and the subsequent hounding of its personnel was logical.

The first skirmishes happened on the lawns midway between the gates and the house. Four of Shizuka's men threw themselves at the so-called firewalkers as they tried to storm the building, cutting and stabbing at them with their swords as they endeavored to force them to retreat. Already, the second wave was coming, hurrying over the gates and into the lodge's grounds. Shizuka and her troops hurried to meet the invaders. The firewalkers were strong, armed with their slingshots and relying on the capacities of stone when drawn into close combat. The Tigers of Heaven did their best to hold ground, but they were unable to repel the attackers. Within just a few minutes, figures were battling on the lawns and in the tranquil garden at the back of the house.

The first hooded attacker to reach the lodge itself knocked something over, setting light to drapes and walls in moments.

In the ops room, Bry and Lakesh had armed themselves from the small arsenal they had stored at the temporary base. As the first robed figure barreled down the corridor and into the room, the two men calmly leveled their pistols and fired, peppering the man with bullets. Neither Lakesh nor Bry was comfortable in this scenario; they were deskmen, employing their intellect in the operation of the Cerberus organization. Nevertheless the hooded figure in the doorway went down beneath the barrage of gunfire, falling backward in a slump.

Both Lakesh and Bry remained poised, their 9 mm pistols held steadily in their hands. The robed figure lay on the wooden floor, silent. Warily Lakesh approached, taking three tentative steps to get a closer look at the man beneath the hood. His simple robes showed wear and tear, and there were several holes across the torso, circles with dark edges where the bullets had struck. The man's face was scrunched up in anger, his lips a thin line where the hood left his chin revealed. He was still breathing, Lakesh could see, fustian robes bunched where he had fallen. Then, without warning, the man moved, his eyes springing open, and he powered himself from the floor and grasped for Lakesh.

The aging cyberneticist jumped backward, grateful for the recent rejuvenation program that his body had been put through. He was old, yes, but at least he wasn't decrepit—not yet.

The attacker's arms cut the air as he drove a punch toward where Lakesh had been standing, and the older man ducked and sidestepped, just getting himself out of the way of the first of those powerful blows. The next fist drummed into the wall beside Lakesh's head, striking with a noise like thunder and drawing away again with a dusting of ruined plaster.

They're strong, Lakesh reminded himself. Drawing on the power of their master, each punch from the firewalker was like a battering ram thrust toward its goal.

Lakesh whipped up the Smith & Wesson pistol as he threw himself out of the way of his attacker, loosing a triburst. The first shot struck the man's torso at the base of his rib cage, burning through the brown robe he wore, but to little effect. The second shot struck the man's face, producing a cloudburst of blood even as the third shot rocketed past him, missing by just a fraction of an inch.

Across the room, Donald Bry was lining up his own pistol on the fast-moving target, waiting for Lakesh to get out of the line of fire. He watched Lakesh duck as he blasted his attacker in the chest and face, and saw the older man spin out of the path of another attack, whipping around a pillar to the far right of the room. Bry pumped the trigger of his blaster then, firing three shots at the firewalker as he staggered in place.

ONE FLOOR BELOW, in the basement of the lodge, Reba DeFore, Mariah Falk and Dr. Kazuka had been examining their patient when Donald Bry had issued his alert. Their patient was Edwards, another ex-Magistrate who had sided with the Cerberus rebels over the past few years, and who had recently been infected by one of the obedience stones. A tall, broad-shouldered figure with a shaved head and muscular build, Edwards exuded an air of menace even lying asleep on the gurney before them.

The two physicians and the geologist were looking at an item of ultrasonic equipment, something akin to a surgical laser that would direct concentrated sound waves on command. The unit featured an eight-inch-wide drum that tapered to a thinner point, which in turn ended in a short tube that was just a little thicker than a ballpoint pen. Kazuka had been mounting the device on a vise arm that would hold it in place so that it could be operated via computer hookup.

"We're entering uncharted surgical territory," he reminded them as he screwed the emitter in place.

The device itself was an experimental model that had been swiftly cobbled together by two of the Cerberus scientists who resided at the lodge. Out of options, it had been mocked up in a matter of hours following Lakesh's initial suggestion. Cerberus employed some of the most brilliant scientific brains on the planet, but even they had been taxed when asked to make the ultrasound emitter a reality.

As Kazuka fixed the emitter in place, Bry's alert came softly over the wall-mounted comm. "There are enemies at our perimeter," Bry explained calmly. "They have entered the grounds, and the Tigers of Heaven are engaging them now. Please be advised that we are under attack, and that this facility is now on level-two high alert."

Wide-eyed, DeFore turned to Mariah. "Again?" she said incredulously.

Mariah shrugged. "We were caught napping last time," she said. "Let's not make that mistake again."

Thus, when one of the firewalker troopers loyal to Ullikummis came hurrying down the staircase, the three doctors were ready for him. Like the other infiltrators, this one was dressed in a thick robe that covered him from crown to ankles. Though thick, the robe was light enough to move freely in, as he proved when he hurtled down the stairs with one of the Tigers of Heaven, tossing the samurai against one wall in a show of strength. The samurai hit it with a loud bang, dropping his razor-keen blade as he tumbled to the hardwood floor.

The blade skittered across the floor before coming to a halt as Kazuka placed the sole of his shoe upon it. In a flash, the Tigers of Heaven physician picked up the sword and entered the fray, running along the corridor and lunging at the attacker even as the man wrenched Kazuka's fallen colleague from the floor by his throat.

"Let him go," Kazuka warned as he jabbed the blade

at the firewalker in a practiced two-handed grip. "Your fight is with me now, monster."

In a split second, the robed figure let go of the other man's throat and spun, batting the blade aside even as Kazuka drove it at his chest. With that, the fight was on.

Though a trained physician, Dr. Kazuka was a Tigers of Heaven warrior, and as such he could wield a sword with the same grace and artistry of any of his samurai colleagues. The blade sang a pure note as it cut through the air, slashing at the face of the hooded attacker. The man in the robe stepped back effortlessly, using the flat of his left palm to bat at the blade once more, knocking it aside with such force that Kazuka almost lost his footing.

Kazuka recovered instantly, turning his stumble to his advantage as he stepped inside his foe's guard and drove the pommel of the sword hard into the man's chest. The man grunted, feet pinwheeling as he staggered back to the stairs.

Kazuka didn't hesitate. He leaped forward, driving his attack and forcing the robed stranger to step up one stair or lose his footing completely. But as the Tigers of Heaven physician brought the long blade down in a straight, vertical strike, his foe breathed the trigger phrase that brought him power: "I am stone."

The blade struck the warrior's skull with a loud clang, like metal striking rock, and Kazuka gasped as the kinetic energy dissipated up the blade's length and shuddered through the muscles of his arms where he held it.

Before Kazuka could recover, the robed stranger thrust his hand out in a vicious open-palm blow, striking the doctor in the nose. Kazuka stumbled back, seeing stars flit across his vision and feeling the hot trickle of blood between his teeth. The robed invader kept at him, his right arm sweeping in a swift arc that ended with a brutal cuff to the side of Kazuka's head. The physician was slammed back into the nearest wall, grunting as the breath burst from his lungs, urgently bringing the sword up into a defensive position. The hooded man struck with the force of stone; fighting him was like trying to do combat with an avalanche.

Kazuka reeled as another blow struck him. This time a sharp knee plunged into his side, followed by a vicious slap across the face.

As the robed attacker prepared to launch another blow, Mariah Falk and Reba DeFore charged out of one of the rooms at the far end of the corridor, hefting the ultrasound emitter between them as they ran up the corridor toward the action. It had taken a few minutes to loosen the nuts and free it from its mounting, but now the unit could be carried—albeit awkwardly—by one or two people. As the firewalker lunged at the struggling Kazuka, Mariah put her fingers to her lips and gave an ear-splitting whistle that resounded down the corridor. The robed intruder halted, turning to see what the noise was, and in that instant Reba DeFore flicked a switch at the side of the sound emitter and blasted a burst of ultrasound at the man.

Other than the faint buzz of the machine itself, the only real hint that the ultrasound was operating was a subliminal feeling of uneasiness in all the people within its vicinity. The ultrasound worked at the edge of the audible spectrum, registering in the inner ears and causing a momentary loss of balance. There was something about the firewalkers, however, that the Cerberus scientists had noticed earlier: while they could seemingly channel the durability of their rock-clad master merely with a thought, the process required some meditative level of concentration, a state that could be disrupted by high-pitched sounds. While the ultrasound emitter had been constructed with the hope of using it as a surgical instrument, right now it disrupted the trancelike state that Ullikummis's faithful warrior had achieved.

The warrior stood rigid as the blast of sound hit, and Kazuka used that moment to take swift action, driving the *katana* into his enemy and drilling the metal through the man's torso until its whole length had passed through him right up to the handle.

Kazuka stepped back as the man stood there, his eyes wide beneath the masking shadows of his hood, the sword plunged into his body just below the line of his rib cage. The robed firewalker stared off into the middle distance, unable to comprehend what had happened to him as blood began to stream between his gritted teeth and pour down his chin. Then, as if his body had finally acknowledged the injury, the man sank to his knees, careering sideways until the left side of his head slammed against the hard wooden paneling that lined the walls. He was dead.

"It seems," Kazuka began, his breath coming in ragged, uneven bursts, "that we have a makeshift weapon to use against Ullikummis's most faithful warriors."

DeFore and Mariah nodded.

"Not especially practical for the battlefield," Mariah lamented. But it would have to do.

THE ROBED FIGURE reeled from the impacts of Donald Bry's shots, dancing an ungainly jig as he staggered back, knocking over one of the desks and sending a computer monitor skittering across the floor. But—

impossible as it seemed—the man recovered in a heart-beat, his hands snapping out for Lakesh where he had retreated behind a support pillar near the windows at the side of the room.

Lakesh reared back. But the hooded figure was faster than Lakesh, grasping a handful of material from the front of his white jumpsuit and pulling the older man to him. As he did so, the man's hood fell back from his face, revealing a bald head and dark, intense eyes. "I am stone," the man announced, yanking Lakesh up with such violence that his feet left the floor.

For a moment, Lakesh hung there, his legs dangling in place as the firewalker glared at him. There was a ferocity in those eyes, Lakesh saw, but also something else—an otherworldliness, as though the man was not quite in his right state of mind, on drugs or in some sort of trance perhaps.

"I am not your enemy," Lakesh blurted. "Please, you must put me down."

The robed man ignored him, shaking the cyberneti-cist in the air like a rag doll. Lakesh was jerked back and forth dizzily, gasping as his swinging arm slapped against the pillar. With his other hand he tried desperately to bring his blaster into place, pulling the stubby silver barrel of the Smith & Wesson around and firing at his enemy's face. The shot went wild as he was spun once more, and Lakesh screamed as his back smashed against the pillar with colossal force, driving the breath from his lungs.

The whole lodge was beginning to stink of smoke as the fire spread from the eastern wing, wisps of gray billowing into the rooms.

Nearby, Bry was screeching, "I can't make the shot. I can't make the shot."

The warrior for Ullikummis whirled in place, hefting Lakesh's form this way and that as if to shake the very life from him. Lakesh watched the room spin about him, groaning as his arms and legs knocked against the walls and windows. In the background, he could hear Donald Bry chanting those words over and over: "I can't make the shot. I can't make the shot."

Suddenly they were at the glass doors that led to the sunken garden at the rear of the property, and Lakesh yelped as he was thrown against them, crashing into the glass with a crack. The glass held as he struck it with shoulders and back. A cobweb of fault lines appeared on its surface and widened as the Cerberus director fell to the floor, losing his grip on the Smith & Wesson as he did. The gun skittered away, retreating beneath a low table containing paper files and computer equipment.

Lakesh lost consciousness for just a few seconds, a great dark wash crashing across his vision like waves on a moonlit beach. When he opened his eyes again, the sounds around him eerily distant, he saw his hooded attacker had turned his attentions to Donald Bry, back-handing the man with a slap so hard that it knocked Bry off his feet.

Lakesh lay slumped on the floor with his head resting against one large glass panel of the French doors. His vision was swimming as the thuggish firewalker strode across the room toward him once more, a streak of red blood marring the left side of his face where Lakesh had shot him. Lakesh struggled to make sense of things as his brutish attacker uncoiled something that he had produced from a pocket of the robes. It was a length of leather, a simple slingshot curled around itself. With his other hand, the robed man tugged at a pouch hanging at his hip, pulling out a clutch of three sharp stones.

Lakesh urged his body to move, trying frantically to get out of the path of that vicious attacker who loaded the slingshot and took aim at his face. His body did not want to respond. It ached and seemed ungainly now, twinges of pain lancing through his arms and legs. Even his mouth didn't want to work anymore, and when he tried to plead for his life it came out as a gurgle from the back of his throat, the sound of a man choking on food too rich for his sensitive palate.

"Faithless nonbeliever," the robed man growled as he drew back the loaded slingshot. "You are now erased from history."

Chapter 10

Lakesh was helpless. Before him, the robed man drew his slingshot back to its fullest extent and began to launch the stone ammunition. But as he did so, all hell broke loose. The window glass behind Lakesh's head shattered with a loud crash and he sank back. Before him, the man with the slingshot toppled backward as a gout of blood burst from his right eye, his own shot pounding into the ceiling as his aim was ruined.

Lakesh lay supine, his neck propped on the wooden frame of the French door and facing out into the garden beyond as shards of glass tumbled to the ground all around him. He screwed his eyes tightly shut as glass splinters peppered his face and chest, feeling like a rain shower as they struck him.

Across the room, the firewalker crashed into the table behind him, a bloody mess where his eye had been. The slingshot hung limply in his hand, its ammunition strewed across the floor beneath the table.

A familiar voice spoke as Lakesh lay there, his eyes clenched shut to stave off the debris. "Hi, honey," Domi said. "Miss me?"

Tentatively, Lakesh opened his eyes as the last of the broken glass tinkled around him, barely believing what he had heard. Standing there, upside down in his vision where his head was stretched back across the ridge of the door's frame, was Domi. The silver length of her

Combat Master was poised at the end of two straight, pure white arms, her sleeveless black top and combat pants in stark contrast to her skin.

"D-Domi...?" Lakesh murmured, the word struggling to break free of his burning throat.

"Tip for you, lover mine," Domi said as she bent to check over Lakesh, her longtime work colleague and current romantic partner. "When facing a firewalker, you need to shoot them in the eyes. They can't 'stone up' there."

Lakesh breathed a sigh of relief, choked and coughed as he tried to push himself up from the floor. Behind Domi, two other familiar figures were making their way into the lodge, stepping over Lakesh's form as they made their way inside. Lakesh recognized Brewster Philboyd and Kudo, the Tigers of Heaven warrior who had gone on the mission with Grant's field team.

"Did everything go all right?" Lakesh asked, his hand reaching for the cuff of Philboyd's pants as he passed.

"The lodge is on fire," Brewster replied. "We need to evacuate right now."

Lakesh closed his eyes in a slow, weary blink. "Donald is around here somewhere," he explained. "You need to—"

"I see him," Brewster said, scampering over to where Bry had been left by the now-dead intruder's attack. "He's breathing. Should be okay."

All around the lodge, the Tigers of Heaven were pushing back and defeating the intruders in a series of small skirmishes. Shizuka lost three men—highly trained warriors all—during the battle, but ultimately her side was victorious. Though how long that victory would last no one cared to wager. The lodge itself was smoke damaged, but for now Cerberus had nowhere left to go. So everyone settled in the ops room—including the double-agent Edwards, who was kept sedated—cordoning off whole sections of the dwelling.

A HALF-DOZEN ANNUNAKI soldiers were battling with a cluster of humans in a courtyard where six arteries met, overwhelming them with brisk strikes from their powerful bodies or utilizing ASP emitters to blast away their enemies. One of the group turned when he heard the sound of heavy footsteps, and he spied Ullikummis striding along one of the streets that led past the courtyard, the redhead and the child in tow. Seeing an opportunity for glory, the Igigi-turned-Annunaki cast aside the human he had been strangling and called to his colleagues, speaking in an ancient Sumerian tongue. The human was thrown high in the air, landing headfirst against a solid wall of the courtyard, snapping his neck and killing him instantly. The Annunaki paid it no mind.

His colleagues did likewise, casting aside their prey in an instant like cats toying with mice, turning the snakelike ASP emitter blasters on the humans and melting them in their punishing heat rays. As one, the Igigi-turned-Annunaki rushed out of the courtyard, running parallel to where their leader had spied Ullikummis.

As the great stone giant turned a corner, the six Annunaki were waiting, and they piled on him, leaping from the low roofs and diving out of the shadows, knocking the powerful figure to the ground by merit of their numbers. Ullikummis grunted as he struck the cobbles with hands and knees, and he shifted his head back in a whip-snap gesture that drove the back of his head into the nose of the Annunaki astride him. Struck, the Annunaki—copper-hued with the tint of emerald to

his scales like copper piping left too long in seawater—
fell back, collapsing as his mouth erupted in a cascade of
blood. He writhed on the ground for a moment, spitting
loose teeth from his ruined jaw, striking with a staccato
of beats as they rebounded from the hard bone cobbles.

Walking a few paces behind her master, Brigid
Haight held her hand up to halt the girl-child Quav,
adopting a protective stance. The copper Annunaki
spotted them as he wiped blood from his chin, and
he reared up off the ground and leaped at them like a
pouncing tiger.

As the other Annunaki used their weight of numbers
to hold down and beat on Ullikummis, Brigid found
herself facing their final member. She ducked, avoiding that opening leap with just inches to spare, feeling
the powerful creature brush past. Her hand was at her
holster instantly, pulling free the TP-9 automatic pistol,
its sleek black lines creating a completed square shape
around her forearm.

The copper-toned Annunaki was behind Brigid by
then, using powerful legs to skitter across the back wall
of the narrow pathway before turning back to face her.
Right arm outstretched, Brigid blasted the reptilian figure with a stream of 9 mm titanium-shelled bullets, their
casings tinkering on the ground as they spit from the
muzzle of the weapon.

In an eye blink, the fast-moving Annunaki weaved
out of the path of those bullets, snarling as just one of
them clipped the ridge above his shoulder blade while
he rocketed toward Brigid once more. She didn't matter, she knew—what mattered was the child.

Brigid bent her knees in ingrained response, dropping as the Annunaki reached her. Unarmed, the An-

nunaki kicked one powerful leg at her face, missing it as she dropped beneath the sweep of his foot.

In that brief instant while the creature was balanced on one foot, Brigid brought her weapon to bear, blasting a cough of bullets at his leg and shattering the kneecap in an explosion of blood. The Annunaki unleashed a senseless howl, crashing to the ground in a tangle of limbs. Brigid was on him instantly, leaping onto his fallen form and driving the nose of her TP-9 into his open mouth before pulling the trigger once more. The Annunaki's head was hacked up as bullets ripped through his flesh, great gouts of blood and offal painting the white cobblestones a vibrant red. Brigid watched the redness spurt across the street, blood licking up the walls as she held down the trigger.

At Brigid's back, Ullikummis was struggling under the fearsome attack of five of his adversaries. They had overwhelmed him by their sheer numbers, and Ullikummis was unable to shake them from him long enough to best them. Trapped beneath their weight, Ullikummis ceased struggling and calmed his mind, searching for his opportunity to escape. With all those bodies upon him, it was like being held in darkness, the heat of them stifling him and snatching at his thoughts. Ullikummis cared nothing for heat or cold, his body genetically tempered so that it need suffer the assaults of neither.

Ignoring the scrum above him, the blows and kicks as the Annunaki strove to bloody him despite his impenetrable flesh, Ullikummis focused his mind on the ground below, the places hidden beneath the cobblestones of bone. There was rock there, he knew, and he reached for it with his mind, passing through the thin barrier to snatch at it with his powerful thoughts. He possessed a form of telekinesis, sufficient to command

and manipulate rock in all its forms, an ability he had employed to build his great stone fortress Bensalem.

In his mind's eye, Ullikummis saw the rock stir, and the ground beneath the dog pile began to tremble.

At that moment, a space appeared before Ullikummis's face, and he looked up to see that the Annunaki huddle had parted just slightly, just enough to allow one of their number to turn his ASP emitter on the great stone scion of Enlil. Shaped like a viper's head, the golden weapon curled around its user's wrist, blasting a vicious beam of heat on the user's command, which came with just a twitch of the muscles. Ullikummis stared into that viperlike face, his magma eyes glowing brightly as he concentrated on the rocks below him.

With a screech, the ASP emitter fired, its persimmon heat beam burning across Ullikummis's stone face for less than a second before a two-inch-wide rock splinter burst from the ground and lanced straight through the user's hand. Still blasting where the sliced-off hand grasped it, the ASP emitter dropped to the ground, sending its red-orange beam into the legs of two of the Annunaki in the dog pile and blasting a third in the ankle. All three lurched back, their weight shifting as they cried out in agony. Ullikummis seemed simply to shrug, shifting his mighty frame enough to free himself from the struggling Annunaki before rising to his full height once more.

Standing, Ullikummis towered over the other Annunaki by a foot or more, and his face billowed with black smoke where the heat beam had struck him. One of them—the one who had held the ASP emitter before losing it and his hand to the rock spear—lay curled up on the ground, clutching the stump of his arm to his chest. Ullikummis took a step forward, stamping down on the pathetic creature's head until he heard a loud crunch of breaking skull.

Another Annunaki was still clinging to his back, and Ullikummis reached behind him, plucking the creature off with no more effort than a man pulling off a sweater. The Annunaki was a female with gray-blue scales the color of rain clouds, a ridge of spines running in twin lines over her scalp. Ullikummis slammed her on the ground, driving the breath out of her with the force of the impact.

As Ullikummis dealt with the gray-blue female, the others were struggling to retreat, their wounds showing in great gashes across legs and feet where the heat ray had struck them before blessedly winking out. Brigid found herself in the path of one of them—much to the lizardlike creature's surprise—and she turned her reloaded TP-9 automatic pistol to blast a burst of fire into his forehead from near point-blank range. The Annunaki crashed backward, slamming into one of his colleagues as half his face disappeared.

The next Annunaki had scales as yellow as the sun. Despite a blistering gash along his left hip, the warrior ran at Brigid, identifying her as an enemy in a heartbeat. With exceptional timing, Brigid kicked off from the ground, leaping high in the air as the pale-scaled Annunaki charged her. Her feet struck the creature high in the chest, and she seemed to run up his body as he fell, whipping the TP-9 around and unleashing a storm of bullets into his torso as she leaped aside. The Annunaki shuddered with the impacts, crashing to his knees and sliding over the cobbles as his momentum dragged him on.

Brigid rolled as she landed, pulling herself into an open crouch as she held her weapon on her fallen foe.

The Annunaki's chest was pocked with blood where the bullets had struck, but he gritted his teeth in a savage snarl as he turned to face her.

Brigid sprang toward the yellow-skinned figure, leaping astride him before he could get back to his feet. Her pelvis slammed against the back of the Annunaki's skull, one knee to either side of his head, and she squeezed. The Annunaki tried to shake her off as Brigid's grip tightened, throwing his head left and right like some deranged headbanger from another era. Brigid clawed at the Annunaki with her left hand, scratching at his face until she found the eye socket.

The Annunaki warrior batted at her hand, trying to remove it from his face. Brigid snapped off another burst of fire from her pistol, the bullets cutting into the Annunaki's reaching arm and snapping against the hard flesh of its scales. Then her fingers were in his eye, plunging beneath the lower rim of the eyeball and scraping upward.

The Annunaki hissed in pain—a sound like an angered snake—as Brigid jostled his yellow eye from the socket in a spurt of viscous liquid.

She dropped back, somersaulting in midair and landing on the ground before the yellow-scaled Annunaki, rocking back on her booted heels. The Annunaki warrior was grasping for his wounded left eye, and when he moved his hand aside the eye stared at Brigid angrily, its luscious egg-yellow turned red with blood, a circle of tears glistening all around it. Brigid pulled the TP-9 up again, rattling off another burst of fire as the Annunaki warrior charged toward her, his lips pulled back in furious determination.

As the Annunaki reached her, Brigid lashed out with her legs, delivering a vicious double kick to his chest and flipping him to the ground. She was on the creature in an instant, delivering a brutal punch to his face with such force that the warrior's head snapped back with a horrible crack. As Brigid retreated from the fallen form, the canary-yellow warrior shuddered in place, struggling to get up again. His struggles looked like those of an insect rolled onto its back and unable to right itself. Brigid's final blow had done something terrible to his spinal column, paralyzing the alien figure from the neck down.

Brigid turned, her red hair like a cloud of fire about her dirt-smeared face. Quav waited, cowering in the shadows of one of the chalk-colored buildings as the scuffle continued. Several of the wounded Annunaki had stopped before her, the wounds from the heat ray glistering on their legs, insects already buzzing about them to feed. They looked at the hybrid child with a mixture of wonder and admiration, as if seeing something beautiful and otherworldly—an angel, a goddess. As Ullikummis crushed the fragile form of the gray-blue female warrior, Brigid delivered two blasts from her T-9 into the back of the heads of the waiting Annunaki, killing them before they even knew what was happening.

The girl Quav was not a goddess yet.

GRANT AND ROSALIA HURRIED up the sloping door hatch of the great ship *Tiamat,* their weapons in hand. Within, more than a dozen of the reborn Annunaki were guarding the entryway from intruders. In short, it was exactly the situation Grant had hoped to avoid. Crouching, he stopped at the lip of the door where it met the inside deck plating, gesturing for Rosalia to halt, too.

Crouched low, Grant peered at the interior, trying

to make sense of what was going on inside. Naked, the Annunaki seemed to be working on the interior walls of the ship. A series of great explosions had rocked the insides of the living ship just a few hours before, and it appeared that these Annunaki were endeavoring to repair some of the damage to the walls. Great flaps of skin had broken away from those walls, hard chunks like metal plating, their surfaces patterned with whirls. Like much of the Annunaki technology, *Tiamat* was organic, grown to their specifications and existing in some nebulous, semiliving state. As such, she was capable of self-repair to a degree, though the Annunaki troopers were working hard to encourage that process. Here and there, the working Annunaki had piled up new plates for usage and were utilizing trolleys to ferry repair materials where they were needed. It looked like a combination of an engineering task and open-heart surgery.

At the back of the room, almost eighty yards from where Grant and Rosalia were poised, a rectangular doorway stood open, pale greenish light emanating from its mouth. There were a few other doorways to the sides of the room, Grant noted, some of them closed but their glowing locks visible amid the charred bone colors of the walls. Large rents were visible on the walls and ceiling, each one rippled and colored the pinkish-red of rare steak.

The Annunaki warriors carried out their repairs in silence, occasionally bumping into one another as they worked in teams of twos and threes. Grant had no idea how he and Rosalia would get past them. There were simply too many, and the room was too exposed to hide from all of them.

Grant indicated the landing deck. "It's too busy," he explained in a low voice. "We wouldn't stand a chance."

Rosalia nodded, her lips pursed in thought. "A distraction, then," she proposed. "Want for me to dance for them?"

"That won't be necessary," Grant assured her.

Rosalia watched as Grant reached into one of the pouches of his belt and plucked out a tiny spherical object. The sphere was small enough to rest comfortably in the palm of Grant's hand, and it featured a metallic shell.

Rosalia smiled, recognizing it. "Of course, you have your little firecrackers."

"Flash-bangs," Grant corrected. "I used up all the explosives breaking in here the first time. But I still have a few tricks.

"You may want to look away," he added, "and cover your ears, too."

Grant rolled the flash-bang ball across the decking before him, watching as it rolled toward a pile of skinlike plating that was waiting to be used for repairs.

Counting down in his head, Grant placed his hands over his ears and waited for the charge to ignite. The flash-bang was a tiny explosive that did exactly what its name implied—creating a big flash and a loud bang but doing no additional damage, a little like a firework. Grant habitually carried a variety of these little capsules, which featured various effects, from billowing thick smoke on command to creating a foul stench. The flashbang would generate a burst of light and sound so bright and loud that it could temporarily blind and deafen an unsuspecting foe, but it left no permanent damage.

With a cacophony of conflagration, the diminutive explosive went off, lighting the large deck like a star going nova.

Grant grabbed Rosalia's hand, pulling her to her feet. "Come on," he urged.

Rosalia opened her screwed-up eyes and followed Grant into the landing deck of the starship. Despite having her eyes closed and her hands over her ears, she had heard the explosion and seen its flash against her eyelids, playing like sunlight across a sleeper's eyes. Now she saw Annunaki warriors rocking to and fro as they tried to recover from the sudden burst of light. Their ears were ringing with the furious noise, masking any sound that Grant's and Rosalia's boots made as they hurried across the metallike plating of the deck. Shouts of confusion came from all about, calls in an alien tongue that Rosalia could not recognize.

In just a handful of seconds, the two Cerberus warriors had made it halfway across the vast cabin, and Grant ducked behind a stack of waiting deck plate, ordering Rosalia to his side.

All around them, the Annunaki were recovering as the effects of the flash-bang dissipated. Several Annunaki paced warily toward where the flash-bang had ignited, peering at the remains—just a little dust and the remnants of the fuse—where they lay by the skin plates. Others were already searching all around, scurrying to the open drop-down doorway that led into the streets.

"What now?" Rosalia whispered.

Grant watched the reptilian figures shuffling all about, trying to tag them all in his mind. "I'll try another flash-bang," he suggested in a low voice, "but they'll probably react faster this time, now they know it's not going to hurt them."

But as he spoke, another startling factor came into play. Three Annunaki had disappeared past the edge of the door to see whether they were under attack just moments before. Without warning, two of them came sailing through the air back into the room, closely followed by their remaining companion. Then the deck resounded with hammer blows as Ullikummis strode into the room, his huge tree-stump-like feet bashing against the plate with crashing beats.

As Grant and Rosalia watched this newcomer, two more figures came in his wake, following as his obedient entourage. Grant recognized them both and so did Rosalia. The child was Little Quav. And the red-haired woman who held the child's hand was…

"Brigid?" Grant blurted, incredulous.

Chapter 11

Grant's utterance was lost to the sounds of Ullikummis's footsteps as he pounded up the drop-down door and onto the plate decking, tossing another Annunaki aside with a sharp flick of his arm. Behind him, the sounds of battle echoed through the city of bone, getting louder and closer. Ullikummis had broken through the ranks, a leader to the end.

Behind the stacked deck plates, Grant raised himself from his crouch, motioning toward the figure of Brigid Baptiste. "What th—?" he began.

Grasping his arm from where they hid, Rosalia hissed for Grant to keep silent. "Remember what we saw in the cavern," she told him, glaring into his eyes. "Your friend can't be trusted now."

Grant bit back a curse, grinding his teeth in frustration. Rosalia was right. A trusted member of the Cerberus fraternity, Brigid Baptiste had been missing for more than two months, ever since the Cerberus redoubt was invaded. Less than a week earlier, Grant and Rosalia, along with Kane and Domi, had bumped into this red-haired woman in a cavern close to Luilekkerville, where she had proceeded to shoot Kane in the chest. Whether it really was Brigid—and the jury was out so far as Grant was concerned—there was something decidedly unfriendly about her now. While he wanted to make contact, to alert this woman to his presence to see how she would react, showing his hand too soon may not be the smartest idea, Grant realized.

Instead, he watched in silence as the red-haired woman followed Ullikummis across the hangar bay, using her familiar TP-9 pistol to blast the living hell out of any Annunaki warriors who managed to side-step the rock lord's devastating attacks and get close to her and Little Quav.

As Grant watched, another of the naked Annunaki, this one shimmering in a rainbow coat of scales with a crest of spines along the Y-axis of his head, ducked under one of Ullikummis's lunging arms and ran at Brigid and the child. Brigid's arm was already raised, holding the TP-9 out before her, its brutal lines like an awful mechanical extension of her own body. The blaster kicked in her hand, delivering a burst of 9 mm bullets into the face of her would-be attacker. The re-splendent Annunaki fell back, spitting like a cat as he fixed the redhead with his gaze.

With no apparent concern for her own safety, the woman who looked like Brigid Baptiste leaped at the Annunaki warrior, charging toward him and bringing her pistol around in an abbreviated arc, its muzzle spitting bullet after bullet into the creature's face and tho-rax. The Annunaki's chest and face popped with sparks where those bullets struck his armorlike skin, whizzing off in all directions as the warrior shook in place.

The Annunaki's vision was impaired in that sec-ond, and Brigid took advantage of that, grabbing one of the spines that protruded from his skull and using it as a handle to pull the creature forward and down. Un-balanced, the Annunaki tumbled forward at the same moment as the red-haired woman shoved her pistol for-ward, ramming it into her foe's open mouth. There was a burst of muffled gunfire, and then the woman stepped back as the rainbow-skinned Annunaki crashed to the deck, smoke and blood mingling as they gushed from his ruined mouth.

Grant winced as he watched the brutal display, trying to recognize his longtime friend in the performance. Brigid was acting as a bodyguard for the child, he understood, placing herself in harm's way against any threats to her charge. But to use such savagery, to dispatch her foes with such utter disdain for them or her own well-being, left Grant feeling sick to his stomach.

Nearby, Ullikummis continued to plow through the other warriors, slapping them aside as they swarmed on him at the halfway point of the hangar bay, close to where Grant and Rosalia were hidden. Working in tandem, two of the Annunaki came at Ullikummis from opposite sides, grasping for the hornlike structures that jutted from his mighty shoulders. Ullikummis spun, trying to shake off the creatures, but both clung on as if their lives depended on it. Then the Annunaki began to pull at their foe, dragging him down and forcing him to bend first one way and then the other. Finally, Ullikummis tumbled down, his stone frame dropping to the deck with the force of an avalanche.

A ripple of excitement ran through the other Annunaki in the room, and they swarmed upon Ullikummis as he struggled beneath the weight of their colleagues. Brigid used her blaster to pick off a few, but Ullikummis disappeared beneath fifteen glistening bodies of scaled armor.

Watching this, Grant held his breath. For a full minute, it seemed that Ullikummis might be defeated, and the room went deathly quiet as he was held in place.

The only sound to echo through the room in those

moments was the sweet voice of the child, Quav. "Is Ullikummis okay, Brigly?" she asked, tugging at Brigid's hand where the warrior woman waited poised with her TP-9.

Brigid didn't answer.

Then, without warning, the scrum of Annunaki bodies seemed to explode into the air as Ullikummis shrugged them off, tossing them this way and that as he rose once more in their midst. His face was an eerie stone mask, no recognition showing there that these lizardlike creatures were in fact his own people, Annunaki just like him.

Grant and Rosalia ducked lower as one of the brave warriors hurtled past their hiding place, crashing against the grown-plate wall with a clang of metal. The reptilian warrior dropped to the floor, a hunk of the ruined hull careening after him.

"Come on, Magistrate," Rosalia urged, getting to her feet. "Time to go."

Rosalia was right. With everyone's attention drawn to the continuing combat with Ullikummis, there was a brief opportunity for her and Grant to escape the room and get deeper into the ship unnoticed. They ran close to the wall, keeping to the shadows, their heads down as they made a beeline for the far doorway.

Behind them, they could hear Ullikummis grunting words in ancient Sumerian, glaring at the surrounding Annunaki with his fierce, magma-pool eyes. As they reached the far door, Grant turned back, his eyes scanning the room for a moment. In that instant, something incredible happened. Ullikummis had retreated a few paces so that he stood before Brigid and the hybrid child, Grant saw, the bloodied Annunaki warriors arrayed before him. His right arm moved in an arc before his torso, drawing a delicate pattern in the air. As Grant watched, that impossible pattern seemed to linger in place, tearing a hole in the air itself. The hole glowed with a swirl of color, lightning crackling in its depths like witchfire. Grant recognized it, or at least he knew something similar enough to make the connection—it was an interphase window, a gateway from one parallax point to another. But such gateways required an interphaser, didn't they? How Ullikummis had created one merely by drawing a pattern in the air was beyond Grant's comprehension.

"*¡Vámonos!*" Rosalia hissed from behind Grant. "No time to watch the floor show."

Grant turned, hurrying into the corridor that waited beyond the hangar bay, grasping his Sin Eater as he ran. Behind him, the quantum window grew wider, allowing Ullikummis and his two companions to step through, disappearing from the hangar deck. The Annunaki ran to follow, halted in their tracks as that incredible rift in space-time winked out of existence. They were alone once more in the hangar, as if Ullikummis and his companions had never been.

SIMILAR TO THE ONES CREATED by the interphaser, Ullikummis's gateway was the product of a clearer comprehension of the world structures around him. The Annunaki were multidimensional beings, their perception of the world far more layered than the simplistic understanding held by humans. While in the Ontic Library, Ullikummis had studied the ways in which space could be folded upon itself, moving the proximity of its geographic points. The trick took concentration, twining two points together like threads on a subatomic level.

Ullikummis had used this trick on several occasions,

most notably when he had launched his attack on the Cerberus redoubt all those months ago, bypassing its sensors and reaching the roll-back doors undetected. He had shown it to Brigid, too, his hand in darkness, and she had employed it to enter the hidden city of Agartha, shifting planes infinitesimally to step through the rocks that masked its door. Most recently, Ullikummis had used the same principle to open the multirift, the one that called on his faithful to come fight in the god war for possession of *Tiamat*.

Any technology that was sufficiently advanced would look like magic to others, after all. That had always been the way with the Annunaki, and even in the twenty-third century their advances dwarfed anything created by the hands of man.

OUTSIDE *TIAMAT*, the war continued apace. Sela Stone, formerly Sinclair, found herself close to the front in the major push toward the grounded starship, driving against the living barricades of the Annunaki warriors. The Annunaki were impossibly strong; strong enough in fact that it had taken less than two hundred of them to repel close to three thousand humans. Statistically, the Annunaki should have fallen by now.

A troop of Annunaki warriors hurried toward Sela from both sides, the gold of their swords flashing in the sunlight as they cut down her colleagues. Sela danced aside as the man next to her—a dark-skinned farmhand who was no more than twenty-one—tumbled toward her in two halves, his body cleaved in two by the swords of the Annunaki. Others were unarmed, but each of their attacks ended in broken bones and crushed skulls, one woman screaming as her spinal column was wrenched from her flesh through her skin, the Annunaki who had committed the brutal attack wielding the spine like a trophy. Sela's Colt pistol blasted, drumming bullets into the Annunaki warrior as his tongue lapped at the woman's blood that had spurted across his face.

Suddenly, Sela fell, a glancing blow striking her in the back and throwing her to the ground. She slammed into the cobblelike paving, her forehead crunching against it with that awful, dull thud of bone on bone.

All around Sela, the human army was making progress. It was loyal to Ullikummis, and those most loyal had been enslaved by the gift of the most potent of the obedience stones, the ones that could transform their flesh into stone like an aspect of Ullikummis himself. It was those warriors—the firewalkers or the new Magistrates depending on your point of view—who led the column that finally drove the Annunaki back into the heart of the city.

Sela Stone pulled herself from the ground, scanning the paving around her until she spotted her Colt Mark IV, the familiar dancing horse engraved on its barrel. Her nose was bloodied and her head was ringing, but there was something else; the beat was gone, receding, leaving her mind clearer than it had been in at least two months.

Sela sat on the paving, trying to gather her thoughts. As she looked around, she felt like a spectator to the battle. Born in the twentieth century, Sela was a "freezie." She had been cryogenically frozen and shipped to the Manitius Moon Base, to be held there in stasis until nuclear hostilities had finally subsided. Sela was a trained naval officer, her fighting prowess was regimented and she belonged in the upper echelon of a human's capabilities. She was in the thick of things now, and yet she could only watch as the firewalkers worked together in teams to pick off each of the unclothed Annunaki who defended the great dragon ship. Sela's own efforts, each tribute to the glory of her master and the New Order he promised, were small and hasty by contrast, shooting at the Annunaki warriors, helping defend and hold the positions as the firewalkers gained territory in the narrow, winding lanes of the dragon's wings.

Sela saw those enhanced humans working their slingshots like shotguns, utilizing their changed skin as a barricade against the vicious assaults of their relentless foes. Many fell, but the numbers were massive now, each warrior pledging his life to Ullikummis and the future he promised. And as she watched, mute witness to the bloodshed on both sides, Sela Stone wondered at the changes in the so-called firewalkers. Had they been blessed with a weapon from their god, or had everyone here been given something else? Was this battle about bodies and numbers and an age-old blood feud, or was it truly being fought with emotion—two sides who had sworn loyalty to something they believed greater than themselves?

Stopped in place, Sela looked around as her fellow humans were cut down, hacked at with swords, bones broken under the brutal attacks of the Annunaki. And, for the first time in months, she saw things the way they used to be. Humans, bloody humans. Caught up in a myth, a trick by the Annunaki. The many following the few, just as it had been millennia ago when all of this had started. Had the humans been duped with a promise of utopia? Was that all that this was for?

INSIDE THE BODY of the great dragon ship, Enlil was observing the battle from the scanning room. So much of

Tiamat had atrophied, whole sections of the wall beside him glistened as if they were weeping.

The Igigi, reborn as Annunaki for his new pantheon, were putting up a solid fight but they were being driven back, cut down by the sheer force of numbers arrayed against them. His enemy had planned well, bringing an almost unlimited supply of troops through the quantum rift at the edge of his territory. Were circumstances different, Overlord Enlil would have admired the planning. Had he not been on the wrong side of it, that was.

As Enlil watched the smoky displays cycle through different aspects of the battle, something flashed in the air and he heard the alert signal, like wind chimes in the breeze. It was confirmation that the ship had been compromised, that someone now walked in the corridors of power, the living arteries of the mother ship *Tiamat*. Enlil narrowed his eyes and they flicked to the side, accessing the correct datastream that would show where the breach had occurred. He saw who it was, familiar even after all these centuries. His son, Ullikummis, here aboard the mother womb, come home at last.

It was time then, he realized. Destiny could be held at bay no longer.

ULLIKUMMIS, Brigid and Little Quav appeared in a swirl of quantum energy, stepping out of nothingness into the ante-nursery of the living starship. The ante-nursery was where genetics could be twisted, where catalysts were triggered. Years before, it was the ante-nursery that had given the signal for the Annunaki to reemerge on planet Earth, broadcasting the signal from far out in space that had resulted in the hybrid barons finally sloughing their false skins.

There were programs here, hypermemories in storage, personality gifts waiting to be bestowed and housed. The room itself was relatively small, a little bigger than the living room of a modest family home or the lady chapel of a cathedral. Like much of *Tiamat,* it looked alive, the columns that held the ceiling winding like the gnarled trunks of ancient trees. The walls were lit by some internal source, scattered pads illuminating the room in a soft creamy glow. The room was dominated by a sunken pit that dropped almost two feet below the rest of the floor. The pit was oval in shape, and its walls and base were made of a light gray substance that looked like pumice stone. A series of regular holes appeared around the edge of the pit's walls, running all the way around, each one no wider than a man's thumb.

Stepping into the room, Ullikummis reached to his left in a loose gesture, and the lights changed, dimming briefly before changing color, adopting a violet shade. Brigid watched as something dropped from the ceiling, descending from a hidden recess at Ullikummis's command. He knew this place, knew its setup and operation. It was Annunaki technology; Ullikummis had grown up using it.

The thing that fell from the ceiling was on a rigid tube, and it halted in place a little below the level of Ullikummis's shoulders, correcting itself with three quick movements. It looked something like a jawbone, a set of long teeth arrayed in a crescent shape that ran roughly fourteen inches from end to end.

As Brigid and the child watched, Ullikummis's crude fingers played in the air, weaving a pattern over the teethlike keys of the drop-down unit. He didn't appear to touch them, but they clearly responded to his subtle movements, lighting in sequence like a child's electronic game. A moment later, liquid began to rush from the holes that circled the sunken pit, and Ullikummis stepped away from the depending instrument, turning back to face Brigid and her young charge as if assuring himself they were still there. The liquid was transparent but cloudy, organic gunk swirling through its midst like sand on the desert breeze.

Ullikummis's hands came together, and he passed them over the pit, drawing from his mighty psionic powers to call on the minerals that existed within the liquid and within *Tiamat* herself. Something sprouted from the middle of the pit, weaving into existence from the subatomic particles at Ullikummis's command. Just as he had made the rock barricades and the lances that had ripped apart Annunaki warriors, now he created a subtler shape, its curved base wide, its sides thin and almost transparent. It looked like an egg, a narrow gap in its center. The liquid filling the pit sloshed against its edges, licking up its curving walls as it continued to take shape. All told, the egglike chrysalis was three and a half feet in height, large enough to hold a human child.

Turning back to Brigid and Little Quav, Ullikummis bent on his haunches, bringing his head level with the child's and openly staring into her pale eyes. "*Tiamat* honors you, Mother," he said, his voice like two great stones being slammed together.

Quav smiled uncertainly, her eyes never leaving those of her once and future son.

"The process will hurt," he warned her. "It is a birth, and as such it must be traumatic for it sees the creation of new life where there was none before. You hold the genetic keys within you, and when they activate you will feel discomfort." He took her hands in one of his great paws, still fixing her with his glowing magma eyes. "This will pass and the world will honor you. I swear this."

Quav nodded solemnly, a child wise beyond her years. "You told me that change was good," she said, "and that it was necessary."

"And you remembered," Ullikummis said, his ghastly rock face moving in the approximation of a smile. "Just as you shall remember everything, our time together before my father betrayed us both."

Behind him, the pool continued to fill with a cloudy, viscous liquid. A pungent stink, like rotting fruit, emanated from it and the weird chrysalis shell towered in its center.

"My father once told me that birth must be painful to prepare us for the pain our lives shall bring," Ullikummis explained. "I have done my best to protect you. The shell will do all it can to dissipate the pain. And you will be safe. Brigid will not be far."

Obediently, Little Quav walked up to the egglike form with Brigid at her side, clinging tightly to the woman's hand as she navigated the step down into the birthing pit. Ullikummis watched—pleased—as Quav stepped inside the chrysalis and let go of Brigid's hand. Once Little Quav was within the shell, it began to seal from the bottom up, the two edges coming together like raindrops, bonding before their eyes.

GRANT AND ROSALIA hurried through the eerie corridors of *Tiamat*. The walls were curved, giving them the impression that they were running inside a series of linked tubes, and each wall was ribbed with great solid bars that glistened like metal yet were calcified like bone. There was liquid on the decking, some of it seeping down the walls and over the sphincterlike connectors that made up the doors between sections. The water gathered in patches, sometimes ankle deep where they ran. The mother ship had been in a worse state when they had exited just a few hours before, when the corridors had been filling with dirty water the color of feces after its main tanks had been compromised. It seemed that the ship had purged herself of that overflow, and Grant could hear great muscles pumping away behind the walls, clearing the remaining water. *Tiamat* was an organic machine, he realized, and there was ethereal beauty to her functions.

Rosalia kept a few paces ahead of Grant, her body tense, senses alert. In that respect, she reminded Grant of Kane, the way his body would tense when he was placed in a dangerous situation, his trusted point-man sense coming to the fore without his even realizing it. Rosalia had spoken a little of being trained, though most of what Grant knew of her was through subtle hints. She seemed unwilling to share too much of her past, although he guessed she came from south of the former U.S. border. He kept speculating that she was perhaps a Magistrate, too, or a lapsed one like himself.

Several times, Rosalia had halted in place, turning on her heel and urging Grant back the way they had come. "Find another route," she had said. "These playmates don't play nice."

Annunaki, Grant realized. She was finding a route into the ship that avoided their enemies as much as possible.

Rosalia took them a long way into the core of the grounded spacecraft, mapping the ship swiftly in her head. Until recently, Grant and Kane had been able to rely on Brigid Baptiste to do that kind of work, and he realized now how much they had needed one another as a team. Whether intentional or not, breaking the trio apart had been Ullikummis's most successful strike against Cerberus. It had crippled their ability to act effectively, and it seemed that they had spent the past two months chasing their own tails as they gradually fractured from within.

They passed doorways and saw items looming in the murk of poorly lit rooms, things intricately fashioned out of complicated angles and curves of metal, instruments or devices of mysterious purpose. Rosalia gestured one way, ducking through a doorway and into one of these rooms even as two Annunaki guardsmen came padding down the far end of the vast, tunnellike corridor they were in. Her movement was so swift that Grant was off balance. It took him a second to right himself, turning into the doorway to follow her before the Annunaki spotted him. This room churned with the noise of turbines, and Grant jogged through it, eyeing nutrient sacs, bubbling pipe work, steam gauges and pressure switches. The ex-Magistrate felt as if he were moving through a vast circuit board or plumbing system, each facet on show wherever he looked. He had been inside *Tiamat* before, back when she had sailed on the cosmic winds in her first form. She had been all sleek lines and glistening panels then. In her current form she seemed rougher, still unfinished, and her walls gave off a faint and alluring smell of spices.

Hurrying through the room, Rosalia spied an exit by a series of pipes that came up together through the floor and disappeared at different points into the ceiling and walls. Rosalia ducked beneath one of the low pipes with Grant just a few paces behind her, holding his Sin Eater ready as he checked they weren't being followed.

"Do you have any idea where you're going?" Grant asked, keeping his voice low.

Rosalia narrowed her eyes in thought. "Toward the center. Little way yet."

Grant nodded, trusting the woman's judgment. She seemed to know what she was doing, and he had to admit he was lost.

At the wall, Rosalia found a door that held a vast cylindrical unit in its middle, like an engorged turnkey. Taking it in both hands, she wiggled it left then right until she felt it bite on the hidden lock and begin to turn. In a moment, Rosalia had the door open and it swung outward, away from her and Grant.

As the door opened, Grant heard a rushing cacophony, like a million kettles all being boiled at the same time. He followed Rosalia as she stepped into the next room. It was huge, a wide gangway running across its center like an elevated footbridge. Thirty feet below, huge, bulging units were arrayed in lines, like the fallen pillars of some great temple. These units were roughly cylindrical, but they bulged in their centers to form beadlike ovals. Running lights twinkled along their surfaces, pulsing in yellows and whites that chased one another across their skins.

Grant stopped, looking down at the strange, bulging pods and spotted figures moving between them. Though distant, Grant could see that they were humanoid, wearing dark garments as they tended to the pods with their tools. Each pod was thirty feet or more in length, and there had to be fifty of them in the room. Engines, Grant realized—they were standing above the engines of *Tiamat*.

As that thought struck him, Rosalia hissed, "Magistrate."

Grant brought his attention back to the present. He looked up and saw four figures approaching. Like the ones working on the engines, these four were dressed in dark coveralls that were ragged and streaked with oils and unguents. The figures looked short to him, not one of them standing taller than five feet high, and they waddled along with an uneasy gait. Even over the sounds of the engines, Grant heard them shriek to one another as they pointed at the strangers making their way through their midst.

"Looks like we're doing the old dance number again," Grant muttered as the group of freakish mechanics came charging toward him and Rosalia, clutching their tools like weapons.

"Then let's mix up the routine," Rosalia said, pulling her sword from her belt.

"*TIAMAT* HONORS YOU," Ullikummis repeated as the egg-like structure bonded together in the birthing chamber, its front sections closing like the teeth of a zipper, knitting together to seal Little Quav within.

A dozen seconds passed as Ullikummis and Brigid watched it close. As the parted sections sealed, locking the girl within, they heard a clatter from somewhere behind them. Combat senses ready, the two mismatched figures turned as one, spotting the newcomer to the room as he stopped in a far doorway.

"And *Tiamat* honors you, too," the figure said. "With death!"

Ullikummis recognized the figure immediately, as did Brigid. Ragged scarlet cloak billowing about his golden body, the newcomer was none other than Enlil, cruelest overlord of the Annunaki.

Chapter 12

Enlil charged at Ullikummis like a runaway freight train, his lips pulled back in a sneer.

"Protect Ninlil," Ullikummis instructed Brigid without taking his eyes from those of his father. Then he began striding forward, picking up speed as he hurried across the birthing chamber to meet with the father he despised, his footsteps driving shock waves through the whole room.

Brigid watched from her vantage point by the stone cocoon as Ullikummis and Enlil clashed for the first time. The stone god struck a low punch to his father's gut while at the same time Overlord Enlil drove his clawed hand at his son's face. Surely he must know that his son is armored, Brigid thought. And then she saw Ullikummis back away even as his father staggered back under the power of his blow. Ullikummis's face was streaming with noxious black smoke; Enlil had used something hidden in his hand to gain a temporary advantage.

Enlil wandered backward, his head down and blood dribbling from the side of his mouth. Ullikummis's first blow had incredible force behind it, blasting through the old man's scale armor. Enlil coughed, wiping bloody saliva from his mouth.

"Better," he spit, glaring at Ullikummis. "I expected better."

Smoke billowing from his face, Ullikummis turned to glare at his father, an approximation of a sneer across his imprecise features.

"You were trained for this, my son," Enlil hissed. "Trained to be the killer of gods. And yet I stand, and I live, and you have failed."

Ullikummis's eyes burned in his face like twin pools of magma as he glared at his father and listened to his mocking tone. "You are no god," he responded. "You have deluded yourself, like untold Annunaki before you, seduced by your own reputation. Narcissus gazing upon his own self in the reflecting pool, never realizing how far you have fallen.

"Look around you. Look at this world our family once ruled. Look at what has become of it, of how you have lost your grip on all the things that made the Annunaki strong."

"And you intend to change this?" Enlil asked contemptuously. "Is that what you plan to do, Ullikummis?"

"No," Ullikummis roared. "I came back here for just one thing—your death."

"Then naught but disappointment awaits you in the bowels of *Tiamat*," Enlil hissed, drawing his hands back in a graceful arc.

The air seemed to shimmer between Enlil's bronze-scaled hands as something took form, solidifying in place between them. It looked like a longbow, curved in a subtle crescent, but there was no string at its inner edge. The crescent shape glowed with an inner fire, like a streak of lightning burned into the air. Ullikummis recognized the serpent lightning, one of the most ancient and revered weapons in the Annunaki arsenal. To wield it took exceptional skill and concentration, taxing its user's abilities to predict mathematical probabilities over more than three dimensions. For Enlil to use it now was as much a statement of his superiority—perceived or otherwise—as his determination to annihilate his son absolutely. The serpent lightning hummed and crackled, like the low rumble of approaching thunder on the air.

Krak-a-boom!

Turning his head, Enlil spit another gob of bloody saliva to the deck. And then he ran, charging across the decking toward where Ullikummis stood with his stone face still smoldering with black smoke. As he ran, Enlil drew back the glowing weapon in his hand and Brigid saw it shimmer and swirl, moving like a stiff cord, whipping back and then darting forward like a striking snake.

Ullikummis raised his left arm, fending away the blow from the striking line of light. A vicious mosaic of sparks rattled across his arm as the snakelike whip was knocked aside, and lightning played across his arm, torso and neck as the angry sparks faded. A moment later, the electricity winked out of existence, leaving Ullikummis visibly rocking, the echo of retreating thunder trembling through the walls of the chamber.

They had history, these two. More than four thousand years of animosity flowed between them like a raging river, and this day its banks had finally burst. Enlil had created Ullikummis from the very start, back when the Annunaki had first walked the Earth. Master manipulator, Enlil had sown his seed in Ninlil during an afternoon of passion and anger, raping her as she struggled against his advances in the back rooms of one of the palaces of Nippur. A festival celebration had continued just two rooms away, and it was said that her cries of fear and pain could be heard all through the palace and beyond. But the Annunaki were decadent, caring little for those unable to defend themselves, and so the feast had continued uninterrupted.

By the time the egg that would be Ullikummis had been laid, Ninlil had already met with Ningishzidda on Enlil's orders, the master genetic engineer for the Annunaki, a scientist who could manipulate DNA with the artistry of a composer penning a symphony. Ningishzidda had changed the makeup of the cells within that egg, altering the creature that would appear, turning it into the monster that would emerge instead. Like all Annunaki, Ullikummis had been born with skin like armor plate, but his was of stone, not scale, a heavy clunking thing that weighed upon his altered bones. Over the subsequent years, at Enlil's instruction, Ullikummis's body had been shaped and reshaped, each manipulation bringing him closer to the ideal monstrous form that the cruel overlord had in mind. A stone pillar of a god, Ullikummis had been sent to kill Teshub, the lord of heaven, on his father's instructions. He had been just eighteen at the time, and already he had killed Annunaki at his father's request, wielding the blade Godkiller that could pierce the fractals that made up an Annunaki's life. The blade itself was a shard of his own body; Ullikummis had carved it from his dismembered arm, tempered it in fires of magma. The arm had regrown, for Ningishzidda had enhanced Ullikummis's genetic makeup in many ways, and at heart Ullikummis was still a lizard.

The attack on Teshub had concerned control of *Tiamat,* and Ullikummis had achieved all he needed to in the sky god's mountain palace. But something had gone wrong, and—along with his guru, Upelluri—Ullikummis had been the victim of a devastating attack that had seen his feet cut off and his body left for dead by his uncle, Enki. When Enlil's forces had found him,

Ullikummis had rejoiced, relieved that his father would
protect him and provide him and his mentor with the
medical care they needed to recover. But he had been
wrong. His plot against Teshub exposed, Overlord Enlil
had distanced himself from the assassination attempt
and had exiled his son from his court, imprisoning him
in a stone chamber that would orbit the cosmos for eternity.

Ullikummis had spoken to his mother briefly, before
he had been locked away in the prison asteroid. Only
then, when everything had come to such a dreadful
head, had he realized that he also had been manipulated,
that his father had done all of this to achieve his aims,
to gain power over *Tiamat*. For four millennia, Ullikummis had drifted the universe in his orbiting prison,
locked inside a shell of stone. And for four millennia,
Ullikummis had said but one word every single day,
reminding himself of his betrayal at his father's hands.
That word had been his father's name, Enlil, and he had
spoken it with all the hate it deserved.

By contrast, Enlil had thought nothing of his son in
four and a half thousand years, paying the matter no
mind since the moment that the child was out of his life.
Ullikummis had played his role, and that was enough.
Enlil had attended his exile from Earth merely as a for-
mality, remaining hidden behind the thick drapes of
his palanquin throughout the ritual banishment, copu-
lating with a slave girl. He had been barely conscious
of the words spoken by his adviser, Nusku, as he read
them from the holographic tablet before the open door
to his son's prison.

"'For the gross failure that you have committed, pur-
portedly in your father's name, you shall be cast into the
heavens. Your name shall no longer be mentioned in this

house, nor shall you be recognized as a deity. Your history shall be known as the story of a failure. No glory shall be visited upon the name of Ullikummis, Son of Enlil,'" the vizier had pronounced.

And then the vizier had spoken Enlil's final taunt, casting the blame upon Ullikummis's mentor.

"'Upelluri dared to turn his hand against Lord Enlil,'" he read, "'poisoning the mind of the great god's son, Ullikummis. He, too, shall be punished.'"

In that moment, Enlil's responsibility to the drama had been publicly assuaged, leaving him clear and free in the minds of both his subjects and all but the most suspicious of the Annunaki.

Now, in the ante-nursery of the reborn starship *Tiamat,* Ullikummis faced Enlil in a conflict that had been millennia in reaching its conclusion. Enlil swung the serpent lightning at him, its shimmering line fluctuating as it cut through the air. This time Ullikummis was ready, punching forward with his right arm and snatching the writhing line midway down its length. The end of the serpent lightning wrapped around Ullikummis's arm, burning everything it touched as it clung to the stone-plate armor that was the prince's skin, clung there like the resin of the terebinth tree, channeling thousands of volts through his flesh. The force was so powerful it seemed to lash against Ullikummis's bones, burrowing deep beneath the stone cladding of his altered skin, the sound of thunder deafening in his ears.

Krak-a-boom!

Ullikummis ignored the pain, dismissing it in the way that Upelluri had taught him, focusing past it and into the wellspring of hate that burned deep in his heart.

Enlil bared his teeth as the serpent lightning trembled in his grip, feeling the awesome power of the weapon looping back and forth from its handle.

Abruptly, Ullikummis pulled his body back, yanking the lightning serpent closer in a flare of sparks and pulling Enlil with it. The scarlet-cloaked overlord had two options now: to let go of the weapon or to follow where Ullikummis dragged him. He clung fiercely, his clawed hand tightly clenched around the weapon's handle.

His right arm alive with dancing electrical flames, Ullikummis used his weight to pull his father back, dragging the fearsome Annunaki overlord forward in a reluctant stagger. He was heavier than his father by far, the stonework of his body giving him the dynamism of a collapsing skyscraper. Ullikummis glanced behind him, past the scythelike protrusions that reared from his immense shoulders, searching for the exit to the room.

"Ungrateful child," Enlil spit as he was forced to take another stumbling step forward. "Your time is over. Your era past. You shone briefly, as was always my intention."

Ullikummis reached out with his free hand, grasping the door frame and anchoring himself there as he drew his father forward at the far end of the serpent lightning.

"Now is the time to lie down," Enlil gritted, "and give your body over to *Tiamat* once more. Accept inevitability. Your moment is over. You are nothing more than a footnote to history."

Ullikummis pulled once more, mustering all his strength to snatch his father forward, dragging him through the door and out of the birthing room.

In a moment the dueling Annunaki were out of the room, and finally Ullikummis released his grip on the burning length of lightning flame. Flames licked along his arm, his dark stone flesh blackened to the color of coal.

Enlil stumbled another few steps into the huge antechamber beyond, staggering like a drunk as he tried to right himself. The lightning weapon flared and dimmed in his grip, cycling through its options as it renewed its fearsome charge.

The room was twenty feet across and designed in a hexagonal pattern, with great jutting arches interlaced high over its deck, each one grown of decorative bone. Ill lit, the room had a faint blue-green glow, like being beneath the ocean. Ullikummis stood in the center of those bone arches, his eyes burning brightly in the gloom as his father recovered himself. Behind Enlil, the door to the birthing chamber sealed shut, metal plates coming together horizontally like a set of jaws.

"You fear me, Father," Ullikummis said, "because I am the one thing you never planned for."

Enlil nodded as the serpent lightning buzzed in his hand like a living thing. "A loose end to be snipped," he agreed, his eerie duotonal voice echoing from the walls.

And then, the two Annunaki charged at each other again, hatred eternal burning behind their eyes.

DOWN IN *Tiamat*'s engine room, Grant and Rosalia stood side by side as the strange, short figures rushed at them along the wide gangway that ran over the engine housings like a bridge. Each figure was dressed in a ragged black one-piece outfit, pockets lining their sides and looped around their waists like a belt sewn into the garment itself. Around their heads, each figure wore a small rig of lights that rested to the sides of their tiny eyes, each light the size of a fingernail but exceptionally bright. Each figure's face proved hard to see behind those lights, but Grant made out tiny, squinting eyes and hooked, beaklike noses with rugged flesh that looked like burned meat.

Grant stepped back, spreading his feet wider in a sturdy position as the first of the strangely garbed figures hurried toward them. Beside him, Rosalia had drawn her *katana* up past her head in a two-handed grip, its charcoal-black blade like a line of shadow in the air. Then the battle commenced, the quartet of figures attacking the Cerberus pair in a flurry of movement.

With a fierce shout, Rosalia brought her body forward and low, swinging her blade in a graceful arc that caught the ankles of the lead figure in a grisly shower of blood. The blood was clear with a black tint, like something that might ooze from a crushed bug. The figure tumbled backward, its pudgy hands snapping out to grab the sword before Rosalia could pull it away.

Behind her, Grant found himself facing the second of the rodentlike figures, and was suddenly dazzled by the lighting rig around its face. This one held a tool of some kind. To Grant's eye it looked like a wrench, brutally curved at the bottom and carved from a creamy bonelike material. Grant stepped back, struggling to see as the wrench rushed toward him, cutting the air just inches from his chest as his coattails billowed before him. Then the ex-Mag blindly raised his right hand—the one that wielded the Sin Eater—and squeezed the trigger, sending a burst of fire in the direction of the ugly-looking creature.

The figure fell back under the gunfire and the bullets went wild.

Grant blinked in quick succession as he willed the effects of the dazzling headlights away. Before him, the strange humanoid burbled something that sounded like an electronic shriek, before rolling across the deck plating and getting back to its feet. Then it came charging at him again with one of its fellow mechanics waddling after.

Grant ejected the spent cartridge from his Sin Eater as he brought his other arm up to fend off the next attack. He didn't look directly at the creature this time, instead timing his blows by a combination of sound, instinct and whatever he could make out from the corner of his eye. It wouldn't do to be dazzled again. Grant sent his Sin Eater back to its hiding place as he fought one-armed against his attacker. His left arm struck against the creature's chest, knocking it with another angry squawk. Grant felt the thing shift against his blow, stumbling just a little. Closing his eyes, the ex-Mag turned, swinging his whole body as he drove a punch into the creature's face. The blow struck with a crack of breaking bone, and Grant heard the creature chirrup as it struggled backward. Then there came a shriek, and he knew he'd knocked his first attacker over the side of the bridgelike gangway.

There was no time to stop. The second creature was already coming at him with what appeared to be some kind of power drill. Grant opened his eyes a slit as he heard the drill bit turn with a high-pitched whir. He smacked it aside with his forearm, slamming the shorter figure across its wrist to keep the whirling drill blade away.

A few paces along the wide catwalk, Rosalia twisted aside as another of the strange creatures hurled a tool at her. Nine inches long, the tool whizzed end-over-end through the air as it cut a path toward her. Rosalia turned her head aside, her dark ponytail swishing behind her as she twisted out of the tossed tool's path. She watched as it clattered to the decking close to her feet.

Then she sprang up, her feet pounding on the walkway span as she lunged at the creature with her sword. Held almost horizontal, the black sword drove through the air and into the humanoid figure as it tried to jump aside. Too slow, the creature found itself skewered on the end of the sharp blade, falling forward as the tip pierced its torso.

Rosalia turned, wrenching the blade free and dancing in place as she swung it toward her other attacker. The creature batted the blade aside with an outthrust arm, a dusty wad of material tearing free as the metal cut through it.

Then the figure was reaching into one of its capacious pockets, pulling loose a thick cord that it wore at its hip. Six feet in length, the blue cord featured a weight on both ends like a skipping rope, and Rosalia guessed it was used to hook items or levers that were higher than the short creature might be able to reach.

With a flick of the wrist, the rope lashed out, one weighted end hurtling toward Rosalia's face. She sprang, feet striking the decking with force as she drove her body up and over the flying weight.

The pendulum whizzed back like a yo-yo, zipping away and behind the dwarfen creature as it marveled at Rosalia's leap. For a split second, Rosalia found herself dazzled by those strange lights that the creature wore around its eyes, and then she was plummeting blindly back to the decking.

The strangely garmented figure seized that moment to strike, whipping the cord at Rosalia's shapely legs as she struck the deck and yanking sharply back on the cord as it entangled them. Before she could react, Rosalia found herself dragged to the deck, the thick cord caught up in a tangle around her lower legs.

Fifteen feet away, Grant leaped over his combatant's next drill attack, kicking out with one long leg and striking his attacker hard in the chest. The shorter figure went down in a cloud of dust from its overalls, screaming wildly like a stuck pig. Grant snapped up a handful of the creature's collar and wrenched it off the deck, at the same time commanding the reloaded Sin Eater into his hand.

Behind Grant, Rosalia grunted as she struck repeatedly against the deck chest-first, the *katana* blade slipping from her grasp and clattering away from her. Behind her, the eerie dwarfen figure was chattering something gleeful, a noise like an excitable fax machine emanating from some orifice in its strange, unearthly face. Grasping the cord with both hands, the creature pulled, dragging the dark-haired mercenary across the deck toward the edge.

Frantically, Rosalia's hand reached for the Ruger strapped to her hip, pulling it free as she slid across the catwalk toward a sheer drop. Then she had the Ruger P-85 pointed at the chattering abomination as it dragged her to the side of the high-up walkway, squeezing the trigger as the creature fell squarely in her sights.

Three loud reports cut the air, their echoes lost to the churning, whirring sound of the engines below. The creature tugging Rosalia by her feet shrieked, toppling backward as the bullets struck it full in the face. Rosalia watched in grim satisfaction as her attacker fell back over the side of the walkway, stepping into empty space and disappearing from view. Her satisfaction turned to horror as she realized that the thing was still clutching one end of the cord, and suddenly Rosalia found herself being dragged briskly across the deck to the walkway's edge.

"Magistrate!" she called, as her hands skittered along the smooth walkway, trying desperately to find purchase.

Fifteen feet along the walkway, Grant rattled off a burst of fire into the gut of the last of the creatures from just inches away, ignoring the troll-like beast as it doubled over in pain. He turned at Rosalia's cry, powering his legs as he chased after her retreating form.

"Go limp!" Grant instructed, shouting to be heard over the cacophonous engines below.

Reading Grant's lips, Rosalia did as instructed, her legs disappearing over the edge of the walkway, and she felt her stomach sink even as her body began to. Grant sprinted toward her, his long legs eating up the dozen strides it took to reach Rosalia, throwing himself forward with his arms outstretched.

As Rosalia began tipping, Grant's right hand snagged around her left wrist, and the muscular ex-Mag gritted his teeth as he was dragged toward the walkway's edge by the momentum. Grant stretched out his left arm, slapping it repeatedly against the hard decking as he tried to bring himself to a halt, the toes of his boots scraping across the bridgelike walkway. Finally Grant stopped, his right arm and shoulder hanging over the side of the catwalk, his hand cinched tightly around Rosalia's wrist. She swung to and fro, the cord still tangled around her legs as the strange dwarfish creature fell from its end, releasing its own grip. Below, a crowd of the strange, dwarfen workers had begun to form, pointing and shrieking at what was going on above their heads. The figure fell amid them with a bone-sickening crack, but the sound was lost to the whir of the engines.

"Thank you, Magistrate," Rosalia said breathlessly. "That's one I owe you."

"Remind me later," Grant said, the trace of a smile forming on his lips for a moment.

Then, gritting his teeth with the effort, Grant pulled Rosalia up until she could reach the catwalk's edge, after which the two of them worked together to get her back on the wide walkway.

"Let's get going," Grant said as Rosalia retrieved her sword from amid the mess of crumpled bodies.

"Good idea," she agreed. "This place is too damn popular for my liking."

ENLIL LASHED OUT with the serpent lightning, the line of light whipping about him in a dizzying display as he charged at the hulking figure of his son. Ullikummis ducked and leaped, deftly avoiding contact with the lightning whip as he powered toward his father.

With a bone-numbing crack, the two foes met beneath the bone arches, their chests crashing together as they drove blow after blow at each other's heads and torsos.

As the serpent lightning cut the air all around him, mighty Enlil struck out with his free hand, driving the heel of his palm at Ullikummis's eye. Ullikummis's head reared back as the blow tried to connect, throwing Enlil's aim off so that his outthrust hand struck high against his cheek instead. Ullikummis took a single step back, creating distance between the two combatants that seemed alive with blinding white electricity. The serpent lightning crackled and spit, the sounds echoing through the enclosed chamber like the sound of rumbling thunder.

Krak-a-boom!

His scarlet cape billowing around him like a bloody rent in the air, Enlil kicked out with his left leg, a double blow against his own flesh and blood. The first kick struck Ullikummis high in the ribs, smashing against his flank with such force it sounded like a shotgun going off. A split second later, Enlil's second blow found its mark, crashing behind Ullikummis's knee and forcing it to bend forward. Ullikummis fell at the blow, lurching forward and dropping to one knee before his father.

Enlil drew the serpent light back and around, describing a rotating arc like the path of a sycamore seed in the wind as it hurtled toward his son's armored body. As the blinding line of electricity struck, Ullikummis powered himself forward, springing from the decking and driving the top of his head up and into his father's chin. Enlil's head whipped back like a skittle in a bowling alley at the blow, even as lightning played across Ullikummis's form from the whiplike weapon that had wrapped around him.

As Enlil stumbled backward, Ullikummis turned his body, encouraging the cord of lightning to cinch tighter about his form. Fire played across his body, and his father lost his footing, the serpent lightning slipping from his grip. No longer under Enlil's control, the cord hurtled around Ullikummis's body like a lit firework, whizzing around and around with a crackling burst of energy and a booming roar of thunder. Ullikummis stood, enduring the serpent lightning as it ran its course, spiraling around his torso in a helter-skelter of unbridled power.

It took five seconds but finally the serpent weapon

unlooped from Ullikummis's stone form, rocketing away from his body and lashing against a wall, its energy spent. It waited there against the floor, twitching like a living thing, dimming and glowing as the energy coursed through it. Ullikummis ignored it.

Enlil lay on the bone deck, his lips pulled back in a grimace, the last vestiges of lightning playing across his teeth. Ullikummis took a step toward him, closing the gap between them, his eight-foot form towering over the fallen figure of his father.

"You had four thousand years to prepare for this," Ullikummis said.

"An eyeblink to the likes of us," Enlil dismissed.

Ullikummis shook his head. "Blood calls to blood, the prince succeeds where the king failed. This world is mine now, and I shall gift it to my mother, reborn in the paradise I am building for her. Your reign is at its end, Father. You are a child of the serpent, but you never left the safety of the kindergarten."

Without warning, Enlil sprang from the floor, striking with the speed of a cobra as he lunged for his son's face. Momentarily caught off guard, Ullikummis tried to step aside as Enlil hurtled at him, a savage sneer on his lips.

"You have no inkling of where the playpen walls end, child," Enlil spit contemptuously as his face loomed close to Ullikummis's. "Nor of who oversees the charges."

In that instant, Enlil's eyes met with those of his son and the two of them began their battle anew, shifting the battle to the next plane as their multifaceted forms warred amid the cosmic whirl.

Chapter 13

Engage.

Kane was starting to lose his grip on what was real. Objectively he knew he was sitting in a chair beneath the hidden city of Agartha, and yet trying to square that information with the reality he seemed to be experiencing was becoming harder by the second.

Physically his body was sitting in a navigator's chair of Annunaki design, a techno-organic symbiote intended to assist in the mapping of pathways through the universe. The Annunaki had come to Earth from the planet Nibiru, traveling across many millions of miles to investigate a new and interesting world on the cusp of childhood. The chair fed the subject with images straight into their brain, bypassing the eyes in favor of the mind's eye, the same part of the brain utilized in dreaming and imagining. This meant that Kane could theoretically open his eyes and see both the world about him and the incredible relay of images being pumped directly into his brain.

But therein lay another conundrum. Kane had been rapidly losing his sight over the past few weeks, and he had reached a stage where he might be struck temporarily blind for extended periods of time, most especially after the discorporation process of matter transfer involved in a mat-trans jump. The problem had become so pressing that Balam, as a telepath, had felt compelled to intervene, using a mind link to grant Kane a form of sight that was a few steps removed from what he was used to.

All of which meant that Kane was now sitting in an alien chair, watching imagery being pumped into his brain's optic nerve while Balam stood nearby, seeing and tapping the same images but only in the role of passive observer.

Kane saw the world opening up in a new and unexpected form, and it reminded him of the thermal-imaging cameras he had used occasionally during his duties as a Magistrate. Agartha waited around him, but it was a different Agartha from the one he knew, all vibrant colors and tabs and arrows. Kane looked at it, feeling as if he was lucid dreaming, walking the narrow streets with the disconcerting sense that he was floating. He was in the streets above the storeroom, his view most likely centered on the approximate position of the astrogator's chair. It was overwhelming, real and yet unreal.

"Stay focused, Kane," Balam instructed from somewhere nearby.

Automatically Kane turned, searching for the speaker of those words where he should be at his shoulder. Balam was not there, and Kane realized he was not surprised. This was a virtual world, or maybe a living photograph, like the kind of live video feed that Cerberus utilized to monitor planet Earth.

As he turned, Kane saw a new range of options open up before him, data hurtling across his vision in gaudy, floating panes of information that tagged everything he saw. Kane could not read the language that was written there, floating in the air like a glass slide, and when he stared at it, the image itself changed, zooming in on the building it had tagged or flipping through a dozen separate still images that somehow related to what he had been peering at.

The information was branching, Kane realized, bringing layer upon layer of new detail for every item he looked at. When it came to charting distant stars, Kane guessed, like earthlings, the Annunaki would need to know what dangers the territory might bring. Could they breathe there? Were there predators? The astrogation chair was like a living encyclopedia, cramming megabytes of information into every inch of space.

Focus is right, Kane told himself. A man could soon get overwhelmed by the oodles of irrelevant detail he was being bombarded with here.

He drew a steadying breath, marveling at the way the image of the streets seemed to roll with the movement of his chest despite the obvious fact he was not actually standing there.

As he breathed out, something else came over Kane's vision, more windows of information hanging in front of his eyes, branching even as he acknowledged them, more panels and tabs opening with every twitch of his eyes. The astrogator's chair was working out the content of his breath, breaking it down into the component parts and relaying information about each one back to him from its capacious databanks.

"Okay," Kane said, speaking the word aloud in an effort to help ground himself. "Let's just take this slow, think it through."

He was viewing a datastream, plunged deep into a cacophony of disordered information that he needed to sort through to get to what he wanted—Brigid Baptiste's location. It was, ironically, the kind of task Brigid was ideally suited to with her archivist background and her eidetic memory. But if she had been here, none of this would have been necessary.

The flow of data pulsed before Kane, adding an extra dimension to everything he looked at. And he stood there—if it could even be called standing—watching as the explosion of data expanded across his mind's eye.

No, Kane reminded himself. He was not watching; he was guiding. He could control the imagery, instructing it to do his bidding, to follow his will. He was here to find Brigid, nothing more than that. It was Kane who decided what to look at within this strange new map— no one else.

With a determined grunt, Kane commanded the chair to seek her out.

LAKESH STOOD AMID THE wreckage of the control room speaking to Donald Bry while Reba DeFore bandaged the latter's wounds. Bry looked more disheveled than ever, with his copper hair in disarray and a bloody smear running down the side of his face. However, despite some superficial cuts and being a little shaken up, he was fine.

"The computers took several knocks," Bry was explaining, "but I think we can salvage something."

Lakesh looked at a wrecked terminal. A stone projectile had smashed through it during their battle with the hooded intruders, and both screen and keyboard had been ruined beyond repair. "What about our communications?" he asked.

Over by one wall, Brewster Philboyd was kneeling before another terminal, running through a reboot sequence to bring the computer unit back to life.

"Just bringing them back online now," Brewster explained. "Booting up okay. We'll be at the moment of truth in about ninety seconds." Brewster's lanky frame looked uncomfortable working from the floor like this, but both of the room's swivel chairs had lost casters during the scuffle.

At that moment, Domi paced back into the room, shaking her head, with Shizuka trotting along behind her. Domi had been on an errand to assess the rest of Shizuka's lodge while DeFore was patching up Lakesh's wounds prior to turning her attention to Donald Bry.

"My love?" Lakesh prompted as he saw her enter.

Domi offered him a haunted look. "Hell of a mess," she stated regretfully.

Lakesh nodded. Domi's conclusions were pretty much what he had expected.

"My men have secured the lodge," Shizuka added, "and they are now surveying the local area. So long as you don't object to the smell of smoke, we should be safe for now."

"Yes," Lakesh acknowledged, "but how long will that last?"

Shizuka said nothing, but her expression showed her concern. The lodge could not be protected for long, as she had neither the manpower nor the armament to hold up a force of determined individuals like Ullikummis's firewalkers. Back in New Edo, her own people were stretched to the breaking point defending against similar infiltrators.

Bry smiled curtly as DeFore finished cleaning the wound on his forehead. "We could move the whole operation again, Lakesh," he suggested. "Not impossible— we've proved that now."

"Yes," Lakesh mused, absentmindedly stroking his fingers across his chin, "but where would we go, Donald? We are running out of safe places to hide."

"Shouldn't be hiding anyway," Domi spit, venom in her voice.

"Now, my dearest one," Lakesh chastised gently, "we must respond to our circumstances or, as the old phrase had it, needs must when the devil drives."

"So?" Domi replied. "Drive out devil."

"Easier said than done, I'm afraid," Lakesh admitted.

Brewster spoke up once more from his position by the wall. "Communications are back online. We're live if you want us to be."

Lakesh looked thoughtful for a moment, gazing out through the shattered glass of the French doors and into the delicately tended garden, so incongruous in this battle zone. "Pass me a headset," he ordered, "and patch me through to Kane. On speaker, if you will."

HIS MIND FED by the astrogator's chair, Kane hurtled across the planet in a rush of blurred sensation. The sun swelled like a great fiery disk in the sky while beneath him the ground seemed to have become a series of straight lines, stacked atop one another like the child's game of pickup sticks. It was a representation of reality, he knew, and yet it felt real to his brain, feeding all of his senses in new and unheard-of ways, making everything novel.

This must be how a baby sees the world, Kane thought. Everything was arrayed before him to be interpreted for the very first time.

He had commanded the chair to locate Brigid Baptiste, but despite the movement he felt no pull. He was flying over a racing panorama, and yet it was nothing like flying. It was like stepping through a waterfall, the water lashing at his body with detail and information, droplets swelling with data he would never have enough time to absorb. Beneath his feet, the ground seemed to swell like the waves of the ocean, an illusion of movement with no physical sense involved. The dichotomy of the two conflicting messages made Kane feel nauseous, and he probed with his tongue, feeling as if that organ was enlarging to fill his mouth. The sense of nonmovement was alien to Kane, confusing his senses the way the early motion pictures had confused their viewers, making them flee in terror as a photographed steam train seemed to hurtle toward them.

The chair was geared to alien senses—those of the Annunaki—and it took some getting used to.

If the chair was locating Brigid, then it was doing so with no sense feeding back to Kane, no noticeable tug. It simply did, without coloring its actions with emotion. And that, too, felt alien to Kane, and it took him a moment to realize why. The navigator's chair was inside his head, running information directly into his brain, and to have information delivered in that way, with no opinion, no interpretation, was inhuman.

Suddenly, a voice blurted in his head, so loud Kane was startled.

"Kane, do you read?"

It was Lakesh, but for a moment Kane couldn't make sense of it. It took him two seconds to realize the voice was not a part of the navigation chair software but was his Commtact springing back to life.

"Lakesh," Kane replied, engaging his Commtact, "what's happening?"

"We've had something of an upset here, my friend," Lakesh explained, "but nothing we can't handle. Wondering how your search is going."

"I'm using a…tracking device to locate Baptiste," Kane stated.

"Her transponder's still not operational," Lakesh reasoned.

"Different tech," Kane summarized. "Annunaki lost and found, something Balam had in storage down in Agartha." As he spoke, the world before Kane's senses hurtled in a rush of color and shape, morphing and blurring as he hurtled toward his destination. Already he was learning to look past it, ignoring the mad paint splatter of once-familiar views. "Takes the wind out of you, though."

As Kane raced across borders drawn in reds and purples and sapphire, his mind expanding far beyond anything he could accurately describe, he saw a sparkling before him like the blinking of an eye. The sparkling was lightning bright, like the twinkling of a star. He gazed at it, feeling a mixture of wonder and confusion, and as he did so his body seemed to be thrust closer, and as it was, the world about him took on familiar shapes and contours once more, solidifying as if it were something that had previously been hidden behind a gossamer-thin curtain.

Kane stopped, the lines solidifying all about him, the strange star glistening in place. In a moment, he was upon it, and he saw what it was.

"Baptiste…" he breathed, the word coming out as nothing more than a whisper.

Brigid Baptiste stood before him, as beautiful as ever, her slender body sheathed in the black leather suit that fitted like a glove, her fire-red hair bursting from her skull like a nuclear explosion. She scowled, and Kane saw dark lines streaked across her face, covering her eyes and darkening her lips. She appeared utterly unaware of his presence, even though he seemed to be standing no more than a foot from her face.

"My *anam-chara*," Kane said as he gazed into Brigid's emerald eyes. "My soul friend."

"Kane?" It was Lakesh's voice once more, searing into his thoughts like acid. "What's happening there?"

"I've found Baptiste," Kane explained. As he did so, his sense of euphoria passed and he started to take in the surroundings properly for the first time. They came into view like a camera pulling focus, blurring into abrupt sharpness.

Brigid Baptiste was standing in a midsize room with sloping walls and a pool of swirling liquid that dominated its center. The liquid was milky-white and its surface glistened despite the chamber's dimmed, purple lighting. The pool's surface was at the same level as the floor, and Kane assumed it was some kind of pit that dominated the room.

Within the pool, placed directly in its center, stood a wide stone structure a little shorter than Brigid herself. Kane recognized the structure, or at least its ilk—it was the same as the stone egg he had found in the fortress Bensalem, where he and Balam had come across the twisted genetic copy of Little Quav.

Lakesh spoke again, his voice intruding on Kane's thoughts. "Kane, where are you?"

It took a moment for Kane to frame his response. "A simulation... I'm not sure," he admitted.

The simulation moved in real time, and yet as Kane looked at it he saw it was imperfect, a blur to the movements, a fractured nature to the areas he was not directly examining.

"I'll pull back," he said after a moment, trusting the Commtact to transmit his words over the thousands of miles between himself, his body and Lakesh.

As he said it, the room became smaller and a tag

appeared identifying it in the swirling script of the Annunaki. Kane had no chance of translating that script,
but if he could have read it he would have seen he was
in the ante-nursery of the starship *Tiamat*.

Kane was fed more information as the image became
larger, seeing the arterial pathways that ran through the
great dragon ship and her location across the banks of
the Euphrates. But something else tugged at Kane's attention as he pulled back, a shimmering red swirl, like
blood, dropped in water.

"What the hell is that?" Kane muttered.

Even as he said it, Kane reacted without meaning
to, turning toward the crimson swirl and, thanks to the
mechanics of the navigation chair, being dragged closer
to it. The swirl rushed in space like a twister, and Kane
saw now that it was just a room away from where Brigid
Baptiste guarded the stone cocoon.

"What have you found?" Lakesh asked over the Commtact, while at the same time Balam's voice came from
farther away asking, "What is it, friend Kane?"

Kane ignored them both, his senses rushing in to get
a closer look at the whir of scarletlike blood. The walls
to the chamber fell into place via the interpretive software of the astrogation chair, building first as trans-
parencies, then blocking into place with lines of solid
color. This chamber was larger, Kane saw, and almost
empty, a series of interconnected arches spanning from
floor to ceiling in an asymmetric hexagonal pattern.

As Kane watched, the red swirl seemed to coalesce,
uniting into first one form and then splitting into two.
Kane's breath caught in his throat as he saw them, recognizing them both instantly. The red swirling mists
continued to curl within them, but the two had taken

on the definite shapes of Overlord Enlil and Ullikummis, his son.

Kane watched as the great rock being was flung across the chamber as if caught in a hurricane, careering a few feet over the decking until he slammed into one of the arching walls. Enlil gestured wildly, but if he spoke then Kane was not privy to the sound.

Instead he heard Balam, his voice filled with trepidation. "Friend Kane," Balam urged, "you should step away from this. You should do so immediately."

"Why?" Kane asked, realizing that the psychic link that the two of them now shared allowed Balam to see everything that Kane viewed via the chair.

"They will see you," Balam explained doubtfully.

"We're hundreds of miles away, Balam," Kane reminded his colleague. "This is just remote observation."

"They will sense you, Kane," Balam explained, and in so doing he explained nothing.

It was as if the First Folk guardian could not quite frame the concept into words, Kane suspected, and he got the sense that he was entering some medium that no human had ever seen before.

The figures moved in their dance of combat, but there was another level to the motions, something Kane had never witnessed before. It was like watching a camera on double exposure, and Kane's brain ached as he tried to decipher all that he was seeing.

Seven feet tall, Ullikummis whipped across the chamber in a spectacular charge, hooking Enlil with one of his scythelike shoulder ridges and knocking the bronze-hued Annunaki back. But at the same time, Kane saw something else happen, a blast of light and color that seemed disassociated with the familiar humanoid figures. It was almost as if it wasn't there at all, like the phantom images left on the eye after looking at the sun—a light of darkness, a color unseen.

Kane tried his best to describe what he was seeing, stunned by the strange depth of his newfound perspective.

LAKESH TRIED to make sense of the information as he listened to Kane's report within the temporary operations room of the Cerberus base.

"It's almost like he's describing some kind of Doppler effect," Lakesh suggested, "though one that can be seen rather than heard."

The Doppler effect referred to the apparent increase or decrease in frequency as an observer neared the subject, and it was best known as the effect generated by an approaching police siren. The effect was achieved by the modulation of the sound or other waves involved, but neither Lakesh nor his colleagues had heard of such an effect being associated with vision.

Sitting at the communications rig, Brewster Philboyd pulled the black-framed glasses from the bridge of his nose and rubbed at his eyes. "Could it be a product of the vision chair that Kane is utilizing?" he asked.

"Undoubtedly," Lakesh agreed, "and yet there's something more to it, I'm sure of that. Call it a gut instinct, if you will."

Across the room, Donald Bry groaned as he brought up information on another of the linked computer terminals that served the temporary Cerberus base. "Kane is a remote viewer to the situation at the Euphrates," he reminded everyone. "With respect to your gut, Lakesh, he is at best a witness to events he has no control over."

Lakesh snorted. "Isn't that always the case with Kane?"

IN THE UNDERGROUND city of Agartha, Balam stood outside the gel-walled room watching Kane's physical body
rock and struggle in the grip of the living chair. With
spiny growths emanating from the chair and worming
themselves under Kane's skin as he held his eyes shut, it
looked as if the ex-Magistrate was suffering from some
terrible nightmare.

"Friend Kane, you must work with the chair and
allow it to work through you," Balam instructed. "The
more you fight against it, the worse things will become."

Kane spit a curse through clenched teeth, acknowledging Balam's advice with poor humor. "I can't make
out what it is I'm looking at," he hissed.

"Kane," Balam said, his voice reasonable and calm,
"are you aware of astral projection?"

"Using meditation to let your mind reach out beyond
the limitations of your body?" Kane asked. "Yeah. Not
a believer."

"The human experience is beyond my capacity to
truly comprehend," Balam admitted, "but I propose
you accept that the chair is augmenting your ability
to achieve such astral projection, or at least something
closely akin to it."

"I'm being fed too much information, Balam," Kane
growled. "I can't make proper sense of it."

"Remember you can still breathe, Kane," Balam said
gently. "Calm yourself. Let the experience wash over
you."

FLOATING WITHIN the hexagonal chamber deep in the
guts of the great dragon ship, Kane drew a long breath
and held it for the count of five before exhaling it gently
through his parted lips. Before his eyes, the messy swirl
of figures and light continued in their vicious combat,

batting each other across the chamber in an ever-changing paint-splatter blur. As he exhaled, Kane saw the blurs become figures again, the burning lights ebb, their blinding illumination turning back to something he could look at without hurting his eyes.

The gods were battling before him, fighting each other to the death. And there was more to it than that, more than Kane had ever seen before. Up to now, Enlil had been a humanoid figure, bronze-scaled with the raiment of a war master. But now it seemed that Kane was seeing so much more, involving a more complete representation of these incredible beings.

"What is it I'm looking at?" Kane growled. "What can I see?"

"The Annunaki are multidimensional beings, Kane," Balam reminded him. "They exist in more planes than the three dimensions you occupy."

Lakesh gasped over the Commtact, hearing Balam's words. "Kane, can you describe what it is you can see?"

Kane looked at them, these two mighty figures throwing each other across the chamber in a Terpsichore of violence. Light seemed to bleed from them, its rays assaulting Kane's eyes yet leaving his vision intact. The two figures seemed to expand, too, growing larger as they fought yet remaining the same relative size to the room. Kane struggled, trying to describe the scene as best he could. It was cognitive dissonance, the sense of two conflicting realities coexisting, and his brain somehow processing both as if they were separate.

"String theory," Lakesh mused, once he had heard Kane out.

"Say again?" Kane asked as he watched Enlil drive Ullikummis to the deck, his talons plucking for his son's eyes.

"String theory maintains that certain objects may exist in multiple dimensions," Lakesh briefed, "and that our own universe is merely a veneer on that grand, multidimensional tapestry."

"You're getting all theoretical physics on me, man," Kane growled. "Care to bring it down a notch?"

Lakesh apologized before continuing, framing his explanation as best he could as he spoke to Kane over the Commtact. "In essence," Lakesh elaborated, "the things we see are merely the edges of multidimensional forms that move through fractal space. If what Balam suggests is correct, that the Annunaki are themselves multidimensional, then what we've been seeing up to now could best be described as the edges of their vast shapes."

"You mean they're bigger than we thought?" Kane asked.

"Not just bigger," Lakesh said, "but operating at an entirely alien set of nodal points that we cannot normally comprehend. I believe what you're looking at—what your brain is trying to process thanks to the chair's input—is a graphical representation of creatures who exist and duel in the dimensions proposed by string theory."

Kane seemed mystified.

"It may be easier to imagine the Annunaki as a pen-and-ink drawing on a sheet of paper," Lakesh said. "Up to now you've been looking at that flat illustration and presuming it is complete, but suddenly you're seeing a third dimension—depth—reaching both into and out from the paper. Compile upon that another level—color—being added, and you can begin to comprehend how a string creature would exist beyond the limits of your earlier assumption."

"And I can see Ullikummis because of the chunk of him I have wedged in my eye," Kane realized. "We're linked, he and I. That's why I was drawn to this place when I went searching for Baptiste. The chair can only do so much, and even with our *anam-chara* bond, the hunk of stone in my head overrode that and drew me like a magnet to its daddy."

While he spoke, Ullikummis came stumbling toward Kane, both hands cinched around his father's throat. As Kane watched, the great rock figure looked up and something seemed to flash deep within his burning magma eyes.

"You!" he rumbled in a voice like grinding millstones.

As impossible as it seemed, astral form or not, Kane had been spotted.

Chapter 14

Calling on his mighty reserves of strength, Ullikummis drove his father's body down against the deck plate once again, his stone hands grasped around the hated figure's throat. Enlil's eyes lost focus for a moment at the force of the blow, and Ullikummis felt him go limp in his hands. Then he looked up and saw the other figure in the room, hidden between the earthly planes, disguised within the hidden angles. It was Kane, the apekin whom he had tasked to lead his human armies and who had rejected that offer, killing First Priest Dylan in the process.

"You!" Ullikummis rumbled in a voice like grinding millstones.

The spectral figure of Kane reared back, surprise on his idiot face. The primitive fool had not realized that Ullikummis could see through the veil of this reality, that the god war occurred on many planes at once.

But as Ullikummis readied himself to snag Kane's astral form, Enlil pulled himself back from the brink of unconsciousness, reaching upward and thrusting his clawed hands in Ullikummis's open mouth. With a savage yank, Enlil pulled his son's head down toward him by his jaw, even as Ullikummis tried to bite off his hand.

"I taught you better than this, Ullikummis," Enlil chastised as he swung himself aside. "Are you lazy or just out of practice?"

Ullikummis slammed into the hard deck plate chin-

first, unleashing a savage grunt of anger as his body
followed. Behind him, Enlil stepped lightly on the balls
of his feet, dancing out of his monstrous son's reach.

"SHIT," KANE CURSED. "He's seen me. But how can he
do that?"

"Kane, you are in grave danger," Balam said from
his safe position outside the cube-shaped room beneath
Agartha's buildings.

"Yeah," Kane agreed. "That's how it generally is."
With that, he had dismissed Balam's concerns and was
turning his attention to his surroundings.

Ullikummis was writhing on the floor as Enlil
danced out of reach, the latter figure stepping back and
forth, keeping his center of gravity low. Pushing himself
up, Ullikummis took a moment to look at Kane once
more, fixing him with his liquid-fire eyes and inclin-
ing his head for just a moment in a nod of acknowledgment. Then the powerful rock god turned his attention
back to his father, powering himself off the floor and
hurrying at the bronze-hued Annunaki like a missile.

AS HE LUNGED at the scarlet-cloaked figure of his father,
Ullikummis jabbed out with his right hand, sweeping
it through the air in a graceful arc. His mother was po-
tentially in danger, and with Kane here—even in astral
form—it would not do to allow her to go unprotected.
She, too, would come to exist in multiple dimensions
upon her rebirth.

SEVERAL DECKS BELOW, Grant and Rosalia were jogging
along a narrow walkway that ran over the water storage
area. Ill lit, the shadow-filled room itself was awash with
spilled water in an area so massive that it had already

adopted its own tidal patterns, breakers roiling back and forth across the vast space. The walkway itself was barely wide enough for one man, its floor arched upward with thin bars like fish bones running along its edges.

As they ran, something hammered through the bottom of the room, sending jets of water violently into the air. The thing continued, driving upward like a striking bolt of jet-black lightning in the darkness, a javelin tossed straight upward.

Grant halted, his hands reaching out for the narrow safety bars that ran along the high walkway even as Rosalia collided with his back.

"What the hell, Magistrate?" Rosalia spit.

Then she saw the javelin-like shards hurtling up and through the walkway, piercing its surface just six feet ahead of where Grant had stopped.

"Automated defenses...?" Grant wondered as the walkway split apart before him.

He and Rosalia clung on as the perilous walkway swung back and forth, its midsection shattered beyond repair. The thick needle of rock continued up through the room and into the ceiling, swiftly followed by a half-dozen identical shards, each one crashing through the roof of the room above the Cerberus warriors' heads, raining debris on the battered walkway.

"We're going to have to find an alternative route," Rosalia screamed as debris crashed down on them from the ruined ceiling.

Grant nodded, the walkway swaying to and fro as it broke free from its mountings. A loud straining noise echoed over the sounds of rushing water below as the narrow path began to career away from its wall attachments.

"Hang on!" Grant shouted.

As Ullikummis powered across the room outside the ante-nursery, a line of rock stalagmites followed in his wake, tracing the curve his right hand drew in the air, bursting through the hull of *Tiamat* and climbing through her decks in a matter of seconds. Each was as wide as a man's torso, ripping apart plates of decking as it hurtled into the room from below.

Rock was his to command, and he used it now not as a weapon but as a defense, shielding that which he wished to protect.

At the same instant, the rock lord's powerful form crashed into that of his father, knocking the older Annunaki backward as he tried to skip aside. Enlil kicked out as he fell, driving himself away from his son's devastating attack.

Past Ullikummis's monstrous shoulder armor, Enlil saw the rock columns burst into view, shattering the bone plates of *Tiamat*'s decking, ripping into her body. Had he time, Enlil would have wept for *Tiamat,* but already his attention was needed elsewhere. There, close to the back wall of the hexagonal chamber where the doors hid the ante-nursery, the rocks were amassing, creating a line of jagged struts like the bars of a cage. And standing beside them was the ghostly, spectral image of someone—one of the apekin, and one oh-so-familiar to Enlil himself. It was Kane of clan Cerberus. And how had *he* gotten here?

"Okay, people," Kane instructed, taking the lead, "let's get our bearings and see what's what."

The first thing he needed to know was where he was. Kane had rushed here so fast, crossing thousands of miles in just a few minutes, it was hard to put a geographical location onto the world that whirred in his mind. The Annunaki figures struck each other again, rushing past Kane's vision as he followed their combat, watching as they seemed to collide with him, pass through him, continuing on as if oblivious to his presence.

"Where am I?" Kane muttered, speaking the words aloud.

His vision seemed to bend as the scene before his eyes moved into transition, the hexagonal chamber swelling as if reflected in a droplet of water before shunting him further away. Kane looked, seeing things he recognized even as a series of illuminated tags rushed before his eyes, adding a depth of data to his comprehension.

"I'm in *Tiamat*," Kane announced as the battle raged before him. "She looks different than before, but…"

Even as he spoke, the cascade of data rushed before Kane's eyes, bringing up fixed views of the great spaceship, a rotating wire-frame model, and detailed information on the ship's stardrive. Kane dismissed the information, unable to take it all in, the language impossible to read.

"Grant and Rosalia are somewhere in there," Lakesh stated, "or they were."

A great many miles away, the figure of Kane strained to activate the Commtact unit hidden along the line of his mastoid bone. Normally he could do that without thinking, but instead something peculiar happened— the vision of the battling Annunaki before him seemed to expand, as if their figures—their presence in the room—were enlarging at an incredible rate.

"Whoa," Kane muttered, gripped by a sudden sense of vertigo. Something about the chair's operation clashed with his control over the Commtact, he realized, meaning that while he could speak into the subdermal communications unit, he could not activate it in the normal manner.

Recalling Balam's earlier advice, Kane took another slow breath, counting through to five before he gently released it through his nostrils. Distantly, he felt the breath brush through the mustache of his beard, but the effect was so dissociated with his form now that it was more like someone reading a story to him, a story about breathing.

He needed to think around the problem, Kane knew, find a way to operate the Commtact without affecting his command of the astrogation chair.

"Can you link me through to Grant?" Kane asked aloud, the beginnings of a plan forming in his mind.

FAR AWAY, in the control room of Shizuka's lodge, Brewster Philboyd worked the communications tabs to connect Kane to Grant. Normally, Kane would be able to do this automatically, but with his mind being all but overwhelmed by the astrogator's chair, the Cerberus ops crew knew he needed all the assistance that they could give.

"Putting you through now," Brewster explained.

GRANT'S COMMTACT burst into life. He was clinging onto a swaying walkway that dangled over the sloshing pool of water at the time, and the voice surprised him as he gripped the narrow handrail with both hands.

"Grant? Where are you?"

The catwalk was hanging at an angle from the wall where it had once been mounted, its distant end clinging to that wall like a limpet. Grant clung to the ragged end of the walkway as it swayed to and fro over the rushing tides within the belly of *Tiamat,* his body arched so that his boots were still touching the forty-five-degree floor. Above him, Rosalia scrambled up the walkway, working hand-over-hand up the railing as she dragged herself back the way they had come.

"Kane?" Grant answered, incredulous. "That you?"

"Course it's me," Kane answered. "Look, I need some help—"

"Busy just now," Grant said, cutting in before Kane could finish. "Me and Rosie are down in the back end of *Tiamat*—you remember her?"

"I'm inside, too," Kane explained. "Well, kinda."

"Hell, Kane," Grant spit as he clambered up the angled walkway with workmanlike determination, "this isn't a good time to hit me with surprises. This ship just got lanced by a shit-storm of rock spears, with us caught in the middle."

"Which must mean I'm directly above you," Kane reasoned. "I need you to make your way here ASAP. I'll fill you in on the way."

"You know Brigid's here?" Grant said. "Somewhere, anyway. I think she's behind us."

"Negative on that," Kane corrected. "I've seen her and she's on the same level as I am."

"Do you know Enlil was in here?" Grant asked.

"Yeah, and he's getting seven bells kicked out of him by Ullikummis," Kane answered, a clear note of satisfaction in his tone. "But this is bigger than either of them, buddy. I'm riding the lightning here and I can't do it alone.

"Let me know when you can see them."

"Shit," Grant cursed as Kane cut the transmission. Above him, Rosalia had made her way to the mouth-like orifice that led from the water room, and she was standing at the door waiting for Grant to join her.

"You going to be long, Magistrate?" Rosalia taunted. "Sounds like a fucking pajama party down there."

"It's Kane," Grant explained as he pulled himself up the last ten feet by the strength of his arms alone as the catwalk swayed, unanchored.

Rosalia's dark eyes widened with concern. "Kane?"

"He's here and he needs our help," Grant elaborated. "My guess is he's up somewhere near the main birthing chamber. We just need to find him."

Rosalia's mouth formed a moue as she considered the problem. "What about zeroing in on his transponder?" she suggested after a moment.

"Negative," Grant replied, pulling himself through the angled doorway to join the dark-haired woman. "From what Kane tells me, that ain't going to work.

"I don't know what he's got himself into," the ex-Mag continued, "but it sure as shooting ain't anything either of us would imagine in our wildest ones. Whatever, he asked for backup so that's what we're going to give him. Change of priorities."

Rosalia nodded in acknowledgment. "Fine, then let's find him."

Grant and Rosalia trotted down the corridor, searching for an alternative route higher into the grounded spaceship.

IN THE UNDERGROUND storehouse in Agartha, Balam watched tensely through the veil of the cube's wall where Kane sat in the grip of the living chair. He had retrieved something from elsewhere in the store, but seeing Kane now made him regret leaving him alone. The man's face was strained with tension, his teeth clenched beneath his drawn-back, white lips, his eyes tightly closed. Sweat poured over the ex-Mag's brow, and his damp hair stuck to his forehead and neck where it trailed over his collar.

Against his better judgment, Balam reentered the cube container, striding over to Kane. The atmosphere within the cube was electric, the air pressure heavy now as the navigator's chair powered up to maximum capacity, flinging Kane's astral self into the void.

"Kane," Balam warned, "you are pushing yourself too hard. You must retreat or you'll be killed."

His body straining against the bonds of the chair, Kane gave no indication of response.

Balam stepped closer, and he felt his robes clinging to him with the static electricity in the air. "Kane, can you hear me?"

Kane's eyes scrunched tighter as he shook in his seat, and then his teeth parted just slightly and he spoke in a strained voice. "I hear ya, Balam," he said. "But I have to do this. Baptiste is relying on me."

"Brigid Baptiste may be lost," Balam reminded Kane with stuffy officiousness. "And you will be, too, if you do not step back from this mad quest."

"Back off, Balam," Kane growled, the tendrils of the chair stretching over his cheeks and closed eyes. "I can do this. I can beat them at their own game."

"No human could ever navigate tesseract space," Balam said with the wisdom of the ages. He was ancient, the last of the Archons who had dwelled in secret on planet Earth for many centuries. While he admired Kane, Balam felt sure the human was being foolish. No son of the apes could possibly enter the multidimensional space and maintain his sanity. Some things were simply not meant for humankind.

"I insist you remove yourself from the chair. Do so now, before you lose everything on this fool's errand."

Kane took a steadying breath, and as he did so the chair seemed to oscillate in time with him. "Balam, can you still see what I see? Are we still linked?"

Balam nodded his heavy, bulbous head. "We are."

"Then I'm going to need your help," Kane explained. "Tune into my frequency, or whatever it is you do with that freaky brain of yours. You're going to be my navigator."

"Kane, I can't possibly…" Balam began.

"The stakes are too high for that shit," Kane growled.

"What you're suggesting," Balam said, the tension clear in his usually calm voice, "is entering dimensional planes that humans have no equipment to even perceive. The dangers are too great—you will be overwhelmed in a matter of seconds and I cannot possibly give consent to that. It is suicide, plain and simple."

"Do you know what they used to say about me back in Cobaltville, back when I was a Magistrate?" Kane asked.

"Is this a rhetorical question?" Balam replied in confusion.

"They used to send me up front on exploratory missions," Kane continued. "They said I had a point-man sense, that I could sniff out danger before it happened. That point-man sense kept me alive, and it saved more than one of my colleagues."

"Friend Kane, with my sincerest respect, the words you are speaking are idiocy," Balam argued. "Whatever your abilities may be in our world, you will be entering a separate plane of reality with no markers or even a frame of reference."

"And that's why you're going to be my navigator," Kane said. "Chair's the engine—you're the map reader."

Kane clenched his teeth once again as another wave of hideous power emanated from the space navigation chair, firing through every cell of his body as it responded to his mental command. Kane was shaking violently in his seat, and Balam was forced to step back as a burst of static electricity zapped across the cube-space. The ex-Mag clenched the arms of the chair with such strength that his fingers dug into the armrests. Then Balam saw a lopsided smile cross Kane's lips.

WITHIN HIS FRACTURING mindscape, Kane saw the different levels of space open up within the battle of the gods. The Annunaki were multidimensional, but it was only now that he began to truly see that. They were shapes and colors and smells he could not describe, things that clashed and morphed and changed. Behind them, the hexagonal chamber of *Tiamat* appeared as solid as it ever had, and Kane clung to it to retain his sense of space. The humanoid figures of Enlil and Ullikummis struck out at each other, their battle raging on the physical plane he knew.

"Lakesh," Kane said, trusting his Commtact to carry the words, "I'm going to need you and Brewster covering my ass for the string-theory shit, okay?"

Close to Kane's ear, Lakesh's voice gave assent. "Okay, Kane, we're with you in spirit."

"Grant?" Kane said, trying a second time as Brewster patched through the communication. "I want you up here ASAP. You and Rosie have got a couple of gods to execute. You read me?"

"I read you, man," Grant grumbled, "but you're asking a lot. We haven't had much success offing the Annunaki before now. What makes you think things'll work out different this time?"

"Because you have a man on the inside," Kane said. "Literally. I'm going into their soulscape to finish this once and for all. But time's ticking, and I'm going to have to start this party without you."

"That's cool," Grant said. "We'll be there as soon as."

Kane's final instruction was merely voiced, engendering the disconcerting feeling of speaking to someone in the same room as he was and yet thousands of miles away. "Balam?" Kane asked. "You have your eyes on, my friend?"

Kane could hear Balam take a steadying breath, even over the sounds of conflict in the hexagonal chamber.

"I will do my best, Kane," Balam assured him. "But I apologize if—"

"Save the apologies for my funeral," Kane told him.

For a moment, the twin figures before him raged and fought, Enlil swinging his son's rock body by one arm before being tossed aside by a flick of his mighty son's wrist.

"Okay, people," Kane said, steely determination in his voice. "We're doing this together. On three."

With that, Kane's astral form charged forward beneath the towering arches of the room inside the belly of *Tiamat,* lunging forward as the Annunaki batted at each other with all their might.

"One…"

As he—ran? floated? swam?—Kane looked past the battling figures, relaxing his eyes and seeing the sparkling lights once more, swirling around one another as they, too, clashed in the folds of enhanced space.

"Two…"

And in that moment Kane dived into the midst of

them, allowing his form to be pulled and reshaped as it entered another plane of existence.

It was a moment that belonged in the history books.

"Three!"

It was the splitting of a man's soul.

Chapter 15

Big things and little things, all of them vying for space, like a whirling mosaic that Kane could just barely make sense of, and only then if he looked at it from the corner of his eye.

The universe expanded before his eyes, a dark blanket dotted with stars. And the two figures danced on the universe, their movements as practiced as an ancient ballet, each one taking his role.

Which was Ullikummis?

Which was Enlil?

Kane could no longer tell. Now they were just two dancers whirling through the cosmic winds, playing each other at the great game of the gods.

For a moment, Kane stopped, holding his hands out before him. The limbs were transparent now, ephemeral things with no consistency. As he looked at the fingers of his right hand, seeing the stars shining through each one, they began to grow, elongating and expanding until they were no longer fingers at all, just a blot on his vision like a sty.

"Hold yourself together, friend Kane," Balam instructed, seeing all that Kane saw via the psychic link they shared.

"C-c-can't," Kane said, struggling with the word.

"You are seeing the universe from another angle,"

Balam told him reasonably, "but you must stay focused or the enormity of it all will overwhelm you."

Kane bit down hard, feeling the sensation of his teeth crashing together in his mouth, bringing himself back from the brink of madness. The multiple images of time and space whirled before his eyes, static and ever-changing, a continual contradiction.

Enlil took on a shape Kane recognized, though he appeared more like a Chinese dragon now, a serpentine line of red-gold scales capped with his sneering face. He lacked substance as Kane understood it, dancing through the universe like a constellation.

Kane turned—his head? his body?—and saw the rock figure of Ullikummis hurtling across the skies like a meteor shower, treading across the blanket dotted with stars before bombarding his father with the mul-tiassault of his component parts, each rock bearing the Annunaki prince's face.

Kane turned once more as the two figures whipped past him, seeing the sun properly for the first time.

"Hold focus," Balam instructed, his voice a steady presence at the edge Kane's consciousness.

Kane watched the sun, saw the dancing flames licking across its surface, reaching out to space only to scuttle back at the very last second, never daring to overextend their reach, like waves on the shore.

And then he was on Earth again, but no longer inside *Tiamat.* It was a ville now, perhaps Cobaltville, where he had grown up, or maybe one of the eight others, all of them strictly following the same design. People were running toward Kane, screaming in fear.

"Molecules," Balam said.

"What?" Kane demanded.

"They are molecules, the debris of the battle," Balam

explained. "Your mind is finding a way to interpret what it is experiencing. These are sights no human has ever witnessed."

Kane watched the screaming mob come running toward him, charging about and past him, knocking into him as he held his place, a rock in the human tide. They were running from something, he reasoned, and so he stepped forward, making his way through the crowd of faces as they surged by.

There, behind them, was the thing that everyone feared. Two great gods striding the skies, their arms gripped together, two hundred feet above Kane's head. Their legs stood like impossible skyscrapers, reaching past the walled limits of the ville, lancing up to dizzying heights. Their faces were lost in clouds. But Kane recognized them as Enlil and Ullikummis, battling at whatever level this was.

They were gods, Kane felt now. They battled as gods, running across space, reaching into the very building blocks of the universe with the urgency of their fury.

"Don't let yourself become overwhelmed," Balam reminded. "Interpret and act, that's all you can do now."

Lightning danced across the clouds—

Krak-a-boom!

Krak-a-boom!

Krak-a-boom!

Each snap darted between the two colossal figures like the reaching fingers of a lover.

Kane searched around him as the crowd surged by, looking for some way to be a part of this war of the gods, some way to be more than an insect in the presence of the almighty.

OUTSIDE *TIAMAT*'s walls, the armies clashed, a thousand voices raised in hate. Numerous figures battled on the streets of bone, lone Annunaki facing down a dozen human beings, rending them to pulp with their brutal, relentless attacks. Pockets of humans succeeded in toppling one or two of their enemy through use of the stone weaponry with which Ullikummis had armed them.

Sela Stone watched from a doorlike recess of a wide column structure. The column twisted upon itself, around and around like an antelope's horn. Bloodshed was all around, the white bone walls and cobbles of the streets awash with red. In her hand, Sela held the Colt Mark IV, its familiar weight providing scant reassurance. She had seen through the veil that Ullikummis had weaved before her and before the eyes of his faithful followers. Though she could not know it, the obedience stone that had been planted inside her months before had become dislodged when she had taken a savage side blow from one of the Annunaki soldiers. Her hair was matted with blood, thick, sticky, semidried gouts of it mixing with her short hair.

With the loss of the stone's grip had come revelation, ironic as it was. The drumbeat, that brutal charging drumbeat, had disappeared from her thoughts where, for the past six weeks, it had raced in her head with all the power of thunder, impossible to ignore. Without its incessant noise, she was beginning to regain her composure, remember what it was to be Sela Sinclair and not Sela Stone, no longer just another "stone wife" in Ullikummis's cheerless army. But still there were plenty of faithful to take up arms in the battle for control of *Tiamat.* All of them fought as if their lives depended on it, and the evidence was all around that in many cases it did—here were the dead bodies of her fallen colleagues, sprawled in street after street, in some places three or four deep.

And what were they fighting for? A promise? Was that all it took? Was that all any war took, ultimately?

Sela turned as a howling Annunaki dashed along the street, a narrow bone club hoisted in one of its gray-scaled hands. The club looked to have been fashioned from a leg bone, gouts of flesh still clinging to it near the grip. As he ran by, the Annunaki turned his head warily to check his surroundings, spotting Sela hiding in the shadows. His eyes narrowed and he halted in midstep, turning to face her, the club raised in one clawed hand.

Standing in the doorway, Sela willed him to move on, to leave her. She was still ordering her thoughts, still trying to remember what it was to be without the merciless drumbeat. "Go," she whispered. She wanted no part of this war now, not until she properly comprehended what it was she was truly fighting for.

The gray-skinned Annunaki took no notice of her whispered instruction. Instead, he drew the club back and charged at Sela, reaching her in two long steps and swinging the simple weapon at her head. Sela ducked, her old U.S. Navy training kicking in automatically despite the lethargy that gripped her mind. The club cut the air, smashing against the back wall with the awful clanking sound of bone on bone.

Without raising her head, Sela's right hand snapped out—the one with the pistol in it—and she slammed the nose of the Colt Mark IV against the kneecap of the Annunaki, squeezing the trigger as it struck. The pistol kicked in her hand, and the Annunaki listed to one side as the cartilage of his knee was shattered. The Annunaki were tough, their scaled skin acting like proxy-armor, but at point-blank range even they could not shrug off a bullet, not one so deftly placed.

Sela watched the Annunaki loll against the wall, falling forward as his leg bent, spitting a furious hiss from clenched jaws. Sela moved swiftly, extricating herself from the falling figure and dancing away in a quick two-step, the muzzle of her gun trained on her enemy.

The Annunaki recovered himself in an instant, clawing against the wall to hold himself up. He shouted something at Sela as his eyes met with hers, and though she could not understand his words the intent in its rage-filled eyes was unmistakable.

Around the two combatants, the sounds of battle reverberated from the hard walls, screams of dying and chants of determination. For one brief instant the battle cry went out:

"For Ullikummis!"

And then it was lost once more to the general hubbub of war.

Sela shifted her aim with the Colt, snapping off a shot at the gray Annunaki's head as he leaped from the shadow-dark recess. He ran with a loping gait now, favoring his left leg. The right leg seemed intact, but the blackened hole where the bullet had pierced it was evident on one side, the shattered remains of the kneecap poking through the fleshlike fingernails pressed against the rubber of surgical gloves. Annunaki blood was oozing from the wound, tracing a line down the scales of the gray warrior's leg, an unguent-like substance seeping out from the bullet hole. Sela blasted her pistol again, sending another shot at the charging Annunaki even as he swung the bone baton at her head.

Two of her shots struck the hobbled warrior in the face, a third skipping off his cheekbone in a blinding shower of sparks. More bullets lashed against the bone walls behind the Annunaki as Sela continued pumping the trigger, trying to fell the broad-shouldered beast.

At the same time, the Annunaki's club raced through the air, slamming against Sela's side with a crack of her ribs. She fell, toppling over herself as she crashed to the ground.

Then the Annunaki was looming over her, struggling to hold himself upright where his knee had been torn apart. Sela looked up, bringing the Colt pistol around in an automatic response.

Sela squeezed the trigger at the same moment as the gray-faced Annunaki brought his simple weapon down on her skull. From nearby, the chant of "For Ullikummis!" drifted to Sela's ears once more, the human army waging battle against the deadly aliens through the mazelike streets of *Tiamat*.

"For humanity!" Sela shouted as the Colt pistol kicked in her hand.

KANE DUCKED as the debris from another lightning blast hurtled to the ground, great chunks of impossible architecture smashing into a million glistening pieces as they struck the floor. The buildings around him were elaborate, more so than the ones he recalled from Cobaltville and the other villes. They towered into the heavens, bloated minarets like crowns atop each one, swirling glyphs and curlicues running up their towering columns in patterns of archaic beauty, all the colors of the rainbow held in every surface, every atom. It was mesmerizing to look at, an image so absolute that it transfixed the human eye. But then, it wasn't the human eye, was it?

Kane remembered how he had come to be here, how he was interpreting the wealth of data that was cast toward him in the many levels of the astral world, trying to make sense of this incredible multiangled war through the dimensions of string theory.

Kane turned away, shaking off the unsettling feeling that he was being drawn in by the colors of the architecture. Everything here was different, multifaceted in such a way that new angles existed that Kane had never seen before, new twists in the cosmic spectrum.

The ex-Mag stepped out of their path as the horrified crowd hurried past, staggering against one of the rainbow-colored walls. It had begun as a vision of a ville, but the whole structure was changing, warping in on itself as Kane looked, each building becoming impossibly detailed, detail within the detail, worlds within worlds. The wall beside him seemed to be changing even as he looked at it, swirling in a miasma of rushing colors, its shapes, its very density altering over and over like a flick book of mismatched imagery.

Kane blinked forcefully, trying to hold on to his sense of perspective. "You were a Magistrate, damn it," he told himself. Magistrates only dealt in absolutes.

Sound was rushing past his ears, a hush-hushing sound like breakers on a beach, the coughing of wind through the mountains. Kane tried to steady himself against that wall as the great shadows of gods moved through space above him, shock waves reverberating through the landscape with each collision.

It was all too much, all too big, Kane realized. He was losing himself to the enormity of the god war, losing his sense of being as he strode in a landscape that man was never meant to see. As he looked at his hands, Kane saw them expand once more, saw his fingers bloom with ghost images, widening and lengthening until they seemed to claw into yet another dimension, bending into an angle that he could not yet perceive.

"Keep it together," Kane whispered to himself. "Just for a minute. Just till it's over."

Above Kane, the towering shadow that was Enlil tossed another lightning bolt at his impossible foe, a hurricane fighting a mountain. The space that was Ullikummis staggered, and the skies seemed to shift with him.

Ullikummis spoke then, and his voice boomed across the skies like a thunderclap. "You made me your Godkiller, Father," he called, "and now I come to execute the one pretender god who knows only violence and hate. Now I come to kill-execute-assassinate you-father-Enlil-Overlord-living shape."

Kane turned away, bringing his hands up to his head, cursing the way his brain throbbed against the casing of his skull. He was hearing the words—some words—but they were many words now, breaking into streams of alternatives like a catalog of synonyms.

IN THE STOREROOM in Agartha, Balam watched wide-eyed as another burst of static electricity emanated from the semisentient chair where Kane squirmed, shooting across the cube-shaped room in a fearsome white streak. Kane shook violently in the chair as the electricity struck against the wall of the massive cube container, dissipating in a circular red glare that fizzled and faded in a matter of seconds.

Balam stared at the wall where the miniature lightning strike had hit. It was getting dangerous in here, and Kane was right in the middle of it.

Balam turned back to his ally. Kane's hair clung to his scalp, thick with sweat, and his body trembled in place, shaking violently back and forth as he was held in the grip of the navigator's chair. Balam blanched as new probes lashed out from the back and arms of the semisentient chair, holding the sitter tighter in place.

In his mind, Balam could see what Kane was seeing, viewing it through their mutual bond in the same way that one may recall a memory when one related an incident in conversation. Kane was struggling with his new environment, Balam saw, the surroundings and even his own sense of self breaking apart as the warring gods battled a mere hairbreadth away from him.

"What is going on?" Kane cried out from the chair, tears streaming down his face past the entwined creepers of the chair itself.

Balam stepped closer to his ally, watching as electricity raced across Kane's body in cruel, jagged arcs here in the physical world even as Kane's body seemed to get discorporated on another plane.

"Comprehension is a fragile thing," Balam soothed, his voice low. "You need to focus, remember who you are and try to make sense of that which is around you but is not you."

Kane shook in place, another burst of energy caroming across the room in a fiery line.

WITHIN THE OTHER PLACE, Kane heard Balam's voice as he slunk against the multicolored tesseract wall, his breathing shallow and fast. Balam's words seemed so close yet so distant, a twin feed of conflicting information, similar to how one tried to incorporate the sounds of the real world within a dream, the mind trying hard to make both things adjust to fit one narrative. Even so, Balam's voice did something. Its familiarity served as an anchor, bringing Kane back to himself in a rush of color and broken scents. For a moment, Kane stood there as the wall behind him continued to alter and stared at his hands, which seemed complete once more, their lost integrity forgotten. He was himself again; he was Kane.

He stared into the skies above, their burgundy color the same shade as spilled blood, bursting across the heavens in a vicious sprawl. The godlike figures smashed against each other like two forces of nature, elements vying for supremacy.

Kane narrowed his eyes as he watched the two mighty combatants slamming against each other high above his head, galactic forms made of flesh and bone. "Come on," he urged himself, channeling all of his will-power. "Either step up or back down." It was the kind of advice drummed into him from the time he was just a boy training to follow in his father's footsteps.

Kane felt his consciousness expanding, felt the new levels of complexity that had taken the place of his old form. With a determined cry, he began to run across the multicolored street, his feet slamming harder and harder against the stones, the shock waves emanating behind him in ever-widening concentric circles. He was in the gods' arena now, and it was time to show what sort of a man he really was.

"Grant, where are you?" Kane asked as he sprinted toward his enemies.

Grant's voice came back after a moment, sounding breathless. "On our way now," he said. "Just trying to find a safe…path."

"You sound like you've got problems," Kane said as he ran, faster and faster across the ever-changing street of souls.

"Nah, nah, nah—nothing we can't handle," Grant assured him. "You give us a few minutes, and we'll be all over your problem like stink on a monkey."

"I'm trusting you," Kane told him as he threw himself at the foot of the gods, using his body like a cannonball to strike at the ankle of Enlil's cosmic form.

GRANT HEARD none of this over the Commtact. All he got was that Kane needed him, and the determination in his voice was unmistakable. The ebony-skinned ex-Mag turned back to Rosalia as the two of them fought off a group of five Annunaki warriors in a wide, four-sided chamber whose walls narrowed to a point at the far end.

"Can we speed this up?" Grant asked.

Rosalia batted away an attacking Annunaki with her black-bladed sword, using a triple strike that turned his attack on himself before driving the point of the blade through his chest. The Annunaki yelped in pain, black blood rushing from his open mouth and amassing along the blade's length as Rosalia drew the sword clear once more.

"I'd love to," she told Grant, "but you care to tell me how? We're outnumbered here and outmatched."

Grant launched a burst of fire from his Sin Eater in a seemingly casual flick of his wrist, peppering another of the Annunaki warriors with shots from groin to sternum. "We're not outmatched," he shouted over the noise, "never that."

Before Grant, the Annunaki who had taken the clutch of bullets stumbled back, clawed hands scratching at the wounds in his chest. The bullets were having some effect, but it wasn't enough to fell a single one of these monstrosities.

Beside the ex-Mag, Rosalia drew her sword back, her chest rising and falling with the exertion of battle. "Whatever," she spit, "we're getting worn down by numbers here."

"You're right," Grant agreed angrily as the Annunaki

regrouped and stalked toward the two of them. As they did so, Grant made a decision. "Stay behind me," he told Rosalia. "We're going to do this real quick."

"Do what—?" Rosalia began, but already Grant was running, building up speed as he charged at the nearest of his foes, the one still recovering from Rosalia's stab with the black *katana*.

Rosalia watched in astonishment as Grant slammed shoulder-first into the Annunaki, batting against the creature with such force that it was knocked off its feet. Grant's pace never slowed. He swiftly stepped over the falling creature and continued down the wide walkway that cut through the chamber, fists pumping. The next Annunaki was still plucking at the weeping wounds on his chest where Grant had shot him. Grant's fist shot out with the force of a juggernaut, slugging the reptilian monster across his jaw with a great crack of bone. The creature turned to react, but Grant hadn't even slowed; he just carried on along the marked walkway toward the group of three who waited by an iris door.

Rosalia hurried in his wake, astounded at the sheer brutality of Grant's attack. They had been caught up in combat almost continuously for a twelve-hour period and yet, somehow, Grant had found his second wind. He was as strong now as he had been when they had first landed in the dragon city, back when laser lights had painted the night skies in searing flashes of red.

Skirting past the first of their fallen foes, Rosalia lashed out with her blade as the second struggled to recover from Grant's jackhammer blow. The alien creature cried out, grasping for her blade with one clawed hand and gripping it tightly.

Rosalia pivoted, twirling on the spot as she pulled her blade from the Annunaki's grip. The blade came free in a spurt of blood, the tips of three fingers dropping free from the Annunaki's damaged hand.

They're getting weaker, Rosalia realized. Somehow, even as Grant had found his second wind, their Annunaki challengers were visibly weakening.

Before Rosalia could impart her observation to Grant, the Cerberus man charged into the remaining Annunaki at the doorway, his arms spread wide to encompass all of them as he threw himself toward the deck. The Annunaki crashed back like bowling pins, crumbling in one great mass as Grant landed on top of them. Then his Sin Eater was back in his hand, jumping as it spit bullets in their faces in a continuous stream that echoed from the hard walls of the two-story chamber.

Rosalia sprinted across the room, joining Grant as he leaped free of the tangled bodies. The Annunaki were struggling to right themselves, ooze spurting down their beautiful, flawless bodies.

"Keep going, Magistrate," Rosalia urged. *"¡Vámonos!"*

Grant didn't need telling twice. He hefted his mighty frame to the iris door, peppering its controls with 9 mm bullets as he ran toward it. In a flash, the controls burst into electric flame and the iris opened, the petals spinning away in a swirl.

Grant leaped through the doorway, Rosalia following just a second behind him.

They were in an elevator now, its floor long and as thin as a plank, a vast drop into the guts of *Tiamat* visible to either side. Like many of the spaceship's faculties, the elevator doors worked like an air lock, a twin set of doors backing one to the other. Grant slapped his palm against the control board, closing the doors and commanding the elevator to ascend.

"You look like you've done this before," Rosalia said.

Grant nodded, though he was paying attention to reloading his Sin Eater while they were safely in transit. "'Cause I've been here before," he explained. "*Tiamat*'s different now, but not that different."

Rosalia looked at Grant as he reloaded his weapon, and she could see that he was breathing heavily. He was covered in gunk, the blood and ooze of the Annunaki marring his black Kevlar coat and shadow suit.

"They're getting weaker," Rosalia told her partner. "You notice?"

Grant smiled, shaking his head. "Not really, but I'll take your word for it," he said as he pushed a new magazine home into the Sin Eater's cartridge slot.

Then the elevator doors opened and Grant and Rosalia found themselves on a higher level, the corridor illuminated in greens and blues from lights running along the floor. Just for a moment, the lighting made Rosalia think of the ocean. And then she spotted the familiar reptilian figures hurrying toward them from the far end of the corridor.

"Here we go again," Grant declared, raising the Sin Eater in a two-handed grip.

ELSEWHERE, IF THAT TERM had any meaning in such circumstances, Kane found himself fighting on the multiplanes of fractal space. At first, it had seemed that the Annunaki paid no attention to him, battling as they were at such an intensity that it reverberated across the tesseract angles of the universe. But as the conflict continued, Kane realized that this was not a battle that would be settled by physical strength—how could it? It was occurring at a level far removed from anything that could be described as physical. No, here was a battle that was defined by willpower, one resolve challenging another.

Kane drew on his own great reserves as Lakesh fed him information via Commtact about the nature of string theory. Kane tried to understand what he was being told, but all he really knew was that—no matter how strange things became—he needed to keep his own grip on sanity. It was his will, his self-image, that fought this battle against so-called gods, man against superior beings.

And as he drew more from his own self-determination, Kane seemed to grow, bringing himself if not to the size of the gods then at least to something that rivaled David facing two great Goliaths.

The Annunaki fought through the angles, appearing and disappearing in ways that Kane could barely follow let alone comprehend, their shadow shapes interweaving with each other as they strove for supremacy, pouring through Kane like water through a sieve.

Kane, for all his strength of will, looked to the familiar to fight his corner. Astride the heavens, fighting atop the ever-changing angles of the city hidden in the cosmic warp, Kane flinched his wrist tendons and called forth his Sin Eater, the handgun unfolding as it slapped into the palm of his hand. The pistol looked different now, no longer made from brutal lines of metal, but bulging and curved, a nipplelike minaret at its end. Kane had the disconcerting feeling he was firing with a temple rather than a gun, and the ammunition was belief—man's belief in his ability to chart his own destiny.

Kane watched as the blaster kicked, a trail of pure whiteness lancing across the heavens to strike the swirling clouds that formed Enlil. The blast hit, shooting through the sky like spilled paint, erupting against the chest of the great Annunaki overlord, and Kane cheered as he saw Enlil stagger and fall under that punishing assault. In that moment, a god fell from the sky, crashing through the universe due to the determination of one man.

Kane was winning. Despite the unbelievable odds, he was winning.

Behind Kane, Ullikummis—whose form here seemed to be a hundred forms with a thousand names—struck a mighty punch, knocking Kane to the ground.

And not just to the ground—through it.

Kane cried out as he fell through another layer of the universe, rocketing through the unfamiliar angles of string space.

Chapter 16

It was like falling. His stomach dropped away from him and he felt that horrible sense of giddiness, the same feeling one got from flying within a dream. All around him, the ten thousand colors of god rushed past as if he were falling through a tunnel or a great winding tube. The colors flickered by faster, giving Kane the sensation that his speed was increasing.

Kane turned his head, trying to look up, but all he saw was the same thing, a great tunnel of color shooting toward him, as if he were falling into it, as if no matter which way he turned he was still falling. The angles were different here, Lakesh had told him; there were more angles than Kane had ever comprehended.

"The conceit of string theory, which has been further developed with superstring theory," Lakesh had said, "holds that the component parts of reality are vast strings that oscillate so as to achieve a charge. That is the charge that we associate with neutrons, electrons and so on."

"Cut the twenty-credit words," Kane had replied as he stared at the towering forms of the Annunaki in superspace, "and just give me the summary."

"Yes, yes, of course," Lakesh had replied over the Commtact with evident embarrassment. "I have been surrounded by physicists and quantum mechanics for too long.

"Superstrings exist in our world, and thus we see them. But they also exist in further dimensions. The very simplified version is that the string loops out behind the facade that we perceive. Each string has a different harmonic, and there had been much debate in the scientific community in the latter years of the twentieth century as to just how many aspects these strings have. Which is to say, how many dimensions they cross."

"By dimensions," Kane asked, "what are we talking? Alternate earths and nutty timelines?"

"No, Kane," Lakesh said, barely concealing the laughter in his voice. "Length and breadth and depth are dimensions, the dimensions that we are familiar with in our world. Now you must imagine others. What your brain is seeing there—wherever there is—are the additional dimensions, ones we have no real means of comprehending."

"How many dimensions are we talking about here, Lakesh?" Kane asked.

"Well, that's a good question. Before the nukecaust occurred, there were a number of competing theories as to just how many dimensions were involved in any string theory," Lakesh explained. "There were even suggestions in the 1990s that several of the popular superstring theories in fact interconnected, that they were each calculating just one aspect of the equation and that all could be joined to create a greater understanding—"

"How many?" Kane butted in impatiently.

"Ten is the base level that all superstring theory works from. Any less than that and the hypothesis would not function," Lakesh explained. "But there have been numerous other theories that contest anywhere upward of twenty facets—or dimensions—to the strings."

"So you don't know for sure?" Kane queried.

"Kane, you must try to understand that this is the stuff of high-end theoretical physics. Superstring is one of those rarefied beasts—a theory of everything."

"And I'm fighting in the middle of it," Kane grumbled. "Good to know."

Now Kane gritted his teeth as he continued to fall in whatever direction it was he was falling, discovering new angles as he was drawn deeper and deeper into the war of the Annunaki.

What it took was focus, he knew. If he could keep his sense of self, then the rest would follow, making reason from the chaos that he was staring into.

With a steadying breath, Kane closed his eyes and let the sensation of falling drift away, like spume on the ocean. He needed to get back to the battle, and to do that he needed to have a cast-iron sense of who he was fighting.

"Kane," he muttered. "Kane."

He could always leave them alone, let these two alien conquerors battle it out. If he did, there was a chance that one or other of them would die, but to do so would be handing the victor the metaphorical keys to Earth, with all those indoctrinated peoples just waiting to bow down before an alien master. No, Kane's place was here, rushing across the angles, bringing his own brand of Magistrate justice to two pretender gods who thought they were better than humankind.

Kane opened his eyes, and he saw the world resolve around him, dark and foreboding. Everything was black now, the line of the horizon a multicolored slit in the far distance, a lone tree waiting there. Enlil and Ullikummis were gone, and Kane needed to find them.

He turned, searching the landscape with a frantic gaze. It was black, everything was black, as if all the color had been torn away. And there was nothing, just that distant horizon line waiting eerily in a thin band of multicolor.

"Grant," Kane shouted, engaging his Commtact, "you want to maybe hurry things up at your end? I can't take both of them on my own." In fact, I can't even see them, he added to himself.

"WE'RE ALMOST THERE," Grant stated as he assessed his current situation. "Hang tight just a little longer."

Aboard the spaceship *Tiamat,* he and Rosalia were hurrying along a corridor that had only a wall on one side. The other side ended in a sheer drop that overlooked a containment bay, eerily half-grown personnel ships waiting there like discarded abortions. The corridor itself was constructed of some kind of bone that had similar qualities to metal plate, and it was too narrow to fit three people abreast.

Up ahead, Grant spotted two more of the Annunaki warriors, their scales rippling in red and green as they hurried down the corridor to meet the intruders.

Grant raised the Sin Eater as he ran to them, swinging it in an abbreviated arc and snapping off a burst of fire at the enemy. Rosalia jogged several paces behind him, her dark ponytail bobbing up and down as she kept up with the long strides of the ex-Magistrate.

Nine millimetre slugs whizzed down the corridor, tearing chunks of flesh out of the red-scaled Annunaki before Grant reached him. Rosalia had been right, Grant realized; they were deteriorating. There could be no question of it now. An hour earlier, the Annunaki would have shrugged off his bullets with relative ease, but now the bullets were capable of cutting into their flesh in great swathes, hacking chunks from their armored skin.

As the two groups of antagonists met, Rosalia kicked out and to the side, her heel rebounding from low on the wall, sending her vaulting up into the air. At the same time as she leaped, Rosalia flicked her *katana* through a wide circle, causing it to meet with the green-skinned Annunaki as she sailed over his head. The Annunaki hissed in pain as the sword caught his shoulder, helplessly turning as the sword pulled him three feet across the narrow corridor.

Rosalia landed in a graceful two point at the very edge of the walkway, her left foot meeting the floor just before her right. The green skin was less lucky. Staggering back under the sword strike under one foot, he went over the edge of the deck. Rosalia gritted her teeth in a bitter smile as the Annunaki dropped over the side, screaming as he fell into the docking bay with its half-formed spaceships.

Grant, meanwhile, was trading blows with the red Annunaki, a female with a single vertical spine jutting from her scalp like a radio antenna. Grant used his weight to best advantage, slamming into the female as her body bled where his shots had struck just moments before. The Annunaki shrieked, a horrible sound in the stillness of the corridor, backing up under the force of Grant's blow until she fell against the wall.

Grant brought the Sin Eater up once more, depressing the trigger and blasting a stream of bullets into the alien's shrieking face. Chunks of her face and skull spattered the wall behind as Grant blew her brains out.

Rosalia's eyes met with Grant as he reloaded his blaster. "Fun being on the rush-rush, huh?" she said.

And then they were off again, hurrying through the unguarded doorway at the far end of the corridor and passing into a small room that contained Enlil's monitoring equipment.

KANE WALKED across that dead landscape for a long time, wondering just what it was he was really looking at. It was almost entirely black before his eyes, and yet he got a definite sense of distance, the unwavering line of the horizon a multicolored band across his field of vision. Whatever the angles were, he was struggling to find Ullikummis or Enlil here.

After a while, Kane spotted something waiting on the horizon to his left, and he trudged toward it, one foot after the other. As he approached, he saw that the thing in question was the tree he had seen from high above, but it was unlike any tree he had ever seen before. The tree was drawn in thin lines, and each one contained the colors of the spectrum. It was as if the tree's image had been carved on the eerie tableau of midnight black.

The tree featured a narrow trunk that reached straight into the air, and its branches stood at regular intervals along its side, the circles of its blossoms running up its sides and middle, with one more blossom poised at the apex of the trunk itself. The blossoms were spherical and, like the tree and the line of the distant horizon, each was multicolored, the colors shimmering and changing in a random pattern that seemed soothing.

Kane looked at it for a long while, wondering what to make of it. "Balam, can you see this?" he asked.

Disembodied, Balam's voice came from very close.

"I see what you see, Kane," he confirmed. "However, I admit to being as mystified as you are."

Kane stared at the tree, walking slowly around it, the sounds of distant wind charging across the otherwise empty plane. There was nothing significant that he could see. The tree appeared the same from every angle, those ten clusters of blossoms arranged up and down its length.

Exasperated, Kane glanced up at the sky, searching for a hint of where the dueling Annunaki were. They had to be here somewhere, it stood to reason—after all, he had been drawn into this dimension by their touch. But there was nothing in the sky, just that simple black sheet identically reflecting the ground.

"Lakesh," Kane said, "I need your input here. I'm lost."

"What can you see?" Lakesh asked, his voice coming loud and clear through the Commtact.

"I'm in a characterless environment," Kane summarized, "and the only thing here is a tree."

"Can you describe it?"

Kane did, and he explained how everything else was simply black.

"I admit that—if you'll forgive a little irony—I am stumped, my friend," Lakesh said. "Many are the cultures that believe in a tree of life, but that is simply philosophy. Despite your spiritual quest, I can see no relation to what you are seeing there now."

"But I'm not seeing it, am I?" Kane reminded him. "I'm seeing an interpretation of your string theory, right?"

"Well, now, Kane," Lakesh sputtered, "it's *not* my theory. Superstrings were first—"

"Tree," Kane interrupted, reminding Lakesh to concentrate on the issue at hand. "What do I do?"

"I don't know," Lakesh admitted. "Climb it?"

"Sure, why not," Kane groused and he grabbed hold of the lowest branch and began to pull himself up. "Nothing else to do 'round here."

GRANT AND ROSALIA PACED warily through the monitoring room. The room had no source of light other than the strange displays themselves, which hung like mist in the air above the crescent-shaped databank.

Grant slowed, his eyes scanning each of the displays, their soft edges disappearing into nothingness. Several showed a feed from outside the ship's hull, where the human army loyal to Ullikummis was fighting for survival against the reborn Annunaki. There, as aboard the ship, the Annunaki seemed to be struggling, their bodies failing them as the hideous combat continued amid streets created by the channels of bone.

Elsewhere among the feeds, Grant recognized the docking bay where he and Rosalia had entered, and next to that display he saw a figure he knew. It was Brigid Baptiste, her vibrant red hair unmistakable. She seemed to be standing in a midsize chamber with a stone item at its center. The stone thing was poised like an upright peanut, standing a little shorter than she was.

"There's Brigid," Grant said, pointing her out on the displays.

"What's that she's standing by?" Rosalia asked, bending to get a better look.

"Not sure," Grant ruminated. "Looks kinda like an egg."

Rosalia searched the monitoring room, looking for the door. There were two: one in the far wall, hidden behind a monitoring bank, the other a hatch set in the floor. "This way, I think," she said, indicating the doorway in the wall.

"In a minute," Grant said as his brown eyes scanned the feeds one last time, searching for anything that may help them, searching for Kane. One feed showed the waterlogged chamber, while another showed the engine room with its strange, hooded engineers scurrying about like rats. Then, after a moment Grant spotted Enlil on one of the mistlike windows, his body showing several new wounds.

"Enlil's still alive, I see," Grant grumbled.

He watched for a moment longer as Ullikummis appeared in frame, driving one of his heavy rock fists into the Annunaki overlord's face and sending him sprawling to the floor. A stream of symbols flashed across the shimmering display, their precise meaning lost on Grant though they reminded him of the biolank data that the transponder beacons broadcast for Cerberus personnel. Now, if he could only make sense of those displays, he could perhaps figure out who was winning. Grant's brow furrowed as he stared at the raindroplike displays, watching their colors flash and change. Then after a moment he shook his head in defeat.

"Screw it," Grant muttered, striding across the control room to join Rosalia at the door.

Seconds later, the two of them were through the door and into another narrow corridor, this one with bulging walls like a flattened hexagon.

OUTSIDE *TIAMAT*'s hull, the rift at the edge of the city continued to disgorge more of the faithful human warriors. Already massively outnumbered, the Annunaki were dwindling now, frankly overwhelmed by the continued push of humans who had been indoctrinated into the cult of stone.

But something else was happening, too. Once powerful, the Annunaki bodies were failing, their near invincibility showing signs of weakness with each successive strike.

Sela Sinclair was rushing at one of the lizardlike creatures in a street close to *Tiamat*'s starboard side. The Annunaki was a silver-fleshed female, with swollen breasts and flaring hips, and she fought with a sickle blade that cut the air with an angry whine. Sela watched as the Annunaki hacked another hooded human to pieces, chopping his body apart in a series of swift, brutal slashes.

Sela ran, blasting a shot from her Colt Mark IV at the silver Annunaki as she turned. The bullet struck the Annunaki in the collarbone, cutting a bloody gash through her shoulder. The Annunaki warrior reared back, reaching up for the fresh wound with her free hand.

Sela squeezed her trigger again, whipping another bullet at the Annunaki female. The Annunaki shrieked as the bullet struck, her shoulder erupting in a shower of blood and ruined muscle.

The Annunaki warrior dragged herself forward, lunging with the sickle to hack at Sela. Sela leaped back, dancing out of reach of that hideous blade as it cut through the air, her pistol blasting yet again. The shot zipped through the narrow distance between them, burying itself in the Annunaki's cheek even as a second slug drilled into her forehead. Sela watched in triumph as the Annunaki dropped the sickle from a grip gone suddenly limp, bumbling backward toward a bone wall.

Something terrible was happening to the Annunaki, Sela realized. Their bodies had been crafted from human DNA, leapfrogging the hybrid stage as Overlord Enlil tried to repopulate the Earth with his brethren. But those bodies had been possessed not by the downloaded minds of the Annunaki but by the living memories of their slave caste, the Igigi. The perverted sum of the parts was something poisonous, creating something deadly to itself.

Sela fired again, her teeth gritted in deadly determination, and the Annunaki warrior went down, slumping to the ground in a bloody heap.

We can win, Sela realized. The humans could win.

IN THE LEAKING ROOMS and corridors of *Tiamat* herself, the clutch of remaining Annunaki were beginning to fail, their bodies rejecting the Igigi memories and simply giving up. Grant and Rosalia ran down the hexagonal corridor, watching in surprise as yet another Annunaki—the third they had seen—crashed to the deck, his eyes going pale as he lost the will to carry on. A genetic time bomb had finally reached detonation, sapping the will from their enemies.

"This suddenly got a lot easier," Grant said, but he couldn't hide the bitterness in his voice.

Rosalia laughed, a cruel, braying sound that echoed down the tunnellike expanse. "Told you so. Typical man—you never listen. Got to see everything with your own eyes."

Behind them, the Annunaki was shaking violently as the life seemed to leak out of him, his body a mess of quivering armored flesh.

Grant and Rosalia pushed their way along the corridor toward the next room, hurrying past the squirming bodies of the dying Annunaki, their clawed hands clenched and twitching, legs bent in pain. Whatever was going through them was causing their bodies to spasm, ripping into them like a stun gun. At the end of the corridor lay a doorway, its hexagonal shape lit in a rich red the exact shade of spilled blood. Lightning blasts came from beyond that open doorway, illuminating the walls of the corridor in staccato bursts of whiteness.

"Come on," Grant said as he hurried toward the open door with Rosalia dogging his heels, the bodies of the felled Annunaki twitching in pain all around them.

Rosalia nodded once, checking that her portable comm device was in place over her right ear.

As they approached the doorway, the two Cerberus teammates heard the distinct sounds of fierce combat over the crackling lightning, grunts and blows as whoever was beyond continued their merry dance of death. Grant checked his Sin Eater with a glance, ensuring it had enough ammunition for whatever he and Rosalia were about to encounter.

Passing through the doorway, the Cerberus warriors stepped into a vast, high-ceilinged chamber laid out in a hexagonal shape, towering arches of bone knotting together high above them. In the middle of the room, two Annunaki masters fought for supremacy, Ullikummis driving one of his powerful fists into Enlil's chest as dark smoke billowed from his face and torso.

Grant took in the room with a quick glance, recognizing the thick rock spikes that lined one wall as the same ones that had smashed through the water room; seeing the way the arches had been bent and cracked where they had been struck. Enlil and Ullikummis were waging a bitter dispute in the center of the room, but there was one thing missing, Grant noted: Kane.

Chapter 17

"Kane, we're here," Grant shouted into his Commtact, striving to hear himself over the sounds of combat. "Where are you?"

Kane's voice came back over the Commtact with an amused edge to it. "Hard to explain," he said, "but trust me I'm right with you. Baptiste is in the next room, prepping a chrysalis-type egg. I need you to get her out of there and stop that from happening."

"Saw that over the displays," Grant replied. Then he scanned the chamber again before he spotted the doorway he would need to access. It was now behind the barricade of rock shards. "Got a wall in the way, though," he explained.

"I'm on it," Rosalia acknowledged, brushing her dark hair from her face.

Grant had no idea what she had planned, but he knew better than to ask for details right now. He watched as Rosalia's lithe figure stepped closer to the fray, stalking around the combatants like a cat as she searched for an opening.

"What about the clash of the titans here?" Grant asked, watching incredulously as the two mighty figures struck each other with savage, bone-jarring blows. Even as he spoke, Enlil snatched something from the deck and seemed to throw chain lightning from his hands, striking his son across his already smoldering rock face.

"We need to split them up," Kane said. "You have any ideas?"

"Hell no," Grant admitted. "But we'll work something."

As he spoke, Rosalia spotted a gap in the fighting. Ullikummis had dropped back under the lightning assault and crashed into one of the towering pillars that held the ceiling arches aloft. She charged through the room toward the spiked rock wall.

Grant watched her run and saw Enlil's head dart to follow her, his clawed hands lashing out to grab her. Grant didn't hesitate; the Sin Eater was already bucking in his hand, sending a dozen 9 mm bullets at his foe. The bullets struck a line along Enlil's outstretched arm, throwing off his aim as the serpent lightning lashed out toward Rosalia. With a snakelike hiss, Enlil spun, fixing his wicked gaze on Grant like a rattlesnake spying its prey.

Grant inclined his head in acknowledgment. "Long time no see," he said.

"Apekin," Enlil spit venomously. "You shall die this day."

"My schedule's full already," Grant snapped as he fired off another burst of bullets from the Sin Eater at the charging Enlil, giving Rosalia ample time to reach her destination unmolested.

Then Grant was rearing back as Enlil kicked out with his clawed foot, the sharp talons sweeping through the air and missing Grant's face by just a quarter inch.

DUCKING BENEATH another burst of electric flame, Rosalia sprinted across the room toward the jagged spears of rock, skidding to a halt before them. Shaped like stalactites, each structure was as thick as a man's torso and placed in such a way that left just an inch or two gap between each. Effectively, the door to the chamber was blocked.

Rosalia had seen this before, when Ullikummis had constructed Life Camp Zero over the Cerberus redoubt, reshaping the innards with growths of rock. Each one could be moved by Ullikummis's mental command, she knew, but there was another way. Those loyal to the rock giant were implanted with a living stone that operated like a key, sending a pulse to the hidden doors on the user's command. Months earlier in the fishing village called Hope, Rosalia had had one of these stone keys implanted beneath her flesh, but she had teased it away from final bonding again and again by use of a sewing needle. Now she glanced down at her left wrist, searching for the almost insignificant ridge that showed there under the brightest of lights.

With a smile on her lips, Rosalia swept her wrist across the stone bars that masked the chamber doors, willing them apart. For a long moment nothing happened, and Rosalia peered back over her shoulder, scanning the hexagonal room. Grant was struggling in hand-to-hand combat with Enlil, lightning firing all about them and Grant's Sin Eater spitting bullets as he shoved the lizardlike Annunaki away. Ten feet from them, Ullikummis struggled on the floor, inky smoke curling up from the wound on his inhuman face. He spotted her in a second, his eyes glowing fiercely through the smoke.

"Come on, you son of a bitch," Rosalia spit. "You want a fucking dance-off? Then show me your moves."

Ullikummis had drawn himself to a crouching position, poised like a sprinter on the blocks. Contemptuously, Rosalia turned back to the barred door, sweeping her wrist across it again and willing it to part. Without warning, her wrist stone found the sensor and the jagged stone shards began to bend outward, shunting out of her way until a two-foot-wide gap appeared in their center.

As Ullikummis began his charge at her, Rosalia worked the lock on the main doors with her hand, commanding *Tiamat* to open them. Ullikummis's tread was as loud as an earthquake as his stumpy feet pounded against the decking, hurrying across the room to where the dark-haired mercenary stood.

Seeing this, Grant ducked in place as Enlil aimed the serpent lightning at his face, arching his back as the lethal cord cleaved the air, crackling with white-hot energy.

Across the room, the newly revealed doors opened and Rosalia dashed through them, slapping her hand against the lock as she did so, commanding the doors to close. Behind her, Ullikummis was just three feet from the ridged bars of stone, reaching for her with his long arms, determined to protect his mother in her chrysalis state. As Ullikummis reached forward, the snake of lightning tickled across his back and shoulder blades, slamming him forward and down with the power of a thunderclap.

ROSALIA CLOSED HER EYES with relief as the doors shut behind her, drawing a steadying breath. Her heart was pounding in her chest, beating against her ribs like a metronome. "Shit, that was close."

Her eyes snapped back open in an instant as she became aware of the sound of boot heels striking against the metallic decking before her. The red-haired woman was running at her, drawing the chunky handgun from its low-slung hip holster, her face a portrait of rage.

The woman was Brigid Baptiste, Rosalia recognized, dressed now in black leather with a long, heavy cloak of furs hanging from her shoulders. They had met many months earlier out in the fishing village of Hope, and more recently Rosalia had been present when Brigid had attempted to kill Kane in a cavern beneath the rebuilt city of Luilekkerville.

Without conscious thought, Rosalia dived aside, launching herself across the room even as the TP-9 in Brigid's hand kicked, blurting a burst of 9 mm titanium-shelled bullets at the space where the dark-haired mercenary had stood. The bullets slapped against the wall and door like cruel rain, missing Rosalia by inches. The Latina hurried on, tracing the curving wall of the ante-nursery chamber, her long strides eating up the space even as Brigid tried to get a bead on her.

Lit in a tranquil violet, an indentation dominated the room, a pool full of swilling liquid the iridescent color of pearl. The pool reminded Rosalia of the Chalice of Rebirth she had seen beneath Luilekkerville, where the young-again-hag known as Maria Halloween had tried to tap the power source of the *anam-chara*. The pool burbled contentedly to itself, and in its center Rosalia saw a great ovoid shape carved from dark stone. Shorter than a man, the stone ovoid looked like an egg.

Tasked to defend the cocoon, Brigid tracked the retreating mercenary, blasting shot after shot at her from the TP-9 pistol. In her first life, when she had been known as Brigid Baptiste, she had been trained in the arts of combat, and using a pistol remained second nature to her. As Brigid Haight she had not been made to forget that life, after all, merely to leave its trappings behind her, to be reborn as Ullikummis's hand in darkness.

Rosalia, too, was trained in the arts of war. Younger than Brigid, she had been schooled in a nunnery close to the border where North America met its southern neighbor. An accomplished sharpshooter and gifted with a longbow, Rosalia preferred an edged blade. Long or short, she felt most satisfied by the silent invasion of a knife to an enemy's gut, or the decapitation of an enemy by sword strike.

Right now, however, as she hurried past the pool, Rosalia reached for the Ruger she carried, sprinting across the chamber as Brigid's bullets followed her. The furious sound of the redhead's blaster was loud in the enclosed space, while the room itself was small, with curving struts running along the walls like spinal columns, each one as thick as a man's torso and twisted in a knot. Rosalia dashed behind these, running around the room as Brigid tried to shoot her, using the weird columns for cover.

After a moment, Rosalia stopped, slapping her back against one of the columns as Brigid continued blasting where she thought the woman would next appear. Bullets drilled through the air, smashing at the walls past where Rosalia had halted, and the mercenary smiled. Checking the magazine of her Ruger, Rosalia whipped out from behind the column and fired at Brigid. Her gun spit three quick shots at the redhead, cutting past the strange stone egg that dominated the room's center.

Brigid moved with breathtaking speed, hurtling across the room as that triple burst of bullets zipped past her, charging along the circular edge of the nutrient pool.

Rosalia had the redhead in her sights, confident that it would be the matter of a single heartbeat to execute her with a well-placed bullet. But she hesitated, making a split-second decision as Brigid's own bullets slapped the walls all about her. The woman was Kane's best friend, Rosalia knew, his *anam-chara*. Kane had spent months searching for her, and no matter how Brigid was acting now, Kane would never forgive Rosalia if she killed her. In the blink of an eye, Rosalia shifted her aim, squeezing the Ruger's trigger and sending a bullet toward Brigid's legs instead.

At the same moment, Brigid leaped, springing from the deck as she lunged over the edge of the pit. Rosalia's bullet whipped past her, kicking up sparks as it caught the edge of the pool. Then Rosalia ducked back behind the spinelike strut she was using for cover as Brigid's TP-9 spit again, sending a burst of bullets in her direction.

Bullets struck the walls in front of Rosalia, gouging splinters of metallike cartilage as they pierced the grown surface of *Tiamat*'s interior. The mercenary paid them no attention, instead glancing down at the Ruger P-85 pistol in her hand. "Dammit," she cursed, knowing Kane and Grant would never forgive her if she killed their wayward partner. "It sucks being a temp."

Then Brigid was beside her, diving between the columns and drawing her own weapon up to shoot Rosalia in the head. The dark-haired woman ducked and turned, feeling the column disintegrate behind her under the barrage of 9 mm fury.

Rosalia backed away, swinging around the pockmarked column and lashing out with a well-placed kick. The blow slammed against Brigid's flank, knocking the redhead off her feet and sending her sprawling into the wall, her pistol still belching titanium-tipped tragedy.

Brigid growled as she slammed into the wall, recovering instantaneously and whipping her gun back up into ready position. Just a few feet away, Rosalia dropped her shoulders, reaching out with her empty left hand in a blur of speed. Brigid's blaster snapped off another burst of fire at her lithe opponent as Rosalia's hand grabbed her below the wrist, forcing Brigid's aim to go wide and sending a half-dozen bullets into the walls.

"I'm really not supposed to kill you, *hermanita,*" Rosalia said as her dark eyes met with Brigid's, "but you sure as shit are going to have to stop shooting at me if you expect me to observe that proviso."

Brigid snarled, her lips pulling back from her gritted teeth. "Get your hand off me, bitch," she barked, flipping her arm.

Before Rosalia knew what was happening, Brigid's flip caused her to lose her grip, sending her backward in a stumble. She crashed down against the decking, her right arm and shoulder sinking into the nutrient bath with a splash of viscous gunk. Beneath the surface, Rosalia felt the Ruger slip from her hand, drifting slowly down to the bottom of the pool in a languid swish.

Brigid was on her right away, leaping onto the mercenary's back and slamming her chest down against the deck with unrelenting force. Rosalia's breath burst from her lungs in a rush, exiting her mouth with a shout of agony.

Rosalia struggled to throw Brigid from her as the redhead brought her TP-9 up toward the back of her skull. Still beneath the swishing liquid of the nutrient pool feeding Ninlil's cocoon, Rosalia's hand flipped up, throwing a handful of the gunk up and into Brigid's face.

"Not today, *chica,*" Rosalia growled as Brigid turned away from the liquid, her bullets going wild. Rosalia heard a familiar dull click, and she smiled inwardly as she continued her assault.

Taking advantage of her opponent's temporary confusion, Rosalia twisted her supple body, forcing Brigid from her back. Brigid rolled, combat instincts kicking in automatically to get her out of the path of Rosalia's follow-through attack. Rosalia kicked out, but Brigid had already rolled away, scampering over the deck and pulling herself back to her feet.

Rosalia lifted herself into a crouch, her dark eyes fixed on Brigid's emerald orbs as the latter woman held her in the sights of her TP-9.

Brigid squeezed the trigger, her teeth gritted as she sent a message of titanium-shelled death at her opponent—only to find her blaster out of ammunition, the trigger clicking on empty.

Smiling, Rosalia reached for the sword she had secured through her belt, drawing herself up to her full height as the black blade was revealed. "Now then," she said, "what say you and me cut to the chase?"

GRANT HAD SLAMMED into Ullikummis with such force that it caused both of them to collide with the closing cartilage doors. Grant rolled, bringing himself up into a fighting crouch a quarter turn across the room from where his opponent had landed, even as Enlil lashed out at his son with the serpent lightning. His eyes fixed on Ullikummis, Grant released the spent ammo magazine from his blaster, discarding it on the floor as he reached for a new one in the inside pocket of his long coat.

Already beaten down by his father's blows, Ullikummis lay against the doors for several seconds, gathering his strength to continue the fight. Enlil had nurtured him to be the greatest assassin of the ancient world, a Godkiller. But this battle had taxed him to his limits.

His face smoldering with dark smoke, Ullikummis turned slowly to face Grant. Grant pounded the new magazine home, flinching his wrist tendons to bring the Sin Eater securely back to the palm of his hand. As if mocking him, Ullikummis mirrored the gesture, flicking his own hand forward as Grant depressed the trigger. A flurry of 9 mm bullets shot across the room from the Sin Eater, cutting through the air toward the stone monstrosity while, at the very same instant, a line of sharp rock columns pierced the floor, emerging from Ullikummis's position across the deck and marching toward Grant like a porcupine's spines.

Grant leaped aside, his legs working overtime as he scampered away from the spiny rocks. He didn't notice Enlil step from behind one of the bone arches, reaching out with one swift, bloody hand to block Grant's path, striking the ex-Mag high in the chest. Enlil's movement was eyeblink-swift and Grant struck his arm and flipped, his legs kicking forward as his head careened downward to the deck. He hit with a mighty thud, sprawling, his vision blurring for a long blink.

When Grant looked up he saw both Enlil and Ullikummis stalking toward him.

"Kane, wherever you are you'd better pull something out of your sleeve," he muttered.

HAND OVER HAND, Kane climbed the tree in the middle of the darkness, working faster and faster to reach its topmost branch. The blossoms waited there, great multicolored circles swirling like glass baubles of mist. Still he could not see his foes. Had he lost them?

Kane clambered higher, reaching out for the lone

blossom that waited at the tree's highest point, its sweet scent cloying his senses. As he reached it, his hand pressing against that multicolored ball, Kane felt the worlds shift around him, multidimensional planes renegotiating the way in which they bonded. The sky opened, the color of a hymn, and Kane smiled as a warmth washed over his skin. He knew that warmth, though he had felt it but very rarely in his thirty-odd years—it was the warmth of compassion.

And then the storm began, bloody reds and putrid greens assaulting his eyes, accompanied by the loud crack of thunder.

LYING ON THE FLOOR of the hexagonal chamber in *Tiamat*'s core, Grant saw Enlil and Ullikummis come charging at him, one on either side. They were so different, it was hard to believe they were from the same species. Where Enlil had sleek lines, Ullikummis was hard and brutal, an assault on the eyes.

They were coming to kill him, Grant knew, and there was nothing he could do about it. He tried to make himself move, to roll aside from the attackers, but they were too close and he was backed up in a corner, with nowhere left to run. So instead Grant did the only thing left to him. He whipped the Sin Eater around and depressed the trigger, spraying the room with bullets.

"Eat it, you evil fuckers!"

The room erupted with sparks as bullets struck, pinging off the towering arches and the walls beyond. And Enlil—savage, brutal, sadistic Enlil—reached out not for Grant but for his own son, turning his blow at the last minute so that he dropped to the floor, tripping Ullikummis as he ran at the Cerberus rebel. Grant watched as the two figures slid past him across the decking, the jagged spikes of Ullikummis's right shoulder missing Grant by barely six inches. Grant's bullets danced across Ullikummis's rock frame, carving tiny splinters from his awesome body as he hurtled by.

Grant had been granted a reprieve, albeit one that might only last a couple of seconds. He didn't intend to waste it.

NEARBY, IN THE ante-nursery, Brigid Haight threw the empty TP-9 pistol at Rosalia as the dark-haired swordswoman charged toward her, her feet splashing through the spilled contents of the nutrient pool. Rosalia ducked, and the pistol hurtled past her, crashing against a distant scythelike column. But the movement cost her, and as she straightened her body, Brigid was upon her, kicking out with one long leg.

Rosalia reared back as Brigid's foot came at her, getting her head out of its path and instead taking a glancing blow across her upper chest. Before Rosalia could respond, Brigid followed through her attack by bringing her other leg up in a perfect snap kick to her face. The pointed toe of Brigid's boot clipped Rosalia across her chin, and the dark-haired fighter went sailing backward in a stumble, struggling to retain her footing. Around them, the panel displays of the room went through their birthing sequences, checking and rechecking the consistency of the birth pool in a whir of pulsing green and blue and golden lights.

Brigid was relentless, following one attack with another, granting Rosalia not so much as a second's respite. Rosalia's mind whirred even as she struggled to stay clear of the path of that brutal assault, kicks and punches powering toward her again and again.

Brigid Haight was a formidable fighter, with hand-to-hand combat skills second to none, Rosalia noted. But still there was a flaw in her technique. So overcome with furious purpose, the woman was following an unconscious pattern, striking from different sides but in the same rhythms—one-two-three, two-two-three—like a dancer at a grand ball. The attacks were swift and fierce, but there were pauses between each, momentary and brief, but pauses all the same. Rosalia began to time these in her head, using the blackened sword in her hand to bat the most savage of these attacks away, keeping barely a step in front of her fearsome opponent.

Brigid herself saw only the threat of the intruder, recalling nothing of Rosalia's background nor the outcomes of their previous meetings. All she knew was that the woman was armed and had entered the sacred presence of Ninlil, the great mother, as her egg was fertilized with the genetic download and fed with the nutrients of the birthing pool.

Brigid drove another cross punch at the dark-haired woman's head, angling it just subtly so that it overshot intentionally and struck instead against the woman's shoulder blade. Rosalia grunted at the assault, but already Haight was bringing up her knee in a savage blow to the woman's pelvis, driving it between the woman's legs with such power it forced her dark-haired opponent upward off her feet.

Rosalia staggered back, the soles of her feet brushing against the floor as she struggled to gain purchase. "Come on," she urged herself as her feet slid. Then she halted, and in an instant sprang from the deck, the sword flashing through the air.

Brigid drove her next kick forward as Rosalia leaped over her, and her foot passed through empty air before sweeping down to the floor once more. Overhead,

Rosalia brought the flat of her sword around, striking the red-haired warrior woman across her back as she hurtled past like a launched cannonball.

Rosalia landed, forward rolling to dissipate her momentum before bringing herself up in a wary crouch. Standing by the pit, Brigid Haight was rubbing at her shoulders where the sword had struck. In a moment, the redhead had unbuckled her fur cloak, and it dropped to the floor in a graceful swish.

Rosalia held the sword poised before her, and as she twisted it in her hands, the blackened blade caught the data lights of the room, flashing blue, gold and green. Brigid seemed to pause for a moment, transfixed by the blade as the lights played across its surface. And then she ran, charging toward the dark-haired mercenary, murder on her mind. Rosalia used the sword to bat the woman away, slicing a line across her leather suit. Brigid stepped back, bouncing on the balls of her feet as a bloody line of red appeared across her chest where the suit had been split by the blade.

Rosalia glanced to her side, checking on the location of the stone egg. Brigid was protecting it, just as Kane had suggested, but it seemed to be just one piece, the whole thing sealed as a single unit. Before Rosalia could think further, Brigid charged her again, and she was forced to defend herself.

The two women fought, struggling to gain the upper hand, the sword cutting through the air in a defensive pattern to stave off Brigid's most fearsome attacks. They were evenly matched, and if either did have an advantage, it was Brigid for she held no compulsion that her enemy should be allowed to live. She was a tool of hate, as her name stated, willing nothing less than ignoble death on any who failed to pledge allegiance to her dread master.

"This is a battle you cannot win," Brigid spit. "Even if I die, a million more will step up to replace me, the priests of the new world."

"Go tell it to the mountain man," Rosalia replied.

And then the two women were charging toward each other once more, Rosalia's charred sword flashing with the lights of the room, the nutrient pool bubbling like soup on the stove, its contents nothing less than the building blocks of life.

GRANT ROLLED OVER and over, hurrying out of the path of the two Annunaki combatants. Enlil was atop Ullikummis where he lay sprawled on the floor, driving the bloodied knuckles of his fist into the rock lord's face. Enlil reached back with his other hand, sweeping it through the air over his head, and suddenly the serpent lightning reappeared with a crackle of electricity like a thunderclap.

Krak-a-boom!

The serpent lightning jostled in Enlil's hand, its lashing head dancing in midair as Enlil brought it down to strike the smoldering body of his son. The weapon struck with a shower of sparks, and Grant watched as lightning played across Ullikummis's powerful frame and the bone deck beneath him. Then, with a loud crack, the floor beneath the two opponents began to break apart, cracking in a long, jagged line.

Grant could only watch as Enlil lashed at Ullikummis again with the lightning weapon, whipping it against his son's body again and again in an unrelenting attack. Ullikummis's body smoldered, smoke pouring from the ridges and valleys that ran along his rocky flesh. Grant trained his Sin Eater on the two Annunaki combatants, waiting for an opening—any opening. To do what, he didn't know.

Crouched astride the beaten body of his son, Enlil drew back the serpent lightning again, its fierce glow like a scar on the air as it whipped back in a crackle of sparks. "You have disappointed me for the last time, loin fruit," Enlil hissed, his cruel eyes fixed on the molten orbs of his progeny. And then he swept the lightning down again, lashing it against his son's writhing body.

But to Enlil's surprise, Ullikummis jabbed out his right arm as the lightning struck again, shaping his hand like a blade.

"No," Ullikummis shouted, driving the hand toward his father's leg. "I am the Godkiller. And you will remember that always."

Then, with a brutal slash of his stone-clad hand, Ullikummis drove his pointed fingers into the flesh of his father's leg, piercing the armorlike scales and burrowing deeper into the limb just above the knee. Enlil shrieked in sheer agony, keeling over but still connected to Ullikummis by the bloody wound that the latter was inflicting. The serpent lightning continued on its own path, lashing now not against Ullikummis but striking Enlil instead, connecting with his hip and sending a potent jolt of electricity through his agonized form.

Ullikummis's hand clawed deeper into his father's limb, splaying his rock-hard fingers as he tore through the flesh.

Enlil crashed to the deck, the lightning playing across his body as Ullikummis wrenched his bloody hand free, bringing with it thick gobs of muscle and skin like a butcher's display. The serpent lightning slunk against the floor, sparking and jolting in a shock of whiteness.

Grant narrowed his eyes to slits, using his hand as a shield to see past the sparking lightning so he could make out what had happened to the pair of them. Enlil's left leg lay at an unnatural angle, a pool of blood forming around the traumatic wound that had been inflicted. Ullikummis had slumped onto his back, dark wisps of smoke still emanating from his face and torso, his right hand and arm covered in his father's blood.

Ullikummis did not appear to be breathing, Grant noticed automatically, the old Magistrate instincts kicking in. Has he ever needed to breathe? Grant queried, second-guessing himself.

FROM HIS VANTAGE point atop the tree, Kane had seen the whole battle as a thunderstorm, with streaks of lightning in ruby reds and emerald greens lashing across the sky, some nightmarish vision of the aurora borealis. He was connected to Ullikummis by the stone implant, and he felt the Annunaki prince's rage as it raced across the black heavens, lashing at his father like a stormy sea.

Then, as suddenly as it had begun, it was over, the storm abating, the sky turning pale.

"Was that it?" Kane asked, clinging to the tree's highest branches.

GRANT STEPPED WARILY closer, eyeing the two forms of the Annunaki as they lay against the deck. Enlil's weapon spewed lightning against the floor, shuddering and snapping as it painted its savage patterns on the bone and cartilage that made up *Tiamat*'s interior.

Neither figure was moving, Grant saw. They just lay there, bloody and exhausted, possibly dead.

As Grant took another step toward the bodies, the serpent lightning flexed again, lashing a burst of white fire against the deck where the cracks had begun to appear. Then, as Grant watched, the whole floor started to split apart, the cracks widening in a rapidly expanding pattern of broken lines, tearing across the hexagonal room in a matter of seconds.

Grant ran for the doorway, but it was already too late—the floor was giving way.

With a loud crack like an avalanche, the floor collapsed, and Ullikummis, Enlil and Grant found themselves falling to the next level of the great dragon ship.

Chapter 18

Vast chunks of bone plate crashed down as the floor gave way, falling like flakes of cooked fish under the touch of a knife. The hole started in the center of the room, where Ullikummis and Enlil had struggled just seconds before, but it expanded in a matter of seconds, huge gaping cracks splintering across the deck, sending great gouges of flooring tipping away into the darkness below.

Grant cried out, sending his Sin Eater back to its hiding place as he grasped for something—anything—to cling to as he was thrown to the deck. The floor was tipping down to the center, slanting at an ever-increasing angle as it collapsed under its own weight, the structural integrity lost, everything falling toward the hole. In the center of the ruined floor, Ullikummis and Enlil were the first to fall, disappearing beneath the ruined line of the broken deck.

Above Grant, those towering bone arches were crumbling in on themselves, the great columns that held them splintering apart.

Miraculously Grant's left hand found a ridged break in the floor as he slid backward at an alarming rate, snagging it with a tight grip as hunks of alien masonry crashed past him on their perilous plunge to the floor below.

Grant hung there with one hand, his breathing coming heavily. He was hanging at the edge of the hole, now a ten-foot-wide gap that dominated fully one-third of the room's floor. His legs hung out over empty space, dangling high above the engine room that he and Rosalia had crossed not an hour earlier.

Grant ducked his head as another chunk of the bone arches hurtled past him, missing his broad shoulder by less than a foot. He watched for a moment as it fell past him, sinking away into the engine room and hitting the distant floor with a crash, sixty feet below. It was pandemonium down there, Grant saw, tiny figures rushing back and forth as the debris rained from the ceiling, the thick cylindrical drives of the great starship now strewed with wreckage.

Grant reached up with his free hand, swinging himself up so that he could grab the edge of the floor. It was rough to his touch, grazing his hand in a biting cut. The deck itself was four feet thick, its strata made up of layered plates of cartilage that glistened like translucent metal.

Grant hung there, catching his breath as he dangled precariously over the huge hole in the flooring, dust and tiles skittering past him amid the ruins of the room.

Then there was another crack, and Grant felt the floor shake, a heavy tremble rumbling through it. Urgently he hurried to pull himself up, legs kicking out as he dragged himself over the edge. Then his chest was on the angled floor, and he was pulling himself up and over the precipice on mighty muscles.

A chunk of bone arch broke away as Grant pulled himself to the floor, collapsing with an almighty boom. The ex-Mag struggled to keep his balance as the already listing floor dipped farther, the column's impact sending a shock wave through the precarious structure.

The floor beneath Grant broke abruptly, collapsing away from the edge. He found himself falling through empty air, the broken ruins of the floor tumbling downward beside him as gravity tugged him toward his doom.

ROSALIA'S SWORD cut the air with a resounding hum like a bird's wing as she drove at Brigid Haight. Then, without warning, the whole room shook and the two women were tossed off their feet. From just beyond the sealed doors, they heard the terrific bang as the floor of the next room fell away.

"Grant?" Rosalia gasped, her head going automatically to the doors where a jagged crack was appearing beneath the violet lights. The doors held, chunks of the wall splitting away from the lintel and smashing against the floor with a resounding bang.

Before her, Brigid Haight was recovering, pulling herself back to her feet and running at Rosalia with a brutal ram's-head punch, the fingers clenched back to drive the heel of her hand into her opponent's nose.

Rosalia avoided the blow by an inch and slashed her *katana* blade around so that it hacked into Brigid's side.

Brigid cried out in pain, but already she was following up her own deadly assault, bringing her open right hand up toward Rosalia's throat. At the same time as Brigid grabbed Rosalia's neck, she kicked forward with her right leg, booting the dark-haired woman in the shin. Rosalia expelled a lungful of air through clenched teeth at the blow, feeling the pressure close on her throat as Brigid attempted to curtail her next inhalation. The dark-eyed mercenary brought her sword back and around, jabbing at her adversary with its pommel because the close quarters prevented her properly utilizing the blade itself. The artistically tooled base of the *katana*'s handle slammed against Brigid's chest, smacking just above her right breast with such force it made her take an awkward step backward. Her grip did not fail, and Rosalia found herself dragged by the throat across the hard decking.

The toes of her boots scraped on the floor as Rosalia was pulled forward, and she lashed out again with the hard stump of the sword's grip, this time striking her red-haired foe across the top of her chest where she had previously delivered a nasty cut from with the blade's edge. Brigid shrieked in agony as the bloody wound was ripped wider, swearing as the pain struck her. Her grip faltered, and Rosalia lunged, using her free hand to extricate herself from Brigid's hold and drive the woman back.

Brigid drove her feet against the deck, springing toward Rosalia with a guttural battle cry borne of pure rage.

Rosalia tried to sidestep, moving out of her foe's path like a toreador. Brigid's arms stretched wide like an eagle's wings as it took flight, and the left arm slammed against Rosalia's gut with enough power to knock the younger woman off her feet. Rosalia rolled backward, the sword skittering from her grasp as she landed in a heap with Brigid astride her. The sword spun through the air, and once again its ebony blade reflected the shimmering lights of the tracking consoles all around as they monitored Little Quav's progress from hybrid girl to Annunaki goddess. The reflected lights seemed to give Brigid pause, and she stared about her in confusion as the sword clattered to the deck, searching the blue, gold and green lights that played across the consoles at the sides of the room.

Rosalia snatched the advantage, twisting her body to

drop Brigid to the deck and rolling herself until she was atop the former Cerberus archivist. There was blood on both their clothes now. Brigid's chest showed a thick line that went from shoulder blade to shoulder blade through the torn front of her outfit. Rosalia bunched her fist and drew it back, striking Brigid in her face once, twice, thrice. Brigid's head slammed back into the deck, and her emerald eyes rolled up in their sockets for a moment as unconsciousness threatened to overwhelm her. Then, as Rosalia drew her bloody fist back for another blow, Brigid's eyes snapped back open and she glared at the woman astride her with savage intent.

"If they rewrote the heroes' rules, who would you root for?" Brigid asked.

"I don't know," Rosalia admitted. "I never cared much about the rules." With that she drove her fist into Brigid's face again, striking her across her smirking mouth.

Brigid's body seemed to lose its strength, and Rosalia felt the woman go limp beneath her. The skin of Rosalia's knuckles was scraped, her hand spattered with the other woman's blood. Slowly, warily, Rosalia lifted herself from her opponent's fallen body and looked up to the stone egg that waited amid the bubbling pool behind her.

As Rosalia pushed herself up, Brigid suddenly moved once again, springing from the deck and powering herself headfirst into Rosalia's gut. She had been playing possum, the oldest trick in the book.

Rosalia crashed backward as the woman's head struck her midriff, pushing her back in a flurry of skipping feet. Then suddenly there was nothing else for her to run against; the deck dropped away and instead Rosalia found herself splashing into the pit that dominated the room, with the lithe figure of Brigid Haight crashing down on top of her.

In an instant, both women sank beneath the pearly white surface of the viscous goo.

The chamber known as *Tiamat*'s ante-nursery fell into an eerie silence as the sounds of violence faded into instant memory. For a moment, the room was uncannily quiet. Even the bubbling pool of liquid seemed to hold still for those tense few seconds.

Then a figure emerged from the pool, clambering out of the iridescent liquid and reaching for the edge of the pit. The woman grabbed the side, pulling herself up and out of the nutrient bath in a swift movement before sweeping the gunk from her face. It was Rosalia, the band that held her ponytail lost somewhere beneath the liquid. She stood there, bent over, taking deep breaths as she ran her hands through her sopping wet hair and wondered, Where is Brigid?

The answer came a moment later, as a second figure burst from the pool, arms striving for the edge as she dragged herself out of the gunk.

"Here we go again," Rosalia muttered.

But she couldn't have been more wrong.

GRANT OPENED HIS EYES, struggling to recall what had happened. There were sounds coming from a source he couldn't pinpoint, a rushing of machinery that simply pervaded the air, like the sound of one thousand kettles reaching boiling point in unison. Grant lay on his side amid a pile of debris, hunks of chipped bone scattered all about like detritus from a crematorium. Orange-red light seeped gloomily into his eyes, and for a moment Grant mistook it for blood, raising his hand to his face to try to brush it away. His arm ached and the hand tensed, muscles locking painfully as he brought it up to his face.

"What happened to me?" he muttered, his body sore and numb.

There were figures moving about, waddling away from him as he watched, their bodies enshrouded in dark rags. Grant watched them, trying to recall how he had wound up here.

He had been in the hexagonal room with the bone arches, he remembered, piecing it together slowly. The floor had given way and he had fallen, fallen a long way. Now he lay sprawled in whatever lay beneath—the engine room, somewhere close to the cooling water tanks.

Tentatively Grant pulled himself to a sitting position, his head reeling. He glanced up, spying the hole far above through which he—along with half the room, it seemed—had come crashing. It was a long way up, fifty feet or more, and it made Grant feel dizzy just looking at it. He had fallen all that way, but he remained alive. The incredible weave of the shadow suit had taken some of the impact, he guessed, along with the thick material of his Kevlar coat, bulletproof and apparently sturdy enough to cushion his fall. The rest he had taken himself, and he could feel his whole right side creaking as he moved, bruises doubtless forming.

He was resting atop a structure high above the floor, Grant realized, and this, too, had to have helped to break his fall, stopping him before he had plummeted the full distance between ceiling and floor. It looked like a huge tube, finished in dark metal with a foot-deep dent where his body had struck it with considerable force. There were similar structures all around, arrayed in rows that ran the length of the vast chamber. The room itself was of dimensions impossible to take in with the naked eye, stretching into darkness at one side, the width alone the size of two football fields laid end to end. It was the engine room, Grant recalled as he looked it over, where the dragon ship's great stardrive was located.

Grant pushed himself up, inching along on his rump to the edge of the cylindrical unit he had landed on and peeking over the side. The floor was a good fifteen feet below, narrow walkways running between the vast tubes where debris from above had come crashing down in a violent hail. Down below Grant saw figures hurrying about as they endeavored to clear away the mess. They were the strange verminlike engineers, dressed in their rag cloaks and wearing the weird lighting units that emanated from their eyes on spectacle-styled rigs.

Grant looked at that drop to the floor, wondering whether he was up for another fall. His muscles ached and it was all he could do to stop from falling.

"Just give me a minute," he told himself.

From behind him, Grant heard a booming sound over the rumble of machinery and turned in time to see Ullikummis leap onto the pipe he was sitting on from its neighbor seven feet away. The stone-clad giant ran across the cylindrical pipe toward Grant, anger in his molten lava eyes.

"Oh, shit!" Grant snarled as Ullikummis stomped closer.

THE WORLD COALESCED before Kane's eyes, a wash of purples and mauves whirring through the sky. Color had returned, the clouds above dancing like spinning crystals, snowflakes of color in the air. There was a beach below, a beach with no sea, just a never-ending shore that echoed with the ghost of crashing waves.

Kane clambered down the tree, sensing somehow

that he should get back to solid ground. As he did so, he saw the man-shape waiting a short distance away, cast in silhouette by the hidden eye of the sun, edges burning away layer by impossible layer.

"Kane, what are you doing?" Balam called from that distant place that was just next to his ear. "Are you lost?"

"I'm not lost," Kane said, dismissing Balam's concerns. "Where's Grant?"

Lakesh's voice piped back from the Commtact in Kane's head after a moment, as he checked Grant's transponder feed. "He's still aboard *Tiamat*," Lakesh confirmed. "Heart rate elevated. What do you intend to do?"

"You called it string theory," Kane replied. "Layer upon layer of dimensions all intersecting, all a part of the whole we never see."

"Yes, but…"

"I'm going to go kill me a god, Lakesh," Kane stated. "I'm going to cut a gash through every one of those dimensions and kill me an Annunaki space god."

At the base of the tree, Ullikummis waited like a statue, his flesh searing away over and over as he stood upon the shifting vermilion sands.

IN THE ENGINE ROOM, Grant sailed through the air as Ullikummis struck him a savage blow from one of his pile driver fists before he could even get himself to a standing position atop the cylindrical driveshaft. Head reeling, Grant looked up to see Ullikummis charging at him, magma veins glowing across his hideous rock form, drawing one of his mighty legs back to punt his foe.

Grant rolled, dodging the kick by a fraction of an inch, rolling again as Ullikummis stamped down at him as if to crush a bug.

"Die, apekin," Ullikummis spit, puffs of smoke leaping from his wounded face as he spoke.

Adrenaline pumping, Grant forced himself to his feet, the Sin Eater materializing in his hand. The pistol kicked in Grant's steady grip, spitting a trio of shots at Ullikummis from just a few feet away. Ullikummis dismissed the bullets, sweeping one of his massive arms through the air and knocking Grant and the weapon aside.

The Sin Eater barrel bent while Grant was thrown backward under the incredible blow, rushing through the air and past the edge of the wide driveshaft. Grant's trajectory took him all the way across to the next tubular container, slamming bodily against it with an expulsion of breath.

Ullikummis charged across the cylinder, springing into the air and leaping the gap that separated him from Grant. Despite his size, Ullikummis moved with exceptional speed, Grant noted as he pulled himself onto the cylinder.

Grant raised the weapon in his hand, saw the bent barrel and thought better of it.

"Damn!"

Then Ullikummis was looming over him, more than a foot taller than the powerfully built ex-Magistrate, genetically designed solely for killing. Grant balked as Ullikummis brought his hands together, clapping them with great force just inches over Grant's dipping head. The sound of those clapping hands was momentarily deafening, like two rocks being broken together, and Grant reeled from the effect, staggering in place.

"Shit, Kane, where are you?" he spit, his hidden Commtact live.

But there was no time to wait for an answer. Already

Ullikummis was reaching for Grant again, determined to squash this thorn in his side once and for all.

Grant ducked, feeling the passage of air as one of those massive arms whizzed by just inches over his head. And then, his head still down, Grant charged forward, driving his shoulder into the great stone figure of Ullikummis.

Balanced on the subtly curving surface of the cylindrical driveshaft, Ullikummis slipped back under Grant's blow, his feet dragging backward and ripping chunks of the surface sheen away as they did so. Grant forced himself on, head tucked in, as if battering down a door, his booted feet kicking out against the echoing surface of the shaft.

Then, incredibly, Ullikummis fell, his hulking body slamming against the roof of the cylinder with an almighty clang. It happened so fast that Grant very nearly lost his own balance, and he staggered forward in a sudden run as he tried to keep himself from falling. After a quick three steps, Grant stopped, and he turned to face Ullikummis once more, his eyes searching all around for evidence of Enlil, too.

"Enkidu," Ullikummis cursed in his own tongue, glowering at the ex-Magistrate as he stood before him. "Always charging like a bull, even after all this time."

Grant looked at him blankly, failing to understand the words Ullikummis spoke.

"Come on, Kane," Grant whispered into the Commtact. "It's now or never, man."

WHILE SHE WAS under the surface of the nutrient bath, a strange change had come upon Brigid. Once a trusted warrior for the Cerberus organization, she had had her mind corrupted and overwhelmed by Ullikummis in his gambit to resurrect his mother and take control of *Tia-mat* and subsequently the world. But the nutrient bath had done something, triggering a change in Brigid that no one could have foreseen. As she stumbled out of the bath, her eyes fixed on Rosalia where the beautiful Latina was reaching for her discarded *katana*.

"Hang fire," Brigid said, spitting nutrient gunk from her mouth as she spoke, placing the recovered Ruger on the deck beside her.

"I don't want to kill you," Rosalia warned, drawing the blade back in a two-handed grip.

"You won't have to," Brigid replied, and Rosalia heard a softer edge to her voice than had been evident just a few minutes earlier. "Rosalia?" she queried.

"Yes," Rosalia said, nodding warily.

"I remember you," Brigid continued, showing no proclivity to attack the woman now. "We were in Hope together. You were a part of Tom Carnack's group."

"What's your point?" Rosalia barked, her eyes scanning Brigid for any sign of attack.

"I have an eidetic memory," Brigid said, a smile tugging at her lips. "You didn't really think I'd forget who I was, did you?"

Chapter 19

Down in the engine room, Grant steadied himself as the juggernaut stone figure of Ullikummis came crashing toward him. Grant was weaponless now. All he had left was his strength—not a patch on Ullikummis's—and his wits, about which the jury was still out.

Grant stepped to his right, flicking out the long tails of his Kevlar duster like a matador as Ullikummis came at him like a rocket. The trick was only halfway successful, and Grant found his left arm going numb as Ullikummis brushed against it.

Down below, the dwarfen ratlike figures were scurrying about in panic, clearing the area as Ullikummis and Grant battled atop the driveshafts.

Hurtling along like a hurricane, Ullikummis took a half-dozen paces to stop, skirting precariously close to the far edge of the shaft.

Grant turned, a grim smile crossing his features for a moment. And then the ex-Magistrate began running, sprinting across the cylindrical unit toward the great stone figure that waited at its edge.

In a plane of reality unseen by human eyes, Kane dropped from the tree and onto the vermilion sands below. He could not help but marvel at the way color had reappeared in this—what was it?—world.

It's the way I interpret things, Kane reminded himself. My brain is getting information shot at it from directions it's never known before, and all it can do is make some patchwork-quilt reality so I can at least function within it.

Is this all reality is? Kane wondered. Is what we're seeing, the trees, the plants—is that too just a way of making sense of shapes we have no real way of comprehending? Is vision itself just an illusion?

Kane glanced ahead and to his right, searching for the statuelike figure of Ullikummis. Enlil had gone, winked out of the multisphere somehow. But Ullikummis remained, his back to Kane as his body flowed with some invisible tide. But as Kane looked, a shape seemed to blur from beyond Ullikummis's form, like a halo cast in shadow. Kane saw faces there, things he had never seen before, things he had no name for.

Keep it together, Kane, he told himself. Keep your head together and work this out. It's an·angle, another line on the graph. That's all this is. String theory—just string.

GRANT'S FEET POUNDED on the surface of the shaft, each footstep like a hammer blow on the cylindrical container. Seeing him approach, Ullikummis smiled—or at least gave what passed for a smile on his ugly features—stretching his arms wide to receive his attacker.

"Come, man bull," Ullikummis growled. "Amuse me for one...single...second."

With a wordless battle cry, Grant slammed into Ullikummis, plowing into him with such force that the two of them first butted, then fell back, the sound of impact like a crack of thunder above the churning noise of *Tiamat*'s engines.

Grant fell back, crashing to the surface of the long

cylindrical unit, his whole body aching like a bruise where he had barged into the Annunaki rock monstrosity.

Ullikummis was not so lucky. Like Grant, he fell back, but standing at the edge of the driveshaft, he had nowhere to fall but straight down, dropping over the side and crashing fifteen feet to the deck below.

For a long moment, Grant lay there, his body crying out with pain from all sides, every muscle strained beyond belief. "Come on," he told himself sternly. "Get up."

With incredible effort, Grant pushed himself from the deck, lifting himself back to his feet and edging along in a pain-filled, shuffling movement. He kept his teeth clenched, and each breath came through them with a hiss, straining for release.

Grant took his time and it was thirty seconds before he reached the end of the cylinder. Slowly, his head heavy with strain, he peered over the edge.

Ullikummis lunged at him from below, clambering up the side of the drive cylinder in great leaps and bounds, literally running up the vertical side of the tank.

"Whoa!" Grant yelped, sidestepping as Ullikummis reached out for him with his massive stone-clad hands.

Grant's feet drummed against the driveshaft as he moved to avoid Ullikummis's attack. The stone giant was atop the cylindrical drive in an instant, reaching forward once again to grab the retreating ex-Magistrate.

STRING THEORY, Kane repeated, recalling the name Lakesh had given it.

Staring at Ullikummis's broad-shouldered back, Kane realized what he had to do. He didn't understand this world, didn't understand this angle he was looking at, but he recognized himself and the things he had brought here.

Reaching down, Kane tore a strip from his frayed denim jacket, tearing the tatty hem away in a swift jerk. The hem was three feet long and about the same width as a bandage. Kane twisted the ends, wrapping them tightly between his hands. The material felt strong enough for what he had in mind.

IN AGARTHA, Balam watched as Kane rocked back and forth in the astrogator's chair, shaking as if he was having a seizure.

"Kane, are you all right?" Balam asked gently, reaching for the Cerberus warrior.

But as he reached forward, another burst of static shot out from the chair, whizzing across the room and catching Balam a glancing blow across his arm. Balam staggered back, patting at the sleeve of his indigo robe where a spark of fire ignited.

Across the cube, Kane continued shaking back and forth in the clutches of the chair.

IN ANOTHER ANGLE, Kane was running at Ullikummis as his statuelike form crackled with energy. Clenched in Kane's hands, the single strip of material was wrapped tautly over the knuckles of both hands, leaving a short length between them, barely a foot across.

Kane's feet pounded on the sands, striking with great blows of sound and fury, spirit and determination.

ABOARD TIAMAT, Grant found himself backing along one of the great engine capacitors as Ullikummis chased him. The great stone monster hurtled at him in great, loping strides, each one encompassing twice the distance that Grant could step.

"My father is dead," Ullikummis gritted, his eyes fixed on the retreating figure of Grant. "He taught me never to leave loose ends unsnipped."

Grant continued running away. "I really don't want to be snipped," he muttered as he rushed along the curved surface of the shaft.

The ex-Mag was close to the end with Ullikummis breathing down his neck as he closed in. He would need to jump to the next cylindrical structure, he realized, because there was nowhere left to run. Head down, Grant drove himself on, his legs screaming in pain as he forced himself to keep moving. But as he reached the edge of the cylinder, Ullikummis just inches behind him, Grant slipped, careening over and over, the long tails of his coat wrapping over his body. His boot had slipped on some leaking oil or something, Grant realized as he crashed down to the cylinder's surface.

At the same moment, Ullikummis was reaching for Grant, his right hand grasping for the back of the ex-Mag's duster. His hand snatched at empty air as Grant sailed head over heels along the last part of the stardrive unit, sending Ullikummis off balance for just a second.

When he recovered, Ullikummis saw Grant lying there, sprawled uncomfortably on the tubular drive-shaft, utterly helpless. Ullikummis paced toward him, his mighty feet striking resounding blows on the metal-sounding shaft, blows that were loud even above the thousand-boiling-kettles symphony of the room.

Ullikummis loomed over Grant, his shadow covering the apekin where he struggled to get up. Ullikummis leaned forward to lift him, but as he did so the

Annunaki prince became aware of another presence just behind him, reaching for him from out of the quantum ether.

Rosalia stared at the red-haired woman standing before her, wondering if this, too, was a trick. Brigid Baptiste, latterly Haight, seemed passive now, offering no indication that she planned to attack. Rosalia was a survivor who lived by her wits, and she did so in large part by being a shrewd judge of character. The woman before her had caught her on the hop less than five minutes before by the old ruse of playing possum. While she seemed genuine now, the thought picked at Rosalia's brain, Might this too be a trick?

"Who are you?" Rosalia asked, the black sword poised upright in ready position.

"Baptiste," Brigid replied. "Brigid Baptiste. And you would be Rosalia, correct?"

Rosalia nodded, watching the red-haired woman intensely. Nothing in Brigid's body language suggested a trick. Indeed, her body language had subtly changed since Rosalia had first encountered her in this small room with its stone egg and pool of genetic gunk.

"Might I ask," Brigid began, making a show of her empty hands, the discarded Ruger still at her feet, "who you are working for? It's just that I get the impression we were fighting."

"We were," Rosalia confirmed. Then, at Brigid's urging look, the dark-haired merc added, "Cerberus."

Brigid shook her head, taking a pace forward. She stopped when she saw Rosalia jostle the sword in her hands.

"I don't intend to hurt you," Brigid said. "Not yet anyway. Jury's still out on the longer term. Ullikummis—you know the name?—well, he did something to me, assaulted me, here, in my head. If you're here with Cerberus, then I should speak with them. I have to figure out what's happened."

"You were trying to kill me is what's happened," Rosalia spit contemptuously. "The innocent act's good, but I'm not buying it."

"Listen to me," Brigid said. "I have what's known as an eidetic—or photographic—memory. It takes a lot to fool my brain, and even then it can't be fooled for long. Ullikummis kidnapped me and tried to get inside my head."

"Yeah," Rosalia recalled. "I was…there," she finished lamely, withholding for now the information that she was a part of the attacking force that took over the Cerberus redoubt. If Brigid was telling the truth, then she didn't want to spook her.

"But, you see," Brigid continued as if explaining it to herself, "you can't brainwash someone with an eidetic memory—they have too strong a connection to their past. What he did was a psychic assault, and I knew I was in no position to beat him off, so I did the only thing I could. I hid."

"Hid?" Rosalia asked.

"I hid my mind," Brigid clarified. "There was a trick I learned back when I was in Russia on a field mission. It involved focusing on a pattern that allowed the viewer to meditate on a set frequency."

Rosalia listened, realizing that Brigid was speaking as much to herself as to her, trying to piece together all that had happened these past two months since she had disappeared.

"Recollecting the meditative tool—the mandala—allowed me to hide my mind in a place called Krylograd on the astral plane," Brigid continued. "It put me somewhere that Ullikummis could not reach."

"You've been 'gone' for almost two months," Rosalia said.

Brigid cursed. "The time sense in Krylograd is all askew. I didn't realize. What happened?" she added, her expression like that of a little girl.

"Ullikummis made you his bitch," Rosalia summarized. "Or whatever was left of you, I guess. We've been working together to find you...."

"'We'?"

"Kane, Grant, Lakesh..." Rosalia clarified.

"So you really are working for Cerberus now?" Brigid questioned.

"Temp position," Rosalia told her, "until something better comes up." She gave a wink.

Brigid turned her head, searching around the room. "Where are we? Looks kind of like a Chalice of Rebirth."

"Big spaceship name of *Tiamat*," Rosalia told her.

Brigid's eyebrows rose. "In space?" she asked.

"No, not unless there's been some colossal fuck up since I last checked," Rosalia assured her.

Brigid shook her head, running her hand absentmindedly through the locks of her wet hair. "I took a dunking?" she asked, staring down at the pit that dominated the room. "A nutrient bath made up of birth stuff. Used to enable genetic download of personality templates in the Annunaki bodies, right?"

Rosalia shrugged. "Big pond, stone egg, that's all I know, *chica*."

"We are all genetic templates waiting for our download," Brigid proposed. "Created in the womb, each of us awaits the facets that will make us individuals, that will make up the things we will carry with us through-out our lives. I'd hidden my mind leaving this shell to Ullikummis, to fill with his values, his truths, what-ever. But the nutrient bath cleared all the crap out of my system—it set me free to reengage my real mind with my body. Without that, I might not have come back."

And then Brigid laughed. "Excuse me, but that's bril-liant."

"It wasn't intentional," Rosalia admitted with a shrug.

"Doesn't matter," Brigid told her, her face the pic-ture of inspired joy. "Do you realize that, thanks to an Annunaki cheat, I've managed to be reborn. That's just incredible."

But Rosalia's happiness was less pronounced. In-stead, her attention was drawn to the thing behind Brigid, the stone chrysalis that stood silently in the middle of the nutrient pool. As she watched it, a seam appeared along the Y-axis of the ovoid structure, top to bottom, and it began to split apart.

"Speaking of rebirth…" Rosalia said, indicating the stone egg.

And then, both she and Brigid Baptiste reared back as the two halves of the stone structure fell away into the pool of genetic debris to leave a single figure stand-ing before them. Six feet in height and of gracile form, the figure was covered in shimmering green scales the color of spring leaves, and she stood naked before them with no sense of shame. It was Ninlil, goddess of the Annunaki, Lady of the Air. She stood reborn, four thou-sand years after her last Earth death. And she didn't look at all happy about it.

Chapter 20

In the engine room, Ullikummis turned back and saw the spectral figure of Kane reaching toward him from beyond the quantum veil. There was a length of cord stretched tightly in the apekin's hands. Before he could move, Kane looped the cord over the stone giant's head, whipping it down until it was snug against his throat.

Ullikummis reached back, grasping for Kane where he'd attacked him from the numerous angles of the unseen dimensions, but his hand swept through thin air. Kane was still in the angles, driving his vengeance through them and into the world beyond.

"You want string theory?" Kane snarled as he tightened the cord around his foe's throat. "Here's what I know!"

With a yank, Ullikummis felt himself pulled back, the air bursting from his throat.

From his supine position on the driveshaft, Grant watched Ullikummis topple backward to the surface of the cylindrical unit. The stone giant was clawing at his throat as if some invisible cord were cinched there, yet it was something Grant could not see.

"Kane?" Grant asked. "Is that you?"

"YEAH, IT'S ME all right," Kane replied.

Within a different angle, Kane was pulling on the

strip of material, pulling it back farther, forcing Ulli-kummis to fall.

Kane pulled harder as the stone god struggled, kick-ing backward to keep Ullikummis from recovering. For the moment, Kane's multidimensional attack was holding Ullikummis, but it couldn't last long; the stone monster did not need air, so there was no way to stran-gle him.

"Balam? Lakesh?" Kane called. "Do we have any-thing to hold this son of a bitch?"

"We're working on it, Kane," Lakesh replied, "but nothing is presenting itself. Short of conducting a bomb-ing raid on the spaceship, we're out of options."

"Can that be done?" Kane asked.

"With personnel as they are?" Lakesh replied. "No."

MEANWHILE, Balam had a plan of his own. He had brought something from elsewhere in the vast store-house, speculating that Kane might use it when the time came. Unrolling the matlike object, Balam laid it out across the floor of the cube by Kane's feet. The mate-rial was a three-foot square of dark green, and marked out upon it in golden thread were concentric circles like a bull's-eye. It was a portable parallax point, the kind that Kane and his team had only ever seen once before.

"There is a way," Balam said, placing himself beside the navigator's chair, "but you'll need to open your eyes. I have a parallax point that can be shifted...."

Squirming in the chair, his body held in place by the eerie, living creepers, Kane gritted his teeth. "You're nuts, Balam," he snarled. "I can't hold on to my pres-ence here, as well as there."

"Once viewed," Balam continued, "you could use the

navigation circuitry to move the parallax point, creating a warp through space."

"Balam, are you even listening?" Kane growled as he struggled in the seat. "If I open my eyes, I'll lose whatever it is I have here. I'll lose Ullikummis."

Balam stared at the parallax point laid out on the floor of the room and he shook his head. "Friend Kane," he said solemnly, "to utilize the parallax point you will need to look at it. I'm afraid that there is simply no other way."

KANE WRENCHED back on Ullikummis once again, dragging him across the abandoned beach in the middle of the desolate angles. Ullikummis had been off balance, but he was recovering, Kane could tell. Even as he listened to Balam explain the situation, Ullikummis reached back and clapped his hands together in a boom like thunder. Kane fell back, struggling to keep hold of the twisted cord around the stone figure's neck.

"You're playing in the big league now, Balam," Kane snarled. "Find a way."

IN THE ANTE-NURSERY, Ninlil of the Annunaki stepped from the stone womb, her face a picture of sadistic delight.

"I live," she declared in ancient Sumerian tongue, "I breathe. The download is completed."

From the edge of the nutrient pool, Brigid and Rosalia watched aghast as Ninlil took another step forward. She was beautiful, her scales a pale green like the spring leaves on a plant, her lines sleek and her skin shimmering beneath the violet lighting of the room. She stood over six feet tall, slender with a pleasing curve to the swell of her bare breasts and naked hips.

"No," Brigid spit, "this can't happen. I won't let it."

More practical, Rosalia simply grabbed her Ruger pistol from where it had fallen and aimed it at the approaching Annunaki, directing a bullet between the thing's eyes. The revolver went off with a loud bang, and the 9 mm slug raced to its target, striking Ninlil midforehead. The bullet ricocheted off the armorlike scales of the goddess's skin, but the shock of impact was enough to make her step back, her feet splashing through the nutrient-filled waters of the pool.

"You can't kill her," Brigid said. "Not like that."

"Then what?" Rosalia asked.

Brigid racked her brains, recalling all she could of what Ullikummis had taught her.

"Hold my hand," Brigid said, running into the nutrient pool, splashing liquid everywhere as she charged at the reborn Annunaki goddess.

"What are you doing?" Rosalia demanded as she was dragged into the pool with the red-haired archivist.

"Ullikummis showed me the Annunaki way of seeing the world," Brigid said as she reached for Ninlil before the stone egg. "They see time as infinite but mutable. Movement is time, and an action can be reversed."

As she spoke, Brigid slapped her palm against Ninlil, striking her chest and shoving her back into the cracked shell of the stone chrysalis. Ninlil stumbled into it, falling back into its embrace.

"There's enough of that other me," Brigid said, "of Haight, to remember how to do this. It's just the same as finding the hidden door to Agartha. But it won't stay with me much longer."

"What are you babbling about?" Rosalia snapped angrily. "You can't live both in their world and ours."

"I know," Brigid replied, flicking her gaze on Rosalia

for just a second. When she did so, Rosalia saw the darkness return to the woman's expression, the sinister fires of hate burning within her emerald eyes. "Anchor me."

Rosalia grabbed the woman's other arm as Brigid pressed her palm against Ninlil's body, shunting her back into the cocoon. Around them, the nutrient bath continued to bubble, dark lines streaming through its milky concoction of amino acids.

Caught in the chrysalis, the beautiful figure of Ninlil seemed to shudder in place, her mouth opening in a silent scream.

IN THE ENGINE ROOM, Grant scrambled back as Ullikummis's body started to crackle with energy. The power was emanating from around his neck, but Grant could not see where it was originating from. The eerie energy ringed Ullikummis's throat like a necklace, sparks blasting out in furious red dots that hung in the air for a second before winking out to be replaced by more of the same.

From the floor level below, Grant could hear the worried cries of the mechanics, and he looked out into the vast engine room to see what they were doing. One by one they were running away from the scene with Ullikummis, scrambling along the aisles that ran between the great cylinders that powered *Tiamat*. Grant figured he ought to take that as his cue and get out of there, too.

Standing, Grant activated his Commtact. "Kane, you got this?" he asked.

"Not sure," Kane grunted back, his voice strained.

As Grant watched, another blast of coruscating energy sparked from Ullikummis's throat. It was as if the god prince was being torn apart.

KANE YANKED BACK on the struggling body of Ullikummis, holding his frightening form on the sand as he fought against him. He looked like a churning volcano now, his magma energies smoldering into the air with relentless rage. Kane held the choking rope in place as Ullikummis lunged for him, one mighty magma arm cutting the impossible landscape as he struck out at Kane.

Kane grunted, feeling the blow cuff him across the left ear, but also feeling it somewhere else, somewhere deep inside. Whatever level this battle was being fought on, it was as much spiritual as physical.

Kane held in place, pulling harder against the cord that strangled Ullikummis. And as he struggled, Kane heard Balam speak from nearby.

"Kane, I have an idea," Balam said.

"Make it quick," Kane spit, struggling with the effort.

"We have been linked at an ocular level," Balam said, "granting you the ability to see despite the infection."

"Faster," Kane growled impatiently.

Beneath him, Ullikummis twisted his mighty body, snagging the cord and wrenching it from his throat in three quick pulls. Kane felt his hands burn as the cord was torn from them.

"I shall reverse the way the link works," Balam explained, "allowing you to see what I am looking at."

"You can do that?" Kane asked, watching Ullikummis pull himself back to his full height, burning lava cascading across his ominous silhouetted form.

"I can try," Balam said hopefully. "Stand by."

Kane watched as the burning form of Enlil's son came charging at him across the cool vermilion sands. Kane stretched out his arms, as ready as he would ever be to wrestle a child of the multiplanes.

Suddenly, Kane's vision changed, and instead of the charging figure of Ullikummis, he saw something else—the thing that Balam was looking at. It was a parallax point, the decorative design sewn onto a simple mat, just like the one he had seen beneath Luilekkerville a week before.

Two realities vied for dominance in Kane's vision, the regular concentric circles and the view of Ullikummis hurtling toward him. Ullikummis burned as he ran, and in that moment Kane had the idea of how to finish this.

STANDING AT THE END of the cylinder, Grant watched as another vicious energy cloud burst from Ullikummis's body, space stuff being borne into the engine room. The energy struck the cylinder beside the one he was on, and Grant saw fire burst to life there in a colossal explosion that shook the whole room.

"I'm going to regret this," Grant muttered as he eyed the sparking form of Ullikummis, "but what the hell."

Then the Cerberus warrior began to run, long strides eating up the distance between himself and Ullikummis where the great stone Annunaki stood, writhing in the energy spewing from his throat. Head down, Grant struck Ullikummis shoulder-first, and it was like hitting a brick wall. Grant grunted in pain, but he didn't stop—his feet kept pounding against the curved surface of the cylinder as he pushed Ullikummis back toward its edge.

IN THE ANTE-NURSERY, Brigid pressed her hand firmly against the reptilian body of Ninlil, applying all the incredible pressure of her corrupted understanding of the universe. Ninlil's body shook in the stone egg, shuddering in place.

Standing behind Brigid, Rosalia watched as the astonishing scene took place. Her brain struggled to comprehend what was happening. It seemed that Ninlil was becoming focused even as the world around her blurred.

Brigid recalled the equation she had used to find the hidden door to Agartha, driving into her mind that different way of seeing, of comprehending. The Annunaki were multidimensional; the static rules of physics did not apply. Backed inside the egg, Ninlil's body wrapped upon itself, becoming smaller to fit the enclosed space, the way her son had traveled the universe in his rock prison.

Time took a half step back; evolution itself was reversed.

Then the stone chrysalis sealed with Ninlil crouched inside it, and Brigid slumped forward, splashing beneath the waters of the nutrient bath.

Rosalia ran a quick three paces forward as Brigid fell, staggering across the pool in ungainly steps as her grip left Brigid's. She turned, pulling herself from the viscous liquid and searching for Brigid. Her red hair spread across the surface, but the woman herself was still beneath the pool.

His head down, Grant drove himself on, leg muscles straining as he barged the towering form of Ullikummis back toward the edge of the cylindrical drive unit. Grant could not see where he was going; he just pushed with all his strength, building momentum and willing the both of them onward. All the while, two words echoed through Grant's mind, over and over: keep going.

Battered from all sides, Ullikummis seemed not to know where to strike, which threat to react against.

His mouth opened wide and his voice rose on a single cry of anguish.

Then, in a moment that seemed to last an eternity, Ullikummis toppled over the edge of the cylindrical drive, even as Grant threw himself to the side. But Ullikummis did not strike the deck below. As Grant watched, the great stone monster tumbled through the air only to disappear in a burst of fiery energy, the great rift of an interphase window appearing to swallow him whole.

WORKING THE astro-navigation program of the Annunaki chair, Kane instructed it to locate the nearest star. In less than a second, he was looking at the sun poised in the center of the solar system like a jewel in space. Elsewhere in his brain, he saw what Balam was looking at, the incredible design for the mobile parallax point. Running through the fractures of multiplaned space, Kane folded the two images together, slapping them against the charging form of Ullikummis as he hurried across the vermilion sands.

ROSALIA DIVED, plunging beneath the surface of the shallow pool until her body was under that of Brigid Baptiste. It was almost impossible to see down there, the liquid was so thick with gunk.

Feeling as much as seeing, Rosalia positioned herself beneath the Cerberus warrior and lifted, bringing her back to the surface. Brigid's eyes were closed, her body still.

"Don't pull this shit now," Rosalia grunted as she hurried through the pool to its edge, the chrysalis forgotten for the moment.

Then Rosalia was at the poolside, hefting Brigid's floppy-limbed form over the edge before dragging herself out. Behind her, the stone egg had resealed, any evidence that it had opened entirely removed.

"Come on, you stupid woman," Rosalia cursed as she pressed on Brigid's chest. "Breathe."

For a moment, Brigid just lay still, not reacting at all. Then there was a sound from her throat and a rush of fluid spurted from her mouth, washing over the already soaked clothing she wore.

"That's it," Rosalia said. "Get it all out."

Brigid's eyelids flickered open, and she stared at Rosalia with bright, intelligent eyes. "What happened?"

"I think you reversed time or something," Rosalia told her. "You were the one doing it. I was just along for the ride, so don't you ask me to explain anything."

Brigid eyed her for a long moment, her breath coming in heaving gasps. "Oh, I had Annunaki thoughts inside me, didn't I?" she groaned.

Rosalia nodded. "They there still? I can shoot you if they are. In the head."

Brigid smiled. "No. I'm me. Or as me as I ever was."

Behind the two women, the strange stone chrysalis began to part once again, a jagged crack running up its Y-axis all over again. Brigid and Rosalia watched as Little Quav emerged, a girl once more. Her dress was gone but otherwise she seemed intact.

Rosalia turned to Brigid, a frown on her face. "Is she going to remember…?"

"Nothing," Brigid said with certainty. "Time can't be turned back but evolution—at least, Annunaki evolution—can."

"Good," Rosalia said with a firm nod, "because I hate killing children."

Brigid draped the fur cloak over Quav's shoulders

and the three of them hurried from the ante-nursery, not bothering to look back.

NINETY-THREE MILLION miles away, a quantum window opened just beyond the corona of the sun like a beautiful lotus blossom, its petals unfurling in the darkness. A single figure emerged from that quantum window, hurtling from it as if thrown with incredible force. It was Ullikummis, his scream lost to the silent vacuum of space.

Languidly, as if he had all the time in the universe, Ullikummis's stone body plummeted toward the sun, its stone surface burning up in a spark of such unremarkable brilliance that no one but the keenest observer would have noticed.

The sun was humankind's first god, a golden ball in the sky, and it cared little for these insignificant lifeforms called Annunaki.

Chapter 21

What happened after that was chaos. The energies that had blasted from Ullikummis had wounded *Tiamat*'s living engines, and it wasn't long before the whole ship began to overheat.

Grant made his way to the exit, keeping in contact with Rosalia as he did so. When he reached the outside, the war was over, all the jury-rigged Annunaki dead, their shoddy bodies corrupted from within. The humans who had waged war for Ullikummis seemed mystified, especially the firewalkers who'd had the obedience stone implanted within them. It seemed that without Ullikummis the stones lost their power. Finally the section of Earth's population who had placed their faith in Ullikummis was free. Strangely, it was Sela Sinclair, one of the missing agents of Cerberus, who led the confused humans from the disintegrating body of *Tiamat,* whose skeletal wings sunk lower into the ground having never had the chance to fly.

Rosalia found Grant on one of the bone streets, triangulating each other via their linked Commtacts, and accompanied by Brigid who was walking slower to allow Little Quav to keep up.

"What?" Rosalia taunted. "You decide just to sit out the final act?"

"I was busy," Grant told her as he limped along amid the mass exodus. "Busy like you wouldn't believe."

Rosalia didn't press the issue. She could see how weary the ex-Mag was. Besides, Grant was more interested in renewing his acquaintance with Brigid Baptiste. Grant slowed, waiting for Brigid and Quav to catch up. They seemed to be in one piece and back to normal, and that was honestly all that Grant could process just now.

HALFWAY AROUND the world, Kane was waking up—for want of a better term—in the Agartha storeroom. Balam watched him with interest, plucking away the strange living growths that the chair had used to interact with its occupant.

"How do you feel, friend Kane?" Balam asked gently.

Kane looked at him, studying the pasty features of this humanoid who had helped guide him amid the cosmic whirl. "I'm alive," Kane concluded after some moments' thought. "Are we saying that for everyone else, Balam?"

"I couldn't really tell you," Balam admitted, shaking his head sorrowfully.

Still seated, Kane brushed his hand against his face as he engaged his Commtact. "Lakesh? Grant? You out there?"

Something flaked away from Kane's cheek like a dried-up scab, and he watched as it flittered down to his chest before brushing it away. It was a part of the stone splinter that had been embedded in him, dried up now with Ullikummis's departure turning to so much dust. And his vision seemed back to normal. Whatever Balam had been doing was finished, no longer necessary.

"Kane?" Grant replied after a pause. "You okay?"

Kane could hear the weariness in his partner's voice. "Better than you," he teased.

Kane waited, but Grant didn't say anything else. "Well…?" he prompted.

"Kane." The one word was spoken by a familiar voice as it came over the Commtact.

Kane's heart leaped, feeling an incredible sense of relief and joy. He steadied himself, taking a deep breath before finally replying. "Baptiste," he said, "you have some explaining to do."

"Yes," she replied, tiredness in her voice.

Kane waited. It sounded like she wanted to say more, but somehow the words didn't come. "Hey," he said, "it's good to have you back on the team."

"Thanks," Brigid said.

And that was their communication over.

Grant came back online a few moments later, telling Kane about Rosalia and about Little Quav, confirming that both had survived intact. Kane related that to Balam, but there was little joy in his voice.

Afterward, Kane paced the cuboid room, shaking his head as he replayed the conversation with Brigid Baptiste over and over in his mind.

"Kane?" Balam asked, sensing the human's distress. "Are you all right?"

Kane stared at him, his haunted blue-gray eyes meeting Balam's. "This is going to take some getting used to."

"We dispatched the Annunaki," Balam reminded him. "You must be thankful for the victories we've achieved today. Remember—everyone survived, my friend."

"Yeah, well," Kane muttered as he left the gel-walled cube, "maybe the jury's still out on that."

But Balam was no longer within hearing range.

ENLIL LAY AMID the debris in *Tiamat*'s engine room, a bloody stump where his left leg had been. He had used part of his torn cloak to patch the leg, creating a tourniquet to slow the blood loss. He felt more than saw the destruction of his son, Ullikummis, although it was difficult to miss the fallout. The whole engine room was alive with flame and smoke where energy had raced out across the dimensions from Ullikummis's wounded body.

Enlil lay there as the verminous engineer slaves hurried to tend to *Tiamat*'s final needs, and he closed his eyes and listened. The womb ship was ruined, dying; Enlil could feel it deep in his soul. He had vowed that the future would be his, back when he had planted the seed that grew to become this great spaceship, but he had not foreseen the interference of his son, returned from his punishment having learned only rebellion.

But what was truly insulting was that the apekin of Cerberus had come, and it was they who had finally killed his rebellious child.

"Cerberus will die by my hand," Enlil gritted as a posse of the verminlike engineers came to spirit him away from the ruined starship. "The apekin had no right to interfere in matters of blood, of family. They will die by my hand, I swear this. It is a debt of honor now, a debt that such puny, jumped-up apes could never possibly comprehend."

Overhead, another great chunk of *Tiamat*'s flesh ripped away from the inner hull, crashing down among the burning wreckage of the engine room. Enlil watched it drop, his bloodied face fixed in a mask of hate.

There was time. There was always time.

WITH THE DESTRUCTION of Ullikummis and the subsequent atrophy of *Tiamat,* Lakesh felt safe in calling his disbanded team home. "Send out the order," he told Donald Bry as the sun began to set outside the ruined French doors of their temporary headquarters. "Bring everyone back—we're going home."

Domi looked up from her perch at a low table, a tentative smile tugging her lips. "To Cerberus?"

"*We* are Cerberus," Lakesh corrected her. "But, yes, we shall be remounting operations at the redoubt as soon as possible."

Domi cheered, along with everyone else in the room: Brewster Philboyd, Reba DeFore, Donald Bry, Mariah Falk and Shizuka and her remaining Tigers of Heaven, too.

IT TOOK SEVENTY-TWO hours to bring everyone back together, and even then the redoubt base in the Bitterroot Mountains, Montana, seemed strangely underpopulated. Hollowed from the mountain, the whole of the base had been overtaken with living rock when Ullikummis had attacked, and now many of the old rooms and corridors were swamped with evidence of that occupation. While much of the redoubt remained under a blanket of rock, the mat-trans unit at least remained intact, and it worked overtime as it shuttled in the surviving members of the Cerberus squad. They numbered close to fifty in all, and a series of strange meetings took place as individuals who had found themselves on opposite sides of the Ullikummis War were reunited.

Lakesh watched it all from his old desk—currently hidden somewhere beneath a veneer of rock—and he smiled. Things would get back to normal in time. Cerberus would survive; it always did.

Ullikummis had left several nasty traps awaiting anyone who tried to take control of the redoubt, but all of them had expired with his death, living rock creatures turned to worthless stones, now nothing more than artifacts of a battle no one cared to dwell on. Already, the staff was working on that ultrasonic beam, seeing whether it might be employed to remove the rocky growths that had overtaken the redoubt like a fungus.

"You look pleased with yourself," Donald Bry said to Lakesh as Farrell reappeared in the mat-trans chamber in the corner of the ops room to be greeted by a very apologetic Sela Sinclair.

"I have every right to be," Lakesh said. "Look around you, Donald. We're back, and our enemies are vanquished."

"Our enemies are never van—" Bry began, but he stopped himself, inevitably looking concerned as he saw Lakesh's look. "I know what you're going to tell me," Bry said, raising his hands in surrender. "To enjoy the victory while we have it."

Bry took a moment to gaze around the altered operations room. "Lakesh," he said, "it's good to be home."

OUTSIDE THE REDOUBT, on the plateau that overlooked the mountain range, Kane joined a number of other personnel as they celebrated their victory, drinks and food somehow rustled up from the battle-damaged canteen.

When he saw Kane step through the open rollback doors, Grant came limping over to him with Shizuka in tow. Behind them, the warm rays of the afternoon sun painted the sandy plateau a rich gold.

"Grant," Shizuka urged, "not so much weight on your leg. Remember what Dr. Kazuka told you."

Grant ignored her, reaching his arms around Kane in a hug. "Good to see you again, my man," he said.

"You, too, partner," Kane agreed. "That was the

weirdest game of rock-paper-scissors I ever played. Thanks for coming through for me."

Grant backed away with a look of mock indignation. "Who, me? What did I do? I heard you were the theoretical physics superhero. Brainiacs here want to kiss your feet."

"You made sure Ullikummis wasn't grounded when we sideswiped him," Kane said, adding before Grant could correct him, "whether you meant to or not."

Grant smiled, looking Kane up and down. The ex-Mag had come straight from the city of Agartha, where he had spent more than two days asleep, simply trying to recover from the emotional and spiritual drain of using the astrogator's chair in the way he had.

"You know something?" Grant asked. "That beard really does not suit you."

Kane stroked his unruly whiskers, eyeing Grant's carefully trimmed goatee. "And what about yours?"

Grant ran his index finger and thumb along both sides of his beard and smiled. "See, mine actually looks good."

As if in agreement, Shizuka linked her arm through Grant's and leaned against him, looking up into his eyes. "You want another drink, my brave hero?" she asked.

"Yeah, I'll help you," Grant said. "Hey, Kane, you—" He stopped. Kane was already walking away across the plateau, making his way to the dark-haired woman who stood at its edge sipping at a glass of water, quietly observing the reunion from a distance.

"You look like hell," Rosalia said cheerily when she saw Kane approach. Around them, the spontaneous party continued apace, with many Cerberus personnel being reunited for the first time in two months.

"Good to see you, too," Kane said.

Rosalia reached up, brushing gently at the place where the stone shard of Ullikummis had been embedded in Kane's face. It had gone, withered and died during the conflict in string space, and all that remained was an ugly bruise that ringed Kane's left eye.

Kane winced as Rosalia's hand touched him. "Hey, careful."

"You big girl," Rosalia shot back. "You never like it when I play rough."

Kane stared at her in surprise, but after a moment he saw her expression warm and she smiled, her even teeth bright in the midafternoon sunlight.

"You did good out there, from what I hear," Rosalia told him.

"Yeah, from what I hear, too," Kane admitted. "Damned if I actually understand half the shit I went through to get us here. Don't tell anyone else I said that, though."

"Ah, don't worry about it," Rosalia said. "Big, strong Magistrate like you doesn't need brains to understand things, does he?"

Kane laughed, shaking his head at the woman's gentle mocking. But after a moment's pause, his expression became somber. "Lakesh told me about your dog," Kane said. "I'm sorry."

"Yeah, well, what does it matter?" Rosalia said with resignation. The hound had died during the initial altercation with Enlil, sacrificing itself to end the battle.

"Mangy mutt saved my hide on a couple of occasions," Kane reminded her. "Did the same for you, and it wouldn't hurt to admit it, you know?"

"Never get close to things, Magistrate," Rosalia told him, "'cause they'll only let you down or get killed in the end."

Kane reached for Rosalia, placing his hand gently on her arm and staring into her chocolate-colored eyes. "You didn't let us down, Rosie. You came through, one hundred percent."

Rosalia inclined her head coquettishly. "Yeah, well, guess what? I'm leaving."

"Why?" Kane asked. "You can stay, you know. You're one of us now. A fully paid-up, secret-decoder-ring-wearing Cerberus member."

But Rosalia was shaking her head. "My place is elsewhere. You got Brigid back. Your trinity is restored. You don't need me anymore, Kane."

"You're wrong. It's not about numbers, Rosalia," Kane told her, but already Rosalia was placing her finger to his lips.

"Never get close to things, Magistrate," Rosalia said. "Then when they let you down or get killed, you don't get soppy and sentimental."

Kane nodded. Rosalia had her own path to travel. She didn't need him or Cerberus. And she was right—they had recovered Brigid Baptiste, and with Grant convalescing after his own battles with the Annunaki godprince, it seemed that they were finally getting back to normal. Which reminded him, where was Baptiste, anyway? Shouldn't she be here?

OUTSIDE THE REDOUBT, Brigid's colleagues were continuing their celebration. It was not just an expression of their joy, Brigid knew, but a way to reappropriate the base that had suffered so at Ullikummis's hands. The next day, the rebuilding would begin in earnest.

Brigid had ducked out of the celebrations early, migrating to her old quarters, which, like everything else in the redoubt, were sprinkled with a light dusting of rock debris, new growths and lumps along the walls and door frames.

She swept wreckage from her bed and sat down, feeling the great sadness inside her. It was a sadness she simply did not know how to address. She had been someone else for a while, her body working to the commands of the shadow self that Ullikummis had created, the character known as Haight.

Brigid had remained largely unaware of Haight's actions, but she sensed the things that had been done in her name, death reaped across the globe, friends turned upon, shot. Haight was some rabid part of Brigid, what happened when disease took control of the body. In this case the sickness was a god, a false god fallen from the heavens to reshape the world for his mother.

Brigid had used a mind trick to hide her true self, focusing on a mandala she had seen months before in a Soviet bunker. The mandala, a meditation tool capable of sending a person's mind to another plane of existence, had been weaved on a Persian rug that now resided somewhere in Lakesh's private quarters. The rug design showed the sky, colored blue with golden rings running through it in concentric circles, highlighted here and there with reds and greens. Brigid's eidetic memory had stored its design, and when Ullikummis had come at her in the cavern cell, breaking her down and rebuilding her thoughts in the manner of the Annunaki, Brigid had re-created the mandala in her mind's eye, sending her personality to that other plane of existence once she knew she could not stop him.

Every time Haight had seen blues and gold and green, it had been like an alarm clock ringing in her mind, trying to reawaken the real woman hiding within: Brigid Baptiste.

Brigid lay back on her bed, trying to remember what it was to be normal, trying to feel at home in a body that had been turned against everything she stood for. There, amid the debris on her bedside unit, Brigid spied an ancient paperback book—*The Bell Jar,* by Sylvia Plath. It was one she had read before, not that long ago. Reaching out, Brigid took the book and flipped it open to the first page. It was a comfort, reading words already familiar.

In spite of her eidetic memory, Brigid knew that sometimes a book only revealed its true meanings on a subsequent reading; sometimes the real story was only clear once you had put it all together for yourself.

Alone in her ruined room, Brigid lay back on the bed and began to read.

* * * * *

The Executioner®
Don Pendleton's
SURVIVAL MISSION

A crime boss turns Prague into a thriving business venture.

When a young American girl is abducted from the streets of Prague, her former navy SEAL father sets out to track down her kidnappers. When he is captured by the same crime ring that has his daughter, no amount of money or U.S. government influence can save him. The only chance the father-and-daughter pair has of getting out alive is Mack Bolan.

Available September wherever books are sold.

GOLD EAGLE®

www.readgoldeagle.blogspot.com

GEX406

Don Pendleton
SEISMIC SURGE

Conspirators plot a massive tsunami set to drown the Western world.

An army of terrorists orchestrating a mission to destabilize the Western world has established a battleground on a volcanic island near Spain—with plans to trigger a tsunami and wash misery across two continents. It's up to Stony Man, Phoenix Force and Able Team to launch a ground assault on the corporation behind the planned tidal wave and its ruthless backers.

STONY MAN®

Available October wherever books are sold.
